THE ADVENTURES OF JASPER JAY HAWK

CHICKEN IN THE BASKET - ALL THE TIME

By Ronald W Stone

Edited By Gavin & Melissa Stone

FOREWORD

When I was a child I remember my father, Ronald Stone, telling my sisters and I stories of the Adventures of Jasper Jay Hawk and his Bicycle in a Briefcase. He told these stories to me, my older sister Gretchen, and my younger sister Gabby. I can't speak for our older siblings Garry, Greg and Gigi.

In my mind's eye I picture hearing these stories in the summer time, when our family had more idle time. I recall hearing them frequently on the back deck of the seagull cottage on Peaks Island while looking out across the sound separating us from Long Island. My father would also tell Jasper Jay Hawk stories during Casco Bay Lines boat rides, while camping at Sebago Lake and occasionally at my Bama's house in Richmond, ME.

Jasper went on many adventures, all of them, with his trusty side-kick Fido Badegleo, a jet black German Shepherd.

Most of Jasper Jay Hawk's adventures take place in the great outdoors of Maine, but not all of them. Jasper and Fido explored Peak's Island, were chased by a Bull Moose near Sebago Lake, got lost in the woods in Richmond, went hiking near Moosehead Lake and foiled bandits on the Saco River. On occasion Jasper's travels took him to more exotic locations like the Grand Canyon or the Redwoods. In all of their exploits Jasper and Fido would help out those in need and meddle in the affairs of wrong doers.

I was little when I heard these stories and at first I believed Jasper was a real person. My father would often borrow from his own life as you will see to fill the details of Jasper's world. This always confused my little mind and led me to believe that at one time in his youth my father was the hero Jasper Jay Hawk. Jasper was always very resourceful and quite cleaver about getting himself out of trouble.

As happens to all things, eventually my father stopped telling Jasper Jay Hawk stories. More than likely my sisters and I simply grew to old to sit still for the stories of a boy and his dog. So for a time Jasper's stories were concluded.

Then in approximately 2005, after my father retired from teaching physical education at King Middle School, he decided to write a new story about the adventures of Jasper Jay Hawk. That is essentially where this story evolved.

He wrote the story over the course of a year and often called me into the office to have me read sections of it or to give me the synopsis of what was going on and ask my opinion. My father rewrote it again, taking out parts and polishing it as best he could. He often asked people to read it and was successful at getting many critiques. I never actually read the entire book from start to finish at that time.

After a while my father stopped working on the novel full time but would still pull it out once in a while. He still longed to have it properly edited and made into a book.

Then, in February of 2014, my sister Gabby's husband, Mike told me he had been given a copy of my father's story and was going to edit it. Mike and Gabby had the wonderful idea of having the book published so they could present my father with his work. This idea resparked my interest and I decided to join forces with them in this project.

We quickly determined that my parents had misplaced the digital copy of the book. They had probably lost it during one of their moves or thrown it away when they replaced their computer. This lead us to determine that the copy of Jasper Jay Hawk that Mike had was the only copy of the book that remained.

Gabby and Mike were gracious enough to give me the copy that they had and over the course of three months, March 2014 through May 2014, I painstakingly retyped the novel. Ironically near the end of May, with less then thirty pages left to type, I found a box of old computer disks. Inside were CDs with the original and revised copies of Jasper Jay Hawk. With them were also many notes my father had kept on the story.

Over the summer, I used the notes my father had kept to write a prequel story. If you enjoy this story, you my also decide to read that one. It tells of the origins of Fido Badegleo and the building of Jasper's original Bicycle in a Briefcase. I then went back and attempted to edit my father's original work. I am not a professional editor. I relied heavily upon my wife Melissa to fix the plentiful grammatical errors left by both my father and me. I think she did a good job. When we were finished, we gave the story back to Gabby and Mike who then had the book published

Melissa and I did make a few minor contextual changes to the story to make it more consistent and to clean up some loose ends. Enjoy.

Gavin D Stone
October 2014

Contents

PROLOGUE

SHANK STELLER was up early this cold February morning. It was no different than any other morning for the past 38 years. He had just turned sixty-six. He ran a successful poultry farm, and it was his job to keep it running that way. He loved the work and enjoyed managing all the different aspects of it.

Jane, his wife of forty years, had just cooked him his usually breakfast of bacon, eggs, and hash browns, with a stack of pancakes. Shank had a hearty appetite. He ate three squares and didn't hedge on any meal. He stood at six feet two inches tall with a strong muscular frame and carried about thirty pounds too many. His hair used to be jet black but now there was more white than black in it.

Shank always sat and chatted with Jane after breakfast before he took off for the day's work. They would discuss the daily scheduled of events, what was being delivered, what had to be done, the priority of things, and so forth. He would do the same with his foreman, Frank LaBreque, later on in the morning, but he always wanted Jane to know the scoop. She was a big part of the business and ran the financial part of it.

This particular morning he had to unload twenty eighty-pound bags of chicken feed out of his truck into the main chicken barn. He had un-loaded half of the feed the night before but it got late and he decided to unload the rest in the morning. He threw a tarp over the trucks bed to protect the feed from the weather and called it quits for that day.

Shank had finished his talk with Jane and was walking down the porch heading for his red Chevy pick up. The truck was three years old and had an over sized bed. He loved the truck because the large bed made it possible for him to haul really big loads. He was carrying his favorite over sized coffee mug with the words "STELLER and SONS POULTRY FARM" encircling the cup. His long time mutt of a dog, 'Maddy,' was running along side him, the dog followed him every where he went.

The sun was just making its appearance. Within an hour the sunrise would be spectacular. In the winter up here in the northern end of Maine the sun came up late in the morning. Shank loved the farm. It spread out over ten acres without buildings for the various phases of the operation. He had laid the buildings out to be aesthetically pleasing but still very functional. He and Jane had started out slow with a small farm and as things progressed and they made improvements the operation just got bigger.

Shank climbed up into the cab being careful not to slip. There it was again, that lower back pain acting up. This time he felt numbness down his arm. He didn't mention anything to Jane. He hated her fussing over him about his health. He put the key in the ignition and turned it. The truck sprang to life with a roar of the engine. Maddy whined and jumped back a few feet. Shank let the truck warm up for a few minutes while he fiddled with the radio dial. He loved the morning talk shows. Maddy liked to get her exercise and run along the side of the truck. She seemed to know where Shank was headed.

Jane was tidying up around the kitchen and putting the morning breakfast dishes to rest in the kitchen cabinets. She wanted to spend the morning catching up on some of the accounting bookwork for the farm so she would be free that evening to go off to Thelma's for a session on rug making. Maddy was outside barking and sounded like her tail was caught in a trap. She looked out the window and there was Maddy making a whole lot of fuss. "Why wasn't she with Shank?" she thought. They had gone out together. She feared something was wrong, so she threw on her boots, grabbed her jacket, hat and went out into the yard where she could get a better look as to where Shank was. She looked for Shank's truck and there it was off the road in a ditch with Shank nowhere in sight. Jane ran the hundred yards to the truck to see if she could make any sense of what had happened. When she got to the truck Shank was slumped down on to the passenger side and the truck had veered off the road onto the side ditch on it's own. Shank was unconscious and not moving.

Chapter 1
The Send Off

Jasper Jay Hawk woke up on a warm June morning. It was a Saturday and he had just graduated from Grondon High School the day before. He had also turned 18 on graduation day. He felt as free as the bird of his last name. It was so wonderful to be through with school. While Jasper loved school; the academics, athletics, social life, everything, he was just glad it was over for a while so he could do some of the things he had wanted to do for so long without any restrictions.

Jasper sat up in bed and dropped his feet to the floor. He scratched at his head through his jet-black hair, rubbed his eyes and yawned. He had a lot to do before tomorrow. He got up and walked down the hall to take a shower. Jasper was a tall young man, around six foot three, he was lean and had a strong athletic body, his eyes were steel-black and he had a dark complexion. He was a black belt in karate and he could handle himself in a tight situation. Today was the first day of the summer and an important day for Jasper.

He had discussed his plans with his parents, Ralph and Marie Hawk. They had become very reasonable people over the years and he loved them very much. They had been great parents.

When Jasper was younger, his father had been angrier and held more of a temper. The summer after their dog, Fido had come along, Ralph had softened and learned to trust his son's intuition.

Jasper discussed things openly with them now and they respected his wishes. He told them he was definitely going on to college, but he needed some time to spread his wings and live a little. That was fine with them as long as he promised to keep in touch on a regular basis and never forgot that he always had a place to call home.

Jasper's first outing was biking to Old Calcutta, Maine where his grandparents, Jane and Shank Steller lived. They were north of Wallgrass Lake and owned a poultry farm, one of the biggest in the state. He had spent a lot of his summers and school vacations there. It was like a second home, a nice familiar start to his trip.

Jasper's dog, Fido, slept in his room and came over to greet him while he sat on his bed after dressing. Fido had been his companion for the past six years. Jasper got him as a puppy the summer before he started the seventh grade. His family had gone up to Indian Island outside of Dairy for a long weekend to visit his grandfather.

Flying Hawk, Jasper's grandfather, was a full-blooded Micmac. He had given Fido to Jasper. When he was first given Fido, his father, Ralph said he couldn't keep him. That's when Jasper began calling him 'Fido', because he didn't want to name a pet he couldn't keep. By the end of their trip, Jasper's father had relented and the name had stuck. Fido was a jet black German Shepherd and was an extremely smart animal. He understood English and was very trainable. Jasper had trained him over the years and they had a unique way of communicating. This alone was the only secret Jasper kept from his parents, as well as everyone else. He felt that Fido's gift was far too unique and powerful to risk sharing with anyone.

After breakfast, one of the first things Jasper did was go visit Stonie. He had asked Jasper to visit him before he took off for the summer. He also had several other errands to do, as well as visits planned with a couple high school classmates and his long time girlfriend Claire Cousins.

Everyone had a favorite teacher, friend or someone in their life that has been a mentor or confidante. In Jasper's life that someone was Stonie. He was his gym teacher for eleven out of his twelve years in school. His actual name was Rocky Pebble Stone. Jasper lived in Landrush, a town in southern Maine just a few miles from the rocky coast. The greater Landrush area has over a half a million people in it.

Stonie's first teaching job was at Longfellow Elementary. Jasper thought back to that first day of school when he had met Stonie and how since then they had developed that acquaintance into a real friendship. Stonie worked at Longfellow for seven years. From Jasper's primary grade right through to his sixth grade. The high schools went from seventh grade to twelfth grade. Stonie was transferred to Grondon High School after Jasper's seventh grade year. He lived across town in South Landrush.

Jasper did not want to get there too early. After his shower he cooked a nice big breakfast and turned on the TV to catch the weather report, to see what to expect for his first day of biking up the coast of Maine.

Jasper was traveling light in terms of clothes. His parents were coming up to Old Calcutta for the Fourth of July for a weekend would bring the trunk packed with his clothes for him.

Jasper grabbed his backpack, jumped on his bike, ready to go. It was a short five mile ride across town and over the 'Million Dollar Bridge' to Stonie's. He usually took Fido with him everywhere, so Jasper flipped the sidecar down and Fido jumped on. He backed the bike out of his driveway and onto Fairmount Street.

Jasper had just finished building his bike. It was a custom made bike he had designed himself at the bike shop where he worked off and on since he was twelve. This was not the first bike Jasper had built.

The owner of the bike shop, Paul Skater who everyone always called 'Paulsie' helped him build his original model six years ago. Jasper had bought all of the parts through the shop discount and with Paulsie's expertise they were able to put together an incredible 10 speed bike that was able to fold up into a briefcase for easy storage. That bike had been Jasper's original Bicycle-in-a-Briefcase. He had many adventures over the years on it. The bike was still in decent condition, besides some minor dings because Jasper took excellent care of it. He had left his Bicycle-in-a-Briefcase neatly folded away and stored in his bedroom.

Today Jasper was riding his new 20 speed, electric bike. This version Jasper had designed mostly with the help of Jonny Skater, Paulsie's son. The bike was equipped with a sidecar Jasper had designed for Fido to ride on. The bike had a lot of special features that no other bike had. Fido could jump off when it was hilly and usually the first hour or so he would trot along side the bike when traffic was right. When he got tired he could jump back on the bike and sit or lie down. Jasper could also set the bike up into its electronic mode and use it as an electric bike for part of a day's trip. When the battery got low, he would then hook it up to a generator and recharge it while he peddled the bike. After charging the battery, he could uses it at night for electricity and then re-charge it first thing in the morning again. The battery fully charged could last for about four hours. Like his original, this bike also folded up. Because of its size, it folded into a good size suitcase rather than a briefcase.

Jasper got to Stonie's in about fifteen minutes. He was out in his garden on his hands and knees weeding his onion patch. Stonie was a tall man, six foot five. He had gotten a full boat scholarship to the University of Tampa for his abilities as a basketball player. He perfected his style of play during his four years playing in the U.S. Air Force. Stonie was now thirty-five years old. His hair was dark brown and just beginning to gray at the temples. His nose came straight down from his forehead with only a slight indentation at the eyebrow. "Nose like a Greek God," was another of Stonie's phrases.

Stonie had a great sense of humor and gardening was one of many hobbies that he enjoyed. He also worked a punch needle and made American Oriental wool rugs, read a lot and worked out every other day. He was always telling Jasper you needed a planned program of physical fitness for life. Him being a gym teacher, that wasn't such a surprise but he practiced what he preached. He said, "I never wanted to be an overweight gym teacher, it would be hypocritical" and "that you had to pick workouts that you enjoyed or it wouldn't last and you would never stick with it."

As Jasper rode up, Stonie looked up from his onion patch and immediately climbed to his feet and said, "Hey Jay, how you doing? Are you leaving this quickly?"

Fido jumped off the sidecar and went rushing over to Stonie wagging his tail so hard it almost knocked him over. He just loved Stonie. He always had a treat for him.

"Hi, Coach. I'm doing fine. I'm leaving tomorrow," Jasper said as he shook Stonie's hand. They walked across the lawn to sit in a pair of adirondack chairs in the shade next to a picnic table. There was a backpack lying on the ground next to the chair Stonie sat in. "I'm planing to get an early start to my Grandparent's house in Old Calcutta in the morning."

"What are you going to do up there anyway?" Stonie asked.

"Well, remember that serious stroke my Grandpa Shank had last winter? He survived it, but it left him in a wheel chair. He can't work the old chicken farm like he used to. My Grandma Jane has been doing her best to hold the farm together. My uncle Robbie is coming home from the Air Force in September. He is retiring after twenty years in and is going to run things for them. She has had help from their trusty foremen, but they could use an extra hand around the farm to help out and what not. Plus I love visiting Old Calcutta. It'll be a nice vacation."

"Well, that's just like you, Jay. Always trying to help someone out. I have a feeling you'll be doing more work than vacationing," said Stonie as he took off his dusty kneepads. Stonie always wore kneepads when he was down in the garden. "My goodness, remember when I hired you to help me prep the driveway for tar? I couldn't stop you for a minute. You're a hard worker, Jay. Hook the dog up on the run and I will go in and fix us some ice tea and we can sit and chat." Stonie jumped up, and glided up the back steps of the rickety old deck.

"Fido won't run off for anything," he called. "He's pretty smart, knows better than to play in the street."

"This corner is too busy with traffic. It just isn't safe, Jay," replied Stonie as the back door closed behind him.

Jasper got up and grabbed Fido's collar. "Sorry boy, I know you aren't going anywhere but Stonie doesn't realize exactly how smart you are." Fido mumbled a growl of understanding and acceptance of the situation, but as Jasper latched the hook onto his collar, he darted an irritated eye at him. Fido hated being leashed up. Jasper sat back down in a chair. Just then, Stonie came back out the door carrying two tall glasses of iced tea.

Stonie reached in his pocket and pulled out a dog biscuit. "Here you go, Fido," he said as he tossed the biscuit to the dog. Fido caught it in mid air.

Jasper took a long pull on the iced tea. Stonie always gave you a big glass that wasn't gone in two swallows. Plus he had brought out a milk jug filled with tea, so there was always plenty. "So," Jasper said, "what are your plans this summer, Coach?" Stonie usually had several things going during the summer. He would run a sports camp during late June and early July. Then typically, Stonie would sail out to Pete's Island and work as the manager of The Evergreen Club, a yuppie club for the high affluent islanders that came up from Massachusetts and New York. Occasionally he would work the whole summer on the Island and leave the sports camp in the hands of its owner. Every forth or fifth year Stonie would take the summer off, if he could afford it.

"Well, this summer I think I will take off," Stonie said, "Penelope wants to go to Quebec City for a few days and see a little of Canada, then maybe come back and go down through Niagara Falls. We've also considered taking the Prince Line up to Nova Scotia and driving back through New Brunswick. Plus I have some work to do on the house. I want to rebuild this old deck and that will take some time. I think I'll be able to keep busy for the whole summer. This house can always use paint. I try to do a side a year, especially on this sunny side where the sun hits it all the time." Stonie pointed to the side of the house that needed paint, but still wasn't that bad. The color was dulled a little by the constant sun and if you looked carefully, you could see it was beginning to peel in places but he could have gotten away with another year without painting it.

"It sounds like you will be plenty busy this summer," Jasper said. "When you're up in Canada, you are always welcome at my grandparent's, so stop by if you can. If it's not too far out of your way."

"Well," Stonie said, "I will have Penelope check the map and see how close we come to Old Calcutta. I have met your grandparents. They are fine people and we just might take you up on the offer. Oh, now Jay. I meant to ask you. What safety precautions are you taking on your trip?"

"Well, I never even thought much about it actually. I do have Fido with me. He's all the protection I really need. He always barks when someone he doesn't know comes near. He's got a pretty good ability at sensing people. I mean he can definitely tell when somebody's no good."

"Well, I'm sure Fido makes an excellent guard dog, but you may want to take some extra precautions. For example, if you take a lot of money with you, don't put it all in one place. Like put twenty dollars in your wallet and twenty dollars in your back pack, and any large amounts should go in a money belt. I just happen to have picked this up at L.L. Bean the other day, figuring you wouldn't think of it." Stonie pulled out a brown macramé belt with a silver buckle from the backpack that had been lying next to his chair. "This is a money belt. It has a place for an ID card and several zipper sections for money all along the inside seam. Always be alone whenever you access the belt for money so no one knows that you have more than you appear to. It looks just like a regular belt and it shouldn't draw any suspicions."

Jasper took the belt that Stonie handed him, and exclaimed "Wow, that's really nice of you, Stonie. You didn't have to pick this up for me. Boy, I really appreciate it." He swung the belt around his waist and buckled it on. It fit perfectly. "Man, this is something. I never really though about a money belt. Thanks again, Coach. You really are the best."

"Not that you're going to get mugged or anything, Jay but there is nothing like being prepared for the worst that could happen. A lot of times when I make plans I think of the worst case scenario and I try to be a little more prepared. You never know what kind of curveball the world might throw at you. I remember one time when I was hitchhiking from Landrush to Tampa, Florida to go back to college. I got 11 different rides along the way. It took me 44 hours. At one point, I found myself hitchhiking on a stretch of highway in front of a 'No Hitchhiking' sign. There were no cars driving past for almost an hour and a half. It was early September and freezing that night. It was on the south side of New York City. Thankfully, I had my down parka with me. Who would have thought to bring a parka with them to Florida? But I had thought ahead and knew there was a chance I might need it. I wouldn't want to be stuck out there without one. Always remember to think ahead. Anyway, eventually a trucker picked me up and drove me as far as a truck stop in Richmond, Virginia. Not only should you always think ahead, but you should never trust anyone until they prove themselves to you."

"Wow, you hitchhiked all the way to Florida in 44 hours?" Jasper exclaimed.

"Yes, I did," he replied, "But in this day and age, I wouldn't do it unless it was an emergency. It just seems like there wasn't so much violence back then as there is today."

"There is one other thing I want to give you for your trips and that is my Jack of all Jacks," Stonie said, as he pulled out his jackknife. He always referred to his jackknife as his 'jack of all jacks'. "The kids gave me a new knife for my birthday so I have to carry the new one around. I want to give you this old one. It has a Native American name on it that I don't understand, COSUNCABUH. See here, very roughly printed on the knife?"

Sure enough if Jasper looked carefully, he could see the letters written out in a sketchy kind of way.

"The funniest thing about this knife is sometimes the name on the knife looks a lot clearer than other times," Stonie said, sounding far away, "It's really strange. I have never sharpened it and I have cut wire and rope and all kinds of stuff with it and it never gets dull. And look at it, it is an old knife but it doesn't look old. There's something very special about this knife and I want you to have it. I found this knife on one of my trips out west with Penelope. She loves Native American folklore and we head out west every chance we get. We go to pow-wows all over the place. Anyway, I want you to have the knife and if you run into any Native Americans up north, ask them about that word on the blade."

Jasper turned the knife over in his hand, rubbing the polished wood between his fingers as a strange feeling of déjà vu came over him. He opened the knife, revealing the blade and read the inscription. COSUNCABUH. Where had he heard that before? Jasper asked himself. He knew he had heard the word before but he couldn't place it.

As Jasper's mind began to wander, the knife began reminding him of another jackknife. The jackknife he'd had with him when he had broken his leg on Green Island, in Moosehead Lake. Jasper could barely remember the events on that island. He had been delirious at the time and only survived because of Fido's cleverness. There was a connection between these two events he was sure. But still Jasper felt wrong taking Stonie's knife.

"Stonie, no. I don't want to take your knife. I know what it means to you," Jasper exclaimed. "I remember the first time I saw that knife in elementary school. At recess the Darwin brothers tied me up with a jump rope and left me hanging up side down on the jungle gym just dangling there. You came over and cut me loose with that knife."

Penelope was just coming outside with a tray of sandwiches and cookies for them and had heard part of the conservation.

"Hi, Jay," Penelope said, "Oh, yes. Take the knife. It means a lot to Rocky to give it to you."

"Hi, Mrs. Stone," he said, as he jumped up and relieved Penelope of the tray of sandwiches. "How are you? It sure is nice to see you."

"I'm fine, Jay. You will take the jackknife won't you?"

"Of course I will," exclaimed Jasper. "It's just that Stonie has done so much for me up to this point and he really doesn't need to give me more things."

Jasper set the tray down on the table and watched Penelope pull a dog biscuit out of her apron pocket and throw it to Fido. The dog jumped three feet up in the air and snatched it up. "You've got to love that dog," Penelope said, with a smile.

"Penelope, tell Jay what Bear Root told you," said Stonie, as he reached out and took one of the sandwiches off the tray.

"Well, Jay, as you know I'm interested in Native American folklore," said Penelope. "Well, I showed this jackknife to an old friend at one of the powwows in Old Town that we went to. His name was Bear Root. He's around 80 years old and can always be found at 'Native Smoke Shopper' in downtown Dairy, that is when he's not at powwow's in Old Town. Anyway, I asked him if he knew what that word meant or if he could identify the tribe. I also told him where Rocky had found it. Bear Root said he thought it was an Indian word based on the style it was written but couldn't tell me more than that. He also told me he had a friend he would ask about it."

Jasper shuttered as he looked at the word written on the blade again. There was something very familiar about the word Cosun-cabuh. "Well, I'll be traveling through Dairy on my way north. Maybe I'll stop by this Smoke Shopper and ask Bear Root if he had a chance to speak to his friend."

"If it interests you, go for it," said Stonie casually. "Don't go out of your way on my account though."

"Oh I know," said Jasper absentmindedly as he fingered the jackknife. "Only if I have time."

Penelope and Stonie exchanged looks over Jasper's sudden de-tached behavior.

Stonie changed the subject and Jasper quickly refocussed. The three chatted for a while until he glanced at his watch. "Wow it's eleven-thirty and I have to be at the bank by twelve. I really have to go. Thanks, Stonie for the money belt and the jack knife and thank you, Mrs. Stone for the sandwiches and iced tea. And thanks to both of you for being there for me and being my friends."

He walked over and unhooked Fido from the dog run. Stonie got up and gave him a big bear hug and shook his hand, then said, "Hey Jay, you're the closest I have ever been to any of my students. It's been a real pleasure watching you grow up and now seeing you strike out on your own. I know that you will always do the right thing."

Penelope kissed Jasper's cheek and hugged him and said, "It's been a real pleasure having you around all these years and remember always come back to see us, won't you now?And Jasper, do be care-ful."

Jasper got his bike and put down the sidecar for Fido. "I sure will and I'll be stopping by the next time I'm in town. And don't you all forget to stop by my grandparent's in Old Calcutta when you go to Quebec this summer." Fido jumped onto the sidecar. He hit the street peddling and waving and throwing them a kiss and was gone.

"Now what did he say about stopping by the Steller's in Fort Kent on our way to Quebec this summer?" Penelope asked Stonie. As she gave him a questionable look.

"Oh, I just said that we were going to Quebec this summer and I would ask you to check the map to see how close it would be to Old Calcutta," Stonie replied, with a sheepish look on his face.

"Well," said Penelope, "if you knew anything about geography you'd know it's about 300 miles east of Quebec." She went in the house laughing and shaking her head. "Yea, Jay. We will buzz right over on our way," she mocked Stonie, using his voice and calling him a 'bonehead'.

Chapter 2
Bike Shop

After Jasper left the bank his next stop was the bike shop. He loved going there. It seemed he would always come out with something new for his bike. This time he had everything he needed for the bike he just wanted that all-purpose tool that would complete his bike repair kit. Plus he wanted to say goodbye to the guys working there. He had learned all there was to know about fixing bikes here. Last year Jonny called him into work on the weekend before Christmas and he earned five hundred dollars commission in two eight-hour days. He pretty much knew everyone that worked there.

Jasper pulled up and brought his bike and dog right into the store. He had told Fido before they went in to be seen and not heard. Fido jumped off the sidecar and greeted everyone. They all knew him. He had his spot in the corner of the shop where he would lie down and everyone would forget he was there. He went right over there and curled up. Everyone was standing around with a coffee or hot chocolate in their hands when Jay came off his bike and parked it. "Hey Jonny, how you doing?Must be break time," Jay said, as he nodded to everyone and shook hands with Jonny. Jonny was the boss and owner of the shop, ‘Jonny's Skate and Cycle Shop’. Bikes and Roller skates were Jonny's main draw and of course all the accessories that go with the two modes of transportation.

"Hi Jay, I'm doing fine. Nice to see you. You know you’ve got a job here anytime you want it." Jonny said to him. "Anyone that can sell bikes and accessories like you can will always have work here"

"Oh gee, Jonny. I thought you liked me for my personality. Shucks I'm hurt," Jay exclaimed, as everyone laughed.

"Oh yeah, that too," said Jonny. "But boy can you sell bikes. Hey bud, are you all set for your latest bike trip? Where are you ped-dling off to now?"

"Yeah, I'm all set, I'm leaving tomorrow bright and early for Northern Maine to my grandparents. I just came by for the torque bar extenuation bit and allen wrench combination that I ordered three weeks ago. Is it in?" he asked.

"Yeah it's in, you know you can make all the adjustments and repairs you need with the tools you have," explained Jonny.

"I know that but this wrench will just make any repairs I have to make go so much faster and easier," said Jasper.

"Hey, I though time wasn't an issue with you."

"It isn't but easy is and I want to make any job I have to do eas-ier. Plus I am scaling things down. Now I will be able to leave ten pounds of tools home instead of bringing all of those other tools along. I will have one tool that will eliminate five others."

"Well, this tool will do that and make it easier. It's a good idea to travel light," Jonny replied. Several customers had come in and the business show room had started to get busy. "We're just finishing our break, Jay. Billie, Bob and Tony you guys take over here. Billy, you get the front desk and Bobby, you take care of the quick repair section. Tony, go downstairs in the dungeon and get that shipment that came for Jay,then go do that fork repair job on the rack in the dungeon that the Terriers are waiting on. They will be back here around 3 p.m. Thanks you guys. You do great work. I will be in my office talking with Jay, and one more thing. When Jill comes in finish your lunch breaks. I don't know who's turn it is for lunch."

Jay said, "I'll go down with Tony and get my order so he won't have to make a trip back up."

"OK," said Jonny, "I'll see you in my office." As he walked to the back of the shop where his office was.

Fido sat up, Jasper looked over at him and put his arm out and his hand up in a gesture to stay. Fido yawned and laid back down to a lying position and rested his head down on his front paws, content to stay there and sleep.

"So how are things going here with you, Tony?" Jay asked, as they headed down to the cellar of the shop called the 'dungeon' where all the serious work took place. It was a really well laid out work area. There was a bench to the right of the stairs that all the incoming orders for parts were put when they came in as well as logged in by one of the workers nicknamed 'the logger.'

"Oh, things couldn't be better.," Tony replied. "Jody had our third kid this past winter and everyone is healthy."

"Wow that's great. You must be up a lot taking care of the baby. I heard the first six months is hell." Jay said, not really knowing much about it.

"Well, you've got to be smart about it," Tony replied, "if things are right you can get your mother and your mother in law involved and you don't have to do as much of the infant stuff. Laura, my oldest, is eight now and she can do all the infant stuff when I am stuck alone with Frank, the new baby. And Joe, the four-year-old follows me around wherever I go and I can handle him. It's all divide and conquer."

"Boy you sure do know what you're doing, Tony."

"Yeah, but you've got to know when to stop. Three is good.That should be the end of the Tony Bree strain." They both laughed.

"Is the shop set up the same as always?" Jasper asked.

"Oh yes," said Tony, "I'm the logger so go ahead and get your part and check it off on the clip board."

"What are Jonny's plans for the shop?" Tony was Jonny's right hand man, and had been working in the shop the longest. Jonny father had hired him originally. He had been a high school acquaintance of Jonny's, but a couple years older. He was a big part of holding the shop together after Jonny's father died.

"He has some plans for winter sports expansion," Tony explained.

"Well don't worry about Jonny," Jasper said, "he'll do right by you. I know that for sure. He owes you a lot for keeping this shop on its feet." Jay picked up his package and put his hand out to

Tony.,"Take care, Tony and good luck with the family. Have a good summer."

Tony shook his hand. “You too, Jay. Drop us a post card here at the shop so we can keep track of you."

"I sure will," Jasper said, as he headed upstairs to Jonny's office with his package in hand.

He glanced over at Fido as he walked over to Jonny’s office. Fido picked his head up and looked over at him. Jasper nodded and Fido put his head down and was content to rest some more. They had this sort of unspoken communication between them.

Jonny was 30 years old. He had been an avid bicyclist. He had been in some big races and knew what it took to push yourself in cycling. He had taken the shop over from his father, ‘Paulsie’, after his father’s unexpected death in a hunting incident that still has everyone puzzled as to just what exactly happened up in Eagle Lake in Northern Maine.

Jonny did not go to college right after high school. He worked with his father in the shop for a few years, spent a stint in the Army and then decided to go on to school. Jonny was attending Tufts University. He was maintaining honor grades and was in the Outing and Bicycle Club. During his junior year he was called home in early November to be with his family during the tragedy of his father's death. He dropped out of school that semester and took incompletes. It took him and his family until the next September to get things back to any kind of normalcy. Meanwhile, with Tony Bree’s help, Jonny took over the shop and kept the business going. Tony was already working there as a full time employee. Billy, Bob and Jill came later. Jonny enrolled at USM where the campus was very close to the shop. He finished up college there with a business major.

Jasper walked into Jonny's office and took a seat in front of the desk. "I am a little concerned about weight and balance, but the saddle bags will be good for weight distribution and, I can put some stuff in the nose of the sidecar. When the seventy-five pound dog jumps on the side-car it makes for a balance problem."

Jonny responded, "That’s when you give your back a rest and put the backpack on the left front for weight distribution and it should ride balanced. Like my father used to say, it's not how heavy a load is, it's the balance of the load."

"How right Paulsie was. He was a genius and all of his ideas made such good sense. The way he had come up with a rotating hinge that allowed the bike to fold up into a suitcase, just like the original, was ingenious. I sure do miss him, I'm sure you do too, Jonny."

"Oh yes, there is no question about that. Just being at this desk everyday is always a reminder of him. By the way I sent a patent in to the patent office so no one can replicate it exactly."

"Good idea. It's such a great bike it would really take off if it was ever marketed and advertised properly."

"Well that is in my plan when I get the patent back. I wanted to let you know, I included your name on the patent," explained Jonny.

"You didn't have to do that," interrupted Jasper, "It was Paulsie's idea."

"No Jay, It was yours." Jonny interrupted back. "You never would have gotten it or the original Bicycle-in-a-Briefcase off the ground without Paulsie but the fact remains it was your idea and you should get credit for that."

"Well, thanks," said Jasper slightly embarrassed by the compliment. "Do you really think you could get them to sell?"

"I sure do. In fact, I'm going to put a child's seat where the dogs-side car is and make a few more changes to try to get a market for young parents. A few changes like that will give the consumer a few more options."

"Good luck with it. Speaking of your father, it's been a few years since his death, Jonny. I have always been curious about exactly what happened up there on Eagle Lake. Do you know any more then what was in the paper? Anyone that knew Paulsie couldn't believe that story." The headlines in the Landrush Evening Express that year read "LANDRUSH MAN IMPLICATED IN DEER POACHING RING KILLED IN A SHOOT OUT WITH LOCAL AUTHORITIES NEAR EAGLE LAKE." Then there was a short article about the incident with big plans to investigate the allegations with the District Attorney involved. And then the story just seemed to die. Know one heard anymore about it for a long while.

"It was a very confusing time." Jonny explained, "Dad had gone up there on his annual hunting trip. He and his buddies had built a lodge up on Eagle Lake twenty years ago. They never missed a year going up there. They used the lodge for all four seasons. Summer they would take their families up separately, dividing the weeks up equally between the six friends and even rotating the weeks. We spent some fun times there for at least a week every summer, sometime two. In fact George Smith, dads best friend, told me Paulsie's share of the Lodge is now in my name and he lets me know every summer when it's my week to go up. I have usually passed on it until this year and I told George that I would like to go up this summer. I have the second week in August. I told George I wanted to do a little checking and try to clear Dad's name of the allegations and charges they have on him. We never could get the exact story straight. All of Dad's friend's say that this Aroostook County Sheriff, Dick Blaire claimed his deputies shot my father out of self-defense. He said that my father started shooting at them in the orchard where he was set up for poaching and that the deputies had no choice but to protect themselves and shoot back. George Smith said that my father had gone to the Ouellette Rod and Gun club for some ammunition and never came back. He and the five other partners in the lodge spent a couple of weeks up there after the shooting, trying to make sense of the whole thing. Sheriff Dick Blaire was ready to put them up on charges of obstructing justice and interfering with an investigation. That for all he knew they were all under suspicions of being part of the ring of poachers. We all agreed that this Sheriff and his deputy were crooked and it was all a big cover up. It was like shoveling shit against the tide to get any answers. Plus, the District Attorney's office's hands were tied because of a lack of evidence. Blaire said that after my fathers' death the rest of the poaching ring vanished, leaving my father as the fall guy and no one to say any different."

"George mentioned there was one deputy up there that seemed like a straight shooter, Ken Silvermen, and to approach him before going up to this Blaire character. However, at that time Silvermen lacked the experience and position to do anything about it. He did say he would be keeping his eyes open. If there were crimes going on he would build a file and do something about it someday. If he said or did anything at the time, he would end up in a ditch with a bullet in this head. So that tells you right there what and who you're dealing with. So be very careful when you go up there snooping around."

"Man," said Jasper, "This thing is such a cover up. Seems to me something has to be done."

"That's how I feel," exclaimed Jonny. "George says,he thinks Paulsie either overheard something or saw something he wasn't supposed to be part of,so they had to shut him up and they chose to do it that way."

"So you will be up that way this summer, second week in August? Do you mind if I come down from Old Calcutta and check things out while your there? My grandparents only live two towns away from Eagle Lake." Jasper replied.

"No not at all", said Jonny, "but keep in mind I don't want to stir things up unless we can come up with something with teeth for my father's defense."

"Oh, I understand. I may stop and talk with this Ken Silvermen when I get there and try to shed a little more light on the situation."

"Well what ever you do be careful. It doesn't sound like this is something for amateurs. I'm only doing it because I can't stand my father's name being dragged through the mud for something I know he had nothing to do with."

"I'm with you, Jonny. Paulsie deserves better than what he got."

"That's for sure," Jonny remarked. A long, uncomfortable silence followed as Jonny appeared deep in thought.

"Hey Jonny, Tony says you are thinking of expanding the business. What's up with that?" Jasper blurted out to try to change the subject.

"Oh yeah, I need more real estate though. I have an eye on the lot next door, which is being sold for back taxes. If I could pick it up cheap, it would be good for the security of this building and for parking. I can always expand later. The winter sports division is at least a year away. I'll try to secure the lot next door, research the winter sports thing and decide everything else later."

"I guess there is a lot to the business end of a shop like this, besides the normal everyday book work of paying the bills," said Jasper.

"There sure is," Jonny said. He stood up and put his hand out to shake hands with him, "Maybe when I do set up something either with an expansion of the bike shop or bring in a new line of winter stock you will be ready to settle down into a real job. It's still a few years away."

Jasper accepted Jonny's hand and shook it and said, "Well, it will be an option to consider when the time comes. I can't say what I will be doing in a year or two. Sometimes things happen and you find yourself in an entirely different situation then you ever could imagine." Jasper picked up the new wrench he was buying and said, "Goodbye, Jonny. Looking forward to seeing you this summer up north." Jasper then walked out of the office and waved.

He walked over to Bill at the cash register. "Hey Billy, can you look up the price of this wrench? I'd like to pay for it." Fido walked over from his corner and seemed ready to go.

Bill looked up the price of the wrench in the catalog and said, "You have a good summer, Jay and don't turn down any stray pussy. If you can find any. That will be $21.55 for the wrench, with the shop discount."

"Here you go, Billy," Jasper said, handing him $25.00. "I think I will leave the chicks to you." Billy always kidded with him about sex and stuff and was about the crudest person he had ever met. Jasper always put the comments back in his lap and ignored him. "See you around and you have a nice summer."

Billy handed him the change. He got his bike and walked out of the shop and waved to Jill over in the quick repair section and said, "Goodbye, Jill." Fido followed along, happy to be leaving.

Jill waved as she responded, "See you eventually, Jay," and winked at him.

* * *

Jasper jumped on the bike and flipped the sidecar down for Fido. Fido was not allowed to run along side the bike in the city, and he knew it. The ride to Chad and Jeremy Blanchard's was only about fifteen minutes from the bike shop and Jasper made it quickly.

It was about quarter til two and he'd told Jeremy that he would be there at one-fifteen or one-thirty. He was running a little late.

Jasper parked his bike along the side of the garage and pulled a one inch pin from the gear crank which simultaneously prevented peddling and steering the bike when disengaged.

Jeremy came out and met him just as he locked the bike. "Hey, buddy. How you doing?" Jeremy said as he patted Fido, who was nudging up to him for affection.

"Oh, I'm doing great. It's been a busy morning. Sorry I'm late. I've visited Stonie, been to the bank and have just come from the bike shop. I probably should have allowed for more time."

"Don't worry about that," Jeremy said, as they walked into the house.

"Claire here yet?" Jasper asked, as he shut the door behind him.

"Yes, she is down cellar in the rec room with Chad. Go ahead down and I will be right down with something to eat."

"Great Jeremy, you don't know how hungry I am. You're the best," he said, as he headed for the cellar door.

As Jasper got to the bottom of the stairs and turned the corner to the rec room, a big "SURPRISE" rang out. "Oh he's a jolly good fellow, Oh he's a jolly good fellow, Oh he's a jolly good fellow which nobody can deny." As thirty of his friends sang out, he stood there dumfounded and speechless. Claire ran over to him and gave a big hug and a kiss and said, "You look so surprised. Did you have any idea we were having a party for you?"

"No idea at all, it never entered my mind," Jasper exclaimed. "I never thought anything about a party, a party for what?"

"Well, Jay when someone goes out to seek their fortune you just never know when they'll be back," Jeremy explained. "Besides, it's a good excuse for a party." Jeremy had been right behind him when he walked down the cellar stairs.

All of Jasper's friends clamored around him for the next ten minutes and slapped him on the back and wished him luck. Claire stayed right by his side with her hand around his waist, talking to people and enjoying the moment alongside him.

Jeremy said, "Everyone brought some snacks and goodies, enough to fill up this table so help yourself." Claire and Jasper walked over to the table and started to fill their plates as the line formed behind them.

Fido was watching all this and thought, I hate parties, because humans are loud and act foolish,but I love parties because there is food and the humans drop it and don't pick it up. Both TVs in the house were on and this always irritated Fido. They are so loud! Why do they need to have two of them on? And why do they have to be on two different stations, the Red Sox and MTV? Human social interactions were also bizarre to Fido. Why did the girls all hover around the MTV TV, while the boys all hovered around the Red Sox TV? Fido didn't understand the point to either one. They're not doing anything, their just staring at a noise machine? I'd rather go outside. Some of the kids were outside playing basketball in the Blanchard's backyard.

Everyone was doing his or her thing. Claire and Jasper had separated for a while. Jasper felt obligated to make the rounds to each group, so Claire decided to talk with the girls watching MTV. Fido was off exploring under tables for lost and forgotten Doritos.

After a while Fido went outside to watch the kids play basketball. The loud televisions weren't as intrusive out here to his sensitive ears. The party went for three hours. Jasper and Claire finally left the party at four-thirty. They took their bikes and headed home with plans to meet for supper.

Claire was a junior in high school at age fifteen and was all academics. She was taking colleges courses at the University of Maine in Landrush. Usually one a semester and sometimes in the summer she would take a couple as well. She had been doing this since her freshman year. She was in a special program for gifted students and had it planned to have her freshman year in college completed by the time she graduated from high school. Course wise she would have twenty-four to thirty hours, by the time she graduated.

She hadn't decided what college she would go to yet, but would be studying pre-med. She planned on visiting colleges this summer and would decide by the fall about where she would go. The colleges were paying for all of her visits. She was sought after by all the major colleges in the country because of her academic achievements. She got a perfect score on the college SATs and had an IQ in the highest range there was.

Claire's relationship with Jasper started out purely platonic. She was just the little girl next door to him for many years. They went to Longfellow Elementary school together for a couple years. She would tag along with the group on the way to school. Then she kept skipping grades and pretty soon she was in the sixth grade and Jasper was in the seventh. He and Claire seemed to grow to be the best of friends which solidified into a really tight partnership. From there it turned romantic a few years later in spite of the three year age difference.

They headed for Stroudwater Park, a place where they could walk and talk privately and spend a little quiet time together. Their relationship was a little unusual for a couple reasons. Jasper would not take advantage of anyone three years younger than him in a romantic situation. They had not had sex yet and he did not plan on that happening until the time was right for Claire, and it definitely wasn't now. Five years from now it would be a totally different situation. Claire was moving through school at warp speed, plus she was involved in so many outside school activities that at first she was happy with him as a boyfriend to ward off the other boys. It started out at first as a relationship of convenience for Claire. From there it developed into more than that and just recently it had moved up a notch or two because Jasper was leaving.

They had peddled over to the bike rack where he chained and locked the bikes together onto the steel bike rack. "Well, that should keep them secure while we take a stroll around the park. Lets go down and sit by the river on one of the benches. We need to talk," Jasper exclaimed, rather nervously.

"Ok," Claire said, equally as nervous, as they headed for the path that would take them to the Goldpan River. The path followed the river and was quite nicely groomed. The city had put a lot of time, money and effort into the area parks, walking trails and bike paths. "Jay, I am really going to miss you. Just how long will you be away for, and can we meet at all in the summer?"

"Well, every Monday and Wednesday night I'll find a pay phone or something and call so we will be in touch on a regular basis. I hope you'll come up to Old Calcutta when your schedule allows." He took her hand on the way down the path. "Fido," he said. "Stay close and don't go off or I will have to leash you. Dogs must be on a leash or in complete control of their owner."

"Jay, people who don't know you will think your crazy if you keep talking to the dog like that. He doesn't understand that much," said Claire

"Yes, he does," Jasper spoke up, not meaning to get defensive but not being able to help it either.

Shut up, Jay, thought Fido as he quickened his pace to catch up with the humans, it only causes suspicion whenever he brings attention to my talent.

They walked along the path for a few minutes in complete silence, both humans thinking of different places to start and unsure of how to get up the nerve. The dog walked along and never went far ahead. The first bench they came to they sat at and Claire decided she'd better start or they'd be there until morning.

"Jay you didn't completely answer my question." Claire said softly, "How long will you be away?"

"That's a tricky question," he exclaimed. "I don't have a timetable."

"That's bullshit," Claire said a little annoyed. "That's all I have been hearing from you for the past month or two. I want you to give me a timeline because it makes a difference in my future plans."

"How does it make a difference in your future? I don't understand," he said.

"Well, for example," Claire explained, "if you're not going to be around much I don't think I want to do my senior year without you. The program I am in is set up for me to advance on to college when I feel socially ready. That's the reason I'm not in college now. I stayed around for the social part of it, to be with you because I love you and wanted to be at Grondon with you."

"I love you too and I know all that so what are you saying?" Jasper asked.

"If you're not going to be around, I think I will go on to college in the fall," she declared. "I mean, what's the point? I am academically ready for college and I was staying around for you and if you're not going to be around, then hell! I might as well get off my ass and on with my life."

"Do you know which college you want to go to?" he asked.

"Well," Claire said, "I have it narrowed down to three schools, John Hopkins, Tufts and Syracuse. I mostly want to stay in the East. I just have to research a couple things and make a decision and I can be all set by the fall."

"Won't you feel a little overwhelmed being fifteen years old and away at college, and away from home?" asked Jasper.

"Just because something is challenging doesn't mean it's not worth doing. My mom and dad have discussed that with the schools. They watch over you like you were the crown jewels. I will have no problem being fifteen and in college," said Claire, confidently. "So Jay, I have been doing a lot of talking. Will you come clean with me and tell me just what your plans are? And how often you will be around?"

"That seems to be the sixty-four thousand dollar question," he said, "and the one most difficult for me to answer. When you go on an adventure like I am going on, there is no timetable, and I know you don't want to hear that. It's important for us to be honest with each other. I will be back sporadically and maybe just for major holidays like Thanksgiving and Christmas."

"I see," Claire said with a sigh and a long pause, "I can see you're not as committed to our relationship as I am."

"That's not true!" Jasper said defensively, "I love you. Our age difference is big right now. I am eighteen and you're fifteen and you look like you're twenty. I want you so bad, I can taste it. Don't you feel the same way? If I stay around, you know as well as I do whats going to happen. I couldn't live with myself if you got pregnant."

“What are you talking about? Haven’t you ever heard of safe sex?” Claire demanded.

“Of course I have but there’s not really any such thing as safe sex. Besides, I’m three years older than you."

“You know, I am so sick of hearing that,” Claire screamed, so loud Fido sat up with his ears perked up and looked at Jasper like he was being a real jerk. Apparently Fido had taken Claire’s side.

He jumped and replied, “Did you know that for the next six months until your sixteenth birthday, I could go to jail if they caught us? It’s called statutory rape. Besides it'll give us time to mature into responsible adults.”

“Oh my god,” exclaimed Claire. “You sound more like my parents than my boyfriend every minute. I am not willing to just sit around for a few years.”

“Think about it,” he explained. “Do you remember what happened to Ashely Warren? You don’t because no one sees much of her any more. She dropped out of school sophomore year when she got so big she was starting to show. She never even went back for her GED. When teenage girls get pregnant, they’re doomed. You have made bigger plans for your life than most people twice your age, to interrupt that would not be cool.”

“Why are you worried about pregnancy? We’re not even doing anything,” asked Claire, angrily. “That's not what this conversation is about. Who says I would even do it with you?”

“Oh c’mon, Claire. I'm just trying to act responsibly.”

“By the way, what are your plans in terms of college?” she snapped.

“What does any of this have to do with me going to college?”

“Well, college seems like a more responsible thing to do than riding around the country looking for whatever,” Claire added.

"I have plans for college. It's just not right now. I wanted to go to a college near where you're going. So we could be closer together,” said Jasper with funny smile.

"Okay, well, do you have any idea when this might happen?" Claire asked.

"The way things are I just don't know when anything is going to take place," he declared.

"Here wc go again," Claire remarked. "Maybe we should just go our separate ways. You get on with your life and I'll get along with mine. And maybe someday we can rekindle this thing, whatever it is." She began to sob and tears ran down her face.

They both fell silent for a few minutes. Jasper new it was best for them to break things off. It wasn't fair to her if he didn't know when he would be back. He just didn't want things to end with her. He didn't like the not knowing. He knew this would happen and he shouldn't have waited until the last minute to do it. He didn't know what to say.

Claire spoke up first, after several minutes that seemed to lag on forever. "You know, I know you have been planning this trip for a long time. Maybe I'm just being selfish. You have the right to go off on you adventure. It just makes me mad, because it feels like you didn't think about how this would affect me."

"Claire, that's all I have been thinking about for the past month," he started quickly, before insecurity silenced him again. "I have been dreading this last meeting with you, when I knew we had to talk about the future and life without each other for a while. I didn't want it to end with you upset or with us mad at each other. I'm not going away forever. I will be back. I think ending things temporarily is probably best. I will always love you. You will always be in my heart. Just don't give up on us completely. I know we have a future together if we want it."

"I do want a future with you and I do love you. I'll think about it, but goddamnit! Jasper Jay Hawk, you need to reevaluate this the next time I see you. Because I won't wait forever." Claire stood up.

"Does this mean you're okay with everything? You're not pissed?"

"Well, I'm not happy because you're leaving, but I'm not pissed. After all, you're going away for an unknown length of time and I have no one around to love," she said as she took his hands and they embraced and kissed a long sweet kiss.

"I'm relieved, I couldn't stand it if anything came between us," he said softly, with a sigh of relief, as they held each other for a long moment.

As the embrace broke, Claire said, "Well Jay, there is a lot of truth in the things you said. I'm sorry for some of the stuff I said."

"I'm sorry too. Are you ready to go home now?" he asked, as he thought how complicated women could be and this one was only fifteen.

"Sure," Claire replied, "we can eat at my house and then do something."

"Can we eat at my house? I think my folks would like that since I am leaving early in the morning. Then we can do something after that. Maybe hang out with some of the gang?"

"Dinner at your house is fine, but I would like to have you all to myself after that, if you don't mind. After all it's your last night in town for who knows how long. She said was a dangerous smile.

Jasper smiled. "You've got it, I'm all yours, Mistress Claire."

They got on the bikes and rode off towards their neighborhood with Fido wagging his tail and chasing them. "Fido,Sidecar," called Jasper. Fido ran over and jumped into the sidecar as it was rolling along.

Chapter 3
A Pit Stop in Bath

The next morning was Sunday and Jasper was well on his way by ten o'clock a.m. He had convinced his parents that he did not want any long good byes in the morning he just wanted to stop at Miss Landrush Diner, his favorite breakfast spot. The diner was a 1949 Worchester dining car which arguably oncc traveled the nearby, and long unused rail-lines, that criss-crossed the older parts of downtown Landrush.

Jasper was up by five a.m. and off by five thirty , and of course his parents did get up and see him off. That was no problem. He just didn't want his Mom fussing over breakfast. Breakfast at the diner had taken an hour and he was on the road by eight a.m. He was taking his first break right outside of Brunswick, Maine. He had stopped at a gas station for a little bit. He was having a tougher time at the peddling than he had expected. This trip was different from the others, he realized. He was carrying considerably more weight, between the electric engine and the sidecar plus the weight of all his gear. It had been only a few hours and he was already getting sore. He loved the strain on his legs and the workout his body was getting. He knew it would take time to get in shape, but he could take it slow.

Jasper's itinerary was to follow Route One downeast through Rockland and Belfast. He planned to stop at some fishing villages on the way. When he reached about Searsport he would find Route 1A and follow the Penobscott River north to Dairy. He would then continue north from Dairy on Route Two, following the river until the turn off for Millinocket and on to Baxter State Park. After stopping at Baxter State Park and Mt. Katahdin, he would go west and north along

Route eleven and make the rest of the trip north to his grandparent's farm.

Jasper planned to camp out most of the time and stop at motels every three or four days depending on the weather. He had made the bike trip once before so he knew where he would stop for breakfasts and where supermarkets, laundry mats and restaurants were. He always made sure he had enough food packed for two days. His plans for meals were to have two good meals a day; morning and evening, and to stop during the day when he felt the urge and eat trail mix or beef jerky. He would throw the dog a biscuit whenever he stopped, also. He carried some dried dog food in case he wasn't near a supermarket. He fed the dog two cups of dog food every evening and one cup in the morning.

The next stop he made was at a gas station outside Bath, Maine. Jasper always liked taking his breaks at gas stations. Cars tended to look out for you more if you were off the road at a store rather then just standing along a country road. Plus if he was low on supplies there was a store right there and probably a water hose around back as well. On a bulletin board near the gas stations front door was a sign for the Maine Maritime Museum. He had been to it with his mother and was thinking of finding it and looking around.
Jasper was pulling on some beef jerky after he had flipped Fido a biscuit said, "What do you say we check out that Maine Maritime Museum in Bath? Then we can hop on the bike and do a couple more hours on the road and find a spot for the night to pitch the tent, after we eat of course." After speaking he looked down at the dog for some kind of a reply. Fido was absolutely still, hadn't touched his bone, ears erect like a pointer, he was looking toward a picnic table and a girl sitting at the table at the opposite end of the convenience store. Jasper couldn't hear her but Fido could. She looked like she was crying but he couldn't tell since they were so far away. Fido looked up at Jasper, whined and danced on his front paws for a second and then remained still again. Jasper started getting curious also.

Jasper said to Fido, "Lets get closer and check this out." She was sitting there all alone. He wheeled the bike and picked up his backpack and moved everything to the corner of the building near the

Ice Box freezer so they were about thirty feet closer. Now he could hear the girl sobbing, hands in her face, very distraught. He looked around further to see if any one was with her. "I don't see anyone with her, do you Fido?" The dog shook his head just like a human and Jasper knew the answer. "Fido, go up to her and act concerned. See if you can get her to stop crying. Give me a signal when I should join you." Fido nodded. He'd played this angle before. He began lumbering toward the picnic table with his head down looking sad.

The girl had a pretty face with a long brown ponytail and she was wearing a blue button-up blouse cut at the shoulders that hadn't been cleaned in a few days. She had full length jeans on despite the warm weather and shoes too dressy for traveling. She was carrying a handbag and had a flannel shirt tied around her waist.

Jasper positioned himself so he could watch Fido do his magic. He pretended to be repacking one of his bags and kept looking up. The dog approached the sobbing girl in a low crouch with his ears back and tail wagging with a soft wine in his throat. He had gotten quite close to the girl and she hadn't noticed. Fido then laid down right near the girl putting his head on his paws. The girl was startled as she noticed Fido. She began to look around to see if the dog was with anyone. Then she noticed him repacking his bag. There was no one else. Fido then continued to whine and nosed her hand to try to get the girl to pat him. As soon as she saw the dog, she stopped crying. She sat back down and started to pet Fido. Soon she started to talk to Fido and the dog became more affectionate and playful. Fido went through all the motions, he sat up with paws out for the girl to shake hands. Fido rolled over and played dead. He had gotten the girl's mind off her problems in just a few minutes. The girl giggled and Fido jumped up and ran around the picnic table, came back and head butted the girl's leg gently. The girl petted Fido for a minute and then Fido began to look around. He caught Jasper's eye and then trotting over towards him.

"This is your signal?" Jasper said to Fido as the dog approached.

Fido rolled his eyes, shook his head, turned around and begin galloping back towards the girl. Jasper got up and walked over towards the girl and said, “I hope my dog isn't bothering you. My name is Jasper Jay Hawk. I see you've met Fido.” He put his hand out to greet her.

“Oh my,” the girl stood up quickly. “I'm sorry, the dog came over to me. To play I guess. I didn't mean any harm. My name is Charlotte.”

"No! No! You've done nothing wrong, go ahead and play with him, he loves people and most people love him,” he said with a smile as she finally took his hand and shook it.

"He sure is a friendly dog and well trained. What'd you say his name was?”

"Ah, Fido, his name is Fido."

“That's defiantly a ‘dog’ name like Rover or a cat named Felix or Whiskers. A smart dog needs a cool name. Not to crap on his name but did you name him?” she asked as she continued to pet the dog.

"Well, um. I did. I kind of named him before I knew how smart he was,” he said apologetically. "Once I named him, it kind of stuck with him and we have grown to like it."

"Who's we?” Charlotte asked, as the dog trotted back over to the opposite corner of the building where they had first spotted Charlotte.

“We is my family and me," Jasper explained, as they were both watching the dog pick up something and bring it back

“Well, I probably would have changed his name. What has Fido picked up?” Charlotte said.

"Oh it looks like the dog bone I gave him when we first got here," he said. "He saw you and never touched the bone. It looks like he just remembered it and went over to retrieve it.” Fido had come back with the bone and laid down about ten feet away and started eating it.

“Well, if you were way down there when you first got here how come all your stuff is so much closer near the ice box?" Charlotte asked, pointing to where he had parked his bike and stuff.

"In all honesty, when I gave the dog the bone down there he wouldn't touch it." Jasper explained. "If you know how animals are when they are given food, they gobble it up so fast it’s gone before you know it, but Fido wouldn't take his eyes of you so I looked closer and saw you were upset about something. So I told Fido we would move closer and he could go over to see you. It seemed like that's what he wanted to do. And now he feels assured that you aren't stressed out anymore so he can relax and eat his bone."

"So you moved closer to spy on me, is that it?" she said with a smirk.

"No, it was as I explained. You appeared distraught and I thought the dog could comfort you a little," Jasper said. "Is there anything I can do? Are you all right?" He stood there awkwardly, "Mind if I sit down?"

"Sure, have a seat. You seem safe enough. With a dog like that I can't go wrong." She gestured to him to sit down and continued. "I don't think there is anything anyone can do and no, I'm not all right."

"Do you want to talk about it? I don't mean to be in your business but sometimes it helps to talk about things and get someone else's opinion or thoughts on things," he said.

"Well, it's a long story and I don't want to bore you with it. I got myself into a situation and now I have to think it through and decide what to do about it," she said. "And I don't want to waste your time."

"Time, that's all I have is time. Let me tell you a little bit about my situation," he explained. He told her the whole story about his bike trip and were he was headed. That this was his first day on the road and that he was free to travel at his own pace and that he had all the time he wanted to do anything he wanted.

"So you're peddling that bike, with the dog, and all your gear all the way to Old Calcutta?"

"Yep, that's right, all the way. I've done it once, without the dog, but this time I have more time and I want to see a little more along the way."

"Well, I'll be damned," said Charlotte, I am from Fort Kent. My father took us, my brother, Buddy and me to Wallgrass Lake to swim once. I know the area pretty well. I lived there with my Grandma Rosa for seven years"

"Old Calcutta is were my grandparents live and I'm spending most of the summer there. What brings you down here?" asked Jasper.

"That's part of the long story I'd just assume not get into."

"Suit yourself. You don't have to tell me a thing if you don't want to. You just looked hungry. Want some trail mix or some beef jerky? That's all I eat during the day. I have my meals in the morning and evening," Jasper explained.

"Well, I am hungry. That's another part of the long story. The last ride I got dropped me off here to use the bathroom and they were gone when I came out. They took my backpack, which had every thing I owned in it, all I had was this make up bag and the clothes on my back. I had fifty bucks in that bag. I was hitching rides trying to make it to Landrush to get a job and work a little to get on my feet and head further south. I have a friend in Landrush to stay with."

"Ok, I've heard enough, you come with me. Fido you stay with the bike and gear and will be right back," Jasper hollered to the dog.

"Why, hey you can't…where are you going? Don't turn me in," Charlotte said, as she was looking towards the gas pumps at a police patrol car that just happened to be pulling in.

Jasper looked over and saw the cop car. "I wouldn't turn you in. Are you in trouble or something?"

"No." she said without making eye contact.

"I was going to offer to buy you a sandwich or something. Like I said you look hungry. So lets go I could use more then this beef jerky myself."

He'll never keep any schedule if he plans to rescue everyone he meets along the way, the dog thought. It's only the first day!

As they walked away toward the restaurant, Charlotte said, "No I'm not in trouble, I just don't like cops. I really don't know you well enough for you to take me out to eat."

"Well, how well did you know those people who took off with your stuff. I think you are safe with me even though I don't have references, except of course Fido."

"You don't have to worry, I will pay you back every cent," she replied as they walked into the restaurant.

At that Fido chuckled to himself, Oh yes, Jasper you're another easy mark. This should be interesting. What will he get himself into this time? I guess this is what he means by adventure. Fido took his place by the picnic table and laid down for a quiet nap.

In the store they went through the line and settled down at a small table in the corner near a window where Jasper could look out and see where Fido was. They said nothing for a few minutes and ate their food. Jasper thought Charlotte was quite beautiful. Her face was young and soft with pretty features. Her hair was brown and dirty but could be nice. It was long and straight and put up with a scrunchy, she was about five feet nine inches, and lean and slender with a full bosom.

Jasper broke the silence and said, “You’re running away, aren’t you?"

Charlotte stopped chewing swallowed and said, "You think you’ve got it all figured out, do you? Look I really appreciate the meal but, hey, I can take care of myself. You can leave now. I am going to sit here for a while."

"Whoa! Charlotte I'm not judging you. It just sounds like you’re running from something and don't really have a plan. It's obvious you can take care of yourself. You got all the way here from Fort Kent, and I don't want to leave."

"Ok, don't leave then. But don't try to tell me what I'm doing and where I'm going. How can you help me anyway? You don't have a car. All you have is that bike and dog. You'd be in my way more than anything else," she replied.

"Ok then, I'll be right back. Will you wait here for one minute? I have to check on something," he replied.

"Sure I'll wait. Where are you going?"

"Nowhere… just give me a minute, Ok?”

Jasper left out the exit and turned right instead of left toward his dog and disappeared. Charlotte thought I’ve got to loose this guy. He's starting to bug me and he can't help my situation one bit anyway.

He showed back up ten minutes later and sat down across from Charlotte. "I just went to the bus station which is over there," said Jasper as he pointed out the window back the way he had come. "They have a bus service," he continued as he laid down a bus schedule in between them. "It can take you from here to Bath, and drop you off at the Greyhound terminal. From there, if you want you can take a bus north or south. Whatever you decide." As he said this he looked into Charlotte's eyes, trying to figure out what she was running from. She had hazel eyes that stared back at him anxiously. She could not hold eye contact with him and looked away as she stirred nervously in her seat.

"I'm going to continue on my trip to downtown Bath," continued Jasper after a couple of minutes had gone by. "Then I'm going to the Maine Maritime Museum for a couple hours. It's twelve-thirty now, there is a boat ride at two that I want to go on. It leaves the museum and travels up the Kennebec River, it takes about forty-five minutes to an hour."

"Yeah," said Charlotte, "well, I'm not interested in the Kennebec River. I told you I'm headed south. I don't have much money and I'm not going to waste the little I have running around with some boy I hardly know. Find another girl to hit on." With that she stood up and marched out the door.

Her remark infuriated him. He quickly gathered the bus schedule up of the table and ran out the door after her. "Wait a minute, Charlotte," he yelled as he swung the door to the store shut behind him.

Charlotte looked back at him over her shoulder as she continued walking up the street towards the bus station. "I told you I'm not interested. Go away, Jasper," she shouted angrily as she picked up her pace.

"You misunderstood me," he protested as he ran up beside her. "I'm not trying to hit on you. I have a girlfriend at home. I'm just trying to help!"

Charlotte stopped dead in her tracts turned to face Jasper, "I don't want your help. I'm going to take a bus south." She yelled and started walking again.

Jasper didn't follow after her this time. "All right, if that's what you want, but it's pretty hard to get on a bus if you don't have any money."

Charlotte stopped again and turned around to look back at him with her hands crossed in front of her. That remark hit home and brought her back to reality. He's right. I need money, she thought.

"Now, I will give you this twenty dollars so that you can catch a bus to Bath. Then to Landrush and go to your friends place there. A loan of course," said Jasper, putting up his hands after handing Charlotte the bill. Charlotte glared at him again. "I don't want anything from you, Charlotte. I just don't want to see you get into more trouble than you can handle from hitchhiking. You can't always trust people willing to give you rides. You've already seen what can happen."

"Well, thanks, but I can't take your money," she said in a much more calm and friendly manner, realizing the truth in his statement, as she smiled and batted her eyes at him.

"I want you to take the money. I wouldn't feel right about it if I just left you here the way things are… besides," he continued as he took Charlottes hands in his. "You could come to Bath with me take the boat cruise as I had suggested, tell me a little bit more about your situation. Maybe I could help you figure out what it is you really want. Then if we figure out a sensible plan. I'll put you on a Greyhound to wherever it is that we decide is the best place for you to go." With that Jasper let go of Charlotte's hands. Charlotte fingered the twenty-dollar bill that he had left behind in her hand, as she looked at him puzzled and trying to figure out what he was up to. "I'm going to get going now. Here is the bus schedule," said Jasper. "Remember its up to you what happens next. You can take the bus to Bath, go to the Greyhound Terminal and get a bus to Landrush, or you can meet me at the museum, it's on Pearl Street. Jasper turned around and walked off before she could say anything more or try to give him the money back.

He felt her eyes on him as he walked back to the picnic table where Fido and the bike remained. He didn't look back at her. Fido looked at him with a questionable twisted head. All that work and she's not coming, thought Fido.

"What?" Jasper said to Fido, "You want her to take your seat and you can run to Bath? She's meeting us there." At least he hoped she was.

Jasper glanced over and saw her watching and waved at her as he pedaled off. She put her hand up and let loose with a short finger wave.

“She is stubborn,” he said to the dog, as he peddled towards Bath. “I can't force her to talk to me. She needs help but I'm not sure I’m the one to do it. I really don't know if she'll show up at the museum.”

Charlotte watched Jasper peddle off and thought, he really has left me with no options. I can't get far on twenty bucks and hitch hiking is really a dangerous way to travel with all the scumbags out there. I really need to consider my little brother Buddy in all of this. Maybe I should talk this out with him. I can probably squeeze a little more money out of him. She took the bus schedule and headed for the teller.

Jasper pedaled to the center of town in Bath and headed for the Greyhound bus terminal. It was easy to find. Whether Charlotte met them or not, a bus locker was big enough to store his gear in one locker. Jasper took the time to fold the bike up into its suitcase and put it into another of the lockers. He locked both lockers and put the keys into his fanny pack he was carrying. He stopped and got a bus schedule of times, places and costs to any of the New England destinations. Then he went into the rest room and got out some more money from his money belt in case he needed it. He would not give Charlotte any more money unless her plan was solid and morally correct.

Jasper went outside buckling up his fanny pack around his waist as he came out the bus terminal exit to where he left Fido. The dog was nowhere in sight. That was very unusual. He began to get concerned. He did a three-sixty and quickly scanned the area looking for the black dog. Nothing! He ran to the corner and looked quickly down the street. There he was front feet up on a sidewalk bench lapping the face of Charlotte. Phew, he exclaimed to himself, I think Fido may have won her over.

Jasper went over and sat down on the bench beside her and said, "Hey Charlotte, glad to see you. I got concerned when I didn't see Fido where I had left him. I guess he really likes you. What'd you do, grab the first bus? Are you going to Landrush or the museum?"

"The bus didn't come for about twenty minutes and I had time to think about a few things you said," Charlotte explained. "I don't have a friend in Landrush, and I can't pin point it exactly but when I thought about it, you made a lot of sense. Like hitch hiking isn't really such a good idea and coming up with a plan seems important. To be honest, I have no money. I think I would like to talk to you about a few things, and I'm sorry about being such a bitch. When you're in a situation like I'm in you have to be careful about a lot of things."

Jasper knew she wasn't too careful about her last ride at the rest stop, but said, "I don't want you to think I'm the savior and can make your world right, but I can listen and possibly help. You can probably think of what would be best for you if you talk about it, also,"

"I'm just so mixed up about certain things that it's hard to really think straight. I am sort of running away but I am leaving my brother, Buddy who's only five with no one to take care of him except a drunk mother. I need to go back for him," Charlotte replied.

"Well, that's where talking with someone can help you think more clearly," Jasper said, as he got up. "Lets go to the museum, stroll through it at our own pace and talk things out."

"Fido," he said, the dog looking up at him. "You know the rules in the city, you need to be leashed." Fido shook his head up and down meaning, Yes.

"Man, that dog seems to understand you," said Charlotte.

"He is smart, no doubt, but he responds to my tone of voice and situations. For example, he hates the leash but knows it's necessary in cities, parks and most buildings," he explained.

"Well, he amazes me. Fido is the smartest dog I've ever met. I worked in an animal shelter and he is the brightest animal I've seen," said Charlotte.

"It's only about six or eight blocks to the museum," Jasper started to say.

"Hey, where's your stuff and bike?" interrupted Charlotte, throwing her hands in the air.

"I stowed it in a couple bus lockers in the station. The bike folds up into a suitcase," Explained Jasper, pointing over to the bus terminal.

"Wow! That's amazing. It folds up?" she said. "Where did you get a folding bike?"

"I worked in a bike shop in Landrush for a few years. The owner and I built it. It's custom made. My boss designed it and helped me put it together. Paulsie, my boss had some parts special made. His son, Jonny a friend of mine, is the owner now. He is getting the bike patented and then maybe we'll selling them to the public."

"That's cool, you're so creative. I've never done any thing like that," Charlotte said.

"Oh you never know, you just haven't had the right challenge yet," Jasper replied, as they walked down the street towards the museum with Fido walking a step behind Jasper who was carrying the leash.

They were walking along exchanging small talk, when Jasper found himself walking alone. He looked back while still talking in mid sentence and saw Charlotte stopped and stiff as a board looking stunned like she had seen a ghost staring at something. He followed her stare as he moved quickly back to her side. "What is it, Charlotte? You look like you saw a ghost. What's the matter?" he said, as he picked up her clammy hand. They were walking past a park in the middle of town not too far from the museum.

"That's the truck that left me at the gas station and took off with my stuff and oh God! There's Charlie, the driver walking towards the car with someone," Charlotte said in a panicked voice.

"Are you sure?" Jasper asked quickly, "Are you absolutely sure Charlotte?" She nodded her head yes. "Tell me something about the truck that makes you think it's the one you rode in. Tell me quick because we don't want them to leave, he is walking towards the truck now, but I need to be sure."

"It was that same color teal blue with that different colored door. It had a silver cross hanging from the interior mirror. It had a ripped back seat were I sat. There were several packs of Camel cigarettes in the glove compartment and a hunting knife, also." The man "Charlie" had gotten to the truck and the other man was waiting in the park. Charlie reached in his pocket and pulled out his keys. He unlocked the door and took out a frisbee and then locked the truck back up. He started towards the park where the other guy went. "Oh yes and that frisbee was in there also in the back with me," cried Charlotte softly. “Too bad he hadn’t left it unlocked, that would have made this simple.”

“Well at least they're playing Frisbee. That gives us time to think of something,” Jasper explained. Then he pointed to a bench beyond the truck. “Let's walk past the truck to that bench over there near the corner. We can sit down get a better view and figure out what to do.”

Chapter 4
The Ferryboat & the Fender Bender

They picked up the pace and walked past the truck. It was a teal blue, Chevy Silverado pick up with an extended cab, one of those three door trucks. The passenger side door looked like it had been replaced and was primed red, like it was going to be painted. Jasper looked over the truck and saw the cross hanging from the mirror and the ripped upholstery of the back seat. There was also a green backpack but the initials on it he couldn't make out.

So at least that part of Charlotte's story had been the truth. He had to be sure. He remembered what Stonie had told him. 'Never trust anyone until you know them well.' They took a seat on the corner bench. The two men were paying no attention to them. They were in their late twenties or early thirties. This Charlie guy was six feet or a little over with an athletic build, the other guy was short but rugged with a goatee.

Jasper believed they would likely give him trouble but was confident with Fido backing him up. However confrontation was always a risk and anything could happen. "Was the other guy with him when he pick you up?" he asked.

"No," Charlotte said, "there were two girls, Patty and Molly I think. I would never have taken a ride if the girls hadn't been with that guy Charlie. They were driving from Belfast to Landrush they told me."

"Is there anything else you can tell me about them from your conversation while you were in the truck?" Jasper asked.

"The Molly girl was Charlie's girlfriend and they were taking Patty to Landrush to meet up with a guy named Jake. Oh yes and there is one other thing. I used a fake name, Crystal, my mother's name. They know me as Crystal. Jasper, I don't want any trouble. I just want my things and my money back."

Jasper looked Charlotte right in the eyes and said, "Look Charlotte, you told me it was $50 before. You've got to level with me on things. I can't help you if I can't believe you."

"I told you, I take precautions for safety reasons when I travel and I didn't want to look stupid by saying I left $100 unattended when I was in the bathroom. I didn't think they would take off on me."

"Then why did you tell me your name was Charlotte and not Crystal?" he asked.

"When you spoke to me at the restaurant you startled me and I didn't have time to think so I just said my own name in a knee-jerk response," she said defensively.

"That's something else to talk about later after we get your stuff back. Let's concentrate on one problem at a time. Just remember, the truth will set you free. But never mind that now. We need to formulate a plan before going to confront these guys. So for this little drama I'll call you Crystal. Now listen…"

A few minutes later they walked back toward the truck from the corner bench. When they got to the truck the two men were over in the middle of the park about forty yards parallel, tossing the frisbee.

Charlotte hollered to them, "Yo Charlie, come here! Hey Charlie, I want my stuff back." Jasper was walking a few feet behind her, with Fido on the leash. Charlie looked over at her during the middle of a throw and completely missed the catch. He started walking toward her.

"Oh Jesus, Jasper, he's coming this way!" She said in a little frightened voice.

"That's good. Don't panic. You want him near the truck, then I will take over. Hang in there, you're doing a good job," said Jasper encouragingly.

"Who are you? What do you want with me?" Charlie hollered, "I don't know you." His friend had gone after the frisbee and was coming up behind. "Hey Jake, you know this girl? I sure don't."

“Hell no,” said Jake, “Never seen her before. What you want with us?”

Charlotte took a few steps closer to the truck and said, “I don't want anything from you Jake-o. What I do want is this Charlie guy to give me my backpack and money that he took from me this morning at the filling station. Don't you remember Charlie? When you took off on me when I was in the bathroom?”

Jasper was standing a few feet behind her looking a little intimidated on purpose. He wanted to get Charlie in the right position before he mounted his challenge. Fido was sitting behind him panting like he didn't give a damn what happened. Charlotte had backed up a few more steps and was even with Jasper when Charlie spoke. “Look sweetie, you seem to have mistaken me for someone else. I've been with Jake here all morning.” He then looked Jasper up and down and didn't see a threat so he continued. “I have no interest in little girls like you, so get the fuck out of here before I really get pissed off,” he yelled leaning in close to her face.

Charlotte jumped back frightened. Fido walked over quietly, not panting, ears up. Jasper stepped forward really close to Charlie and said calmly, “You know, I don't like the way you're speaking to her. All she wants is her stuff back. You give it over nice and I won't send her to get that cop over there. I’m sure he could settle this easy enough.” Jasper nodded, gesturing towards a policeman fifty yards away who is writing parking tickets on the other side of the park.

Charlie and Jake glanced over at the cop and looked back and smiled at him. “You can do whatever the fuck you’d like to, I’m not giving that bitch back anything.” Charlie took another half step towards Jasper as he clenched his fists tightly.

“We’ll kick both of your asses before that pig even notices,” Jake added with a cocky look on his face.

“So you're saying that you do in fact know her and you did take her things?” suggested Jasper.

“I didn't say anything.”

“You said, ‘I ain't given that bitch back anything,’ which implies that you took something,” Jasper explained.

Charlie had a confused look on his face and said, "The only thing I tried to take from her was her virginity and someone else beat me to that. But she was pretty sweet, even for sloppy seconds." Charlie and Jake both broke out laughing. "Why don't the two of you get the hell out here before I really lose it?"

"You bastard. You have no right to say shit like that," Charlotte interrupted and screamed at Charlie.

Jasper held up his hand to calm her down and said to Charlie, "So now we're getting somewhere, you do know her. What's with this charade about not knowing? I think it's pretty obvious that you've taken her stuff. I'm giving you two choices. Give us her bag and money or I'll send her over to get that policeman." The officer was still standing at the same car writing a ticket.

"Five seconds to decide, Charlie." Jasper starting counting down from five as they stood toe to toe. Charlie's face turned red and his fists tightened. He stepped back planted his back foot and came around with a sluggish roundhouse punch with his right arm. He aimed for Jasper's face but the punch never reached its mark. Jasper stepped in, blocked the punch with his left forearm and drove the heel of his right hand into Charlie's jaw knocking him to the ground. He pivoted on his right foot and came across the left side of Jake's face with the back of his right-hand. Jake went down on his knees. All this happened in a split second. At the same time Fido jumped out in full fighting form bearing his canines; growling and slobbering on Jake's face. "Hold, Fido," Jasper said and the dog moved back six inches still growling and showing his fangs. "I'll have that dog tear you a new asshole if you move a muscle, Jake." Jake didn't move. Jasper turned back to Charlie who was lying on his back just recovering from the blow he had taken. He pointed his finger into Charlie's face while staring down at him. "I didn't want things to go this far but you gave me no choice. You listen and you listen well."

"Jasper," Charlotte interrupts, "I know where my bag is in the truck. Have him give you the keys and we can get my bag and get outta here."

"Hold up, Crystal. I want to give this guy some final advice." A few people had started to gather while he and Fido held the two men on the ground. "Look, we're drawing a crowd. Unless you want the cops in on this you'll cooperate. I'm going to let you two get up and we're all going to walk over to your truck. The dog will attack if you try to run or get aggressive. I promise you he will attack the first person who gets out of line. Do you both understand?" The two men nodded their heads in agreement. Jasper stood up and said, "Back, Fido. Stay on defense. You two get up and walk slow over to the truck and sit on the front fender." The dog backed up slowly and the men stood up even slower. They all walked over to the truck. "Okay people, just a small misunderstanding. You can all move along now," Jasper explained. About six people had gathered together to watch. With Jasper's assurances they all began to turn to leave.

Charlie and Jake sat on the fender of the truck, Fido coming with a low growl and a show of teeth now and then. Charlie said, "Listen man, we don't want any trouble with you or the cops. This Crystal bitch, umm, girl is lying and trying to take our shit."

"What do you expect him to say?" Charlotte interrupted. "First he claimed he didn't even know me, then he claimed he slept with me. Which he didn't, by the way. I can prove it's my backpack. You'll find my initials on it, CWB."

"Those are my initials, you lying bitch. Lady, I'm going to get you if you take that pack," Charlie swore. "And I'll get you too if you let her pull this off," he said to Jasper as he pointed at him. He looked over the cop who is even closer now.

The officer was coming down the street ticketing cars and was moving their way. "Well, Charlie, it's your call. The cop or the backpack?" he asked. "Give me the keys so Crystal can get the bag or talk to the cops about it."

Charlie was really sweating the closeness of the cop so he reached into his pocket and brought out the keys.

Charlotte snatched them out of his hand, unlocked the truck and opened the door. She saw Molly's sneakers and sweater on the floor. She quickly unzipped the first section of the backpack and stuffed them in. She pulled her wallet out of the bag she had earlier told Jasper was her makeup bag and put it in another section of the backpack. She had been planning to do this as soon as she realized he had control of the situation. It only took a few seconds and Jasper was too engaged with Charlie to realize what she was doing.

Charlotte emerged from the truck with the backpack. "See, Jasper? My initials are right here, CWB." She pointed to them with a confident smile. "And look. My sweater and sneakers are here too." She pulled them out and showed them to Jasper and then stuffed them back in. She unzipped another smaller section of the backpack and pulled out her wallet that she had just placed there. "Here's my wallet that they tried to take. Now is everyone convinced this is my stuff?"

Jasper looked at Charlie. "I'm convinced, her stuff is in the bag. Her wallet is in there, it even has her initials. You're just pissed because you couldn't get away with her money. You're a sad son of a bitch of a man to leave a girl by herself with no money or way to get along. Now you listen here, you get in the truck and move on out here or I will call that cop over here and let him straighten this out." The cop was getting too close for Charlie's comfort.

"Let's go, Jake. We'll get the backpack later and I will get both of you for this. Watch your back, Jasper," Charlie said pointing his finger one more time into his face as he and Jake scrambled into the truck and drove away.

Jasper committed his license plate to memory and would definitely jot it down in his address book later along with the make,model and description of the truck. He had a feeling he may see them again.

Charlotte said, "Let's get the hell out of here. We've got to put this town behind us. They'll be back, you can bet your ass on that."

"Look Charlotte, they'll never expect us to go to the Maine Maritime Museum, we'll be safe there. I think you are right we should get out of this area. They seem at home here. If we can get to the museum before two and take the boat ride across the Kennebec River to Woolwich I think will be safe."

"What are you saying? The boat is a ferryboat?" asked Charlotte.

"Not really but my mother told me it stops at the little town of Woolwich across the river when there are a lot of tourists so they can hit some of the antique shops over there," he explained. "This is really the first big day of the summer season because school got out for most everyone last Friday. I am banking on a large group of tourists at the museum. Let's hope so. We need to move fast. I have to go get my gear and bike. Do you want to continue on to the museum with Fido or wait for me here?"

"Hell no. I'm not leaving your side as long as those guys are around," said Charlotte as she looked down the street for the truck. After seeing Jasper in action against those dip shit guys she felt more secure.

"Okay then," he said. "Let's get going. We've lost a lot of time. The museum tour is half over and we need to be there for the boat ride by two o'clock." Jasper turned toward the bus station and headed for the terminal to get his gear from the lockers. Charlotte held Fido's leash and was following behind him, she had put the backpack in place on her back. As they approached the bus station, Jasper saw a cab. "Charlotte, grab that taxi. We'll take it over to the museum. It'll save time. Fido, stay with her." Jasper disappeared into the station.

Boy, thought Fido, another change of plans. Jay is really going off the deep end. Now we got tough guys that want a piece of us. I'm not totally convinced that Charlotte Princess is leveling with us either. It seemed to take her some extra time to get her bag out of the truck. Well, Jasper's the boss, he knows what's best.

It only took him a minute to get his gear. Charlotte had the cabbie open the trunk and Jasper threw his stuff in on top of the backpack and got in. The cab took off down the street toward the museum.

A boy that Charlie had intercepted in the park after his encounter with Jasper and Fido stood across the street from the bus station. He wore a red Boston Red Sox baseball cap with the 'B' logo in front and the hat on backwards. He stood outside of the phone booth he had used after calling Charlie back and telling him that the two people and the dog the boy had been told to follow had just gotten into a cab and taken off. The boy told Charlie what direction they were headed in. Charlie was three blocks away at another pay phone and took off after the cab. He was able to catch up with it and kept it with in sight. He stayed well back from it. Charlie was only keeping his distance because of the dog. He and Jake had to figure out a plan as to how to get the dog out of the picture. They were on their ass and he was determined to get his drugs and money back and most of all his personal notebook. If that notebook got in the wrong hands, he would be in deep shit. Plus, he wanted to teach those two a lesson. The cab stopped and the three were getting out at the Maine Maritime Museum. Jake got out and Charlie went back to pick the kid up, keeping out of sight of the entrance to the museum.

Jasper, Charlotte and Fido piled out of the cab at the entrance of the museum. Jasper paid the cabbie. They got their gear out of the trunk and went into the museum. All this with no words spoken. He was reaching in his fanny pack to get money for the museum fee. Charlotte piped in proudly, “I can pay for this. I will pay you back for the cab ride and lunch and here is your twenty dollars back you gave me at the rest stop. That should make us even.” Charlotte handed the clerk twenty dollars and handed a twenty to Jay with a sincere smile on her face.

“It’s not about money, Charlotte,” he said as he took the twenty. “Thanks.” He shook his head. There was no arguing with her.

The clerk handed Charlotte their tickets and change and said, “The dog must stay on a leash and the boat leaves at two. You can catch up with the tour guide or just wander through at your own speed. The boat will be making a stop in the town of Woolwich for those who want to check out the shops. You can get a ride back to the museum on the three o’clock run.”

“Thank you,” he said to the clerk. “This worked out perfectly.” He looked at Charlotte as they picked up all their gear and headed into the museum. “In light of everything that’s happened, I’m not really interested in the museum anymore. Lets just get a cup of coffee over by the docking area and wait there. It would be hard to lug all this stuff around through the different buildings.” Charlotte agreed and they took off for the docking area and found a bench to sit down on. Jasper tied the leash to the bench and went over to the snack bar for their coffee. He could see the dog from where he stood. You weren’t really supposed to leave them unattended. Charlotte took the backpack and went to the ladies room.

Charlotte got into the ladies room and went right into the stall to be by herself. She went through the contents of the backpack. The first section of the backpack was full of dime bags of marijuana and some other assortments of various colored pills sealed in sandwich bags. There were also two quart sized bags of a white powder that she assumed was cocaine. She had no idea how much it was worth. She opened up the other zip section where she had shoved the sneakers and sweater in and she now saw it was filled with money, mostly twenty dollar bills. Charlotte thumbed through the money to get an idea of how much was there. It seemed to be about three thousand dollars. Oh My God! she mouthed silently as she unzipped the smaller front, remaining section of the backpack. There was a nine millimeter pistol with a box of cartridges and a black notebook. She had seen them open the backpack up and take out a dime bag to smoke in the truck while they were driving and she had also seen some of the money but she had not realized there was all of this. Charlie must be a big time drug dealer. She had thought he was just some country boy toking up with his friend. Someone she could hit up for some money. The money was all she was after and she hadn't expected this much. She had heard them say something about going to the park while they were all in Charlie's truck. She had known where they would be. She knew they were from Bath. They had actually gone out of their way to give her a ride to the gas station. When they left her at the rest stop she had been exactly as Jasper had found her, minus the tears. Her only hope was to get ahold of some money and get back to Fort Kent. She had not talked much during the ride in the truck so they actually knew very little about her, except an incorrect first name. When she saw Jasper at the rest stop she had come up with this plan. He had a naive, eager to help, boy-scout look about him. Charlotte figured she could play on his sympathy, get a ride to Bath and find the unassuming Charlie at the park. Then with a little luck, and a teenage boy dying to be her hero, she could somehow steal his bag. She had rationalized that it was okay to steal the money from Charlie because he gave off this creepy vibe in the truck. She figured that he was a little sketchy and if he was out selling pot from his truck he probably deserved to be robbed. But now, everything had changed. These were serious drugs and a lot more cash then she ever would have thought. The nine millimeter pistol also made her nervous. If he had a gun like that he probably would be willing to use it, especially to get his property back. She had to make a decision. Should she tell Jasper how serious this shit had gotten or just keep him in the dark. She liked how he fought and how he was cool under pressure but he was way too honest. Charlotte did feel she owed him something. He had treated her well and helped her when he didn't have to. If he didn't know what he was dealing with, someone could get seriously hurt. She figured she'd better tell him the truth. Charlotte sat on the toilet seat staring into Charlie's backpack for several minutes. Should she tell Jasper now before they leave or wait till the boat ride? She knew the answer even as she was asking herself the question. She could not tell him until they were on the boat. Things had gotten out of hand. This situation was dangerous. If she started to tell him what was going on before they boarded the boat there was little chance in her mind that Jasper would continue with his original plan. He would not get on the boat, he would keep her right here in this Maritime Museum and wait for her to explain herself, then he would turn her into the police if they didn't run into Charlie first. She had to wait until he had already committed to taking her to Woolwich then she could tell him the truth on the boat ride. That would give her a half hour with him as a captive audience to convince him she was leveling with him. It might be hard to do because she had lied so much recently, especially to Jasper.

Charlotte took the sneakers and the sweater out and zipped up the backpack. She then put them into the ladies room trashcan. She nervously headed towards the entrance of the museum to look for Charlie's truck. With the drugs, notebook and so much money involved she knew Charlie and his cronies would be close. She walked up to one of the two large windows that were on either side of the main entrance and looked out. The glare from the sun on the glass should conceal her from the street, she thought. Charlotte scanned the nearest area to the museum, just in case, not expecting the truck to be so close. She then focused on the area to the left of the building and looked further and further down the street towards the park. She saw nothing. She then looked over to the right and had to squint because of the sun coming through the window. She thought she glimpsed the front end sticking out of a side street but the sun had been too intense.

She looked away, closed her eyes for a few seconds while the after image of the sun's glare burned across her retinas. When it had faded she opened he eyes again. Standing next to her was a touristy looking middle aged man with a tweed cap and a pair of binoculars hanging from around his neck. He seemed to be waiting for someone. Charlotte saw them and said to the man, "Sir, I'm looking for my little brother. I think I see him way down there across the park. Can I use your binoculars for a second to see if it's him? It won't take but a second."

"Why sure, dear. Go ahead," said the man graciously. He took them out of the case and handed them to her.

"Thank you so much," said Charlotte smiling sweetly to him as she grabbed the binoculars, almost too fast. She focused them back over to the spot where she thought she had seen the truck. She cupped her hand above the binoculars to prevent the glare from the sun scoring her eyes again. Sure enough, it was the truck. She could see it clearly this time. She could tell it was the same truck because of the red door and the teal body. A kid with a red cap on backwards got out of the truck while Jake got in taking his place. The kid started walking toward the museum. They've had surveillance on us ever since we left the park, thought Charlotte. Shit! I knew they'd play hardball. There's way too much involved.

Charlotte handed the binoculars back to the man and said, "Nope, it's not him. Thanks anyway. I'll find him, plus he knows where I am." She glanced out the window to see the kid getting closer. She left quickly waving to the man, not giving him a chance to respond. As she left the lobby she heard the clerk Jasper had spoken to earlier speaking to a couple at the head of the line. "…it's only four dollars, half price, but I'm afraid we're not selling any more tickets for the boat tour. The two o'clock is sold out and the three o'clock is only a return trip."

Oh good, thought Charlotte, the kid wont be able to get on the boat. Charlotte went straight to where Jasper was sitting.

Jasper had been sitting with Fido for about ten minutes. He had finished his coffee and Charlotte's was growing cold. "Is she coming back, Fido?" he said finally. Fido looked up at Jasper, cocking his head to one side. Fido nodded his head twice and stood up. He looked in the direction Charlotte had left and lifted his left front leg, standing point. Jasper looked in the direction Fido was pointing. "What? I don't see her," he said.

Fido whined in what sounded almost annoyed. "Woof," said Fido, without dropping his gaze, as if his response was sufficient to explain himself. Charlotte darted around the corner an instant later. Fido looked at Jasper with what looked like a smirk on his face. He sniffed the air and winked at Jasper.

"You smelled her coming? Of course you did," said Jasper.

"There you two are!" announced Charlotte as she approached the duo. She came from the left the direction of the main lobby, not the bathroom.

"Where've you been?" he asked, seeming slightly confused. "I thought you went to the bathroom?"

"I did," said Charlotte with a shaky voices. She seemed nervous to Fido. Her body language was tense and she was too fidgety with her hands. She smells of suspicion and alarm thought the dog. Fido whined at Jasper and looked up at his friend with concerned eyes.

Jasper caught Fido's cue that something was wrong. "Charlotte, what is it? You look like you've seen a ghost, again."

"I did go to the bathroom," she answered, "but I got thinking, what if Charlie and his friends aren't through. I mean, what if their mad at being caught stealing my bag and they want to get even with us? They might've followed us. So I went to the front of the museum to take a look around."

'That was a lie!' Fido thought as he listened to Charlotte. He didn't know what the lie was, but the dog's instincts told him Charlotte was hiding something.

"I saw Charlie in his truck on a side street talking through the window to a kid in a Red Sox cap. The kid pointed to the museum. Charlie drove off and the kid crossed the street coming straight toward me. I hot footed it back here to find you. I don't think he saw me."

Jasper looked down at Fido who seemed tense and suddenly irritable. The dog was making a steady low growl that Jasper almost couldn't hear. He was definitely suspicious of something. "I don't get it, Charlotte. Why would Charlie, some country boy risk another confrontation with us over your bag? I'd think he would just assume cut his losses for the time being after what happened last time."

"Well, I don't know," Charlotte said, defensively. "but, I'm sure it was him and the kid's coming this way."

"This kid must just be following us to see where we're going. I can't imagine Charlie would be stupid enough to pick a fight with us right in the middle of a crowded museum."

"Well, he wont be able to follow us for long," Charlotte added. "He can't get on the boat. I heard the clerk telling some people that the rides were full and they were only selling museum tickets."

"Ok, that's good! We'll lose him on the ferry. We'll have to figure out what to do when we get to Woolwich. We'll have some time on the boat to come up with a plan. With this many people riding, lets move up so there no issue with us getting on."

They got up and started walking closer to the river where the boat was docked. They sat down on the grass. Jasper watched the kid in the Red Sox hat as he got up and moved closer, apparently so he could see where Jasper and Charlotte had moved to.

"I wonder if he knows the boat stops in Woolwich across the river?" Jasper said, as the boy stood back up and walked over to a pay phone ten yards behind him. Jasper leaned over to Fido and pretended to interest himself with patting the dog while he whispered into his faithful companions ear. "Go over there and see what you can hear." Charlotte wasn't paying attention to Jasper and Fido. She was absorbed in watching the boy with the cap.

Fido picked up the leash in his mouth and covertly slinked over to where the boy was standing and laid down a short distance away. Fido seemed too far away from the boy by Jasper's reckoning to hear any more than mumbles, but he reminded himself that Fido was a dog with sharp senses. His hearing is far more developed than his own.

The boy didn't notice Fido at all as the dog settled into his recon post. "...getting on the boat. I couldn't get a ticket. The boat rides are full for the day," <pause> "...So, you want me to stay here and when they come back I'll keep on their tail," <pause> "Ok Charlie, you've got it."

The boy hung up the phone on the receiver. He looked up to see if Jasper had moved. Fido took this as a good opportunity to slip away. He stood up and walked away from the boy to the left circling around to come up to Charlotte and Jasper from the opposite side. The boy would not be able to tell where he'd been skulking from. "Hey! Where were you off to?" Charlotte asked as she noticed the dog returning to her side. She bent down and patted Fido on the top of the head and behind his ears.

"He's been on a reconnaissance mission," Jasper told her. "but now he's back." He stood up and looked down at the dog. Fido turned around and nuzzled his head into Jasper's outstretched hand.

"Was he talking to Charlie?" he whispered.

Fido nodded his head up and down almost imperceptibly.

"Is Charlie going to wait out front?"

Fido neither nodded his head nor shook his head. He must not know the answer to that, thought Jasper.

"Can the kid get on the boat ride?"

Fido quickly shook his head 'no' to that.

"Ok, good we knew he wouldn't. Did he tell Charlie that the boat drops people off in Woolwich?"

Fido shook his head 'No'.

"Ok," continued Jasper. "They may not know that. We'll have to hope they don't. One more question. Is the kid going to stay and wait for us to come back?"

This time, Fido nodded 'Yes'.

"Great," said Jasper in a more conversational voice. "We'll have to move fast on the other side. You were right, Charlotte. He can't board the boat but he'll be waiting when the boat returns."

"How do you know?" she asked. She hadn't noticed Fido and Jasper's exchanging of words.

"I just have a hunch they are holding a grudge over your back pack. Once the boat returns without us, they will quickly discover where we've gone."

"Yeah, we'll have to keep moving. I guess we'll have a lot to talk about and discuss on the boat ride," she said nervously. She certainly did have a lot to explain, she thought as she flexed her grip on the strap to her backpack.

It was time to board the boat. It was pulling in and letting off the one o'clock riders. Jasper, Charlotte and Fido got up and found a place near the front of the line. Charlotte had the leash and the stolen backpack and Jasper had his gear and suitcase. The deck hand stopped them and asked "Can you stow all that gear on this side? This isn't a ferry, its just a tour boat."

Jasper piped in, "My grandfather lives in Wiscasset and is going to meet us on the other side, this is his stuff. We won't have it on the way back. We can sit on the bags and not take up any seating if that's all right."

"Well, okay, but don't make it a habit." The deck hand took the tickets and let them board. Jasper glanced back at the shore and saw the boy weave through the crowd and then gape at the boat as it pulled away.

Breathing a sigh of relief, the group then lumbered with their gear toward the front of the boat. They found an open corner where they could put the suitcase and sat down. A few minutes passed. The river's edge pulled away and the boat picked up speed. Jasper and Charlotte both contemplated what had happened over the last few hours and what to do. Jasper scowled and frowned. He looked puzzled.

"Jasper, I have to tell you something," Charlotte exclaimed. "It's not my fault and you can't get mad."

"What? What are you talking about?"

"You have to promise first."

"What? Promise what?"

"Promise not to get mad."

"Charlotte, I don't know what you're going to say. I doubt I'll be surprised at this point, so fine! I promise to try not to get mad."

"I hope you can say that in a few minutes. We are in deep shit. This bag is not mine, it's Charlie's. Everything I said is a sham. I was trying to steal his bag. When we were riding, he got into his bag and I saw he had couple hundred bucks in there. I'm so desperate, Jasper!

You have no idea. My brother, Jasper! I need the money for my brother!"

"You stole his bag and you don't want me to be mad?" Jasper was befuddled. "You're a thief and you don't want me to be mad? Stonie was right, he told me not to trust people."

"No, Jasper," interrupted Charlotte. "It gets worse than that. Hold on. I just went into the ladies room to count my winnings and looked through the pack...."

"Well?....."

"There are drugs in it. I mean a lot of drugs. Marijuana, pills, some white powder. I think it was cocaine."

"What?"

"There's at least a few thousand in cash in the middle section. Also there's a gun, a pack of bullets and a small notebook in the front pocket. I think this Charlie's a big time drug dealer and I'm scared."

"Bullshit. I don't believe you."

"I'm serious, Jasper. Look if you want."

Jasper snatched the bag from the floor next to Charlotte's foot and held it in his hand before Charlotte could think to react.

"Hey!"

Jasper unzipped the top of the big section and looked in. His eyes widened. He closed the big section and quickly glanced in the middle section. Jasper looked in the small section and gasped. "Jesus Christ, Charlotte! A gun, you have a gun."

"I don't have a gun. It's Charlie's," Charlotte argued defensively.

"Keep your voice down," warned Jasper looking around the deck. When he was satisfied no one had heard he continued in a lower tone. "How do I know these aren't your drugs?"

"I might have made some mistakes but I'm not a drug dealer. Do I look like that kind of person to you?"

Jasper looked at Charlotte for a few seconds with a hard eye. "So you got desperate and got in over your head? Is that how it is? You think that makes it okay?"

"I didn't mean to."

"Of course you meant to," said Jasper angrily. "You meant to rob some poor hillbilly farm boy of his money."

"You don't understand Jasper. I had to. I had to for my brother. He can't stay there. We can't stay there."

"You have to keep quiet or someone's going to hear."

"Sorry"

"I should turn you in... better yet I should turn you and Charlie in with this bag." Jasper thumbed the shoulder strap of the backpack he still held. "What's so bad that makes it ok to steal from someone? Someone nice enough to give you a ride?"

"Nice? You think Charlie's nice? You met him. You punched him in the face and you think he's nice. He's a drug dealer."

"But you didn't know that then," interrupted Jasper. "You didn't know he was a drug dealer when you robbed him. You found that out in the bathroom fifteen minutes ago."

Charlotte looked up at Jasper as tears began to pool in the corners of her eyes. She held them back from falling. She tried to hold his gaze for another moment and couldn't. She looked away, wiping her eyes with the back of her hand.

Oh geez, thought Fido who had been listening to every word of his two companions exchange, she's crying again. Jasper's too much of a sucker for this.

"If you think I'm going to help you instead of turning you into the police then I want to know. I want to know what's so important that it justified stealing," Jasper sputtered.

"My brother, he's worth stealing for. My stepmother is awful. She's absolutely crazy. She's a drunk, Jasper. That's not even the worst of it. You never know what you're going to get with her. Sometimes you come home from school and she's passed out or just mellow watching TV or staring off into space in a stupor. Those are the good days. Those are the days you can just keep quiet, keep out of her way and mind you own business."

"Charlotte listen,"

"If Buddy would get too loud or start acting silly she might yell but that was usually it. But other days she wouldn't be that easy to get along with. You'd come home and she'd be in a rage. It would be over different things. She'd be mad about the noise in the house. How hot it was. How stupid we were. Whatever it was, it didn't matter. She would be ruthless and vicious. She would reduce Buddy to tears crying on the floor. She would scream, throw things and threaten us. Once she knocked my father down the basement stairs. I don't think she meant to knock him down a flight of steps, but she was hateful. She's a complete and utter nightmare."

"I don't understand."

"Let me start at the beginning. My mother, Crystal Baker, died when I was three in a motorcycle accident. I remember her vaguely. My father, Fred Baker, took me to his mother's, Grandma Rosa in Fort Kent to live. I loved her. I lived with her for nine years. My father would come and go. He never stayed long. Always off to a new job or some other equally vague endeavor. When I was twelve, my father hooked up with Karen Towle and they had my brother Buddy. They set up house keeping in Frenchville, Maine a few towns over from Fort Kent. My father made me come live with them. She was nice the first week, made me sandwiches and even braided my hair once but she quickly turned. She's not all there. Last week I came home and she had locked Buddy out of the house. He was crying on the porch with sunburned shoulders and face. He's only five years old, Jasper. He told me he had been naughty, so Mommy had put him in time out. I broke the door latch in and found her passed out on the living room floor. She woke up after a couple of kicks. I couldn't help it Jasper. I was so mad over what she had done. I kicked her twice, hard as I could. She was all right though and hell on wheels when she got up. She grabbed me by the hair and threw me down and began yelling about how ungrateful I was. We got into a yelling match and she dragged me by the hair out the door and told me to get out. She threw a few of my things out the door. Mostly what little I have with me now. So I left. She hadn't meant it. She was just ranting, like she always did. But I ran anyway. I ran away because I couldn't take it any more. She's evil and I hate her. I wanted to get as far way from her as I could. I had a little money. I walked four miles to the grocer where you can catch the bus. The first one that came was headed for Dairy. I hitchhiked the rest of the way to the rest stop you found me at."

"Wow Charlotte, that sound awful. I can't even imagine."

"But then I got to thinking about my little brother. How my step mother is just going to ruin his life, so I realized I had to go back. I needed money. I had run out and had no way to get home. What was I even going to do when I got there? I have to find a way to get my dad to let me take Buddy to Grandma Rosa's. I needed money and a plan. I wasn't going to live one more night in that house. I couldn't think of any other way of getting money. Then Charlie and Jake picked me up. They were nice enough to give me the ride but I got a really creepy vibe off of Charlie. Some of the comments they made along the way left me feeling like I got off lucky to make it to the gas station without being raped or worse."

"That doesn't make it right, Charlotte."

"I know. I was wrong and had no right to steal but I had my reasons. I couldn't do nothing. I'm sorry. I shouldn't have gotten you involved."

"Does she have a phone?"

"What? Who?"

"Grandma Rosa?" suggested Jasper.

"Oh, She'll take us," said Charlotte. "It's a matter of Karen giving up Buddy. I have to convince my father that she's no good for us," she said. "He's still off chasing dreams half the time. He doesn't see the worst of it."

"Look we're almost there. I'm still not sure if I can trust you or if half of what you're saying is true. But I'm going to take a chance here and not turn you in. But you have to come with me and we'll figure this out together. You're not walking off with this backpack. We'll figure out what the right thing is. Understand?"

"Okay, Yes. Thank You," Charlotte sounded a little relieved and surprised.

"Right now we need to get a ride north to Wiscasset. It's about twenty miles. There's a campground near there we can stay for the night. I think we'll be safe there. I have all the camp gear we'll need. We can get a good night's sleep and figure out the next step. I figure we have about thirty minutes to an hour to get out of Woolwich, before Charlie and Jake make it over here to look for us. Our friend in the baseball cap will be back on the pay phone as soon as this boat returns to port without us."

"If we can get a ride, shouldn't we go as far as we can?" asked Charlotte.

"I think if we do that we could get stranded on the side of the road somewhere late at night out in the boonies, with Charlie and his guy's driving round looking for us. It won't be just him you know. He'll have everyone he knows out looking. If this is all true those drugs are worth thousands of dollars, maybe tens of thousands of dollars. Then there's the cash and that notebook. That notebook probably could implicate him. He must be a little frantic. Our best bet is to lay low and move slow, only if we're sure it's safe. We should keep Fido out of sight. He's a giveaway in our description. And Charlie's not likely to forget him."

"Ok, you're the boss, but we've got to get trucking," said Charlotte.

"Hey they're docking now," said Jasper. "Lets get off and find an outside cafe to sit down at and find a ride going north fast." They disembarked the boat and they headed straight down the main street of Woolwich, past most of the shops and sat at a corner outside picnic table of a variety store. A good spot with traffic. Across the street was a gas station. "If anyone gasses up over there I'll go over and chat them up for a ride. You stay here with Fido and look for any possibilities. Remember, we can't be fussy. Take any ride north"

Jasper went in the store and bought some sodas and snacks so no one would bug them about sitting at the picnic table. Soon someone pulled into the gas station. It was an older man driving an old car. "I'll be right back," said Jasper as he got up and started across the street.

The attendant was filling the car's gas and washing the windshield when he reached the lot. As Jasper approached the vehicle, the driver got out and exchanged a few words with the attendant. Neither one noticed him as he stopped to wait a few paces away. The attendant turned away from the older driver and popped the hood to check the oil.

"Hey mister, how you doing?" asked Jasper, taking his opening. "My sister and I are looking for a ride to Wiscasset. You headed north by any chance?"

The old timer looked at him and Jasper nodded to him and pointed across the street, back towards Charlotte and Fido.

"I'd be happy to give you a ride, but I'm headed south, sorry."

Jasper thanked the man and turned to leave. Suddenly, an old, beat up, rusted Ford pickup truck roared into the station and smashed into the trash barrel that was sitting near the gas pump. Old oil cans and dirty paper towels littered the concrete as the barrel spilled over. The display of windshield washer fluid got rattled and fell over as well. Jasper jumped back a step and bumped into the old timer's car, thankful he had not been two steps ahead of himself. He would have been laying on the concrete instead of the trash barrel and washer fluid.

"For Christ's sake, Freddie! Why don't you slow down and stop hitting everything you see on the road with that goddamn worthless truck?" said the attendant to the driver as he started picking up the mess.

"Hey, let me do that, it's my mess. I'll pick it up," said the big man who was jumping out of the truck. A little boy was following him. The little tot was a spitting image of the man, just smaller.

Jasper jumped in and started to help pick up the windshield bottles knocked over by the man. "Hey mister, why you helping my Dad?" said the boy.

"Well kiddo, I thought it would be the right thing to do," he replied .

"You know who he is?" retorted the boy.

"No, I don't believe I do. Should I?" asked Jasper with a sideways smile for the boy. He continued picking up bottles.

"Well, he's known as 'Freddie Fender Bender' round these parts. And that's his truck," said the boy proudly as he beamed at his father and pointed to the rusty Ford.

The man came up to the boy and put his hand on his shoulder with a grin. "Hi, my name is Freddie Fender," said the man giving Jasper a dusty hand to shake. “I can’t judge those barrels very well, I guess. I’m always hitting them. Hey Joe, fill er up, will ya?”

The attendant was collecting his fee from the old timer. “Ok Freddie, just one minute,” he said.

“This is little Freddie Junior,” said Freddie as he indicated his attention back on the little boy. “And that’s my truck, the ‘Fender Bender’. You from round these parts?”

“No actually we’re from Landrush.” explained Jasper, “My sister and I are headed for Dairy, but our car broke down in Bath. We’re taking the museum tour. Hey, you’re not headed north by any chance are you?”

“Hell yeah, we live in Wiscasset. Headed there right after this.’

“You wouldn’t be willing to give me and my sister a lift there, would you?” he asked attempting to look and sound as pathetic as possible. “There’s a campground right outside Wiscasset to the north, off Route 27, I saw it on our map.” He pointed across the street to Charlotte “There’s my sister over there with my dog. We can all sit in the back, no problem, we wouldn’t get in the way.”

“On the Gardner Road? Shit yeah,” said Freddie jovially. “My wife’s brother runs that campground. It’s called Pinetree Acres. Tell her to come on over. The dog and your bags will have to go in the back but we can make room for the two of you in the cab.”

Thank God, Jasper thought to himself with a sigh of relief. He signaled Charlotte to cross with a wave. “Great, I’m gonna go help her with our stuff. Thanks again.”

He went over to Charlotte and Fido and together they carried everything to Freddie’s truck. “I told him you were my sister and we broke down in Bath.”

Everyone shook hands after they had gotten the gear and Fido into the back of the truck. “Charlotte, this is Freddie Fender, Freddie this is Charlotte and I’m Jasper.”

Freddie Junior had climbed into the bed of the truck and was patting Fido.

“Freddie Junior? That’s Fido,” Jasper said to the young boy.

The boy smiled at that and Fido began licking his face. The boy giggled.

"Sorry, Fido. You're traveling back here this time," apologized Jasper.

Fido laid his ears flat while he considered this and than with a dissatisfied groan he laid his body down as far forward in the bed as he could get. I'll be lucky to survive this ride with someone named Fender Bender at the wheel, thought Fido. I'm not a sack of potatoes, I'm your best friend.

The four humans then piled into the rusty Ford. With Freddie Junior sitting on Charlotte's lap, they peeled away from the gas station, undoubtedly leaving tire screech tracks in their wake.

"So, your car's in Bath? What're you going to do about that?" asked Freddie, as the truck backfired its way down Route one.

"Oh, I called my father about that and there's some kind of transmission trouble. He told me to have it towed to the nearest dealership. It's still under warrantee,"explained Jasper, surprised at how easily lying was coming to him. Charlotte, he thought, was a bad influence. "...Then he said we should catch a bus to Dairy. On the way back to Landrush we can pick up the car."

"Makes sense, I guess. Except there ain't many buses out of Wiscasset"

"Yeah, well we have to stay somewhere and we already have the gear. This trip's turning out more costly than I'd originally thought," said Jasper truthfully, "We could take that boat back to Bath in the morning."

"You know," Freddie replied, "I have to go to Dairy in the morning tomorrow. I'm leaving around noon. You guys are welcome to ride with me. I own a pig farm in Wiscasset and I have to go to Dairy to pick up some new hogs I just purchased. I have a better truck at home. I'll be taking that and pulling a trailer but there will be plenty of room. My new truck is my pride and joy, a doublewide Ford truck with an extended cab. This here's my 'Fearless Freddie Fender Bender' Junior mentioned earlier."

"That would be great!" Charlotte blurted out, a little too anxiously.

"Yes, that would be really nice," agreed Jasper.

"It's all set then," Freddie said joyfully. "I'll pick you all up at eleven thirty in the morning at Pinetree Acres. It will give me time to do my chores and clean up." They all agreed and the conversation zeroed in on Freddie Junior for the rest of the trip.

Chapter 5
The Trek to Millinocket

It was only twenty odd miles away to Pinetree Acres campground but in Jasper's mind it was their escape. If they were careful and laid low they might get out of this thing yet. They picked a campsite that was the furthest one in from the road. The manager Jocko, Freddie's brother-in-law put Jasper and Charlotte on a flat bed pulled by a tractor and took them to their site. They were taking their gear off of the flat bed when Jasper said, "Jocko, if some guys stops by and ask if two kids and a dog stopped to camp here tonight could you cover for us? It's my sister's ex-boyfriend and she's trying to get away from him. He's a real SOB, if you know what I'm saying."

"I hear ya. Never saw ya in my life," Jocko smiled. "I'll tell the misses back at the office. What about Freddie? Should I call him to tell him to say the same?"

"Yeah, would you?"

"Sure thing," Jocko said as he spit out tobacco juice on the ground. "I'll drop the firewood by before dark with some kindling."

"Thanks," Jasper gave him a few dollars for firewood. He thought a fire might help them relax. The campground was real nice it had some amenities that not all campgrounds have; hot showers, indoor plumbing, electric hook up at each site, an outdoor pool and a playground.

He got to work putting up the two-man tent. Charlotte was making noise about taking a shower. She had to walk about a quarter mile to where the out building was for showering. "Jasper, I'm going to take a shower. Can Fido come with me? And..." Charlotte's face reddened with embarrassment. “Do you have some shorts or a T-shirt or something I can wear? I want to wash out the clothes I’m wearing.”

He chuckled, “Sure. Fido, go with her but stay out of site while she is in the shower.” He dug through his bag and found a pair of shorts and a t-shirt. They would be too big for her but they would do. He also pulled out a towel and his bath kit. “This may come in handy.”

She took the stuff and smiled meekly. She hadn’t even thought about a towel or soap. “Thanks,” she said with a bashful smile and headed for the shower.

“See you in a bit,” he said as she walked off.

Wow, Jasper thought, she hadn’t packed anything for her trip. He thought about her story. He tried to imagine getting in a fight with his mother that would result in being thrown out of the house and had difficulty conjuring the images. He felt skeptical toward her. Was this new story the truth or just as false as having her backpack stolen? She lies so much I don’t know what to believe. As he put the campsite in order he thought of the events of the day. He still wasn’t sure why he had stuck with her after she told him she had lied and that the bag was stolen. I guess, he thought as he unfolded the tent, that it was the desperation in her voice. Or the fear and love she spoke of for her brother Buddy. That, if nothing else in her story, felt genuine, felt real.

He had a rain fly over the tent. The fly extended out further to provide a dry canopy space if a shower came up. He moved the picnic table under the dry space. He then strung a clothes line in a sunny spot, ten or fifteen feet from the table. He stood back and looked over the site to admire his work. He had put all the gear under the picnic table where it was accessible but not in the way. The pole with the electric hook up was right behind the dry space. The faucet for water was just beyond that with a downhill slant away from the tent.

Jasper sat back to think things through. He needed a workout. He had a rule, he never let three days go by without working out. It was actually Stonie’s rule that he had taught him. He didn’t count biking as a workout because it was like walking, your legs got used to it. Today he thought he would jog the campgrounds and mix in a martial arts workout. He would work that in before dark. He figured he would leave Fido with Charlotte. He still didn’t trust her. She might take off with all that drug paraphernalia. It seemed like a big temptation to him. All that money and Charlotte with a poor track record.

Thank God for the ride with Freddie. It really couldn't have worked out better. Tomorrow they would go to the Dairy police station and turn in the backpack with the drugs, money, pistol and notebook. That would get these guys off their tail and hopefully, off the streets. Then Charlotte could get on a bus for Fort Kent and he could continue on to Mount Katahdin.

He couldn't believe all that had happened in a day on the road. He knew they weren't safe in this area until Charlie and his cronies were off the streets. He had no idea how long that would take. He had to scratch the plan to follow the coast to Searsport and just take a giant leap to Dairy. He knew that Charlotte would have a different outlook on what they should do. He would have to put all his effort into manipulating her like she had played him in Bath. He shook his head not believing how he got sucked in by her. He trusted people too easily.

Jasper heard them coming before they got back to camp. The snap of twigs and the scuffing of feet on the worn path were unmistakable to Jasper's well attuned ears. Fido was more stealthy in his approach than Charlotte but the dog also made tell-tale noises if you were listening carefully.

Charlotte rounded a corner made by two lean pine trees and came into view. Her hair was wet and hung limply on her shoulders. She was wearing his white Landrush track and field t-shirt. It hung so long on her the shorts he'd given her were concealed beneath, giving the illusion that she wasn't wearing them. The shirt didn't hang shapeless on her though. She filled it out in her own way. Her breasts looked even bigger than I remember, thought Jasper as his mind wandered over her body. She wasn't wearing a bra which made her hard to ignore. He could see her left nipple standing out through his t-shirt. It looked nice enough to pinch. Her hair was tossed on her right shoulder and was staining the shirt with water. Her eyes were a beautiful dark green.

She was staring at him with an amused grin on her face. He'd been caught, just like that. Jasper dropped his eyes to the ground and could feel the heat flushing into his neck and face.

"You look like you're about to go somewhere. May I suggest a cold shower for you, Mr. Jay Hawk?" teased Charlotte as she turned away from him to hang her clothes and towel on the clothes line.

With her back turned, Jasper traced her long smooth legs with his eyes until they disappeared under the t-shirt. She had a perfect ass, he thought as he stared at her backside. She reached up over her head to adjust the clothesline and tighten it. The t-shirt rode up a few inches in the process and Jasper could see the blue trim of her underwear and the curve of the right side of her bottom. She wasn't wearing the shorts he'd given her, he realized.

As he gawked at her and this new information computed in his head, Charlotte looked over her shoulder and grinned mischievously.

"Hey, I was thinking of getting a little workout in," he said trying to break the awkward tension he was suddenly feeling.

"I bet you were," said Charlotte turning around, grinning knowingly and crossing her arms under her breasts.

"Yeah, I do, I mean I was... I am," Jasper stumbled over his words. "I am going to go for a jog. I'll only be gone a half hour. When I get back I'll take a shower and go to the camp store and buy some burgers and we can have a cookout and eat."

"Sounds good to me," said Charlotte. She walked over to the picnic table pulled out Jasper's bag and replaced his shower kit.

"I will leave Fido here to watch, I mean protect you." Fido sat up straight and his ears were standing erect, in alarm. He barked softly and shook his head 'No' at Jasper. The dog stood up and bounded over to Jasper pretending to act excited about the idea of going jogging.

"Oh, he wants to go with you, what a good dog," said Charlotte.

Jasper kneeled down and patted the dog's head. He bent in and kissed the dog's forehead and whispered into his fur so Charlotte couldn't see. "I don't trust her, Fido. She might take off or do something stupid. You need to watch her for me."

Fido nodded is head discreetly and padded his way back to Charlotte's side. The dog sat down on his rump, whined and groaned and then slid into a laying position.

"No, see? He's fine, he probably just wants a bone." Jasper reached into his pocket and pulled out a dog bone and threw it to his furry friend. Fido caught the bone in mid air and gobbled it up as Jasper trotted off, waving back to them.

Charlotte went over to the picnic table and got the backpack she had stolen from Charlie. She took it to the tent. Fido watched her suspiciously until she went into the tent and closed the flap. The dog padded over to the tent and found it unzipped. He stuck his head in the tent and laid down in the entryway. He was half in and half out of the tent.

"What kinda watch dog are you?" said Charlotte, "No one is going to approach from inside the tent. You could at least turn around and pretend to be on the look out." The dog stood up when she was finished speaking and did exactly that. Charlotte stared at him in amazement. Did he just understand what she had said? That's impossible, she thought.

Charlotte had decided to count the money in the bag and think things out. She counted for a few minutes and came up with a total of three thousand two hundred and eighty-five dollars and no change. She then thumbed through the black book and read a few pages of IOUs, addresses and numbers of people to call for certain drugs and notes on other people. What kinda drug dealer accepts IOUs, she thought? Well, maybe the type that always got paid back she guessed not really knowing anything about the subject. She had never done any drugs. She'd smoked a few cigarettes with friends but after watching what drugs and booze had done to her stepmother, they hadn't really interested her. She continued looking through the notebook. It had some coded figures and terms she didn't really understand. It also contained a list of the drugs that were in the backpack. That part was easier to follow There was eight thousand dollars worth of drugs in the bag and another twenty-thousand dollars worth at a hold mentioned in the book. The address of the hold was even listed in the notebook. This notebook almost seemed too good to be true. Charlie was meticulous with his book keeping, but didn't seem to have any common sense.

Charlotte zipped the backpack back up and rolled over on her side. If we can get away from here she thought, I can split the money with Jasper and give the drugs to my stepmother as payment for my little brother. Then Buddy and I can get away from her and go live with Grandma Rosa. The money will make all the difference. I can live normally and not tell anyone at home about the money and just use it when I need it.

She figured Jasper would have a different idea. She thought again about running away from him. This would probably be her last best chance to do so, she realized. He wouldn't be back for another twenty minutes or so. She could tie up Fido and just run. Hitchhike outta here and then... It wouldn't work. She'd never get out of here without risking running into Charlie or one of his cronies. This time she would be alone and he would be unforgiving. If Charlie was smart at all, he'd kill her to keep her quiet. Plus, Jasper didn't deserve to be deceived again. He had stayed by her side and saw her this far out of harms way, even knowing she'd lied to him. He was a stand up guy which was rare, especially in someone so young. Charlotte would have to think of a more creative way to deal with Jasper. Then again, perhaps she already had.

Sweat was running down Jasper's forehead and into his eyes. He had been running hard ever since he'd left the camp. He ran hard because he was irritated at himself. He was irritated for being duped so easily by Charlotte, for getting into a fight without knowing the situation and most of all he was irritated because of his feelings for Charlotte. He hadn't been able to pry his eyes off her when she'd come back from the shower. She had looked startlingly sexy when she'd walked back to camp. He hadn't been prepared for that. What disappointed him was not so much that she'd caught him staring. He guessed she'd wanted him to stare. She hadn't put on the shorts deliberately, he thought. He was disappointed in himself for wanting her. In that moment he had wanted to take her in his arms, kiss her and take her into the tent for more. Was he really that weak? Was his relationship with Claire that insignificant that he would toss her aside when the first pretty girl walked by?

No, he thought, He had been with Claire for several years. He wouldn't throw that away. Certainly not like that anyway. Claire was beautiful, smart, hard working and above all honest. Charlotte was beautiful, yes, but she was also a liar, a thief, a runaway and what else? He didn't know enough about her to be traveling with her. But he knew enough about her to know he should get as far away from her as he could. This whole thing was a mess.

I guess that was part of what he found attractive about her. She was a few years older than Claire and her body showed it. Her breasts and hips were more filled out. The way she walked around the camp, she knew how to be seductive, unlike brainy Claire. But mostly she was bad news. Strangely, thought Jasper, thats what's most attractive about her. She was unpredictable to him and she was in trouble. He rolled his eyes at himself. She gives me the chance to be a hero. How dumb I am, he thought. So caught up in rescuing someone I've completely lost perspective. He hurdled a fallen log on the path he was jogging. Well, I've found some perspective and I can still set this right.

Forty-five minutes later, Jasper came walking into camp from the showers. He had returned to the camp briefly earlier, after his jog. He had picked up his toiletry pack, taken a shower and visited Jocko's wife at the small store near the campground entrance. He had brought back with him the fixings for a cookout; hamburgers, cheese, buns, soda and condiments. Both he and Charlotte were starving.

Charlotte came out of the tent as he was setting up his propane stove on the picnic table. Charlotte had apparently put on his athletic shorts while he was gone. Jasper noticed as well that she was carrying Charlie's backpack. "I hope you're not making too many plans for what's in that backpack," he said.

"I was just taking an inventory of what's there."

"Oh, I'm sure you were," said Jasper.

"Honest, I haven't taken anything. I just counted it and put it back."

Jasper glanced at Fido when Charlotte wasn't looking and the dog nodded 'yes'. Well, at least she was telling the truth for now, he thought disparagingly. "Fido, sit over there beyond the tent so you will be out of site of the road. This time of day Charlie and them will be out looking for us before dark." It was usually getting dark around eight-thirty or nine this time of year. Jasper put the hamburgers on and then got Fido's food out to feed him. He ate and was content to stay behind the tent and sleep.

Charlotte had been nervous all along and suggested that they eat in the tent. Jasper agreed and as soon as the food was ready he brought it in the tent where Charlotte was waiting.

As they were eating, Charlotte told Jasper how much money and drugs they were dealing with. Jasper looked over the black note-book while she was explaining. Charlotte sounded excited and the fear she had been showing seemed to be fading away, for the moment.

"Look Charlotte, I know you probably have some other idea but we have to turn this in to the police."

"Well, wait!" Charlotte interrupted. "I know these guys are trouble but we have a chance to use this money to do something good."

"This is a lot of money Charlotte. You think Charlie is just go-ing to forget about it or about the people who stole it? If the police can pick these guys up soon we will be safe and there will be a drug dealer off the streets. If there is any argument it should be, how will we turn it in and to what police station." Jasper remembered the last words Stonie had said to him; Always do the right thing.

Charlotte began to wring her hands and said, "Jasper, the one concern I have is how to get my brother away from my stepmother. I know I could trade the drugs for my brother. She is that much of an addict that I know she'd do it. Please, Jasper. I need this." Charlotte scooted the short distance between them until they were side by side with their shoulders touching. "You don't understand. There's no other way." Charlotte cried as tears started to run down her face. She held eye contact with Jasper for a few seconds and then put her head in her hands and sobbed.

"C'mon, Charlotte," he said sympathetically, as he put his arms around her to console her. "There's another way, there has to be an-other way to help your brother. What about if we told your father?" She's using me again, thought Jasper less naive than before.

"There's no other way. My Dad knows exactly what's going on. That is why he stays away." She leaned into him, stretching out her arms and wrapping them around his neck, pressing herself against him.

Jasper hugged her back. He felt bad for her and for Buddy. He could feel her tears moistening his neck as she sobbed and her warm body against his as well. He could feel her breasts heaving against his chest as she whimpered. Was this for his benefit as well, he thought, is she playing on my sympathies again? “It’s okay Charlotte, we’ll find away to set this right.”

Charlotte pulled back slightly and looked him in the eyes. “Thank you,” she said as she leaned in and kissed him on the lips. Jasper was paralyzed for a moment and she kissed him softly again. Then something in his mind exploded and he was kissing her back. Their mouths opened as they kissed and Jasper could feel her soft tongue.

They were laying on the ground of the tent now. Jasper held himself on his elbow above her. He didn’t remember pushing her down. Her hands were rubbing the bare skin of his back and chest. He didn’t remember taking his shirt off either. It didn’t matter how. He just needed her... now. He wanted all of her. They kissed and groped at each other. Jasper felt her legs wrap around his waist as his hands moved up her side. He realized she had lost the shorts again and couldn’t recall if she had them on when he entered the tent or taken them off in the last few minutes. Then he felt her breast in his hand and his thumb caressed her nipple through her shirt. This was moving fast. Too fast, but he didn’t care, it didn’t matter. He was out of control. This is wrong, he thought.

Charlotte heard a growl at the tent door and looked over Jasper’s shoulder. She could see the silhouette of a dog’s head staring in at them.

As she moved Jasper became aware of the low growl as well. He leaned more heavily on one arm and lifted himself half off of Charlotte. Fido advanced half into the tent and barked at them and then whined.

“He’s the only one with any sense around here.” He climbed the rest of the way off of Charlotte and handed her his shorts.

“What do you mean?” she said as Jasper searched for his shirt. “You don’t want this? You felt like you wanted it a minute ago.”

"Oh, I wanted it all right," he said as he donned his shirt and exited the tent. Charlotte pulled on her shorts and followed him. "But it's not right."

"Do you have a girlfriend or something?" she asked.

"That has nothing to do with it," he continued annoyed. "This isn't right because we don't really know each other. And you're only doing it to try to persuade me to go along with your idea of stealing the money."

"That's not true," Charlotte began.

Jasper turned half around and gave her a questioning eye.

"Well, it's not the only reason," she finished.

"You're desperate to help your brother, you said that before. I'd be taking advantage of you if I let you do this."

They stared at each other for several seconds in silence. Almost a full minute went by. Jasper began to become aware of the crickets chirping and he saw a bat swoop down from the trees.

"You're a sweet boy, Jasper," Charlotte said, breaking the silence. "I took advantage of you earlier. I'd have thought you'd appreciate the opportunity of returning the favor."

"Ha!" he laughed cynically, "There's no honor in that. Now lets try to figure this out. Where was Buddy when you left?"

"I took him over to Grandma Rosa's in Fort Kent. Karen and I had just had a hell of a fight and she hit me and threatened to harm Buddy. She was drunk out of her mind. A friend of mine gave us a ride to Fort Kent from Frenchville. Then I left him with Grandma Rosa and took off. That's why I had nothing packed. I just grabbed a ride with some University students that I knew and kept hitching rides until I ended up in Bath shortly before I saw you. Thats about when I realized I needed to get some money and get back and take care of Buddy."

"Where is your father?"

"Grandma Rosa knows how to get a hold of him. I'm sure Rosa called him and he is either there or on his way. I'm sure they're cursing my name for leaving."

"I saw a pay phone up outside the store, lets call Grandma Rosa."

"I don't know."

"If we can get a hold of your father we could make a deal with him. Tell him the only way you'll come back is if you can keep Buddy with you at Grandma Rosa's and he has to file for custody and give it to you and Grandma Rosa so Karen can't come take him back. It seems to me that if he cares for you at all he should go along with it."

"He might but there's something about Karen that scares the hell out of him and he can't stand up to her. It has to do with her brother in law, Clinton Perry. There are three Perry brothers and Clinton is the oldest and runs a chicken farm in Frenchville. Frenchville is near Long Lake, east of Fort Kent. My father works for them and they have something over his head and he is scared of them."

"Hey!" exclaimed Jasper confused, "I know that family. My grandparents have had run ins with them over the chicken business. Like price wars and stuff, little things but always something. My grandfather, Shank Steller, has tried to sit down with them and reason things out but they were not very nice and he ended up having it out with them and has had nothing to do with them for years now. What a small world that we met."

"Your grandfather is Shank Steller? I thought he got sick and died?"

"Well, he had a stroke actually, but he's still alive. Anyway back to your father."

"Ok, well they have something on my father but he won't talk about it. I could ask him about Buddy and Grandma Rosa. I'm not sure it will work but, I guess, it's worth trying.

Jasper and Charlotte walked up to the small store. It was around seven-thirty and it was still light out. Jasper was a little nervous about coming so close to the main road but with the entrance to the shop and pay phone on the back side of the building facing the campground, away from the road he figured it was relatively safe. He told Fido to stay at the camp for safe keeping. He'd been unable to convince Charlotte that the dog would do as he was told and stay no matter how long they were gone. She kept looking back over her shoulder, expecting to see Fido running to catch up.

When they got to the shop, Jasper led the way straight to the phone. He looked around more than once to make sure there wasn't anyone around. He occasionally could hear Jocko's wife inside the shop moving around but that was all. She appeared to be alone. Jasper lifted the receiver and inserted a few coins while handing it to Charlotte.

"She called out the numbers as she punched them in. Jasper wrote the number down on a loose scrap of paper to put in his own notebook later in case he needed to refer to it again.

After several rings, Grandma Rosa answered. Charlotte held the phone sideways to her ear so Jasper could get on the other side of the receiver and listen in. "Grandma Rosa this is Charlotte," Then the tears and the 'I'm sorrys' started. Then the small talk and 'let me speak to Buddy', then more tears and eventually Grandma Rosa was back on the other end. "Can I speak to Daddy? Is he there?"

Freddie - "Where the hell have you been for Christ sake?"

Charlotte - "I ran the hell away you bastard."

"Hold it, Charlotte, hold it," interrupted Jasper as he put his hand over the receiver. "Don't fight with him. You'll never get anything out of him if the two of you are yelling at each other."

"He brings out the worst in me, I have to defend myself."

"Be calm and reasonable and he's more apt to be the same way. Try it, please." She nodded her head and took a deep breath.

Freddie - "...the hell did you go? You there? Don't hang up on me you ungrateful little..."

Charlotte - "I'm right here Daddy, sorry. I'm just a little upset."

Freddie - "You should be for Christ sake, sticking you grandmother with this wild little brat."

Charlotte - "Daddy, Buddy is a good boy. Try not to swear so much." Jasper was impressed she had said it calmly.

<pause>

Freddie - "Well when are you coming back? Rosa is too old to take care of, Buddy. You need to be here. Damn it to hell."

Charlotte - "What about Karen? Can't she take care of him?"

Freddie - "You know damn well that she can't even take care of herself."

Charlotte - “Why not Daddy? What’s wrong with her?”

<pause>

Freddie - “You know exactly what’s wrong with her. Don’t make me talk about it in front of your grandmother. You get your ass home.”

Charlotte - “You know Karen hit me and threatened to hit Buddy. I had to get outta there and I had no place to go. So I went to Grandma’s and left Buddy there and then I just took off.”

Freddie - “Ok, well now that you’ve come back to your senses get back here.”

Charlotte - “No.”

Freddie - “What? You can’t say no to me!”

Charlotte - “I’m not coming home unless you meet my conditions.” She looked over at Jasper with concern and uncertainty. He nodded his head ‘yes’ and motioned for her to continue.

Freddie - “And what the hell are you demanding?”

Charlotte - “I have two conditions. Number one, Buddy and I both stay to live with Grandma Rosa. Karen is not a fit mother for Buddy and I will not live with her and that is final.”

Freddie - “C'mon Charlotte, you know I have trouble with her and her brothers.”

Charlotte - “Well too bad, I don’t know and don’t care what that’s all about. But you need to stand up to Karen and her brothers for the sake of you son. You’ll just have to grow a pair of balls.”

Freddie - “You goddamn little shit, you think you can order me around?”

Charlotte - “Well, it’s either that Daddy or they’re both your problem and I won’t be back. Either you give me Buddy and deal with Karen yourself or I’ll stay down here and you can deal with them both.”

Freddie - “Where are you anyway? You sound like you’re a hundred miles away.”

Charlotte - “I’m in Landrush, I hitchhiked down here and am staying with some friends. They’re encouraging me to stay. It’s quite appealing to be honest.”

<pause>

Freddie - "Whats your next condition?"

Charlotte - "Number two, you have to get legal action started on Monday morning to give custody of Buddy to me and Grandma Rosa."

Freddie - "You little, bitch. Do you realize how complicated that will be?"

Charlotte - "Well, you should have thought of that before you had children."

Freddie - "Ok, fine. I'll see what I can do. But you need to get your ass over here."

Charlotte - "I will. I'll get on a bus tomorrow morning and be home by the end of the day. But remember, if you try to renig on this deal then I will leave just like before. I'm serious about this."

Freddie - "You got to let me talk this over with Grandma Rosa. Can you call us back in a half hour or so?"

Charlotte - "Ok, Daddy but these are my terms. Non negotiable. I will only call back to make sure it's alright with Grandma Rosa, not with you. You already know my terms." Charlotte hung up the receiver

Jasper stepped away looking at her and said, "What if he won't buy your terms?"

"They were reasonable terms based on the situation. He needs to talk to Rosa and she will tell him to do as I say. What else can he do? He doesn't want to be 'stuck with Buddy' as he calls it. I'm his only bet. He's a horrible father. People who don't want kids shouldn't be allowed to have them," she said.

"I know what you mean," he said. "Lets hope your father goes along with us. We still need to talk about Charlie's bag."

Suddenly they heard an engine start and turned around. Jocko was getting onto his tractor. He spotted Charlotte and Jasper by the pay phone and waved.

"He's probably about to go deliver us our wood for the fire." Said Jasper as he waved to Jocko.

"Oh, that's right," said Charlotte. "But we have to wait to call Grandma Rosa back, we're not ready to go yet."

"That's fine," said Jasper ideally. "Jocko strikes me as a pretty trustworthy guy, besides Fido is at camp and wouldn't let anyone go prying through our stuff."

"You put an awful lot of faith in your dog."

"He's a smart dog."

"Hey," said Jocko as he pulled his tractor up to Charlotte and Jasper. I was just headed out to see you, want a lift back to camp?"

"Thanks Jocko," said Charlotte "but I have one more call to make."

"Ok," Jocko replied with a look of concern on his face. "I'd make it fast though, that Chevy truck you talked about? It stopped by and asked if you two and your dog had stopped here for the night. I told him no. The only people here had small dogs and I didn't have any teenagers staying here either." Jocko laughed, "The guy in the truck described your dog as mean, not at all the way I remember him."

"Thats because he kicked him every chance he ever got," said Charlotte.

"Where is your dog anyway?" continued Jocko.

"Oh, we left him back at the camp," replied Jasper.

"Well, you should be careful with that. He could bump into a skunk or a porcupine left on his own like that."

"You're probably right," Jasper humored Jocko, thinking how absurd it would be to find Fido in that type of trouble. He was smarter then seventy-five percent of people Jasper knew. But Jocko and Charlotte didn't know that and he hoped no one but himself would ever find that out about Fido. "He's usually pretty good but you can't be to careful. We'll make our call fast and head back to camp. Thanks for putting that guy off, Jocko. He's relentless, he may come back"

"Of course," said Jocko, "You know, he gave me a number to call if I were to see you."

"Really?" said Jasper as an idea came to him. "Can you give me that number? I may be able to call him and reason with him and get him off our back."

"All right, listen. I'll give it to you because you seem like an honest young man. But I don't want any trouble around here. If you call him, you do it before you leave tomorrow. I don't want him coming back here tonight if I can help it. This is a family place and I don't tolerate any hot heads."

"Oh, don't worry," Jasper replied. "I have no intention of calling him tonight."

"Alright, well lets see," Jocko pulled a small notepad out of his flannel shirt pocket and thumbed past the first few pages. "Here it is ," he said tearing it from the notepad. "You take the original I don't want any part of that creep."

"Thanks," said Jasper accepting the offered scrap of paper with a small smile.

"All right kids," Jocko continued. "Have a safe evening. You'll have wood waiting for you back at camp.

"Thanks again, sir." Charlotte said as she and Jasper waved as the old tractor drove off.

"So, you see," said Jasper sounding far away as soon as the truck went down the road, "we're not out of the woods yet. We have to be far from here tomorrow. We'll ride with Freddie to Dairy and then drop the bag off at the police station." Jasper turned to look Charlotte in the eye and judge her response.

Charlotte was silent for several seconds. "I don't know. Can't we just keep the money? The cops will just lock it up and it will be wasted"

"You don't understand the concept of honesty or trustworthiness do you?" In the past few hours we've been doing a lot of lying to get away from these drug dealers. I'm not stupid and saying be honest in this situation, because we're dealing with dishonest people and we need to get away safely." Charlotte looked uncomfortable and wouldn't make eye contact with him. At least she can feel guilt, thought Jasper. "We lied to Freddie about our situation to get here and we also lied to him to secure a ride to Dairy. And then we lied to both him and Jocko and Jocko's wife. And then dragged them into lying for us. See how all these lies just keep building on each other in order for us to keep it going? All this goes completely against my character. Freddie and Jocko could get hurt by these lies. When we see Freddie in the morning, I'm going to level with him on what's going on. If he got caught helping us... what would they do? Maybe kill him! I can't live with that."

"I guess," said Charlotte sounding unconvinced and still staring down at her shoes.

"It's the responsible thing to do. If you make a habit out of lying, everyone loses. You have to keep making new lies to cover your old lies. Eventually you can't remember all your lies and soon your house of cards is ready to fall. So, to answer your question, yes. We have to turn the money in."

Charlotte shook her head and smiled at Jay and just looked at him for a minute, then said, "You know you're much different from Grandma Rosa but you sound just like her. Living with Karen these past five years I have lost a little of what Rosa taught me. She always talked about character and integrity. I think fate brought us together,"

"If Rosa really taught you that, then there's hope for you yet. I feel a little better about your plan to move there with Buddy. I have Rosa's phone number and if this all works out I'll call you there periodically. Make sure you're doing all right."

"You will? Really?" said Charlotte, looking up at Jasper for the first time since he had gotten on his soap box.

"Of course," he said chucking. "So can I take it you agree we should hand the bag over to the police?"

"I don't trust the police," Charlotte protested. "I'm afraid that once they have my name somehow the drug dealers will get it and their friends will come after us. Right now they only know me by a wrong name and they think I'm headed to Landrush not Fort Kent. Plus if we turn the backpack in and tell the cops the whole story they will want to hold us for questioning. Then we could get held up for weeks. Grandma Rosa could think I was involved in drugs and rethink my moving back in. You'll get held up from your summer adventure too. Your spotless record won't look so flawless then either. Can't we just leave it on the police station steps or on a bench outside the police station headquarters?"

Jasper pondered over what Charlotte had said, the possibility of being detained by the police was one of his concerns. That very well could happen. He thought about what it meant to 'do the right thing'.

He had trusted her before and wanted to be sure this time. He decided he would test her between here and Dairy and make a final decision there. Meanwhile they could come up with a workable plan. He finally answered, “If you’re sincere about going to Fort Kent, taking care of Buddy, living with Grandma Rosa and start living honestly; then maybe we can draft up a letter to the police chief of Dairy. We could put the backpack in a locker at the bus station or something and notify them.”

“I promise, Jasper. That’s exactly what I intend to do. I have changed, you’ll see.” He decided he would have to take her at her word. It had been more than half an hour since they had gotten off the phone with Charlotte’s father. They needed to finish their business with him and get out of sight for the night. They could finish their discussion about the backpack back at the tent.

Charlotte picked the receiver back up and dialed the number. Grandma Rosa picked up the line they talked for a few minutes and hung up. “It’s all set. Grandma Rosa said she’d take us in. She said her health isn’t great and I would be responsible for Buddy a lot of the time, but that’s nothing new to me. He will be in school next year and I can get a job. Rosa also said she would work on Daddy about the custody thing. She told Freddie off and he realized he had no choice. It was either that or becoming a Dad and he never really wanted that.” At that point Charlotte stopped talking and became very quiet.

She began to cry softly. This time she pushed Jasper away when he tried to comfort her. They turned from the shop and pay phone and began walking back to the campsite. As they walked, Jasper reflected on the situation that was before her. She was little more than a kid herself and she had to raise a brother practically on her own. Thank God for Rosa willing to help. He reconsidered his opinion of Charlotte. Her devotion to her brother, despite the sacrifices it was forcing her to make showed its own strength of character. Charlotte might not always be honest but she was honorable. “You know,” Jasper began, “I’m sorry for the morality lesson. You might have been wrong to steal the backpack and this is one hell of a situation we’re in but you are doing the right thing for Buddy. You haven’t been thinking about yourself all this time. You’ve been trying to help him.”

Charlotte cried a little harder and took ahold of Jasper's arm, leaning on him as they walked. "The thing is, I'm crying now thinking about myself and all that I'm missing. Like why me? Why couldn't I have had a solid family? Instead of a dead beat, absent father and a drunk psychopath step-mother?"

"You have the right to feel selfish once in a while, especially with what you've been through. Everyone wants a little stability and a chance to live their dreams. Hang in there. I think your chance is coming soon." Jasper did his best to sound reassuring but to his own ears his statements sound cliche. The words seemed nonetheless to help. By the time they had arrived back at camp, Charlotte had dried her eyes.

They found Fido not far from where they had left him. He came slinking out from behind the tent stretching and yawning. There was a small pile of wood near the fire pit. Jasper prepared the fire pit and got a fire going. Jasper filled Fido in on what had happened with their phone call to Grandma Rosa and the news he had received from Jocko. Fido reported back no strange activity from the campsite during their absence.

Soon the trio was comfortably sitting around the fire. Charlotte's mood had improved and she was joking and telling funny stories while Jasper drafted a letter to the Dairy Police Department. When he was finished he held it up and read it allowed.

Note to Police Chief:

There is a green LL Bean backpack with the initials CWB on the front. It is in the Greyhound Station on Main St. in locker ____, here in Dairy. It was taken from Charles Washington Baldwin. He is a drug dealer. He is after me, but doesn't know me. He just knows my first name and I want to keep it that way. That is why I can not trust anyone, even the police. I fear that his gang will find me. He needs to be picked up fast. They are dangerous. Charlie drives a Chevy truck with an extended cab and a third door, I'm not sure the year. The right front passenger door is painted red like a primer coat. The license plate is '420 THC', Maine plates. I found out his phone number is 366-2571.

This Charlie guy operates out of Bath, Maine. In the backpack you will find over $8,000 worth of assorted drugs and paraphernalia, three thousand plus dollars in cash, a 9mm handgun with cartridges and a black notebook. The black notebook should give you plenty of information on his operation. I hope you get this guy off the street. I will call you to make sure you got this letter and the bag at some point in the future. Sorry I can't talk to you in person but these drug dealers scare me. I don't want to get involved anymore than this. You have the information, hopefully you can make it useful.

Thank You

"It sounds all right to me," responded Charlotte. "What about mailing the notebook along with thc key? The book will tell them everything and maybe get them moving a little faster."

"Thats a good point," said Jasper. "When we get to Dairy we can ask Freddie to let us off at the Greyhound Bus Station. We can then lock the backpack up in a locker and mail the letter, notebook & key to the Dairy Chief of Police. Then I can resume my trip to Baxter State Park on my bike and you can go to Fort Kent," Jasper explained.

"Yeah, this sounds much better. I like having a plan. I'm starting to feel safer than I have since I ran away two days ago."

"Lets not get ahead of ourselves. We are still very much in Charlie's territory and could still be spotted. I think we can breath easier once we're in Dairy on a bus riding north."

Charlotte nodded her head and then put everything away and zipped up the backpack. They stayed up for a while after dark. Charlotte told jokes and ghost stories until she ran out of tales to tell. Jasper pointed out constellations and explained astronomy until Charlotte and Fido were throughly bored of the subject.

Fido was bored far sooner than Charlotte for he had difficulty following Jasper's logic. The night sky was entirely dark to Fido except for the moon which was a magical thing that he both feared and awed over. Jasper's notion that these mythical stars were somehow suns in the night sky was preposterous. If there were millions of suns in the sky then how come the night sky was dark and the day sky so bright. Humans had some peculiar notions about certain things. Eventually they turned in for the night. They had picked up a bed roll for Charlotte at the camp store.

"Sleep well if you can and try not to worry," instructed Jasper. "Fido will wake up and warn us if anyone comes within fifty yards of the campsite. We're as safe as we can be."

"Thank you, for everything Jasper, really," Charlotte said as they settled onto their bed rolls. Jasper had unzipped his sleeping bag so they could spread it out and share its warmth. The night was turning cool. They huddled in the tent and the dog slept on the tent floor a few inches away. Jasper accepted Charlotte's kiss cautiously but was quick to remove his hand from her hip when he realized it had drifted there unconsciously. They wished each other good night and lay there silently.

Jasper lay awake for over an hour before he could fall asleep. He perceived that Charlotte was likely awake for a good portion of that time as well for it was a long while before her breathing relaxed and became slow and rhythmic. He thought about Charlotte's body being so close to his and did not dare let on that he was awake. He was unsure if he could restrain himself again if she reached for him as she had done earlier in the day. Eventually sleep found him and he slept soundly.

The next morning Jasper awoke to find himself in the tent alone. His heart jumped into his throat. Charlotte must have decided to take off with the backpack in the middle of the night after all.

As the cobwebs in his head cleared it occurred to him that this could not be the case. Fido would have warned him if that was happening. Jasper stuck his head out the tent door and found Charlotte warming one of his pots, filled with water over the campfire. He breathed a sigh of relief.

"Hello there, sleepyhead," Charlotte teased when she spotted him. "I thought we should start with some coffee. What do you think?"

"That sounds great," Jasper croaked, as he climbed out of the tent. They had a leisurely time of making breakfast and packing up Jasper's camping equipment.

By eleven-twenty, Fearless Freddie was true to his word and arrived at the campgrounds to pick them up. He drove all the way in to their campsite. When he pulled up, Jasper was finishing tying up the last of his bundles. Charlotte was dressed again in her clothes from the day before that she had washed and hung to dry the previous evening. They were ready to go.

Freddie got out of the truck and said, "No rush you guys, I'm just early. We have a three hour drive and I just wanted to be off by twelve."

"We're all ready to go," Jasper spoke up.

"Yes, the sooner we're out of here the better," agreed Charlotte.

"This is a nice truck," Jasper continued, trying to sound casual. "Certainly in better shape than the other one."

"Yeah, the Fender Bender is my beater. I'm really careful with this one. Say, Jocko called me last night and said if anyone contacted me about dropping you two at Pinetree Campgrounds to tell them different. Well, just after Jocko called this guy pulled in my driveway and asked me that very question. His name was Charlie, he said the serviceman at the filling station said I gave two kids and a dog a ride. I told him I dropped you off in Wiscasset and you all started hitchhiking from there."

"Thanks for doing that," said Jasper glancing at Charlotte, who appeared unnerved by this new information.

"I've seen this Charlie guy around before. This is a small town and everybody knows each other's business. I don't know his angle but I do know he's been in trouble with the law before. You two should be careful around that sort."

"Trust me," put in Charlotte. "We want nothing more than to get away from him. He thinks we've slighted him somehow and wants revenge. It's all a big misunderstanding but he won't leave us alone."

Jasper gave Charlotte a sideways glance and scowled at her when Freddie wasn't looking. Charlotte shrugged her shoulders in response, suggesting 'what else could I say'.

"He had a whole army out looking for you three. I heard from 4 people in town saying they had similar visitors last night."

"Four other people know we're here?" Charlotte blurted out in alarm.

"No, no. No one else knows you're here," Freddie explained. "It's just a small town and whenever anything unusual happens, the town gossipers start singing."

"Well, we're really sorry about all this," Jasper added. "I hope he doesn't bother you again." Jasper started loading the truck with his gear and suitcase.

"It's no real bother, just seems a little unusual for a guy like Charlie to be so out spoken in his search for you. You must have really pissed him off for him to be so desperate to find you."

Jasper and Charlotte exchanged worried, knowing looks while Freddie tied down their gear with a bungee cord and complained about things rolling around in the bed or the truck.

"We're all set to go, I think," said Jasper doing his best to sound upbeat which he did not feel this morning.

They drove to the campground entrance and Freddie stopped at the camp store to gab with Jocko's wife while Charlotte and Jasper went to the restroom to wash up before hitting the road. "Lets level with Freddie," Jasper recommended as soon as they were out of ear shot. "We can tell him the truth on the way to Dairy. I know we can trust him. Look what he has done for us already. He should know what he's gotten himself into and what we're carrying before he drives us all that way."

"Are you sure?" Charlotte asked. "What if he decides he'd like to take the money? How do you know we can trust him?"

"Look what he's already done for us," said Jasper. "We don't have to give him an inventory of the backpack but he should know Charlie is a drug dealer and we're planning on turning it in as soon as we reach Dairy."

"I suppose so. He is taking a bigger risk for us then he realizes."

A few minutes later they were back in Freddie's truck. To get to Dairy, they needed to travel north up the Gardner Road. Freddie planned to travel through Gardner to Augusta. Once in Augusta they would get on I-95 north for the remainder of the trip to Dairy. They turned left out of the Pinetree Acres campgrounds onto the Gardner Road. They drove for a few minutes in relative silence. With a reluctant sigh, Jasper spoke up and proceeded to tell Freddie an abridged version of what had happened. He modified some details. He left out the part of Charlotte stealing the backpack and instead explained that her backpack had somehow gotten accidentally switched with Charlie's. He wasn't sure how convincing that aspect of his retelling was but it was the only way he could get Charlotte to agree to come clean to Freddie. Jasper finished his confession by explaining their plan of turning everything in to the police and he read Freddie the letter he had drafted the night before.

Freddie was quite engaged during the story. He asked Jasper a few questions and then was quiet for a time after. Eventually he replied that he thought their plan was a good one but why wait until they got to Dairy? They could easily turn in the backpack in Augusta.

Freddie explained that he didn't really like the idea of drugs being in his truck. "If it's all the same I'd rather turn the bag into the Augusta authorities, instead of driving all the way to Dairy."

"Sure," said Jasper. "It didn't occur to me we'd be going through Augusta. Are you sure you don't mind stopping? We don't want to waste any more of your time."

"Believe me, I would feel a lot better with that bag outta my truck. I don't want to have to explain that to the police if we were to get pulled over."

"What do you think, Charlotte?" Jasper asked. "We could just as easily get you on a bus to Fort Kent in Augusta as in Dairy."

"I guess that sounds fine to me," said Charlotte, feeling weary of any change in plan. "You'll be able to resume your bike trip all the sooner as well."

"Well, I'm glad you told me," Freddie put in. "I should stop in a little bit and use a pay phone. I should call my wife and tell her to go over to her brother's for the day. Maybe I'll tell her if those guys stop by again she should tell them I'm picking up hogs in Lewiston, not Dairy."

"You should tell her to call the police if they show up, too." Jasper added.

Freddie found a spot to make a call and they were back on the road in a couple minutes.

When they arrived in Augusta, Freddie and Jasper exchanged addresses and Freddie dropped Charlotte and him off at the Augusta Greyhound bus station. They quickly paid for a locker and stowed Charlie's backpack in it as planned and took the key. They said their goodbyes to Freddie and thanked him for all his help. Freddie pulled away and narrowly avoided hitting a crosswalk sign on the side walk. He honked one last time as he sped off.

The drop off plan went exactly the same way they had planned it, only in Augusta. Jay rewrote the letter addressing it to the Augusta Chief or Police instead. They mailed the package containing the letter, key and notebook to the Augusta Police Station special delivery to the Chief of Police. The teller told them that the package would be delivered by the following morning.

Charlotte and Jasper soon returned to the bus station and checked the itinerary. It was only one o'clock in the afternoon. There was a bus headed north up I-95 to Millinoket that was scheduled to depart at two-thirty. According to the schedule, Charlotte could buy a ticket in Millinoket on a bus that would continue up I-95 to Houlton. From Houlton that same bus would then take Rt 1 through Caribou and eventually arrive in Fort Kent.

"So what do you say, Jasper?" asked Charlotte. "Do you want to take a bus with me to Millinoket? You'll be on the doorstep of Baxter State Park."

Jasper was tempted, it was a good excuse to spend more time with Charlotte. "No, I'd like to honestly. As crazy as the last twenty-four hours have been, I'm glad I met you. But it would defeat the point of my trip. I think we're out of Charlie's jurisdiction and I'm not trying to rush my way to the state park or to Old Calcutta. I'm trying to see where the road takes me."

"I understand," said Charlotte looking slightly disappointed. "Thank you for everything you did. And I am sorry I got you involved."

“It’s all right, I got myself involved,” Jasper said cheerily. “Besides, right now the road is telling me it’s lunch time and you have an hour and a half to kill before your bus. Lets get your ticket and then find a place to have lunch before we say goodbye.”

Charlotte grinned happily and stepped up to the ticket booth to buy a one way ticket to Millinoket.

Chapter 6
Baxter State Park

Charlotte left the bus terminal by the main exit and found Fido waiting for her outside the door "Oh, hey buddy! Where's Jasper?"

Fido woofed softly at Charlotte and turned way to begin walking up the street. When Charlotte failed to follow the dog, he turned around and woofed a little more forcefully.

"I guess you want me to follow?" Charlotte asked the dog. Fido again turned and began walking up the street. "Jasper is a fool to give you such freedom, one of these days you'll get hit by a car." Fido groaned and Charlotte would almost have believed the dog rolled his eyes at her, if such things were possible.

Fido led Charlotte to the building across the street from the bus station. The sign indicated it to be 'Gretchen's Diner'. It was a small diner and served breakfast all day. Charlotte found Jasper sitting in a booth looking over a menu. Fido laid down on the floor near the exit. The waitress, scowled once at the dog but then seemed to forget about him. Charlotte joined Jasper in the booth, "For someone so cautious and law abiding, you sure allow Fido an awful lot of leeway. Aren't you afraid he'd run away or get lost roaming around like that?"

"Fido is very smart and would never run away," said Jasper. "Besides I wanted to make sure we would get a seat."

Charlotte considered the ridiculousness of his statement as she looked around the diner, there were plenty of open tables. Soon the waitress came over and took there orders.

They ate their lunch and said their goodbyes over coffee. Jasper told Charlotte that when he got to Old Calcutta he would give her a call and they should get together. He would like to met Grandma Rosa and Buddy.

After they had eaten, they walked around the neighborhood near the station for a while and waited. When it was nearer to two-thirty Jasper walked Charlotte back to the bus station and gave her a final hug and wished her luck. As the bus pulled away, they waved to each other and Jasper thought he saw Charlotte wipe away a tear before the bus bounced up the road and out of sight.

After Charlotte's bus had left he opened his bicycle in a suitcase and organized his gear, put the side car down for Fido and prepared to resume his road trip.

Jasper needed to consult his Maine atlas before they could get under way. His original itinerary had not included traveling near Augusta. After several minutes he determined that he could follow Route 202 through Waterville, Pittsfield and Newport. Following several smaller roads that together made up Route 11 north he would then travel through Dover-Foxcroft, past the 'Penobscott off Reservation Land Trust' and finally arrive in Millinocket.

Jasper calculated that the trip to Millinocket was approximately one hundred forty miles. He figured he could bike that distance in ten to fourteen hours. It was almost three O'clock in the afternoon. If he wanted time to make camp he should start looking for a camping site at the latest by seven O'clock. With luck he believed he could make it to the Dover-Foxcroft area in that time.

The first two hours of his bike ride his road followed parallel to the Kennebec River. The countryside was beautiful on this warm June day and he passed several farms and a few large ponds. Half an hour beyond Waterville, he pedaled over a picturesque covered bridge which straddled the small Sebasticook River in the town of Clinton. There he saw two men fishing from the dock and he remembered he had not restocked his supplies for the road after his excursion with Charlotte.

This wasn't a problem for he had saved plenty of money. He thought though that for only two days on the road he had already eaten out plenty. The fishermen gave him an idea. He would set up camp near one of the ponds or the small river that flowed by Dover-Foxcroft.

After Waterville, the countryside became far less populated and there were fewer and fewer houses and farms. Jasper's imagination began to get away from him and he imagined seeing a Chevy Silverado with a red primed passenger side door come around a hidden corner or into view over the next hill. Lucky for Jasper, alone with only Fido no such thing occurred.

To get his mind off of it, Jasper decided to turn on the electric motor and give his legs a rest. He sped through the county side past Pittsfield and soon was approaching Newport.

Jasper looked at his watch, thinking he was making good time. He realized then that it was already seven. He had miscalculated the distance and would not reach Dover-Foxcroft today. He needed to find a place to set up camp if he had any hope of doing so before dark.

Fido and Jasper continued for two miles beyond Newport and found a clearing on the right hand side of Moosehead Trail,which was the portion of Route 11 they were currently traveling. The clearing went all the way down to the edge of Sebasticook Lake, which according to his atlas was fairly large, almost three miles across. The duo stopped there and made camp fifty feet or so from the lake's edge near a small grove of birch trees.

Jasper having been in the boy scouts and taken several wilderness survival classes including hiking the Hundred Mile Wilderness was a decent woodsmen. He had packed some nylon string and fishing hooks. Using Stonie's Jack-of-all-Jacks, he was able to fashion a small branch into a suitable fishing rod. He dug in the soft soil near the trees and carried away several worms to use as bait.

It was already after eight o'clock and dusk was approaching. After starting a small camp fire, Jasper headed to the water's edge. By the time it was full dark he had been able to catch two decent sized trout. He prepared them, again with the help of his jackknife and cooked them over his fire. Jasper ate the fish with a wild salad he had made from the vegetation he found in the field.

Most people, Jasper thought, saw the woods only for its trees and a field only for the grass. They walked by completely unaware of the resources available.

The next morning was a Tuesday and he and Fido were up at dawn. It was hard to sleep in when camping in a tent, especially when your tent was not in the shade. As soon as the sun hits your tent it starts to warm up.

Jasper went fishing again and made himself and Fido another meal of lake trout with a potato he found in the bottom of his bag.

By eight o'clock he had broken down his tent and repacked all of his gear. He consulted his atlas a second time to make sure he knew where he was going. He wanted to make it to Millinoket by the end of the day. Jasper calculated that the rest of the trip was about eighty to ninety miles and that he should be able to do that in six or seven hours.

His battery for the bike was partially drained so he decided to pedal and recharge the battery for a while. The trip quickly became hilly when he arrived in the foot hills of the Appalachian Mountains. It took him two hours to reach Dover-Foxcroft.

Between Dover-Foxcroft and a small town known as Milo, the road followed a small river. It was a quiet journey with nothing to see but a half dried up riverbed and an unchanging forest. The landscape was the same for miles with hardly a house or field. During this time Jasper remembered that he had not called Claire on Monday. A stab of guilt ripped through him as he recalled his last conversation with her when he had said he would find a phone to call every Monday and Wednesday. He had found a phone on Monday night but he had been so preoccupied with Charlotte and her phone call to Grandma Rosa that he had not thought to call Claire. Between kissing Charlotte and forgetting to call Claire, Jasper was beginning to feel like a real jerk. He decided he would call Claire either tonight or tomorrow morning.

The rest of his trip there was relatively uneventful. He did manage to get himself lost once by accidentally taking a logging trail. He only realized it was a wrong turn when he reached a dead end.

His bike tires sank into the mud at the edge of a marsh that was overtaking the logging road. In his attempt to free the bike he slipped in the mud and fell. As Jasper and Fido turned around, he discovered he was covered in mud. He laughed it off but soon became discouraged as he wasted two and a half hours back tracking and taking two additional wrong turns before he finally gave up and asked Fido to follow their scent and lead him back to the Millinoket Rd in Brownville, where Jasper had first steered them in the wrong direction.

* * * *

It was five o'clock in the afternoon by the time Jasper reached Millinocket. Millinoket was a small but successful rural town that was largely tied to the paper industry. The Great Northern Paper Company had built a hydroelectric dam on the Penobscot River in 1899. That dam was still in operation today, almost eighty years later. Its proximity to Baxter State Park and the Moosehead Lake area had also developed the town into a launching point for vacationers and adventurers seeking to explore the Maine wilderness.
Jasper decided to spend the night in a motel. He was dirty and wet and needed to shower and launder his clothes. He could also, more easily, check his equipment and repack his gear for the continued bike trip from a motel room than while out camping.
Jasper stopped briefly at the side of the road and spoke to a man sweeping the patio of Garry's, a restaurant that appeared to serve breakfast and lunch that appeared already closed up. The man gave him directions to a nearby motel. After a one mile ride further up the Millinocket Road, he found the Smith Brook Motel on the right hand side of the road. He consulted his map and was pleased to find he'd gone in this direction.
In the morning he would be able to continue north, past Millinocket Lake, onto Baxter Park Rd which would take him to the Togue Pond gate entrance of Baxter Park.
The first thing he did after paying for his room was to check that his bike did not need any adjustments or repair work after the delay on the logging road. Then he locked it outside his motel room on the bike rack. He found an outlet nearby and was able to plug in the bike's rechargeable battery. By morning it should be fully charged.
The motel room had a phone but Jasper decided to wait until morning to call Claire and his parents back home.
He was glad to have the first three days of his trip over with. He hadn't expected so much tension and he certainly had not expected

things to go as they had. When he had decided to make the trip, he wanted to get some peace and solitude. Being chased by drug dealers halfway across the state was not what he had expected.

During his trip from Augusta he had found some solitude but found himself distracted by the constant need to look over his shoulder, expecting to find Charlie Washington Baldwin baring down on him. Hopefully it would be more peaceful in Baxter State Park. Jasper went to bed with those thoughts in mind.

He awoke at seven the next morning. Jasper would have to wait until the Baxter State Park Authority opened to check and see if there were any openings for overnight camping in the park. The Park Authority had an office in the small downtown area of Millinocket. He had made reservations for a couple weeks later, because he never expected to be at the park so soon.

Jasper took the short bike ride back to Garry's Diner and had breakfast with Fido on the patio. When they were done eating he sat there and wrote a couple of letters on beautiful Baxter State Park postcards. He sent one to his parents, Jonny and the gang at the bike shop, Stonie and Penelope, Chad, Jeremy and Claire. He was able to mail the postcards right there from the restaurant.

After breakfast, Jasper went back to the motel to make a few calls before turning in his key and setting out for the Park Authority. He decided to call his parents and Claire now since he would be camping out in the park and didn't know when he might next have a chance to use a phone.

He decided not to tell them about the drug dealers or about Charlotte. He just said he had decided to travel inland through Augusta instead of by the coast. He told them he was more excited about hiking in the Park than traveling up the coast. It was good to hear their voices.

Jasper felt guilty lying to his parents and Claire. His folks trusted him to be honest and knew he would always do the right thing. He felt he had handled the situation but wondered if his parents would agree. He didn't want to worry them or make them question his judgment.

Not mentioning Charlotte to Claire was an obvious move. It would only make her jealous even if he succeeding in painting the picture as platonic. Despite his reasoning, he still felt bad about his dishonesty. It was, however, good to talk to everyone.

After checking out of the motel he headed for the Park Authority in Millinocket. Once he got there he cancelled his reservations he had made for later in the month. He checked to see if there were any cancellations for the next three or four nights. The clerk told him that the park still had reservations open and that if he needed more time he could visit a ranger station and let them know.

The clerk was impressed with Fido's search and rescue certificate and that Jasper was a junior ranger. Normally pets were not permitted in the park and the clerk wanted to restrict him from bringing the dog. Jasper told the clerk that Fido had been involved first hand in several rescues over the years, which was true. The clerk decided that Jasper could bring the dog to the Ranger Station near the Touge Pond entrance and ask the Senior Ranger for an exception.

Jasper also asked about getting a wilderness pass which would allow him to go beyond the designated trails.

The clerk frowned at him and told him that traveling alone even on some of the marked trails deeper in the park was not advised but he could take that matter up with the senior ranger as well.

Jasper was done at the Park Authority and headed up the Millinocket Rd to take on the State Park. Weather wise it was fantastic with no clouds in the sky and the temperature in the high seventies and sure to get higher by mid-day. The scenery was like a page torn out of a picture book. Jasper would often stop at designated areas to look around and see the views. Most of the park roads were dirt.

He started biking the twenty or so miles to the park entrance. Fido had a bright orange and gold search and rescue jacket on to try and impress the senior ranger and make him easier to spot.

Jasper knew the park well. His family had been going to Baxter State Park for years on hikes and outings since he was a kid. His parents would stop there on the way to their grandparents every year.

Jasper approached the Togue Pond Gate to check into the park. There was only one ranger on duty.The ranger was a woman about thirty years old with dark curly brown hair and freckles. On her name tag it said 'Ranger Butler"

"Good morning, how are you today?" she said.

"Just fine," replied Jasper. "It seems like a really nice day." He handed his ID card to her and she started to log him in.

"Will you be tenting out or just on a day trip?"
Jasper handed her the paperwork from the central ranger station, "I will be hiking and tenting for three nights to a week."

"Ok, thats fine because the park hasn't been full. Make sure that you stop at one of the ranger stations on your fourth day and state your intentions so we know you haven't gotten yourself lost. I see you have a dog with you," said Ranger Butler sounding surprised as Fido pushed the front door open with his head and walked up to the counter to join Jasper.

"I do actually. This is Fido and he is search and rescue certified. I was told in town at the Park Authority to talk to the senior ranger on duty to see about an exemption for taking my dog in the park. I was also interested in getting a wilderness pass and maybe doing some bushwhacking and sleeping in non designated areas."

"Well then, you'll need to speak with Terry. I can radio for him to come down and meet with you. Don't get your hopes up though. It's not often that we allow bushwhacking in the park."

Jasper and Fido waited outside and familiarized themselves with the park map they got from Ranger Butler. When Jasper had come here over the years, his family had typically stayed in the Kidney Pond area of the park and around the southern side of Mt. Katahdin. This time Jasper was interested in exploring something new and wanted to visit the central and northern parts of the park where it was less explored.

After fifteen minutes, a dark green pickup truck with a state of Maine emblem on the side pulled up to the ranger station at the entrance.

A man of about six feet tall with a well tanned complexion and black hair stepped out. He was wearing a park ranger's uniform and hat. He saw Jasper and Fido watching and came up to speak with them. On his name tag Jasper read that his name was Ranger Bearroot.

"Good morning," said Ranger Bearroot. "I hear you've come to explore the park?"

"Yes, we have. My name is Jasper Jay Hawk and this is Fido". Bearroot, he thought. His name sounded familiar to Jasper. Then he remembered Penelope Stone's story of the old Native American friend she had in Dairy. The one who she had asked about Stonie's jackknife. His name had been Bearroot. Jasper wondered if this could be the same person. Somehow he doubted it. Penelope described him as being much older. In his eighties Jasper believed. She certainly didn't mention him being a park ranger either.

"Well, pets are prohibited in the park; domesticated animals can get lost, disrupt wildlife and make messes," replied Bearroot.

"I understand that," Jasper said. "But Fido is no ordinary dog. He is a certified search and rescue dog. He has been involved with several rescues and lost persons cases over the years. He would not cause trouble, I can swear on that." Jasper handed Bearroot Fido's credentials that he had remembered to bring with him.

Ranger Bearroot examined the document with a skeptical look on his face.

"I've also been trained in wilderness survival through the boy scouts." Jasper pulled out his own documentation and handed it to the ranger as well. "I did the hundred mile wilderness with my troop in the eighth and tenth grade. The last two years I was in the outward bound program and became a junior ranger."

"Well, thats all very impressive and makes me feel a little better about a young man of eighteen coming alone to the park," said Bearroot, giving Jasper a long look. After what seemed like an eternity, Ranger Bearroot spoke again. "Jay Hawk you say?"

"Yes, sir," replied Jasper.

"Oh, call me Terry, I'm nobodies Sir," said Bearroot with a chuckle. "I seem to remember a story in the paper a few years ago about a boy and his dog rescuing two small children lost in the woods. I remember it was a brother and sister like two and four years old. I think it was near Bethel. If I remember correctly the dog was sent out into the woods late at night to find them and then stayed with them over night and brought them to safety in the morning."

Jasper smiled remembering the events and nodded to Bearroot. “It was near Bethel on the Androscoggin River. The children were actually three and five.”

“I thought I recognized your name but couldn’t place it,” said Bearroot with a smile. “If I remember from the article the police on the night the children went missing had criticized you sending the dog out alone. How could you have trusted a dog to keep to his duty and search for those children unaided?”

“Well, it was a little more complicated than that,” Jasper said, rubbing his head, “But I know Fido, he’s a unique animal and is quite intuitive and I think I’ve trained him well. He knew what he was doing.”

“I guess he must have,” said Terry. “I’ll give you an exemption and let you bring the dog with you into the park. Obviously he needs to stay with you and you need to clean up after him.”

“Of course, Ranger Terry. You don’t need to worry about that. Thank you.”

“Ranger Butler told me you were also hoping for a wilderness pass as well. I’m afraid I can’t give you that. It’s too dangerous to go alone. Even on the marked trails experienced hikers have gotten hurt and lost when traveling alone. You have an intelligent canine that is quite a resource to you if half of that article I read was true. That makes me feel better about you hiking alone but we’ve only ever given out wilderness passes to larger groups with expert guides with them, usually doing environmental research on the park or watershed. I’m sorry.”

“I understand I guess. Thank you for letting me bring my dog, you won’t regret it.”

“I’m sure I won’t. You’ll find there is plenty to explore even without leaving the trails. Many of them are pretty isolated. Be careful.”

“We will,” replied Jasper. “Can I ask you something else?”

“Oh? What is it?”

“Your last name is Bearroot?” he ventured. “That’s not a very common name. Are you Penobscot Indian by chance?”

“Yes, I am.” said Terry confused. “How did you know?”

"A friend of mine told me she knew an older man who was Penobscot. He lived in Dairy and they met at a powwow in Old Town. His name was Bearroot also. She told me he could usually be found at a Smoke Shoppe and tobacco pipe shop in Dairy."

"That sounds like my grandfather Albion. I'm afraid he died this winter."

"Oh, I'm sorry, I didn't know," said Jasper embarrassed he'd charged in so quickly.

"Oh, don't be. You didn't know. What made you bring him up?"

"Well, my friend, she had a jack knife that had a Native American word engraved on it and she had asked your grandfather what it might have said. He had not known at the time but said he knew someone who could speak quite a few native languages and that he could asked his friend for her. I was curious to track this information down."

A dark shadow of suspicion crossed over Terry Bearroot's face. It was gone so quickly that Jasper had not noticed but Fido had. Bearroot smelled of fear and caution. "My grandfather was a great one for tall tales," he said, and handed Jasper his ID card and other paper work including the letter of exemption for Fido. "One of my grandfather's favorite stories was about an old Indian who had been banished from his tribe and lived up in a remote part of Mount Katahdin. The old medicine man was supposedly over one hundred years old. He had migrated over a number of years to Maine from a Western tribe. The story says he came up here to die. His name was Buffalo Man. It sounds to me like my grandfather was spinning one of his yarns about him. The legend goes that he was the best in all the nations at bringing down buffalo. They say he is still up there in the mountains. That's the legend, how much of it is true is hard to say.

"So no one has ever seen him?" asked Jasper taking his paper work and ID card back and putting them away.

"Well, I don't think there is anything to see," said Terry snapped back. "And don't get any ideas. I won't have hikers going off trail bushwhacking for anything, especially not a mythical Indian Shaman."

"Don't worry, if you said I can't have a wilderness pass then I can except that," said Jasper. "We should get going so we can get started on a hike before it gets too hot. Thanks again."

As they walked back to Jasper's bike, Fido looked over his shoulder several times. Terry was watching them leave. There is something else he knows that he's not telling us, thought the dog. He knows where to find this Buffalo Man, I'd bet my tail on it.

When they reached the bike, Jasper got on and Fido jumped in the side car. They headed left down the Park Tote Road. They biked to the Katahdin Stream Campground. At the ranger station located there, Jasper met Bud Swayer another park ranger and was given permission to store the bike at the Ranger Station. Jasper was thinking they would more than likely camp at the Katahdin Stream Campground but wanted to keep his options open. If he decided to stay at one of the designated lean-tos or a different campsite he didn't want to have to worry about whether his bike was secure.

After securing the bike at the ranger station, Jasper grabbed his backpack that he had repacked at the motel the night before with his survival gear and camping equipment. He had gone grocery shopping before he left Millinocket and had backed up everything he needed. What gear he didn't want to weigh him down while he and Fido were on the trail he left packed in the suitcase with his bike.

Fido and Jasper headed up the Appalachian Trail until the reached the summit of Mt Katahdin. The view was breathtaking. While they were there, a group of hikers asked him to take their picture in front of the Mt Katahdin sign.

Shortly after that, the two companions hiked the Knife's Edge Trail to the Helon Taylor Trail that lead them to Sandy Stream Pond. There was another campsite at the Sandy Steam Pond and with Fido's urging Jasper decided to stop for lunch there before continuing on.

After lunch they followed Chimney Pond Trail past the Basin Ponds and then took the Hamlin Ridge Trail to the top of Mt Hamlin. The view there was equally breath taking.

Jasper took a deep sigh as he realized he had not thought of Charlotte, Charlie or the bag of drugs until this moment. This was what his trip was supposed to be all about. He enjoyed being outdoors hiking. It was one of his favorite past times. He liked that he had to use his own power to get somewhere and being out in nature, in the woods gave him the chance to let the weight of the world leave his shoulders. Hiking was a great way to clear your head.

After a short rest, he looked at the time, it was quarter til five. He thought out loud for Fido's benefit. "We should really head south down the Northwest Basin Trail. According to the map," he continued pointing at the Baxter State Park map he had gotten from Ranger Butler, "it will take us right back to the Appalachian Trail and Katahdin Stream Campground."

Fido looked at the map and gazed around the Mountain top. He never really understood maps or words. He could read but he did best with signs or short phrases. He had used human words before to figure out which way to go. Once he even read a letter someone had written to Jasper. A few sentences, that was fine. He had difficulty understanding how humans could read a book and learn a story about something from it. What did a book filled with paper and words have to do with a knight fighting a dragon? How could a page of words convey that?

Maps were much the same. They ware a meaningless page with lines and pictures. A map had fewer words than a book but Jasper acted like with its help he could never get lost. It sounded like bologna to Fido. A nose with a fresh scent, that was how you properly found your way. Why stare at a piece of paper and scratch your head when you could put your nose to the air and find the answer flowing through it.

Still to humor his friend Fido woofed in confirmation. It was late and he voted for heading pack to the campground and scoring a few of the hot dogs that he could smell in Jasper's backpack.

"I'm curious about the northern portion of this trail though," Jasper continued, ignoring Fido's woof. "Look, it goes past the Caribou Spring for about a mile and then seems to just end. I wonder what is that way."

Fido had an inkling of what Jasper was not saying and he began a cautionary low throaty growl.

"Oh don't worry, boy," he answered. "I told Ranger Bearroot I wouldn't go bushwhacking without his permission and I'm a man of my word. But he did say in the legend this Buffalo Man lived in a remote part of the park. I keep getting this feeling of déjà vu. You know what I mean?"

Unfortunately Fido did know what Jasper meant. He felt it too, more importantly he smelled it. It was a smell he didn't like. It reminded him of events he'd rather not recall. It reminded him of his friend injured and trapped. Fido would rather not face the trickster again. Still, Jasper was his boss so Fido would follow where he lead. The dog did give an annoyed growl and gave him a sideways look for good measure.

"All right then," said Jasper excitedly. "It's not even far. We'll hike to the end see what's there, if there's nothing we'll turn back around. Deal?"

Fido nodded yes. Here we go again, thought the dog.

They hiked north for half an hour before reaching the end of the trail. Jasper was surprised to find it ended at a lean-to site. It was clear that it had not been used this season. Jasper kicked a punky log that the lean-to was made from. It didn't seem trustworthy. There was a Baxter State Park sign designating it as an official site but the sign was awfully faded. Jasper was surprised it had not been replaced and the site was not better kept up.

He pulled out his map and looked again. "Its funny, this isn't shown on the map. It doesn't seem like it should be here."

Fido whined softly, attempting to urge Jasper to turn back. If it doesn't seem right, thought the dog, then maybe we shouldn't stay here.

"I think it's a safe site," responded Jasper. He didn't have to be telepathic to read his friend's mood. "I still have that feeling, I think we should clean up the site, set up the tent and spend the night."

They did just that. After they had made camp, eaten and prepared for bed Jasper hung their food with a rope from a tree to keep it away from animals, just in case.

It was an eerily quiet night and sleep came with difficulty to Fido and Jasper. When it did come Jasper dreamed that he was standing in their current camp site but the site was much better maintained and the paint on the sign was fresh. It was day time and the sun was out. It was a beautiful day. Jasper looked north and was surprised to see that instead of a wall of saplings and undergrowth, there was a path. The trail continued north.

Jasper began walking up the trail. His steps were unnaturally long and he covered a mile with one stride. He continued up the trail and it past several peaks in the park and then past a large pond. As he walked the day faded to night and became cold. He began to feel that someone was watching him.

Soon he began to hear laughter. It was an oddly familiar cackling laugh of an old man. Jasper was sure he had never heard the laugher before but he couldn't shake the sense that this wasn't the first time. He stopped short when he looked ahead and saw a very tall, very old Native American man standing in the path ahead of him. He was struck with a feeling of frantic terror and turned to run away. He tripped and fell.

He woke up still griped by his panic. He shot up out of his sleeping bag and out of the tent in what felt like a single motion.

It was early morning and the sun was shining through the trees at a low angle. Fido was standing in the center of the campsite staring at the wall of saplings intently.

"What is it, Fido?" Jasper said. "Is someone out there?"

The dog shook his head 'No'.

"Have you been awake all night, standing guard?"

Fido looked him in the eye for a long moment and then nodded 'yes'.

"This place gives you the creeps doesn't it?"

Again the dog nodded 'yes'.

"It's beginning to do the same to me. Lets pack up and move on. What do you say?"

"Woof," the dog said happily with his tail wagging.

They packed up the tent and the rest of the campsite and ate a light breakfast. Before an hour had passed they were heading south down the trail to continue their exploration of the park. They took the Chimney Pond Trail east to Sandy Stream Pond and then followed the

Russell Pond Trail north to Russell Pond. The hike took a little over five hours. They spent the remainder of the day hiking around Wassataqouik Lake and camped for the night at Little Wassataqouik. There were two other groups of hikers camping there as well and Jasper and Fido listened to their stories for a while before going to bed. Ranger Sawyer stopped by to check on the group of hikers while they were trading stories and Jasper showed him Fido's exemptions papers again.

Before going to bed, Jasper, again, got a feeling that pointed him north. He felt like a compass being drawn off towards the center of the park far from any of the existing trails. He went to bed determined he would follow the Pogy Notch Trail north and explore the area around Matagamon Lake.

The next morning was Friday and Fido and Jasper packed up to set out for Russell Pond where they could find the trail north. It was so quiet and peaceful that Jasper slowed down to enjoy the hike. Fido walked along seaming to enjoy the hike, as well. They had been walking for about twenty minutes when Jasper heard an engine and thought to him self, "Gee, it's so hard to get away from that sound. Even in Baxter State Park, it's present." Soon the noise was upon him. Jasper turned around and it was a ranger on a four wheeler waving him down. He stopped and said, "Hi Ranger Sawyer," recognizing the man they had met two days earlier.

"Hi, Jasper Hawk? Right?" he asked.

"Yes, what can I do for you?"

"I got a message from TB, that's Ranger Bearroot, to find you and your K-9. He's a tracker? We have a lost nine year old boy in the Great Basin area of the park."

"Actually that's his specialty, He has a noise like a blood hound." Fido was listening and was already to get going.

"Would you have any objections to us using him to find this kid?"

"None at all, in fact I'll go with you," said Jasper.

"Great, hop on," said Ranger Sawyer. "Bud is my name, Bud Sawyer, nice to meet you Jasper."

Jasper threw his backpack in the back and hopped into the two seated four wheeler. "The dog can ride in the back." The four-wheeler was similar to a small truck with a back for carrying gear. Fido jumped up into the back and they were off.

"They have a chopper back at Russell Pond Campground waiting for us. In cases like this, time is really important," said Bud. Jasper had noticed the helicopter pads at several of the sites. When they got there, Bud introduced him to Bill Rounds, the helicopter pilot and in no time they were in the air.

As the chopper was setting down at the Great Basin ranger station near Chimney Pond, he saw Terry come walking up toward the helicopter. He put out his hand to greet him. Fido jumped out of the chopper and TB said, "Hey there Fido, I'm glad I gave you that exemption, after all." After he shook hands he pattered the dog warmly. "So do you have a piece of the boys clothing?" asked Jasper, eager to get into action. "Just how long has the boy been missing?"

"Well, he hasn't been missing all that long. I got the report from his father, Ray Verrill, less than an hour ago. Thats when I remembered Fido and you being here, that the dog was certified tracker. We had this helicopter available so I got right on the phone while Ranger Sawyer went out in search of you two. Luckily, Ranger Sawyer remembered seeing you up near Wassataqouik last night. The father is right over here and we have a description of the boy, Bobby Verrill, so let's go so we don't lose any more time."

TB hollered to Bud over the sound of the chopper, "Bud were going to start over on Saddle Trail where the boy was seen last, you ride with Billy in the helicopter and follow the direction or the dog and look around by air. If the chopper gets out of site I'll send up a flair."

Billy ten-foured him and headed back over to the helicopter.

TB introduced Jasper to the father and they went over to the place where the boy had been seen last on Saddler Trail, not too far away. Jasper had a shirt belonging to the boy and said to Fido, "We need to find this boy fast but don't out run us. Go fast enough so we can keep up."

Fido barked and put the shirt deep into his snout and took a couple of long sniffs of it. He then started to circle until he got the scent of the boy and then took off in a straight line, until he got to the woods. Fido slowed up a little and just went where the scent took him.

They took off in hot pursuit of the dog, but not until TB asked everyone except the father, Jasper and a couple other volunteers he knew to stay behind. The going could become real treacherous given the direction the dog was headed in. TB didn't need to rescue more than one person at a time. "With the air patrol and the five of us, we can cover a lot of area fast and to many people would be a burden. Everyone can keep searching the campgrounds and paths too, but basically stay put. We will report back as soon as we find anything." The fifteen or so people who had gathered seemed to understand the situation as Terry Bearroot explained it.

The search was on and Jasper figured they would be able to be on top of the lost boy in less then half an hour or sooner, if he stayed on the trail.

The pace was steady for fifteen or twenty minutes. If Fido got too far ahead he would bark a few times so that they would know what direction to go in. Fido had to slow down a few times to circle. One time he came back with a t-shirt in his mouth. He went out to the edge of a cliff and looked down and then followed the tracks back and caught the scent again and took off down a slope. They were off the path by this time. The scent led Fido off Saddler Trail and into the woods.

Bushwhacking was now the order of business in the search. It was starting to get hilly and steep in places. Next thing he brought back was one sneaker. "That will slow the boy down a little," TB exclaimed. The radio began to bark on TB's hip. He answered the radio while he moved along with the search party. "The chopper has located us and is headed in the general direction. It's hard for them to keep a steady eye on us, or the dog because of the trees and underbrush. Bud has the glasses on us and is keeping us in sight." They could hear and sometime see the chopper occasionally. TB radioed to Bud, "The dog veered off the path and is headed for Hamlin Ridge. I don't see how he would ever get to Hamlin Peak, so check out the ridge area. There isn't as much over growth there, ten-four."

"Roger that," Bud replied. As the group heard the chopper veer off in the direction of Hamlin Ridge.

All of a sudden, Fido came up with a series of very aggressive barks and took off like a bat out of hell. He kept barking as he ran. Jasper said, "We're either getting close or he has picked up an intruder's scent to add to the mix. Fido's clearly agitated and wants to get to the boy in a hurry. He'll keep barking to let us know where he is but I doubt he'll stop till he finds the boy."

TB radioed up to the chopper and told them to scan for something else besides a boy and a dog. "We better pick up the pace or we'll loose his bark." TB said.

They all picked it up and did their best to keep the dog's bark within earshot. The search party was now making very good time with TB and Jasper up front covering a lot of ground despite the bushwhacking conditions.

He was a step or two behind TB when all of a sudden in the quiet run of the search the radio barked out "TB that bear is in the clearing over by Caribou Springs. You know the one that has been ripping apart all the tents and bothering the hikers this past week." Bud continued on the radio. "The dog is here now. He's tearing across the field towards the bear. I don't see the kid anywhere, instructions? Over?"

TB had to slow up now to instruct Bud, "Go ahead, Jasper. I'll be right behind you. But stay clear of that bear. He's dangerous when cornered, and it looks like he might be, because there is a cliff beyond that clearing. We're about a mile away." Jasper took off like a shot as TB grabbed the radio and kept running and said to Bud, "Keep looking for the boy and watch the reaction of the dog. He is trained to put himself between the bear and the boy. Look behind the dog!"

TB paused for a minute while he jumped over fallen log. "Bud keep giving me status reports. Jasper will show in about ten minutes. Have the thirty-three and tranquilizer gun ready. Shoot to kill if the boy is in danger."

They all picked up their pace. Jasper was way up ahead and the father and two other volunteers were well back but not losing sight of TB. TB hollered back, "I have to pick it up. There is some action about a mile away. Keep in a northeast direction and you will find us." TB took off like a shot.

Jasper lost Fido's bark for a few minutes but as he picked his pace up and the going was easier. He began to hear it faintly. It was all up hill and he was sweating profusely. He was tiring but couldn't stop. The thought of a bear up there must be frightening for the kid, he thought.

As he got closer he could hear the chopper, barks and growls clearer and clearer with every step. As he ran he scanned the forest for a club or a heavy stick. All he had was the Jack of all Jacks Stonie had given him. That was no match for a bear.

Fido had caught up to the bear and stopped barking so the bear wouldn't hear his approach. The bear was clearly concentrating on a giant boulder about twenty-five feet from the cliff. Fido charged the bear and nipped it in the ass and jumped back before the giant bear could react. He then reacted with a barrage of barks and growls trying to get the bear to chase him.

The bear wanted what was under the boulder, but it was too far under for the bear to reach. It started to push the rock, and it move slightly. The dog took another charge at the bear and this time the bear turned just in time to face the dog.

The bear had stood up on its hind legs and threatened the dog.

Fido stopped within lunging space of the bear and waited for the follow through of the big bear's swing with his right paw. When the bear swung and missed, Fido charged it and bit hard into the bear's right thigh and then retreated as quick as he charged.

This infuriated the bear. Fido had taken a good bite of the bear and it was pissed off and started to chase the dog. Fido ran till the bear stopped, about thirty feet from the boulder. It still wanted what was under that boulder and turned back. Fido launched the attack again to stop the bear from going back. The bear turned and faced Fido again. He stood up and growled at the dog.

This time Fido didn't wait for the bear to swing or do anything he ran straight under the bear's legs so fast the bear couldn't react. The dog was now between the boulder and the bear.

As Bud relayed what was happening TB grabbed up the radio. When Bud had finished he said, "Bill, position your chopper over the boulder and behind the dog so the bear thinks he will have to go through the dog and the chopper to get to the kid. The kid has to be under that boulder, I'll bet money on it. The dog knows it."

Bud replied, "Roger, line open."

Bill did exactly as TB had said and continued to report on the happenings. "We are in position and the bear is looking in wonder, trying to figure what is next."

"Bud," Terry continued. "Jasper should be showing up at the end of the clearing. Look for him and get the microphone out and tell him to wait for me. If the bear sees or smells us back here, it will be truly cornered and no one knows who he will charge; the dog or us. Repeat, Tell Jasper to wait. We have to circle the area and give the bear an escape route or someone will get hurt or we'll be forced to shoot the bear. Have your weapons ready. Over?"

"Roger that," Bud replied.

Jasper was approaching the clearing and had found a big stick. He stopped to see what to make of the situation. Fido was holding off the bear with the chopper behind the dog. Jasper quickly assumed the dog was between the boy and the bear. Realizing he better start circling so as to give the bear an out he started going left as he heard Bud blast over the chopper microphone, "Jasper, stop and wait for TB." More noise confused the bear. It started to look around.

Bud blared over the intercom again, "Stay still and the bear won't see you."

Jasper stopped and did what Bud said and watched the standoff between the bear and Fido. After a few minutes, he sensed someone standing beside him. It was TB. He never heard him come up.

"Ok, good job Jasper," TB whispered as he put the radio to his mouth. "Bud, we need to move down wind of the bear, otherwise he will smell us before he sees us. We need to let the other three know to move in the same direction as we are. I'll have Jasper stay here to tell them which way to go when they show up. It shouldn't be to long. We have to give the bear a corridor to escape through that would be the left side towards Klondike Pond."

"TB, what about tranquilizing him here, in this wide open field?" asked Bud.

TB answered back, "We still haven't had a sighting of the boy. Remember, I just assumed he was under that boulder. I still think he is, but he might need medical attention. If not we can do the bear as soon as the boy is safe with his father. I am going to circle right and get behind the dog to get the boy out. Jasper, if the bear comes your way when the other three are here, spread out and let him hear you and see you. He should turn to the left and take the left corridor we leave open for him. Let the bear go Bud, but stay close in case we need to take the boy to the hospital. If not and the bear stays close you can tranquilize him once we have the boy safe. We'll see what he does."

Jasper stayed put and waited for the other three. TB started to circle to the right. The bear starred at the dog and with the helicopter there started back a little and then rushed for ten feet. Fido stood his ground and looked fierce with his barking and growling. The helicopter let out a deafening shrill loud noise that stopped the bear. It got up again on its hind legs and let loose a horrific display of frustration, and then turned and went straight back towards Jasper and TB.

TB was circling right and started waving his arms and hollering in Abenaki at the bear, Jasper followed suit and started waving at the bear. It stopped again about fifty feet from him, looked left and then right and did exactly what TB had expected. The two volunteers, Chuck, Buck and Ray were just coming along and Jasper said, "Make noise and wave your hands. We're trying to drive it to the left." They started in, hollering and waving.

The bear started going left more and soon was going exactly in the direction of Klondike Pond. By now TB had begun sprinting for the boulder and the dog was still about thirty feet behind the bear driving him to the left. The chopper was aiding the dog in the drive.

"Jasper, hold the dog. Let the bear go, everyone else just spread out and stay close. The bear will get the idea not to double back." TB then went under the rock to look and see what was there. He had his flashlight out and saw the boy. "Bobby, your father is here and the bear is gone, are you all right?"

There was no answer. TB repeated what he had said. He could see the boy move.

"I think I'm all right, but I'm stuck. The bear scared me so I jammed myself in here. Then the bear moved the rock a little and it came down on me and now I'm stuck for good."

"Not for good, Bobby we'll get you out," said TB. "Here's your dad. Keep talking to him, while I organize a way to get you out."

TB gestured to the father to talk to the boy as he grabbed the radio and called to Bill Rounds. "Bill, forget the bear for now and get over here. We'll trap him later and tranquilize him and get him out of here. For now we need to put a chain around this boulder and lift it just enough to free the boy. The bear has moved it enough to really wedge the kid in there good."

The chopper was there fast with a chain dangling over the boulder. TB signaled to let more out and they sent it down. Jasper, Buck and Chuck secured the chain around the boulder.

TB said through the radio, "Bill we don't need much height just enough for Jasper to get under there and pull the boy out." TB had nodded to him to ask if it was ok with him in going under after the boy.

Jasper nodded back 'yes'.

TB had selected him because he was the slimmest and most agile and could do it the most efficiently. He had noticed it was a tight fit for himself when he was talking to Bobby under the boulder. "I'll give you the go ahead as soon as I get a couple logs or rocks to wedge under the boulder after you lift it so it won't come down on them if he doesn't come out quickly."

The guys found small boulders and a log they could wedge under there after the big boulder was lifted. "Ok," TB said over the radio, with Bud, Bill, Jasper, Chuck, Ray and Buck listening. "Bill you take it up only about a foot or so, not much. Chuck and Buck, you jam the logs and small boulder under the big boulder. Jasper, you go under only when Chuck and Buck have the log and small boulder in place. Ready?"

Every one was in their places as TB double-checked the chain and then said, "Up." The boulder moved up a little more than a foot and Chuck and Buck jammed their pieces in place. "Hold, Bill,"

called TB over the radio, "Ok Jasper, go!" He was in there like a snake. He went so far in that only his feet were visible.
Jasper said to the boy, "Hi Bobby, my name is Jasper. Have you loosened up any?" Both Chuck and Buck had flashlights pointed in the wedge of the bolder. Jay could see the boy pretty well.

"I think so I can move my legs now."

"It might hurt a little while we start out, grab my arm and we can start to wiggle out. Ok?"

"Sure I'm ready."

Jasper took the boy by each arm and pulled the boy towards him while he inched backwards. Jay was moving out slowly when Chuck and Buck grabbed him by the ankles and belt and pulled him and the boy out in one quick motion. The boy's father, Ray Verrill came over and the boy was soon in his arm, sobbing and hugging him tightly.

"Everybody stand clear! The chopper is letting the boulder down," TB reported. Every one stood back as TB talked to Bill Rounds the pilot. "Ok Billy, bring her down and then land that thing in the clearing." Billy did just that and the bolder settled down. Jasper and Chuck unhooked the chain and Bud pulled it up and the chopper landed in the clearing.

Everyone's attention was on the boy at this point to see how bad the leg was. Fido wiggled in and licked the boy's face. The boy knew the dog had kept the bear at bay and gave him a big hug.
"What's his name?" Bobby said.
"It's Fido," Jasper said. "Trained to save kids like you."

"Well, he sure did. If I had been that bear, I would have taken off too."

Bud Sawyer, the ranger medic of the crew said, "The foot and ankle area have been crushed but only an x-ray can tell how bad." He was applying an ice pack to the swollen area.

"Ok, here is what we'll do," said TB. "Jasper, Fido and I will walk back. The rest can fly back in the chopper. There is only enough room for six passengers. Bud, radio ahead and let everyone know at Chimney Point that the boy has been found. Then get him to the hospital for an x-ray. We'll regroup at CP Ranger Station at 2:00 pm and debrief the situation."

"Ok," Bud Sawyer said. "Lets pile in and get going. See you guys later. Everybody buckle up and lets go."

TB chuckled and said, "I love it when a rescue is successful. It gives you such a good feeling. There are some that aren't so rewarding and that's a killer. You keep wondering what you could have done to make it turn out right. Sometime there is nothing you can do." TB pulled out some beef jerky from his backpack and handed a stick to Jasper as they walked along.

He took the jerky graciously and said, "It sounds like it would be a very satisfying job and on the other hand, a very frustrating one. Depending on how things turn out."

"Well, over all it's a great job if you like the outdoors and if your significant other is with you on it. This type of work is right up Tolerance, my wife's, alley. She's a ranger also, but right now she's pregnant with our third child. We have two boys and this one is going to be a girl. Tolerance lives back on the reservation with her mother. I go there on my time off."

"Wow that must be a handful."

TB now had his water bottle out and handed it to Jasper as they walked. "Not really," exclaimed TB, as they walked along. "On an Indian reservation, everyone helps especially the grandparents." Tolerance and I work split shifts. Like I work Sunday to Sunday and she works Wednesday to Wednesday, so we always have three days together. Winter shifts are different with less vacationers." The small talk continued as they made their way back to the start of the hunt at Chimney Pond.

Chapter 7
Buffalo Man

Jasper and Terry Bearroot walked slowly up the trail that lead towards Chimney Pond. They were both exhausted from the chase. Jasper could tell from their small talk that Terry had something on his mind.

Eventually Terry turned to him and said, "Jasper, I set it up this way so you and I could talk on the way back. I didn't exactly tell you the whole truth the other day. You have to understand. I can't give a wilderness pass to a lone hiker, it's just not safe. But... volunteering Fido to help us probably saved that boy's life, so I feel I owe you something. Will you tell me more about what you're looking for?"

He told Terry again about Stonie's jack knife and Penelope's interest in Native American Pow-Wows. He showed the knife to Terry. "This is the jack knife that Stonie gave me. He found it out in the Midwest, in the Badlands of South Dakota. He told me he thinks it's a Native American word, engraved into the blade. COSUNCABUH, do you know what it means?"

"Well, Jasper," replied TB. "There are at least 200 American Indian languages that are still spoken today. It's possible it is a word, but it is not Algonquian. That's my language."

"It wouldn't matter so much to me," Jasper began. "If I didn't keep getting this feeling. I feel like I should know the word Cosun-cabuh. Like I've heard it before."

"Buffalo Man is far wiser than I," said Terry. "Perhaps he will be able to give you some answers."

"So he is real?" said Jasper with a grin.

"Some of the legends of Buffalo Man are quite true." TB continued. "But your friend Penelope is also correct in saying that the tales are often embellished into a good story. My grandfather introduced me to Buffalo Man when he first arrived here. He is a very interesting old man. The best way I can describe him is as a medicine man or a shaman, though he would never claim to hold such a title. He had a way of understanding the natural world that is far different from the way in which we have all been brought up. He knows the plants and animals in the park in a way that know one could know them. I can't explain it, but he seems capable of unnatural abilities. I have had many conversations with him over the years. There is just no one wiser in terms of Indian knowledge and the ways of what he refers to as the dreamworld. One time, we were in a bar in Old Town, when I first met him and some locals came in to one of our spots to raise some hell or something. Things just started to get rough and this big guy took a punch at Buffalo Man. Well, he ended up on his ass before anyone could explain how he got there. All I saw was a flash of light. Buffalo Man had put up his walking stick like a shield and the guy was on his ass. After that, they all walked backwards out the door, picking up their friend and leaving. He is truly the oldest and wisest man I have ever known. When I talk to him, things don't really sink in until I have had time to think about all he has said."

"I really would like to met him Terry," Jasper said. "After talking to Stonie and Penelope an interest in my heritage has resurfaced."

"I could help you seek him out. After all, I have the authority to give us both a wilderness pass, but you would have to travel with me. No one should bushwhack alone."

"Really?" Jasper said excitedly. "You'd take me to see him?"

"I'll try," TB replied. "But you will only find him if he wants to be found. What about your on Indian heritage?"

"My own heritage wasn't exactly kept from me. I'm a quarter Micmac, I guess. But it wasn't often discussed. Penelope asked me questions occasionally about the Micmac but I felt I couldn't really talk about it. I asked my father about my grandparents. My grandmother lives with my uncle Charlie in upstate New York. She moved there after she divorced my grandfather. Flying Hawk, my grandfather was a full blooded Micmac. He gave me Fido as a puppy. Then he was killed a year or so later in a car accident. I wanted to meet my Micmac family after my grandfather died. That's when I was told there was a big brew-ha-ha over it. My father said without his father, he'd never be able to mend the bad blood. I'm not even sure what the issue was, its something my father won't talk about. I always felt that if I knew a little more about the Native American way of life, I could mend the problems between the Micmac tribe and my family. I haven't made much progress."

"Maybe you are looking in the wrong places." TB handed the knife back to Jasper and said. "I will take you to Buffalo Man's summer camp if you're interested, but as I said he will seek you out if he is interested in talking to you. I have to round up the bear first."

"That would be great, Terry. Can I help in capturing the bear?"

"As a matter of fact you can help," replied Terry. "The bear should be in a trap we have set up at Klondike Pond by morning. The bear is headed in that direction now. We can tranquilize him and air lift him to the section of the park that Buffalo Man is in. Before we do anything, though, we have to debrief at Chimney Pond and work out the details."

They walked on at a faster pace now since the first stick of beef jerky and water put a little energy back into their systems. TB had thrown Fido a stick of jerky and he was able to find his own source of water. The dog would disappear and reappear in the underbrush now and then. Jasper didn't give him a thought knowing he would be fine.

They talked some more about the Indian way of life and about Fido. Jasper was careful, as he always was, not to mention anything about Fido's special skills.

TB talked more about Buffalo Man and what good he had done for the park. TB had talked to Buffalo Man ten days ago and told him about the bear. Buffalo Man had told him where to set the trap and what to put in the trap to attracted the bear. He had told TB too, "Drive the bear in that direction and you will have him within twenty-four hours." He also had told TB to air lift the bear to Sable Mountain just north of Mahar Pond, where Buffalo Man's summer camp was. There was plenty of food there and not many people in that are of the park. He would be content there and would not bother anyone for the rest of the summer.

"I will bring you to the general area where we drop off the bear," explained TB. "It was just a coincidence that the bear showed up during the search for the boy. Everything worked out in driving the bear towards Klondike Pond. If all these coincidences work out we should be able to get the bear out of here. Sometimes things just go your way." He smiled as they walked the rest of the way up the path to Chimney Pond.

Everything had gone just as TB had said it would on the way back from Chimney Pond. The bear was in the trap at Klondike Lake the next morning. They had tranquilized it and air lifted him to Mahar Pond. The helicopter had dropped TB, Fido and Jasper off at the site where the bear was. They had cleared the net away and put an identity band on the bear's ear. They gave it the antidote for the tranquilizer. When the bear functioned properly after about thirty minutes, they would call the chopper back to come and pick them up.

Jasper, Fido and TB waved to the rangers as the helicopter lifted off and headed southwest to go land a few miles off and wait for their call.

They first decided to get down wind of the bear so it wouldn't smell them. They got about fifty yards away and were partly concealed by the underbrush. They set up a vigil to watch the bear until it was on its feet and ready to roam. The bear had been out like a light but was starting to move now, about ten minutes after the rangers injected the antidote. Jasper hadn't taken his eyes off the bear. All of a sudden about thirty feet from the bear, upwind from it, he saw the image of a man standing, facing the bear and himself. Jasper rubbed his eyes in disbelief. He was still there. "Fido, do you see that man?" Asked Jasper. The bear was moving now. His only conclusion was that this was Buffalo Man. He was taller the Jasper had expected. He had long silvery grey hair hanging free in the slight breeze. He had a face that looked made of stone with strong features and sharp eyes that seemed to catch everything. Jasper figured his lean frame did not have an ounce of body fat. He was skinny and wiry looking. He had a jogger's headband around his neck with a Nike logo on it. He stood, solemnly with his arms folded in thought, like a wise old chief. His chest was bare and he wore deer skin pants and beaded moccasins on his feet. Jasper held back the urge to holler at the man to get away from the bear.

Fido stood at attention like a pointer watching tensely as the bear moved even more. Jasper soothed the dog and told him to relax. Fido sat down and sighed audibly, clearly displeased with the relaxed approach he, TB and now this strange newcomer were taking towards the bear.

Jasper was dumfounded. The bear was now swinging its head back and forth as he woke up and Buffalo Man continued to stand solemnly still. He was looking through the bear without any indication on his features that he was concerned about his proximity to it. The bear was up on all fours now a little unsteady and still swinging his head. That action seemed to helping the bear regain its equilibrium. His first couple of steps were wobbly but he was gaining strength as he walked.

The bear walked back and forth, four or five steps to the left and then it would turn and walk to the right, always looking around. He looked straight at Jasper, TB and Fido, who weren't moving and didn't seem to notice them. He looked at Buffalo Man and could smell him but continued to ignore him. The bear stood up apparently to stretch. He let out a growly sounding yawn, dropped to all fours and brushed past Buffalo Man and faded into the forest cover.

TB got up and followed the bear to the edge of the woods and gestured to Jasper to join him. The ranger veered to the left of where the bear had gone but seemed to know where he was going. They reached a perch where you could look down over the canyon and see for a long way without walking very far. Jasper soon caught sight of the bear as it lumbered along, stopping and checking things out as he explored his new environment. Jasper had his backpack sitting beside him as they sat and watched the bear. He took out his pair of binoculars and watched the bear moving along.

TB pointed to a spot about a hundred and fifty yards down a ravine, ahead of the bear and said, "There's a nice alcove down over there. It would make for a suitable den for our lumbering friend." Jasper put his binoculars on the spot and looked around and saw what TB meant. There were plenty of boulders and crevasses a bear could disappear into. They watched as the bear roamed and lumbered along, headed straight towards the spot that TB had pointed out. Sure enough the bear walked around, checking out various boulder and crevasses for a place and soon disappeared into one of them. They waited but soon determined he wasn't coming out.

TB got on his handheld radio and, after speaking briefly to the pilot, turned and told him that the helicopter would be back in about ten minutes to pick them up and return to the Central Rangers Station. "That should give you a few minutes to decide if you're returning with me or planning to bushwhack your way outta here."

"Bushwhack my way?" said Jasper, confused.

"Well, I can't keep the chopper up here all day. You found Buffalo Man. If you want to stay to talk to him you'll have to bushwhack your way out."

Jasper looked at TB questioningly, "I thought you couldn't give wilderness passes to lone hikers?"

"You'll hardly be alone. Buffalo Man has found us and he will watch over you until you reach the trail. You're a good woodsman. I wouldn't consider leaving you here if we hadn't found Buffalo man, it's pretty remote. You'll want to head southeast." TB pointed in the direction the helicopter had flown off fifteen minutes ago as he spoke.

"Are you sure he'll speak with me?" asked Jasper. "He looked angry and didn't even make eye contact with us."

"He'll talk all right, he wouldn't have shown himself if he didn't want to talk." TB said reassuringly. "He's not an angry man either, Jasper. He's... contemplative."

TB and Jasper walked back from the small ridge and rejoined Fido who appeared to be held in a standoff with Buffalo Man. The hair on Fido's back stood on end and he was growling softly. Buffalo Man had not appeared to have moved from the spot where he had first laid eyes on him.

Before long they could all hear the chopper approaching and soon it was overhead. TB radioed up to Bill and he threw down a rope ladder, which TB grabbed and began to climb. Part way up, TB stopped and looked down over his shoulder at Jasper. "It was nice meeting you. Thanks for all your help with the boy. Check in at Central Station when you get back so no one worries. And I'll owe you a beer." With that, TB winked with a grin and continued up the ladder. As soon as he'd pulled his legs into the helicopter it soared off to the Southeast and was gone.

When the Helicopter was out of sight, Jasper turned back to look where Buffalo Man had been standing. He was gone. Jasper looked around for several minutes without being able to figure which way he had left until Fido barked and pointed with his nose at a bolder only 10 yards ahead of them. Buffalo Man had been standing in plain sight and yet had completely vanished in the shadows of the trees. It gave him an eery and uneasy feeling.

"I know who you are and why you've come Mr. Jay Hawk... Do you?" said Buffalo Man as he turned and leapt the eight feet to the ground and landed without a sound. He quickly began to walk away without waiting for a response from Jasper.

Jasper hurried to follow him.

"Bearroot is glad that our brother Bear is home and safe. He is a smart man, not afraid to see truth. Do you fear truth, Hawk?" Buffalo Man looked sideways at Jasper as he asked, making eye contact with him for the first time. Jasper felt a chill go down his spine as the old Indian's eyes left him.

There was something familiar about the old Indian, but Jasper couldn't place it. It was like out of a dream.

"Buffalo man, I..."

"Is it Buffalo Man you came to speak to or Cosuncabuh?" said the old Indian.

Jasper was puzzled and alarmed. "You've heard of Cosuncabuh?

"Heard of him? I know him," said Buffalo Man, as he continued to walk away from the ridge towards a stand of trees down hill.

Jasper couldn't believe his ears as he followed Buffalo Man. He took out his Jack of all Jacks and looked at the name again. It read COSUNCABUH in the same type it always had. There was a subtle difference, however. The letters were much clearer than he had remembered. Anytime he had looked at it before the name had appeared dull and faded, almost unreadable. Today the letters looked as bright and polished as if the knife was brand new.

Jasper stopped in his tracks and looked ahead at Buffalo Man. The indian continued to walk seemingly unaware that Jasper had stopped. He had remembered a dream from long ago. He remembered an old, lanky man with a cackling laugh. He remembered there had been chanting. In the dream, the old man had tried to kill him. Jasper remembered the chanting had been the name, 'Cosuncabuh, Cosuncabuh,' over and over.

He realized that finding the knife had not been by chance. Nor had finding Buffalo Man in Baxter State Park. He's been stalking me somehow in my dreams, thought Jasper.

"Who are you?" he called to Buffalo Man suspiciously. Jasper spread his feet and stood with his fists clenched. "Are you Cosuncabuh? How can you be real?"

"I am not Cosuncabuh, but he is very close," said Buffalo Man as he stopped thirty paces up the path they were taking and turned around. He folded his arms on his chest.

Fido rushed ahead of Jasper toward the indian baring his teeth and growling. The hair on his back raised as he challenged Buffalo Man.

"I have not brought you here to harm you or your master, Fido." Buffalo Man opened his arms with his palms out towards Fido to show his sincerity. "I've brought you here to answer your questions."

Fido put his fangs away and slowly stopped growling. He cautiously sniffed Buffalo Man's hand. As Fido relaxed, Buffalo Man began to pat his head.

"You do have questions, yes?" said the old man as he looked up from the dog to meet Jasper's eyes again. He had a slightly amused look on his face.

Jasper was uncertain but decided he was not in immediate danger from the wiry old man. He wanted answers certainly. He would withhold judgment until Buffalo Man explained himself. "I do. I want to know who or what Cosuncabuh is."

"And you should," continued Buffalo Man as he abruptly turned back around and marched around a bend in the path made by the small stand of trees. "We will continue when we are sitting at camp. Come, it is just ahead."

They made it to Buffalo Man's base camp after a brief walk. There were two medium sized wigwams probably about 6 feet in diameter at the bases. They were canvased with birchbark and the frame was made of medium thickness flexible branches tied together with some sort of natural twine. They were well made and would keep out most weather. As Jasper looked around, it occurred to him that all the materials to build the wigwam was within twenty paces of the camp. There was also a bright yellow LL Bean tent, a cold fire pit, and several various sized bundles of supplies Buffalo Man had gathered while foraging. There was also a hand crank radio, a collapsable camping chair set up near the fire pit and a pilc of broken junk. The pile had several aluminum poles sticking out of it and a torn blue trap as well.

Buffalo Man spoke when he saw Jasper looking curiously at the pile of junk. "So many people come here, to the park, to worship and commune with the forest spirits and to see the abundance given to us by Mother Earth. Then they leave their trash behind. Perhaps one of these days I will travel into one of the towns near the park. I will go to a... church? Is that what you call it?"

Jasper nodded.

"I will see that day if you always leave your trash and junk behind when you're done worshipping." Buffalo Man chuckled, apparently finding something funny and continued. "I have been waiting for your arrival for several years. I was never sure how it would be. The future, I am sometimes blessed with seeing, in my dreams. Your coming I have long dreamt, but never with clarity." Buffalo Man sat in his chair at the fire pit and Fido scurried forward to sniff at the old man's boots and his hands when they were eventually offered again.

Jasper walked to the fire pit and sat on a small boulder near by. He was anxious to get talking again. "Buffalo Man, what can you tell me about Cosuncabuh?"

"Beef jerky?" he said pointing at Jasper.

"What?" Jasper responded confused.

"Let us eat together and discuss."

Jasper pulled out the package of beef jerky he had in his pocket and offered some to the old man. "How'd you know I had that anyway?"

"I didn't know you had it. But Cosuncabuh did," said Buffalo Man as he took a piece and passed the bag back to Jasper. "Cosuncabuh knows and sees a great many things. He watches things and places and people. He watches animals too. Your talking friend here, he is very special," Buffalo Man continued, still petting the dog. Fido appeared to be in heaven, basking in the attention he was getting. "Yes, he is very special and very welcome here. You brought the knife too, didn't you?"

"Um, Ahh, Yes," said Jasper weakly. "I brought the knife," he confirmed with more certainty in his voice. "But... he can't talk. The dog I mean. He can understand English perfectly but he can't actually speak."

"Fido can talk," Buffalo Man said matter-of-factly. "The question is, can you listen? I don't doubt he has said many things to you. Sound advice, I'm sure, he has offered. But of little good it will be if you cannot quiet yourself enough to hear his advice."

"Huh, I... He's never spoken, have you?" Jasper said confused. Fido looked at him out of the corner of his eye. He was enjoying his scratch but did stop long enough to furrow his brow at him.

"Cosuncabuh can see many things in his dreams." Buffalo Man continued, sounding far away. His face looked like it was made of stone. "He shares his dreams with me, Hawk."

"How can he? Who is he? I don't understand."

"He is a spirit. A dreamwalker from the Spiritworld and very powerful. He cannot come into our world. He can only see into it through someone's dreams."

"Dreamwalker? But that was you in my dream." Jasper said.

"Through meditation and practice you can learn to dream in the Spiritworld. I found Cosuncabuh there or, more to the point, he found me."

Buffalo Man pulled out a long wooden tube with a dark red pipestone bowl attached to one end and a mouth piece carved in the other for smoking tobacco. The pipe was beautifully carved and painted with an animal scene. Buffalo Man reached in a pack near his chair and found a leather pouch containing tobacco. He packed the pipe and took several tokes off of it to clear his mind before continuing. He passed the pipe to Jasper, who attempted to turn it down politely. Buffalo Man gave Jasper a sharp look of irritation and Jasper changed his mind placing it to his mouth. He did his best to take a few small puffs without choking.

"Well, what is it he wants?"

"I do not fully know Cosuncabuh's objective. He is very old and he doesn't share everything with me. All I know is that he has been searching for you for a long time. Probably longer than you've been alive."

"But how can that be?" said Jasper skeptically. "He couldn't have known about me before I was born."

"He's forgotten more than you will ever know," insisted Buffalo Man. "I have been on many dream quests over the years. This first was when I was ten or eleven. It was then that I decided I wanted to be a student of the Spiritworld. I wanted to learn of my ancestors and teach others the ways of my people. I did not encounter Cosuncabuh until I was twenty. The first time I met him was in the sweat lodge, on my third day of meditation. I was frightened by him, as you are now. It took a long time for me to learn how to commune with him. When I did, he told me to go on a journey. Over the years I have travel far over much of this continent. He eventually led me here. I have been here for twenty years. He never told me directly but I believe now we've been waiting for you. Cosuncabuh sees something in you. That is why he gave Fido to you."

"What?" blurted out Jasper, not believing his ears.

"You think English speaking dogs are common? Fido comes from a world within the Spiritworld," Buffalo Man explained. "Fido was given to you,to aid you in your journey. You two are a balancing piece between good and evil. Together it is your task to fight against greed, hate and misdeeds."

"I can't believe it," Jasper said rubbing his hands through his hair. "What can I hope to do against the evils of the world?"

"Look at what the two of you have already accomplished," Buffalo Man replied spreading his arms. "And you're only getting started. It is up to you, you can believe it or you can reject it."

"I'm in shock, it's a lot to take in, but... of course I believe it," said Jasper looking over at Buffalo Man. "I have a dog that understanding English, and a jack knife with his name on it that seems to have fallen out of the sky and you knew who we were before we introduced ourselves."

"You must learn to dreamwalk if you are to succeed. Dreamwalking will help to guide you and help you commune more with Fido. You can be of the same mind if you practice discipline. But beware not all dreamwalkers are friendly. Dreams can be a very pleasant place or they can be filled with nightmares. I will attempt to guide you, while I can."

* * * *

Jasper woke up the following morning, which was Saturday, in Buffalo Man's camp. He felt surprisingly rested with a lot to think about after the discussion the day before.

Buffalo Man had Jasper practicing exercises all afternoon and evening the day before. They had sat and Buffalo Man had guided him through some meditation exercises. The old indian had Jasper stand and practice martial arts forms and poses. When Jasper had gone to bed, he had strange dreams. This morning after waking up, he remembered the odd dreams taking place but could not remember what had happened.

Jasper looked around the campsite. He was sure Buffalo Man was already up. His watch read seven o'clock but he imagined Buffalo Man coming straight out of an old western with John Wayne. The kind where the wise old indian got up half an hour before dawn. He packed his backpack for the hike and took down his tent. He left his backpack and went off in search of the old indian. As he had expected, he found the older man tending to chores around the camp. Jasper also found his breakfast, still warm, waiting for him near the fire pit.

"Good morning, Hawk," Buffalo Man said. He referred to Jasper by his last name. Buffalo Man said that Jasper should embrace his Micmac heritage. So, at least for now, Jasper was answering to the name of 'Hawk'. He saw no point in arguing the matter. He would respect the man's ways, after all it was him who had sought out Buffalo Man.

"Good morning," said Jasper. "How long have you been up? Breakfast smells good."

Buffalo Man had his hair in a ponytail, using his Nike headband like a scrunchy to keep it out of the way while he tended to his chores.

"I just got up a half hour ago to get breakfast ready."

"I thought Indians got up at the crack of dawn or something?"

"Ha!" laughed Buffalo Man, "That's only in John Wayne movies. We are as varied as white men are. I am quite modernized. I pick up the practices that make sense. If I encounter a technique that works better than the older, traditional ways then I adjust. So long as it doesn't take away from what is important."

"And what is important?" asked Jasper. "John Wayne, movies?"

Buffalo Man gave Jasper an intentionally exaggerated, disgusted look. "No, our connection to each other, to the other creatures that inhabit this world and to Mother Earth. This LL Bean tent, the written language of your ancestors. These things aid me in enhancing my connection to this holy place. But there are many innovations that subtract from our fellowship with Mother Earth. And those I reject..." after a long thoughtful pause he continued, "That is the Indian way, adapting yourself to the situation at hand."

"How old are you, Buffalo Man?"

Buffalo Man grinned and chuckled, "That is on a need to know basis and no one here needs to know. I will give you this one clue. I was a four-year-old Arapaho boy when I fled with my mother after the Battle of Little Big Horn. I am old enough to have many enemies."

They sat there quietly and Jasper ate the breakfast that Buffalo Man had prepared. He was not sure what his breakfast was but it was good and there was plenty of it. Jasper had put out some dog food for

Fido. They talked for a while longer and their conversation led to more ideal things. Buffalo Man was telling him how to tell when fiddleheads were ready to be picked when all of a sudden Jasper began to have a nagging feeling that he needed to leave. Some barely perceivable force was telling him that something was going on and he needed to be on the move. He wished there was a phone on top of this mountain. When he couldn't stand it any longer he turned to Buffalo Man and said. "Buffalo Man, I can't stay. The outside world calls."

Buffalo Man smiled, "You have started to separate the two worlds. That is good. They defiantly need separating, until they are joined. Trust your senses they will prove more reliable than you know."

Jasper scratched his head not understanding Buffalo Man. He was encouraging him to leave? He had expected the older man to try and persuade him into staying.

"I see you are all set to travel. You have your backpack ready to go. You are using your senses wisely even if it is subconsciously. Use them wisely and consciously and you will flourish. Watch your blade closely. It will guide you."

Jasper took out his Jack of all Jacks and looked at it. Satisfied, he said, "Thank you, Buffalo Man. I have something I think I need to attend to. I will keep your words in mind." He held out his hand to shake hands with Buffalo Man.

They grasped arms just below the elbowed bid each other a fond farewell. "I am relieved that you are with us," said Buffalo Man. "Goodbye for now, we will meet again."

Jasper hiked out of the deep forest. It took about half the day. He stopped at a small stream around mid-day and had a light lunch out of his backpack. He climbed over boulders and bushwhacked his way to Russell Pond.

Once he reached Russell Pond, Jasper took the Chimney Pond Trail to Katahdin Stream Campground. Then Jasper went to the campground Ranger Station. He went inside and found it empty. Bud Sawyer would be the ranger on duty for this area. It was about half past three according to Jasper's watch. Bud must be walking around on patrol. He went to the pay phone and picked up the receiver. Who was he supposed to call, he thought. He knew something was going on but didn't know what. He needed to talk to someone who did know... Mom and Dad, Jasper thought. Whatever this feeling is about it has to do with my parents. I will call home.

Jasper dug in his fanny pack and found a dime. He inserted the coin and dialed the number to home. It rang for what seemed like eternity before it picked up.

"Hello?" said his father sounding far away through the phone.

"Hi Dad, It's Jasper. Is something wrong?"

"Well, nothing's wrong. It's not an emergency or anything... have you been speaking with your mother? His father sounded slightly annoyed.

"No, I just woke up this morning and had a feeling I should call home. Like maybe there was something going on."

"Goddamnit, I told her not to worry you with this stuff." I wish she'd left well enough alone.

"Never mind that," interrupted Jasper. "What's going on?"

There was a long pause. After a time he heard his father let out a long sigh and then he explained. "There is something fishy going on at Grandma Steller's place and I wondered if you could get there a little quicker then you previously planned."

"Sure, I could, but whats up. Is Grandma ok?"

"She is fine but concerned. In the past week about fifteen chickens a day have been found dead in the yard after the morning feeding. There were no physical signs as to what killed them. According to Frank LaBreque, after two or three days of it the Sheriff took a couple of the chicken corpses. The sheriff sent them to the state laboratory. Dan Cooper, their long time veterinarian, wasn't happy when he found out what the sheriff had done and neither was Shank. Dan knew the state would have the health department down on us and sure enough they are swarming all around the farm. Jane is in a tither and mad as hell at the sheriff for acting so fast and jumping to conclusions. Sounds like she could use some help."

"I'll head out right away. I'll try to get a ride up there. Maybe I can get in a day or two."

"Thats great, Jasper. Shank has it under control. I just thought you being there may make your mother feel a little better."

"Ok, I will gather my things and head right out."

"I hate to screw up your trip like this but I thought something should be done. I can't take the time off from work right now or I'd go up there. It's been almost a week of dead chickens. Close to eighty birds. Something is wrong."

"No problem, Pop. Don't worry, I'll check it out. And you aren't screwing up my trip. I was close to leaving anyway. Goodbye, I'll call again soon as I can." Jasper hung up the phone and leaned against the pay phone to think for a minute. Eighty dead chickens in a week. Holy cow, thought Jasper. Thats crazy, it could only be the Perrys causing trouble. Jasper retrieved his bike from where he had locked it up and then hiked to the Tote Road. Once he reached the road he could pedal the rest of the way.

He rode his bike to the Togue Pond Gate entrance to the park. Ranger Susan Butler was on duty. "Well, hello, Jay Hawk," she said with a smile. "I guess that rescue was a big success. Had you heard? That little boy has a broken leg, I guess."

"Really?" said Jasper, a little surprised. He had essentially forgotten about the boy after meeting Buffalo Man and then this news from his father.

"Yes, Bill told me this morning that the doctor said he'd broken his fibula. Apparently when his foot got trapped it put pressure on his leg and the smaller bone, the fibula broke."

"Will he be all right? I mean, he'll be able to walk, once its healed?"

"Oh yes, it is too swollen to cast right now but in a few days they will and in about six weeks he'll have it off and be running and jumping like nothing happened. That dog of yours is quite the bloodhound."

"Well, he deserves all the credit. We never would have gotten there to the boy in time without him. Say, could you do me a favor, Ranger Butler?"

"Sure. What is it? Anything for you two. You're heroes."

"I have to leave in a hurry and I didn't get a chance to see TB on my way out. I have a semi-emergency at my grandmother's in Old Calcutta. I need to be off sooner than planned. When you see TB will you tell him I said thanks. I have a letter for him, here." Jay held out a short letter that he had written at the Chimney Pond Campground. The letter read:

Bearroot,

I have a semi-emergency up to my grandparents in Old Calcutta. I was planning to visit you again before I got word from my father to head north. I wanted to thank you for introducing me to Buffalo Man. I had a really worthwhile talk with him. Next time I'm up in the park I will look you up. You still owe me that beer. Oh, and by the way, Buffalo Man is a man of many words when he has something worth saying.

Many Thanks

-Jasper Jay Hawk

Jasper handed Ranger Butler the note. She took it and he jumped onto his bike and started to pedal off. Ranger Butler frowned with a confused look but waved to Jasper.

He waved back as he flipped down the sidecar and Fido hopped in. Dark clouds were closing in as he peddled on to Millinocket.

Chapter 8
On to Old Calcutta

It was lightly raining by the time he pedaled into Millinocket. He had a hundred and twenty-mile trip to make and he wanted to do it fast. He decided to stop and eat at the same place he had breakfasted three days ago, Garry's diner. He would put a sign up on the table in the restaurant/truck stop for Fort Kent and maybe he would get a ride. If not, he would push on with his bike. Steady biking for a day and a half or two would get him there but a ride of course would be faster. Jasper and Fido sat in the truck stop with a sign on the table. 'RIDE TO FORT KENT, W/DOG, THANKS.' He was so confident he would get a ride he had his bike folded up into its suitcase.

Well, it happened. After he finished his lunch he had three choices. A logging truck going to Eagle Lake, a pick up going all the way to Fort Kent or a ride going to Ashland, which was about half way. Jasper picked the logging truck. He went over to the two guys that offered him rides and thanked them but said he would go with the logging truck. Jasper thanked the driver of the logging truck for the ride and said he would be ready anytime, just to holler on his way out. The dog could get in the cab with him and Eagle Lake was exactly where he wanted to go.

Jasper wanted to try and find the Aroostook County Sheriff, Deputy Ken Silvermen. He was the only honest sheriff in the county according to his friend Jonny Skater, owner of the bike shop in Landrush.

Jonny's father, Paulsie's hunting lodge was also located west of Eagle Lake. He wanted to check it out but probably wouldn't do that on this trip. He would wait until Jonny came up in August.

So he did have an agenda. He was going to get to the bottom of all this and get on with things. He wanted justice for Paulsie's murder. And he wanted to fix the chicken farm right for Robbie when he got discharged from the Air Force in September. He also wanted to check in on Charlotte Baker and her brother Buddy and Grandma Rosa. He felt that Charlotte's father Fred Baker had some good in him and wanted to see if he could meet him and feel him out.

As Jasper sat there thinking things out, the logging truck driver tapped him on the shoulder and said, "Lets go boy. I'm ready to roll." Jasper jumped up and paid his bill, grabbed his packs and went out the door . He walked across the parking lot and climbed into the big cab of the logging truck with Fido following close behind him.

"M'names Hank. Hank Mercer from Eagle Lake," The driver said as he lunged into the cab with his hand outstretched in a friendly gestures. Jasper put out his own hand and it disappeared in the big man's palm.

"Hi, I'm Jay Hawk and this is Fido. Thanks a lot for the ride. It's hard to get a ride with a dog. I really appreciate it. We're from Landrush," Jasper said trying to be friendly. "You lived here all your life?"

"Pretty much. Did a tour of duty in Vietnam back in sixty-six and been here ever since," Hank said, as he down shifted the eighteen wheeler trying to pick up speed.

He was watching Hank maneuver the big rig and was impressed. He often wondered if it was hard to drive something this big. "How long you been driving a logging truck?" He asked.

"For North Atlantic Paper, about twenty years. I just dropped a load of pulp off at the mill in Jay, Maine. I got three days off then I go over to Grand Lake Stream and get another load. It goes on and on like that. Steady work, but driving is an awful life for a family man." Hank shifted again. The rig was finally getting up to cruising speed.

"You got family in Eagle Lake?" Jasper asked.

"Yeah, I got family here. A nice little set up on the lake. What about you, what are you doing hitchhiking up north from Landrush?"

"I am headed up to see my grandmother and grandfather. They own a chicken farm in Old Calcutta," he said, as he watched Hank maneuver the big truck down the road.

"I did some independent driving before I hooked on with this company twenty years ago and I used to haul some chickens. There are the Perrys in Frenchville and the Stellers in Old Calcutta. The two biggest chicken farms up here. So you're Shank Steller's grandson."

"Wow, you know my grandparents, what a coincidence." The truck was now doing seventy miles an hour on this small road with Hank very comfortable behind the wheel.

"No son, it's not such a coincidence, because I have lived here most of fifty-five years and one time or another you run into people or hear about them because the population is so small. It's spread out but it's not wicked populated, and anyone that runs as big an operation as your grand folks are going to be known by most folks in these parts. They probably employ over sixty to eighty or so people, as do the Perrys. I probably have relatives working for Shank or Clinton."

"When you hauled chickens, who did you haul for?"

"I hauled for both farms. But I will tell you this. Shank Steller was a hell of a lot more fair than Harry Perry. Clinton Perry runs the business now, the father Harry is retired and in a nursing home in Frenchville. I heard that Clinton is worse than his father. Whatever price Shank gave us for hauling, we all would go by his prices and force Harry to pay proper. It was that way with hauling feed and a lot of other things." Jasper knew the rift with the Perrys well, they had lived with it a long time. It was nice to hear that the general public knew the score also.

"I heard Shank had a stroke last winter," said Hank.

"Yeah, he did last February. He is wheelchair bound, but does ok. He can't do the work he used to be able to do though. His left side is slightly affected but it affected his legs and walking the most. He claims with physical therapy he will be walking by the end of the summer. We're all hopeful that he will walk again. He has dropped twenty pounds since the stroke and has a great attitude. His mind is as sharp as ever and he still makes everyone toe the line."

"What a rough break. You say his mind is still sharp?"

"Oh yeah, it's a lot of the physical stuff he can't do."

"Well, that will affect Shank a lot. He was all physical. Liked doing for himself."

"True, but he has turned a lot of his focus on walking again and he is really working hard at that. I think he'll do it."

They went for a time just being quiet. Jasper wanted his reaction on Paulsie's murder six years ago. He knew he would know about it. He also wondered what he thought of Sheriff Dick Blaire. Jasper decided to come right out and ask him. "Do you remember about six years ago a man, Paul Skater, was killed over in Ouellette, right up from Cross Lake, west of Eagle Lake? He was supposedly linked to some deer poaching ring?"

"Oh yeah, I remember that real well. It was across the lake from me. There had been a lot of poaching going on back then. We would hear shots at night all the time. And that incident sort of nipped it in the bud. Why do you ask?"

"Well, that guy killed was the father of a good friend of mine. We just couldn't imagine him doing that sort of thing."

"I didn't know the particulars about the case, just what I read, but after that incident the deer poaching stopped completely. It just seems to the locals and myself included, that there had to be a connection somewhere. Sheriff Blaire seemed to have the whole thing under control."

"Yeah," Jasper grumbled. "Unless this Sheriff covered the whole thing up to protect someone."

"Yow boy, don't let too many people hear you say shit like that. Sheriff Dick Blaire is the law around here and if he gets word someone is talking like that you won't last long around these parts."

"Well, when you know Mr. Skater like I did and his family does you just know he wasn't like that. He wouldn't even think of doing something like poaching deer. There has to be another explanation."

"I always say you don't really know someone until you've been in their boots. A word to the wise, just don't let anyone hear you talk about the sheriff that way, and don't go looking for another explanation."

"Are you trying to tell me something about Sheriff Blaire?"

"Only what I've already said. Be cool around him and don't get him on your wrong side. He is no one to mess with. I've seen him mad. He takes no prisoners. There was this one time two years ago. A couple Canadian guys came down to Frenchville. They were getting a little rowdy in at Peggy's, this local bar out of Rt 45. Peggy called the Sheriff cause they were starting a little trouble. Nothing serious mind you. They just needed a uniform to point them in the direction of home. Well, Sheriff Blaire showed up personally. I heard he was out for blood, used his car door to ring their bells. Story goes they ended up in the hospital back in Canada. The official report of the Canadian police was that they got into a fight in Canada with each other and ended up in the hospital. No mention of Peggy's Bar or Sheriff Blaire, but everyone knew the real story. Another time a reporter came up from Dairy to do a report on the Peregrine Falcons and their declining numbers. Sheriff Blaire sent that man home with a broken camera and a sudden found interest in the Lobster Industry in Camden."

Jasper found out what he needed to know about the sheriff. The people fear him and his word is final around here. He would have to tread lightly.

He got off the subject of it all and they just discussed light stuff until Hank announced his turn off. Jasper thanked him for the lift as he grabbed his stuff and he and Fido got out of the big rig.

Hank had let him off in a good spot. He needed a pick me up and there was a big sign, Wields Extra Mart & Coffee Shop with a gas pump right on the corner. There were outside picnics tables that Jasper piled his gear on. It was well lit and he went into the store with instructions for Fido to stay with the stuff.

Jasper walked through the door and greeted the lady behind the counter, "Hello, Miss. Sure is a nice day, isn't it?"

"Yes, by golly it is," she said in a nurturing tone. "The humidity this afternoon isn't near as bad as this past week has been." The store was empty and she was wrapping up fresh baked cookies that smelled like they just came out of the oven.

"Ma'am, do you mind if I use the hose outside to give my dog a drink? I have a bowl and won't make a big mess."

"Call me Penny and sure, go ahead and use it. Just wrap it up when you're done.

"Hi Penny, my name is Jasper Jay Hawk. Thanks a lot for the use of the hose. Boy, it sure smells good in here. "

"Thank you. That's my secret recipe," She said as she finished up with the last package of cookies.

"Thanks for your help," Jasper replied as he turned and walked outside to take care of Fido and filled his own water bottle. He sat down on the edge of the picnic table to put his bike together. Fido looked up at him with worry just as he felt a presence behind him.

"It's a slow one today, not many customers. Mind if I watch? I brought you some cookies." Penny handed him a plate piled with several large treats.

"Sure, have a seat."

Jasper pushed over on the bench and said, "I'd be happy to pay you for these," as he took the plate and put it on the picnic table between them.

"No need, I over bake as a rule. What kind of a bike is that?" Penny asked.

"It's specially made. It has a sidecar for the dog to lay down on." He was just about done putting it together.

As she examined how clever the bike appeared, a pickup truck and a smaller car pulled into the pump station. The smaller car was faster. The short older man filled his tank and walked over to Penny. She made change for him out of her apron pocket. "I try to keep a little change in my pocket," Penny explained as the man walked back to his car. "If I'm out here taking a load off, I won't have to interrupt myself unless the customer needs something in the store."

Jasper chuckled at her inventiveness as the two men from the pick up truck approached. "Hey Penny, can we get in the store?" one of them said.

"Sure thing, Jake. Follow me," replied Penny as she made a spectacle of the interruption he had caused her on such a fine afternoon.

Jasper continued eating the cookies and looked closer at the man pumping gas. It was Clinton Perry and the guy that went inside was

Jake Perry, his younger brother. He recognized them from past summers. They're still driving that old pickup, Jasper thought. The word 'PERRY CHICKENS' was painted on the both doors but not that clear to read. The words wouldn't jump out at you unless you looked carefully. Jasper studied it after recognizing the two brothers. They might have recognized him if he got up and started to talk to them but they were looking right past him and didn't really look him over. Fido was sitting under the table and they didn't even notice.

The brother, Jake, came out with a carton of GPC cigarettes and a case of PBR, the cheapest beer on the market and a bag of ice. Jake put the case of beer in a cooler in the back of the pick-up and then dumped the ice on it. Clinton was just finishing up with his gas. Sam, the youngest never got out of the truck. They took off down the road like they were late for a meeting.

Penny came out and said, "Those are the three Perry brothers, Clinton is the oldest and a mean one. Jake is a close second to Clinton. Sammy, the youngest isn't too bad. They just act tough when the older brother is around."

"Sam is the nicest kid when he comes in alone. And Susie Mae, the sister is just the sweetest thing. She just has nothing to do with the older brothers. Her and Sammy chum around together a lot. The two oldest are just no good, they'll probably lose the chicken farm their father worked all his life to build. I guess the father was no gem either."

"What makes you say that'll loose the farm?"

"Oh, I'm sorry. Do you know the Perrys? I shouldn't shoot my mouth off to strangers," said Penny.

"Yes, I know them but I am a Steller. My grandmother is Jane Steller. I've come up to help her out for the summer. Let's not be strangers." Jay put out his hand and shook hands with Penny. "Nice to meet you."

"Penny Wields is my name." She took Jasper's hand and said, " Good to know the Grandson of Shank and Jane Steller. Why, the Perrys will probably lose the chicken farm, one reason they treat their workers like shit. Pardon my language, but they do. Number two reason is the living conditions are horrendous for them. I hear it all the time. Workers from both farms come into this store and you can't compare the two farms. If the board of health ever went through their farm they would close it down. That's what the workers say. But I keep my mouth shut. Yes, I do."

Jasper chuckled and said, "I see you do and thanks for the vote of confidence in my grandparents farm." Fido had all the water he wanted and had eaten the biscuit Jasper had given him. Jasper had eaten the cookies and beef jerky and was ready to roll. He picked up the bowl and his water bottle and stowed them in his pack. "Well, Penny, I have to roll. I am forty miles away and would like to get home before the end of the day if possible. See you later and thanks for the water, cookies and the chat."

"Thank you Jasper. You see, I don't get much business until the weekend. It's steady but it's really busy on Friday, Saturday and Sundays. I usually have three of us in here then." She got up and waved to him as he pedaled off toward the next town, Plastid.

It was getting close to dinner time and Jasper still wanted to flag down a sheriff cruiser, but he wanted to be selective because he didn't want to talk to Sheriff Dick Blaire yet, anyone but him. The countryside in Aroostook County was flat. Farm after farm, there were rows of potatoes. He could really get up some speed. There were few interruption, the traffic was light and the road was ok. It was just a little harrier when the logging trucks stormed by. He was going through the town of Plastid when he spotted the Steller Chicken Farm truck, his grandfathers, parked at the Brass Rail Bar and Grill. Jasper figured he would know the driver, whoever that would be, so he pulled over to the side of the bar. He parked his bike and stashed his gear in behind the bike and locked everything up with the bike. Whoever it was probably stopped there after work. He ordered Fido to stay outside.

Fido woofed and pushed his head towards the rear.

Jasper looked and he saw what Fido saw. The Perrys truck was parked in the back lot of the bar. "Thanks, Fido. Stay close and let's go in." He decided to take the dog in with him. He was very curious about this coincidence of the two chicken farm trucks being in the same place.

Jay walked into the Brass Rail. It was an L shaped bar. One side of the barroom had a food service opening for the grill in the kitchen, and food was served at the bars with some tables on the floor area with low lighting. The bar itself had lighting behind the it and tables on the floor with no lighting and at the end of the room was a pool table. Over all, it was a dark place.

Jasper told Fido to disappear in the room and pointed toward the table he wanted. Fido went to the table and got under it and Jasper sat down at the same table. He had grabbed a hat out of his pack so as not to be noticed and slouched down in the booth, facing the bar section. At this point he could see two people playing pool. It was too dark to see anything else. His eyes would have to adjust to the lack of light.

A skinny but tall redhead came over with an apron over her torn stone washed jeans. Her top looked to be two sizes too small. "Can I help you, Mister?" Her name tag read Judy.

"Hi Judy, I will have a hamburger and a Miller Light."

"Do you want fries with that? And do you want bottle or draft?" Judy asked.

"No fries, thanks. Umm bottle is fine," he said, hoping he didn't sound forced. It was usually easy to get served he had found. No one really cared, especially up here near the border. He was 18 anyway, which was practically legal. It was in Canada anyway.

"Ok, Miller bottle with a burger. Take about seven." Abruptly she twirled around and disappeared with his order out the back door to the kitchen.

Jasper's eyes were now starting to adjust and he was still unnoticed by anyone but the redhead. He could see ok now and started to scan the patrons. Jake Perry was playing pool with a seemed to be local and he noticed Frank LaBreque and Clinton Perry in a booth nearest the pool table, the pool table light making it possible to see who it was.

The redhead set the beer down and disappeared again. Jasper sipped his beer which tasted kind of good after the long twenty mile pedal from Eagle Lake. He stayed put and just watched for a while.

Judy came over and set his burger down a few minutes later and disappeared around the corner of the kitchen door. He broke his burger in half and gave half to Fido who mowed it down like a starved dingo. Jasper continued to watch Frank and Clinton talking. He wished he could get closer but knew Frank would notice him. Clinton let out with a big howl of laughter. They both stood up and Clinton slapped Frank on the back, and Frank walked out toward the side door at the other end of the bar. As he headed toward the door, he looked over in Jasper's direction for a second and slowed up a little but kept on going.

Jasper couldn't tell if he'd recognized him or not. He told Fido to keep cover and to follow him. Clinton had gone to the men's room behind the pool table.

Jay left money to pay for his burger which was now gone and stood up carrying the Miller Light he was nursing. He walked over to the jukebox and began looking through the songs. Most of the songs were old, but classics. Jasper selected Twist and Shout by the Beatles and Jail House Rock to follow by Elvis. Then he casually sat in a booth near the jukebox only two away from where Clinton Perry had been before his trip to the head. After a minute or two Fido stole under the table, stealthily.

Clinton came out of the men's room just as Jasper had sat down. He had his back to them and settled in to the booth and pretended to drink his beer. In all actuality he didn't really like beer all that much but figured it might be helping him blend in.

Jake took his shot as Clinton approached. "I don't like you being so friendly with that guy, LaBreque." said Jake as he looked up from the table.

"You know the score. How else are we going to get what we want without collaborating with the enemy? Anyway, he wanted to talk to me about improving relations between the two companies." Clinton was eyeing Jake's next shot.

"Yeah, but can you totally trust him? I mean he has been working with Steller for twenty years or more. He must have some loyalty to them," Jake said while eyeing his next shot and banking it off the rail and sinking it in the side pocket.

"Look Jake, this isn't about loyalty to the Stellers. We've got the health department all over their ass by Blaire taking those chickens. That's a good thing, it slows up their operation and will have the public wondering about their product. Plus we've got Blaire on the payroll. Just stick to the plan and we'll have the monopoly in the chicken business around here soon."

"I just don't trust the guy," Jake said outright. He was lining up the next shot. It was a bunny he couldn't miss. "Plus, Blaire will shoot us if anything goes south. He's just plain someone you don't mess with."

"Look Jake, LaBreque knows that. That's why he let Blaire take the birds. You think anyone is going to say no to Sheriff Blaire." Clinton said. "It's not about loyalty it's about having the balls to stand up to Blaire." He laughed as he thought about it. "Pull your ball back with backspin English so you can line up the eight ball and finish this game. We've got to get out of here."

"No shit, you don't have to tell me how to play pool, Clint," said Jake, "by the way, when is Freddie going to make his next feed drop? Oh yeah, little brother's going down," As he looked at his opponent.

As he listened, Jasper realized that the local playing with Jake was actually the younger brother Sammy.

Clinton replied, "Freddie is going to cool it for a bit. I am thinking about hitting the other end of the operation. He has had a lot on his mind lately I'm thinking of opting him out and leaning on him"

"You mean whacking him? What's up with Freddie these days?" Jake asked.

"No, not whacking him just leaving him out. That Charlotte daughter of his has got Freddie hopping through hoops to get custody of Karen's son Buddy. Then you know damn well if that happens Freddie will wise up and divorce her ass. Then I'll have to take care of the bitch. With Karen being my wife's sister and all, Maggie thinks she has to take care of her whole family. I'd rather have Freddie stay with Karen. I don't want that trouble making, drug addicted bitch in my house and that's what will happen."

"Well, maybe Freddie needs to be slapped around a little to keep him in check," suggested Jake. "That looks like the game,

Sammie boy." Jake sunk the eight ball in the corner pocket and yelled " Rack'em up, short stuff."

"No, don't start another game. We gotta blow this place. Let's go," said Clinton. "You're right, Jake. Maybe we need to visit Freddie and slap some sense into him. Meanwhile, I think I'll keep him away from this dead chicken deal. He's libel to screw it up."

"Maybe slapping him around isn't the answer," said Sammy as they got up and headed for the backdoor to where their truck was. "Well, what do you suggest, college boy?" Clinton said, as he put his arm around Sam's shoulder. "Should we kiss him and ask pretty please, Freddie? Help me out here." Jake and Clinton started laughing as the screen door slammed behind them. "Haven't you learned anything from your big brothers?" was the last thing Jasper had heard them say.

"Wow," Jasper said to Fido. "We got an ear full. I'll have to discuss this with Grandpa Shank. He'll know what to do. Let's go boy."

They were pedaling down Route eleven and Jasper was deep in thought when he heard a woof from Fido, which brought him back to reality. A sheriff's cruiser was sitting in a blind spot on the road about fifty yards away, waiting for some would-be speeder to drive by.

"Nice spot, Fido. I was daydreaming. I've gotta get a look at the officer on patrol. Look, you run up to the patrol car and jump up and down in a friendly way and I will come over and make up some reason why you're being so hyper. He won't shoot you if you wag your tail and smile."

Fido shook his head and thought, dogs don't smile, Bozo. They pant and that looks like smiling. Then he shook his head in agreement and jumped up off the bike and was over to the cruiser hopping like a jackrabbit and wagging his tail and smiling, panting.
With Fido's quick move, the bike almost knocked over. Jasper recovered and pedaled the bike toward the cruiser. The policeman had rolled down the window as he saw him coming. "Stop Fido, stop. That isn't Uncle Charlie. Sorry officer, the dog sees a cruiser and thinks it's his past Master. My Uncle, he was a police officer from North Carolina and then retired and gave the dog to me until he gets back from

vacation. He and his wife went on a cruise to Europe for most of the summer. Boat, train, plane, the works. They're stopping at every place they can. Then he says he's going to buy a camper and see the good old U. S. of A."

The sheriff had been in the comfortable air-conditioned car and didn't seem to want to be bothered. "Yeah, Yeah, Yeah, he'll be back in a couple weeks so don't go far with that mutt. Cops like the idea of traveling but they really would just rather stay home and put their feet up and throw down a cold one."

Jasper was busy trying to cool down Fido who was getting a little carried away with his acting. "All right, all right mutt, go easy." Fido stopped when he heard the word mutt. It was one thing this cop calling him a mutt but not Jasper. Jasper could tell and patted his head nicely as he talked to the officer. Fido remained quiet. "Oh well, I think his wife is the driving force in this one."

"Well, in that case he might last a month." The cop chuckled and laughed under his breath and thought he heard him say, "He's probably pussy whipped." Jasper was able to read the officers name tag and it said Deputy Brian Dauber.

"Hey Deputy Dauber, where is the Sheriff's main station? I am Shank Steller's grandson and he wanted me to check on a report from the State on a health related situation regarding his farm."

"The grandson of Shank, the chicken man, really? Well, that's interesting. That very subject came up at our briefing this morning. I'll save you a bike ride. Headquarters is in Fort Kent and the report isn't in yet. You probably have four days to a week, and you know if the report comes back on the negative side, positive for a virus we're going to have to close down the farm until further testing is done. It will be in the state's hands then and it will be a minimum of a six-week shutdown. How will that effect the business?"

"It will pretty much close it," Jasper said. "My grandparents could sustain a hit for a few weeks but six weeks will kill them and the business."

"Sorry to give you the bad news. It really isn't bad news yet. Just pray a lot and hope for a negative report. Maybe Sheriff Blaire will visit you with good news."

"What does this Sheriff Blaire have to do with it?"

"He has an order to deliver the results directly to him with know other person seeing it. He's afraid of contamination of the report. Well, sonny. I have to make my rounds. You and the dog have a nice summer and don't play too hard."

"Hey,Deputy. One other question. Where does Deputy Ken Silvermen patrol? He's an academy friend of my brother's and he wanted me to look him up and give him his mailing address."

"Out of luck again. He is on vacation and won't be back till this coming Friday. He patrols east and west of route one on the Canadian border. See ya. Gotta go." As the window was half up and the patrol car shot up rocks and dirt as it sped off.

"Wow, Fido. This is serious stuff. I hope Shank knows his Congressmen, because that report better not get in the hands of Blaire. I have a feeling he's in cahoots with the Perrys in more ways than one."

The Wallgrass Lake turn off was less then ten miles away and they would be home soon to the Old Calcutta farm. Jasper was very eager to see his grandparents.

Chapter 9
The Steller's

The Stellers met some forty years ago. They were in California at the time. Jane was finishing up her college at UCLA and Shank had just finished his tour in the Army. He was being discharged now that World War II was coming to an end.

Jane had to laugh when she thought of when they first met. Shank was ashamed of his first name. His name was Shannon and he would only answer to S. Steller for his mail and on the duty roster. He basically drove a tank in the army so the boys started calling him Shank Steller and it stuck.

They had met at a United Service Organization (USO) club party being given to honor all the GI back from Europe and celebrating their arrival home. Most GIs were waiting on papers like Shank was to ship out. Both Jane and Shank were dreadfully shy and were sitting in the corner with this party going on and began to talk. They were both from the east coast and found out that they were both finishing up their business at the same time. Jane LaClair was headed for New Brunswick, Canada and Shank was headed for Fort Kent, Maine.

After they met at the USO Club they kept in touch and ended up arranging their travels together on the same train all the way across the country. They never stopped talking. Shank told Jane about his plans to start a chicken farm and Jane was going to teach in Canada for a couple years and see where it took her.

Shank had built up a savings and hadn't spent much of it during his eight years in the service. Plus his discharge money he got when he musters out of the Army. He was going to buy some land and then build his farm.

His father had been a migrant worker and a long haul truck driver. His mother worked in the Fort Kent library. She refused to go the last time his father went out to pick and got a job in Fort Kent. He decided to give up following the harvest and moved back to Fort Kent and they lived there the last ten years before Shank went in the service.

Jane moved to Fort Kent after a year teaching in Canada. She had missed Shank too much and moved to where he lived. They got married that next year. Between the two of them they had enough saved to buy the land, two hundred acres, in Old Calcutta near Wallagrass Lake and establish financing for their house and got started on Shanks dream. It had turned into Jane's dream by then.

Shank and Jane Steller put all their time into planning and building the farm while Jane taught school. Jane working allowed Shank time to throw up a coop for a hundred chickens and build their house. Shank had done his homework and knew exactly what he wanted and how he wanted to do it. He got in good with the local veterinarian, Dan Cooper, Sr. He had seen several operations in Europe and in the US. He knew how to lay out the farm but started small, with plans to add on as time went by.

The Stellers had their first child a year after they got married, Robert Austin Steller. He was presently in the USAF and due to get discharged in September after twenty years of service. Five years later they had their second child, Anne Marie Steller. She was a beautiful baby girl.

Both parents had talked it over with Ann Marie and Robbie about the distribution of the farm in the future. Robbie was to take over the day to day operation of running the chicken farm when he got discharged. Rob had a wife and three kids.

Shank had a lot picked out for Robbie's family to build on. He left the planning of the house up to Robbie and his wife. He would also inherit the farm and its operations.

Everything had been going so good and the farm was prospering. Shank and Jane were looking forward to September.

They hadn't seen much of the grandchildren because of Rob's military commitment. He only got leave about once a year and they were eager to see more of all of them in the near future.

Ann Marie would inherit the house and its contents and a small portion of lake front property that the Stellers owned on Wallgrass Lake.

* * * *

It had been five months since the stroke and heart attack and Shank's prognosis was good for a near full recovery. He had Coronary Artery Disease and his left anterior descending artery and his right coronary artery were both eighty percent blocked. He had had a heart attack in the truck. The heart attack had caused a clot to break loose that then caused him to have a stroke. He had triple bypass surgery to correct the problem. His left side and legs had been affected but since the surgery but he had made some great advances. He had gone to an inpatient rehab center for physical therapy. He had starting to use a walker with the nurse's aid but didn't trust himself not to fall. He had lost forty pounds and looked really slim to those that hadn't seen him in a while. He was home now on the farm. His attitude was great and he went to physical therapy three times per week.

Jane was bent over the desk working on the accounting end of the farm business. The whole operation had gotten so big Shank had urged her to hire some additional office personnel shortly after his stroke and she had. She was looking forward to turning it all over to Robbie when he came home in September. Jane looked out the window and saw Shank's old truck coming down from the main road. Frank LaBreque had gone to town for some supplies and was just returning. You could see all the traffic coming and going from the back windows of the farmhouse.

It was close to three and Shank had begun to stir from his afternoon nap. He was going every other day for very strenuous physical therapy and it wore him out after. Only two hours are called for but he insists on three. He then comes home and collapses for an afternoon nap after lunch.

"Was that my truck?" Shank asked Jane.

"Yes," she replied, "Frank went to town for supplies."

"I will be able to do all that soon," he answered. "I'll be walking within a month. Therapy is going really well. I have to learn to balance on my feet. It's like I forgot everything. You have to learn it all over again."

"I'm sure you will be walking soon enough. Just don't rush it."

"Can you stop what you're doing for now and go out and sit under the tree in the back yard?" Shank asked. They'd had a ramp put in off the back deck so Shank could come and go freely.

"Sure, I can stop," Jane said. "I'll meet you out there in about ten minutes, with some ice tea and food."

"Great, I'm looking forward to it."

It was one of those gorgeous June days with no humidity and a slight breeze. The temperature just hovering over eighty and the breeze enough to keep it cool.

Jane brought out a tray of sandwiches, fruit, pretzels and ice tea. The stroke made them both more conscious of what they ate. Everything they ate was low in cholesterol, low in sugar, low in fats. You began to like it as much as the fatty stuff and you were better off for it.

Shank asked Jane, "Any more dead chickens since I laid down for my afternoon nap?" There hadn't been any in the last two days and that had helped the tension around the farm some.

"No! Thank God," Jane replied. "I couldn't take another week of that.

I am still mad as hell at Frank for letting Blaire have those two chickens. He sent them right off to the State you know. I suppose with Sheriff Blaire breathing down his neck who knows what anyone would do. It seemed a little premature to be panicked about it so soon. Why was Blaire here anyway? There should have been no reason for him to even come out."

"I asked Frank why Blaire was here and he said the Sheriff wanted to talk to someone about the Perry's complaint. Frank said he didn't know about any complaint they had with us and said that I must have heard about it because he hadn't. The next thing he knew, Blaire saw the chickens in the truck and said he had to confiscate two of them. Grabbed them and left. Frank said he started to protest and Blaire gave him that look and said it would be wise to mind his own business." Shank was shaking his head about the whole thing. "Maybe I should let him go. You can't let people bully you like that."

"Well, he has a family to support and what else would he do?" Jane replied.

"It's not about that. He screwed up and I don't think he even realizes it. When I spoke to him about it, he was apologetic but not very remorseful. He said 'How would I have handled it'? I told him that I would be handling it very soon."

"Oh dear, Shank. I don't want you having anything to do with that Sheriff. He is bad news."

"Everyone is scared as hell of this guy but let me tell you mister, he is mistaken if he thinks he can come on my property and push us around."

Just then Jane jumped out of her chair and hollered, "Jasper's arrived!" She was happy to be off the subject. Fido was running across the lawn with his tail going even before Jane saw Jasper coming down the farm driveway. Maddy, Shanks dog, was all over Fido, jumping on him and barking. Fido jumped on Shank with his front paws up on the wheelchair, licking Shank's face and wagging his tail. Shank greeted him and patted his sides. Fido then went over to Jane and got his hugs from her.

A moment later Jasper appeared around the corner of the driveway. He pedaled right up to Jane and gave her a big hug as he dropped the bike and embraced her saying, "Boy Grandma, it's good to see you. You look so good."

He turned to Shank, who had stood up very carefully before Jasper saw him. He walked over to him and shook his hand and said, "Grandpa, I see you've been doing well with your rehabilitation. Look at you standing up and everything." He shook his hand and gave him a big hug and a pat on the back. "It sure is nice to see you both."

"I though you were going to take about three weeks to get here biking all the way and enjoying the country. It's only been a week and here you are."

"Well, I got on the road and some things happened. I got a chance to catch a ride with some folks to Augusta, from Bath. Then I biked to Millinocket."

"Huh, I see," said Shank. "I thought you were going further up the coast to do some salt water fishing?"

"Well, I was," Jasper explained. "But I had a spur of the moment opportunity to travel with some friends to Augusta and decided biking north inland would be interesting." Jasper felt guilty leaving out such a larger part of the story.

"I see, so how long did you stay in the park?"

"We tented out for three nights, Wednesday, Thursday and Friday night. Oh, I have to tell you something!" Jasper said excitedly.

"What is it?" Jane and Shank said in unison.

"Fido was involved in a rescue," Jasper explained. He then relayed the story of the missing boy, Bobby Verrill and the stand off with the bear.

He was glad to have a tale to dive into. Jasper wasn't used to keeping things from his parents or grandparents. He felt he had to keep Buffalo Man secret for obvious reasons. It was an unbelievable tale. He was also weary of casting light on Buffalo Man. He was a private person and would not appreciate being revealed.

The issue with the drug dealers and Charlotte was another story. He was afraid of Charlie and didn't want him to find out who he was. He also did not want attention pulled away from the important issues at the farm. Jasper rationalized that leaving the evidence in a secure location and going well out of his way to write a letter and send the smoking gun notebook to the police made up for the fact that he was not coming forward.

"Well, that is an amazing story, Jasper," said Jane. "It sounds like you were part of it all too,"

"Huh... Well it was mostly Fido. I was just running with the rangers," he said as soon as he realized his grandmother was talking about the lost boy and not Charlotte.

"Thanks again, Grandma," Jasper said. "What I really want to do is tell you both about the last fifty miles on the trip from Eagle Lake. I did some detective work on the way up. This is serious stuff."

"How did you know we had any problems?" asked Shank.

"To tell you the truth, when I was in Baxter State I just had a funny feeling I should check in at home. When I called my dad, he told me about the dead chickens and the health department," replied Jasper. "He wanted me to get here a little early if I could, and I was concerned, so I got here as fast I could. And from what I learned I'm glad I did."

"Jasper, there was no reason to rush for this. I have everything under control and Dan Cooper is pretty sure the birds were poisoned. We just have to find out how and why and the circumstances. We haven't had any incidences in three days."

Well, Grandpa maybe you'll feel differently when you hear what I learned."

Jasper told them about what the logging truck driver, Hank Mercer said about Paul Skater's suspected murder, and the 'good-ole-boy', bully attitude of Sheriff Dick Blaire. He also explained all about seeing the Perrys at the extra mart, seeing Shanks truck outside the Brass Rail Bar and Grill, seeing Perry's truck in the back lot, going in the bar, how friendly Clinton and Frank were, Frank leaving and not recognizing him. Then he told them about moving his seat closer to the Perrys without being noticed.

Shank was really interested at this point and started to say something. Jasper held his hand up and said, "there's more."

He told them all about the conservation during the pool game. Sheriff Blaire was on their payroll. They were definitely out to damage the farm any way they could.

Jasper continued on to tell Shank and Jane about what Deputy Sheriff

Brian Dauber had to say and how he'd gotten into the conservation, then what he had to say about the State health report and the results going excessively to Blaire. He thought Dauber was a straight cop but that Dick Blaire was as crooked as they came.

Jasper ended with, "I think this Sheriff Dick Blaire is in the Perrys pocket to take down this farm. He is behind the poaching ring and framed Paul Skater for it. Paul heard or saw something he shouldn't have and got murdered, I am sure of it. He is probably behind a lot of illegal stuff around here."

That was a lot to digest. They all sat there for five minutes just thinking. Finally Shank spoke up, "What you say about the Sheriff is all probably true, but lets keep it between ourselves for now. Without evidence, what you say isn't worth a tinkers damn. We have to have proof."

Jasper explained to Shank about what his friend Jonny, at the bike shop in Portland told him about Assistant Deputy Sheriff Ken Silvermen. "He was too green to take on Blaire at the time, it would have been suicidal. He would keep what fishy information he had on file and build on to it and when he gained some seniority and clout he might be able to help Jonny out.

"Well, you feel this Silvermen out," said Shank. "You seemed to get a lot out of this Dauber guy. Just make sure this Sheriff Silvermen doesn't go running to Blaire."

"Oh, I don't know Shank. He said this Sheriff Blaire is no one to cross. I don't think we should get Jasper involved." Jane explained.

"Grandma, I'm already involved, I will be careful like I was with Dauber."

"Yes Jane, Jasper is involved and look at all the information he found out on a fifty mile bike ride. He knows how to handle himself and he will be all right. He isn't a kid anymore and Fido will be with him all the time. I feel ok about him doing this."

"All right, Shank. You be super careful Jasper. If anything happened to you I don't know how I would explain it to Marie or Ralph," Jane said.

"Well," Shank paused, "you best get used to it, because if we put our heads in the sand we could lose the farm. I won't let that happen and I know you Jane. You won't either. I have a meeting with Dan Cooper at seven a.m. tomorrow morning. He has his findings on what killed the chickens, says they were poisoned, and he has a theory on what's going on. We are going to have a walk through some of the coops. Maybe you should come with us Jasper."

He jumped at the chance, "Yeah, sure I'd love to."

Jane put in, "What about having Frank go along? After all he is the foreman."

"You've got a point there." Shank picked up the phone and called Frank. "See Jane, you're right into this. You come up with all these suggestions and then cry CAREFUL. I know it's just the woman in you." He smiled lovingly at her.

Frank - "Hello"

Shank - "Hey Frank, Shank here."

Frank - "Hey boss, what's up?"

Shank - "I got Dan Cooper coming in bright and early tomorrow at seven a.m. He is giving me his findings on what killed the chickens and his theory about it. We're going to do a walk through some of the coops and see if his theory holds water. Are you interested in joining us?"

Frank - after a long pause "Yes, sure. You said seven a.m., right?"

Shank - "Jasper's up from Landrush. He is going to be with us, also."

Frank - "Ok, but what do we need the kid for?"

Shank - "He's not a kid anymore and he's helping out for the summer until Robbie comes in September. I'd love to give him some experience in these matters."

Frank - "Ok then, you're the boss. I'll see you at seven a.m."

"Well, that's done," said Shank after he hung up.

"Grandpa, can I bring Fido into the coops with us? He doesn't upset the birds. I have been in there with him before and they're calm," he asked.

"Call me Shank from now on, son. When we're at work or talking shop. The birds are fine with Maddy too because she doesn't chase. What would be the point of Fido being there?"

"He notices things. Stuff we might miss or never think off. I would just feel better if he came along."

"Ok," Shank said, "I'll keep Maddy out, we don't want too much confusion in there. But if the dog bugs me, he's out."

"Fair enough, he's great at disappearing." Jasper explained, while Shank looked at him a little unknowing. "You'll see."

"Jasper, Frank questioned me why you had to be there. I'm going to give you a clipboard to take notes of all this. I want to document everything from now on. We can give the notes to Doris to type up afterwards."

"It's not a bad idea, Shank. We need to grab this thing by the tail and shake the hell out of it," Jane put in. "What if they start on the other end of the operation and taint the final product? The public hears that someone dropped dead eating Steller Chickens and we all go down the tubes." She threw her hands up in the air, almost ready to cry.

Shank thought this over and said, "You're absolutely right Jane. We do need to tighten up around here. See Jasper, why she is so valuable to this farm?"

Jasper put in, "I can see where all your great ideas come from, Shank."

"Careful boy, but you're right. Behind every successful man is a brilliant woman. Here is what we've got to do. Both of you pipe in if you've got any good ideas. It's called brainstorming. After we meet with Dan Cooper, we'll organize meetings with the whole farm. We'll call it 'Our new security plan'. We can finalize it later. It will take time to work out the new policies and procedures. I'll meet with the coop managers and have them write up policies on the live part of the operation. Incoming deliveries, receiving, coop managers, day workers, feeders, cleaners, and health/disease control. Then the other end of the operation, I can get administration to work on the outgoing end; death row, sanitation disposal, chop shop, packing, and outgoing delivery. We'll get the policies and procedures all worked out and then have a few smaller meetings. Frank can run some of these meetings as well as myself. Jasper, you can follow Frank around to his meetings. I'll tell him I want you to get some live experience at running meetings. Then I'll put Frank in charge of checking sign in and out logs. Or we can work that out later. Maybe I will set up a security division.

Well then, there you go. It's all set." Shank looked at them with puzzled looks, when he saw Jane and Jasper looking at each other, shaking their heads. "What's wrong?"

Jane put in, "Your idea of brainstorming, Shank Steller, is talking and not stopping for anyone else to say something. You're basically on the right track though. So we can close this meeting and talk about it later. Right now I want to stop the shop talk and visit with my grandson."

They did just that.

Chapter 10
Investigation Coop

The next morning Dan Cooper was at the breakfast table at six thirty am having coffee with Shank and Jane. Jasper had just come down with Fido from his room. His grandparents had two guest rooms and he'd always used the one facing the farm out buildings in the back of the house.

"Good morning, everyone. Boy, you guys sure do get up early," said Jasper.

"Hi there, Jasper. It's been a long time," said Dan Cooper ass he stood up and put out his hand in a friendly gesture. "Nice to see you."

Jasper shook his hand in a manly fashion and said, "Nice to see you also. What's up with this chicken problem here?" he asked.

"I'll go over everything when Frank gets here so I don't have to repeat myself," replied Dan.

"Ok then," replied Jasper as he got up and let Fido out and threw a couple of dog biscuits out to him.

Jane was putting down his breakfast. "Here you go Jasper. We usually eat at six, but it's your first day so I let you sleep."

"Thanks grandma. Don't give me any special privileges. I'll get use to the early rising."

Shank threw his truck keys across the table at him and said, "Here are my truck keys. It's yours for the summer. I have my van I can drive. It's set up as handicapped accessible. I should be back in the truck by the end of the summer."

"Thanks, it will really come in handy."

"It's not only handy, it's a necessity. To get from one end of the farm to the other it takes thirty minutes to walk it. You won't have that much time to waste," Shank explained.

"So you're working full-time huh, Jasper?" asked Dan.

"Yes, we arranged it last March when Grandpa had his stroke. I said I'd stay on until Rob came home in September."

As Jasper was finishing his breakfast, there was a knock on the screen door of the kitchen and Frank LaBreque walked in. "Hi, everybody. Looks like we're all ready to go."

"Well, not quite Frank. You sit down and have a cup of coffee." Jane gestured toward a chair.

"Thanks," Frank replied, as he took the seat offered.

"Now that you're here Frank," Dan paused, "we can go over my report here and then we can walk through a few of the coops to see if my theory holds any water. Is that all right with you Shank?"

"Sure. Sounds good to me, but this thing is only a week old and if Frank hadn't given those chickens to Blaire no one would know about it and we could have kept this all in house, now we have the state out here checking on our every move."

"Look Shank, I told you Blaire took those chickens and me by surprise and I was sorry about it," Frank shot back. "If you had been around a little more I……"

"Well, I wasn't here. I was at physical therapy, but you didn't even check with Jane," he said louder.

"Ok! Ok!" said Dan. "Enough. What's done is done. I think we can head the state off."

They both looked up and said almost at the same time and said, "HOW?"

"Well, if you two will let me give my report. I think we can set up a meeting with the state and nip this in the bud, are you two ready to listen?"

They both nodded and the Doctor continued.

Jasper let Fido in as he wanted the dog to hear the report too.

"Ok I already indicated to Shank that the birds had been poisoned. How, is the question. I think we can figure that out in our walk through, but right now let me give you the medical report part." Dan fell silent for a minute while everyone nodded and quieted down. Then he continued, "I took blood and feed samples from all the birds that died except the two Blaire took. I would like to have samples from those birds also, maybe it's still not too late. I'm calling Augusta to see if I can get them. What I did was keep track of which coops the birds came from. Maybe we can figure out a pattern from that information. So far we have seventy-four birds dead. Cause of death was the chicken feed laced with arsenic poisoning. Whoever spread the seed had to wear rubber gloves, or they would have poisoned themselves. There was a high level of arsenic in the food in their stomachs and in their blood. Enough to kill them. This was intentional. I'm betting a handful of feed laced with arsenic was thrown through the fencing out in the closed in out-pens in the yard. It looks like after they were fed their first feeding at first light in the holding-pens. Then let out in their out-pens the scattered seed was gobbled up quickly by the first ten of fifteen birds out and they would be the effected ones. The symptoms are, bleeding from the openings, anus, mouth and eyes maybe depending on the amount of arsenic present. After feed is ingested the birds would walk around, mix and mingle for twenty or thirty minutes and then drop. Sixty-three were dead in the morning after the first feed and probably the other eleven dropped during the day. Probably eating seed that was carelessly dropped while poisoning the others. We could have a person or persons on the farm sabotaging the operation also."

Everyone looked at each other in wonder as Dan continued. "The coops involved so far are the even numbered coops in the back two, four, six and eight the odd number coops in the front are untouched so far. This gives us a pattern. It suggests that someone entered from the back woods and did their thing and left. Threw a handful of feed laced with arsenic through the wire fence into the holding pens and then took off. This is a very likely scenario. The out-pens closest to the woods were the ones we got the dead chickens from. They could pull off the deed without having a key."

"We have a turn key security system. A watchman drives the grounds and walks through the coops every hour and a half. He turns an electric time clock, which punches the time he made his walk through. We've checked the time tapes and there are no irregularities on those nights," reported Frank and Shank nodded in agreement.

"In a situation like that the culprit could lay low under the cover of darkness, back in the woods and wait till the turn key left, then walk up and throw a handful of tampered seed through the fence in the out-pens and then be gone. That's my report and a couple of theories to think about," Dan said in conclusion.

"Well," Shank said, "that sure clears up a lot of unanswered questions. It gives us a lot to look for during the walk through. Jasper, get that clipboard and take some notes and we'll brainstorm some ideas."

"Brainstorm like we did yesterday," Jane said with a smile.

"No, this time everyone has a say." Shank grinned.

Frank put in, "I'm thinking we should check the perimeter of the woods that start a hundred yards beyond the coops." Jasper set to work taking notes. "If someone was there for four straight nights there's bound to be something left behind."

"Also," Jasper added, "if someone was there, Fido can pick up the scent and follow it to where it came from, most likely."

Dan said, "Let's not forget the outside of the out-pens. There might be some feed carelessly dropped outside of them and we can gather that for evidence samples."

Shank piped in, "Do we know anyone in the sheriff's office that we can trust to be here so as to be an authoritative witness? It could be said that we all collaborated together and thought up all of this. If we do find evidence of any kind of tampering, I think we should have a law man here."

Frank said, "I agree, Shank. I've been here a long time and the cleanest cop on the force is Ken Silvermen."

Jasper put in, "I've heard that clear down in Landrush. Back when Paul Skater was murdered, he was said to be an honest cop by my friends."

"Can he be persuaded to keep any information that we gather under wraps until we can prove something?" asked Shank.

"I've had dealings with him also," said Dan. "He won't break the law but he doesn't have to report anything if a law hasn't been broken. We're just gathering evidence on a possible criminal act. Plus, we haven't put in a complaint yet."

"If we do put in a complaint Sheriff Blaire, he'll make himself the chief investigator and bury all the information we gather," said Shank. "We just won't put in a complaint until we have enough evidence in Silvermen's hands."

"I know for a fact that Ken Silvermen is on vacation till Friday," said Jasper.

"I know him pretty well," Dan put in. "I will give him a call at home and explain the situation to him and if he is around he might come over."

"I don't want to put this off, Dan. Could you call him now and see if he is around? Maybe he is just lying around and didn't go anywhere on vacation. There is a slight chance of that," Shank said.

Jane said, "You can call from the study Dan beyond the kitchen."

"Thanks, Jane. I'll make that call to Augusta also," said Dan.

"Any other ideas while Dan is making the calls?" asked Shank.

"Without ruling out sabotage, should we make a confidential list of anyone that should be checked out or watched?" asked Frank. "We have a lot of workers and there are a few shady characters. When you employ as many people as we do there are bound to be a few bad eggs, so to speak."

"You've got a point there, Frank," said Shank. "Why don't you make out a list and run it by us? I am out of the loop now since the stroke and Jasper just got here. Jane and Dan just don't work around the farmhands like you do. Get some of our trusted colleagues and run it by them. You know, like Lefty Bridges and Dan Snyder, Johnny Prue and Sid. Guys like that who have been here twenty or more years and we know wouldn't put the boots to us. Those are the guys that we can trust to scout out the rest of the employees. Sid and Jonny live in the employee quarters and know all those guys"

"Ok, Shank. I'll do that. You're right, most of those guys together could sniff out a skunk. I'll talk to them."

"Frank, I'm sorry about at the beginning of the meeting when I got on you again about the dead chickens Blaire took. I know exactly how he can be. This whole thing just pisses me off and I'm finding myself coming up short a lot lately."

"Don't mention it, Shank. I think I can understand how it must be to go through what you're going through," Frank said.

"I do want to talk to you some more about something else. Maybe later when we have a little more privacy." Just then Dan came back into the room from making his phone calls.

Dan got everyone's attention and said, "I just talked to Deputy Silvermen. I told him flat out about our mistrust for Blaire and he understood. I told him about Blaire taking the birds off the farm without a search warrant and sending them to the state. He doesn't always agree with the way Blaire does things but holds his tongue. He said he could just treat this as a complaint and look into it. He could hold off on a report until there really is evidence of foul play. Then he would have to act on it. In the case of evidence against a superior, he would have to go to the District Attorney. He has to have convincing enough evidence and handle it properly so anything collected would stand up in court. He isn't about to sick the district attorney on his boss and have it not stick. He is coming in at ten a.m. He suggested I call in another veterinarian, not one that works for you, Shank. I just called a colleague friend of mine, Frank Cunningham. He has to be back at Soldiers Pond at twelve and will be here by nine forty-five. I also called the state and talked to another colleague of mine, Charlie Whipple, of the health department. He granted me a meeting at five p.m. in Augusta. He said he needed to see me about the health report anyway and he would get me samples of the blood and feed of the two dead chickens."

"Great job, Dan with making all these arrangements. Isn't that going to be a strain getting on to Augusta by five?" Shank asked.

"Yes, it is Shank." He looked around and saw that the others were involved in individual conversations and not listening closely, he bent over and whispered to Shank and said, "Charlie said something about the AGL virus." Shank new instantly the urgency of the meeting.

"What AGL virus?" he whispered too loud. Dan immediately put his fingers to his lips to keep it hushed. This was something he was told in confidence, so Shank stood and said, "Ok then, everyone we've got a lot to do in an hour. Frank, you go find the good old boys and make up a confidential list of shady employers. Jane can get Betty and Shirley from the office building and whip up some food and coffee for after the meeting."

"Shank, I can do that myself," Jane replied.

"Ok, suit yourself. Dan and I will put together some paper work with some clout to it and make some copies of the medical report for Silvermen. We'll all meet outside the front of coop two at ten o'clock. Dan, I will meet you over at the administrative building and we'll talk about this other thing."

Everyone split to go do what he or she has to do and after the room was cleared out, Jasper leaned over to Shank and said, "What's AGL virus?"

"You overheard Dan, did you?"

Jasper nodded his head yes.

"Well, you better not mention it again on this farm. On a chicken farm that virus is worse than hoof and mouth disease on a cattle ranch. It can wipe you out,so don't mention it again. Our farm doesn't have that virus. Blaire is up to something. I'm not making any accusation, but he must be behind this. You proved that at the Brass Rail in Plastid when you overheard Clinton Perry. If you must know, the AGL virus is Avisgastrolousis the most feared disease for barnyard chickens. The virus attacks the gastrointestinal tract and causes internal bleeding. It can go dormant in chickens for long periods of time and then something triggers it and birds suddenly die. It is spread through contact with chicken feces that is already contaminated with the virus. If one chicken dies from the disease, it is likely that all chickens on the farm are carrying the virus. Consumption of meat from an AGL virus caring chicken will result in severe intestinal problems and sometimes death to humans. Research is being done right now and there's some progress being made. So there you have it. Don't mention it again. Now give me a hand and let's go. Help me out to the van and you take the truck. I will meet you at coop two at ten."

Jasper helped Shank into the van and he headed for the administration building to meet up with Dan.

He had some time on his hands so he drove the truck back to the main house with Fido just to think about things for a bit until it was time to get over to coop two. He began talking out loud to Fido, "So Blaire is on the payroll of the Perrys. He must be getting paid off to ruin the Steller Farm. Thats a lot of pressure on my grandfather. I'm already convinced that he had a hand in Paul Skater's murder. The poaching ring was broken up after Paulie's death. I'm sure that it was Blaire's poaching ring and that Paulsie found out about it. Blaire or one of his inside boys killed Paulsie, then they stopped the poaching to try to give the effect that all the poaching being done was by Paul Skater."

Now if the health report comes back with this AGL virus, the two chickens Blaire took from Steller farm had to be switched with two other chickens infected with the virus and turned into the state as the Steller chickens. None of the Steller chickens that Dan checked had the virus. The question remained, what did Blaire do with the chickens he took from the Steller farm? This was haunting Jasper as he sat there in the truck.

He was remembering one time back in Landrush, a cat had been run over near his house. His Mother asked him to take the body of the dead cat to the police station, so he did. He put the cat in a box and brought it in. He went inside and told the officer that he had found this dead cat in the road and what should he do with it? The officer said to give him a description of the cat, color, size, and markings, location found and any other identifying things about the cat. If anyone called about a lost cat with the same description then they could tell them to stop looking.

"What should I do with the body? I have it in my car in a box." The officer said, "There's a dumpster in the back of the station for road kill.. You can put it in there."

Jasper remembered commenting about it and the officer said every station he knew in the state had a dumpster for road kill in the back of the station.

He decided to ask Ken Silvermen if they had a dumpster for road kill in the back of his station. If so, he was going to check it to-night. Jasper had wanted to go to Fort Kent anyway to see Charlotte and meet her Grandma Rosa and Buddy.

When Jasper and Fido arrived back at the main house, they went inside and Jasper found his grandparents phone wasn't being used. He looked up Charlotte's number in his notebook and called.

Charlotte answered, "Hello Charlotte, this is Jasper. I'm back from Baxter State Park. How you doing?"

"Oh Jasper, I'm great. It's really nice to hear from you. I'm glad you called. Aren't you back early? I didn't expect you for at least a couple weeks."

"I got another ride after I visited Baxter State Park."

"Thank God you have that motorized bike with all that long dis-tance peddling," she said sarcastically.

"Hey, I've got some business in Fort Kent tonight and would like to see you and meet your Grandmother Rosa and Buddy. I've talked so much about them with you I'd love to finally meet them."

"Is this a date, Jasper or is it them you want to see?" she said in a playful, little tone.

"Call it a date. I'd take you out anytime, but I also want to meet your family," Jasper replied, remembering not to trust her. "I'm still not sure I can fully trust you, remember. Plus I said it was business."

"Oh Jasper, since I met you I always do the right thing. What kind of business?"

"I might have to stop in at the sheriff's office for a few minutes to check something out. Answer this one question. When my back was turned at the Pinetree campground, did you take any money out of that backpack we turned in to the cops in Augusta?"

"Oh, you suspicious thing, you. I won't answer that without seeing you face to face so I can slap you silly for even thinking that." She laughed a long laugh and said, "What needs to be checked out at the sheriff's office?"

"I'll tell you about it when I get there and maybe you can help me if you want," he replied.

"Oh boy. This should be fun. I don't like sheriff's offices."

"Well, you can stay in the truck then."

"Can I decide when you tell me more about it?" Charlotte asked.

"Of course, so is that a yes then?"

"Yes, yes come. I'll have supper ready at six, is that ok?"

"Yeah, that's just right. Can I have your address?" he asked.

"Forget the address, that just confuses things. Go straight through town till you pass the sheriff station, can't miss it, and go a mile beyond that to a big building on the left with a sign 'ANTIQUES AND MORE' and turn right on Pleasant View Road. Grandma Rosa's house is a quaint little Red Cape Cod about a half a mile down on the right."

"Well, I'm looking forward to it. I will see you at five thirty then."

"Great. See you then," Charlotte said.

That put a smile on Jasper's face. It sure was nice talking to her.

* * * *

With that done, he decided to go on over to coop two and wait for everyone. People were starting to gather. Word had gotten out about the walk through and curiosity was starting to gather among the employees.

Deputy Silvermen had arrived and along with him was an Assistant Deputy Jean Barker and Frank Cunningham the veterinarian friend of Dan's. Shank and Dan were briefing them on exactly what they were looking for and what their suspicions were. They wanted to rule out or find evidence to prove it was an outside intruder that poisoned the chickens or if the evidence pointed at an insider. They could then focus on finding the person inside. Frank had a confidential list of suspicious personnel gathered by the good old boys of the farm. After everyone was briefed and Shank sent all the curiosity seekers back to work, he put Ken Silvermen in charge.

Ken spoke up authoritatively, "I want this to be an independent investigation so we will make up three teams headed by myself as team one and Assistant Deputy Jean Barker as team two leader and independent veterinarian Frank Cunningham as team three lead investigator. The purpose of this is to rule out any tampering by the Steller employers. It's the only way any evidence would stand up in court if it ever goes that far. Everyone understand the importance of this? My report has to be free from biases." Everyone nodded their heads in agreement.

"Now Shank, you join team three with Frank C, and Frank L you join Deputy Barker of team two, and Dan and Jasper, join team one with me. Team two and three should each take one other Steller employee to witness and help record. That will make three teams of three people. The team leaders are obviously in charge of each team. Write down everything the team leaders indicate in the report. Do not influence the independent leaders. Jasper, Shank tells me Fido is a certified tracker."

"Yes, he is."

"Good, you will start out with me and if any of the teams find any evidence of a possible infiltrator into the grounds, then they should contact me on the hand held. They are set on channel thirty-two. Each team leader will have a hand held radio. I will send Jasper and Fido over to possibly pick up a trail if the situation arises. If this happened four days in a row, there's bound to be a pattern of some sort. Jean, can you get the equipment bag with the evidence kits out of my Blazer?" Ken had brought his unmarked civilian Blazer only about twenty yards away.

"Ok Ken, I'll be right back." Deputy Jean Baker went over to get the bag.

"Now everyone will get evidence kits. They have label stickers, rubber gloves, tongs and tweezers. Make sure you use them, don't handle anything. Bag it and tag it. Is that clear?" They all nodded.

Jean arrived with the equipment bags holding the evidence kits. "There are clipboards and pencils as well for each advisor. Each evidence kit has a dog whistle to call the dog back and a regular whistle to call for human help."

"Now, we're covering coops two, four, six and eight. Each team should look for blood samples from the holding-pens and out-pens, especially in coops six and eight. They were the last two hit. Look for feed outside the out-pens. Bag and tag everything. Remember, look for cigarette butts, look for anything that looks suspicious to you. Look around for marks on doors, windows, etc. Evidence of breaking and entering. The intruder may have lost his lighter or jack knife. Walk the grounds behind the coops near the woods as well."

Deputy Baker finished handing out the evidence kits and walked back to Ken with the last one.

"Ok, we've all had a quick course in looking for evidence so lets go." My team will take coop eight. Team two with Deputy Barker will take coop two."

Jean nodded at Ken.

"Team three?" continued Ken. "You take coop four. Coop six can be covered by who ever finishes first. Remember to identify the coop where you tag any evidence. Jasper, you take a radio and come with me. Keep it on until you are called out on a track run. All radios are on. Don't be afraid to ask questions, my handle is, silver bullet."

"Our handle is Barker," said Jean.

Ken said, "Frank C. what's your handle?"

"I don't have one."

"Take FC then. When you ask a question or talk to a person use their handle or you'll get two or three answers back or none at all. Lets go."

The investigation teams groups took off to the coops assigned to them. Jasper went with Ken and Dan, radio on, evidence bag over his shoulder. As he walked along, Fido at his side, he decided to chat up Ken Silvermen. It was a half mile or more away to coop eight at the opposite end of this section of the farm.

"This must be a very interesting job," Jasper said to Ken.

Ken looked at him and said, "Usually, but on this particular case it is sort of a sticky situation. You have to be really careful when you go over the boss's head." It was common knowledge to the group investigation teams that Sheriff Dick Blaire was under suspicion. "One slip up and your career is over"

"I know Shank really appreciates your honesty as an officer. He asked Dan to call you because everyone on the team knew of your integrity and strong sincerity against crime," he said.

"Well, I appreciate that."

"You have the border run on Route one, don't you?"

Ken looked questionably at Jasper. "How'd you know that?"

"I ran into Deputy Dauber outside of Plastid on my way here yesterday. I asked him about you. He told me you were on vacation and that you'd be back next week. That's why Dan called you at home. He knew you weren't at work."

"How do you know me and why were you asking about me?" Questioned Ken.

"Jonny Skate, the son of Paul Skater who was murdered six years ago said you were the only honest cop in Aroostook County. He wants to clear his father's name and I told him I'd help him. He is coming up the first or second week in August."

"I remember Jonny. He was pretty upset when the investigation slowed down. Well, don't you two do anything stupid. You might be messing in an area you don't belong. I know the case well, and it isn't closed as far as I'm concerned. I'll talk to you later about it, maybe. Right now coop eight is right here."

They walked into the coop and looked around. The coops were like a big warehouse. They were two hundred feet long and at least hundred feet wide. They were about forty feet high with a slight pitch going up to fifty-five feet at the top. There were four large rooms on each side at least fifty feet by fifty feet called holding-pens. Each pen held around fifty chickens.

There were eight coops that brought the farm chicken total to roughly three thousand birds. There was one chick coop called 'hatches' where they raised chickens, two egg coops where they held chickens for laying and the other five coops were for meat hens. Every six months the name of the coops changed. The second six months the chickens were called 'peepers'. The next six months the coop named changed to 'yearlings'. The next six months the coop was named 'One-and-a-halfs'. The next six months the coop was called 'Deuces'. Then it went to 'Deuce an a half'. And finally to 'Tres'. The Tres would go to the slaughterhouse and the peepers would take the Tres coop. That was the evaluation and rotation of the chickens.

There was a steel walkway that went the length of the coops thirty feet up. You could walk the walkway and observe all the holding-pens. The coop manager could manage the bird's lives from the main panel board at the half way point of the coop.

The coops were completely automated, except for cleaning. The cleaning was done when the four double garage doors on each side opened up to let the birds into the out-pens. Crews go into the holding pens and clean each coop. Each holding pen was white washed and all the chicken hutches and roosts were partially enclosed under the steel walkway.

In the evening, the lighting in the coops would go dim, imitating the sunset and the birds would be on the roosts by the time it was dark. The coops were staggered by one hour. Two coops at a time would be cleaned and then the next two coops would be up with a false sunrise and fed and cleaned, and so on down the line. It took four hours to complete the process of feeding and cleaning the eight coops.

The hoppers, feeding containers, would be lowered at the opposite end of each holding-pen at first light. They were controlled electrically by the coop manager at the central panel. The birds would eat for forty-five minutes to an hour inside and then the double doors would open to the out-pens where the birds would continue to eat outside in the out-pens. The double doors would stay open and the cleaning would begin.

After the cleaning process, the birds would usually stay out side. Watering troughs were inside and outside. The cleaning crews groomed the out-pens on a weekly basis, they would take one coop a day and do the out-pens in the afternoons after the morning cleaning shift.

The coop manager met them at the top of the walkway and explained the operation and how it worked. It was ten fifteen and the birds were out mingling. We were welcome to walk around the inside of the coops with the birds in them. That was fine.

The team's concentration was on the two pens closest to the back of the coop. Jasper and Dan followed Ken down the iron walkway to the very back of the building. Ken walked down the iron stairs to the holding-pens.

Just then, his handheld went off, "Silver Bullet, this is Barker of team two. We could use the tracker. I have a couple of signs of a possible intruder. I am at the back of coop two."

"Ten-four, Jasper is on his way," Ken said. "Jasper, you're up. Turn on your radio and get on your way."

He took the lower door out and headed for coop two. There were dirt roads behind the coops for tractors and trucks and other machinery so the going was easy. Jasper ,moved at a slow jog and was there in a few minutes.

"Hey Jean, what you got?"

Jean was walking back from the wooded area and said, "Well, we have bagged and tagged nothing but cigarette butts. Several different brands around the road here, but the concentration turned to GPCs over there in the wooded area. There's a place where someone stayed quite a while and smoked close to a pack of GPCs. Let's take the dog over there and see if he can pick something up." Fido took off like a shot toward the woods. "Christ, does he understand English?" Jean asked.

Before they got to him, he was coming back with his nose to the ground, following a scent he had picked up in the woods. Fido was headed for coop two. "Lets see where he goes," said Jean.

Frank L. was just coming back from the woods and told us he had bagged and tagged a couple of Coors light empty beer cans in that same spot where we found all those cigarettes.

They followed Fido around to the side of the out pen of coop two. The dog backed off and barked. There was some bird seed on the ground outside the out-pen. There was also some of the same seed on the inside of the pen that the birds inside couldn't get to because it was in back of the feeder. Jean said to Frank L, "Go inside the pen and bag that seed behind the feeder and I'll bag this seed outside the pen. The thing is that it's not the same type of seed that the farm uses. I think we have something here."

Fido was told to retrace by Jasper so they headed back toward the woods to see where the intruder went from there. The hand held started to yak. "Jasper, this is FC, I am behind coop four in the woods. I need the tracker."

“I’m headed your way,” Jasper said through the radio as he continued in the direction they were already going.

“Well, we’ve bagged cigarettes and Coors beer cans,” said Frank C. “There is a large deposit of GPC butts in the woods behind coop four.”

“Lets have the dog pick up the scent and see if the intruder is using the same method as over at coop two. He followed the intruder over to the corner of the out-pen,” explained Jay.

Frank C said, “Look, he is going over to that same corner. Lets see if there is anything to bag and tag.” They went over to coop four and sure enough there was birdseed in the same places as coop two.

Jean said as she walked by, “I am going to check that same corner in coop six’s out-pen to see if this is the pattern.”

“Jasper, I need you and Fido at coop eight,” said Ken over the radio.

“Roger that,” he said back.

“Have him check the corner of the out-pen, and tell him what we’ve found,” Jean said.

Jasper gave the dog whistle a blow and headed to coop eight. Ken was over at the corner of the out-pen bagging and tagging seed. “That’s just where the dog tracked the intruder at the other out-pens. Looks like a pattern to me,” He gave Ken an update on basically what everyone had been finding. The dog had been tracking the two and sometime three and four day old tracks just fine.

“Let’s call everyone in, Jasper. We’ll meet over behind the woods of coop eight,” said Ken.

Fido just arrived from the woods. “Fido, back track from this point and go slow. If it takes you to the woods, wait for us.” The dog did what he was told. He turned on his hand held and called everyone in to meet behind coop eight in five minutes.

When they got to the edge of the woods, Fido was there waiting. Ken asked, “Shank, what’s behind the trees and where does your property end?”

“We have a security fence that runs along a dirt camp road that abuts Wallgrass Lake then it goes back up to the main road. From these woods, the fence is about a quarter of a mile away. It’s not rough going. There are some paths." Shank was driving a four wheel ATV and was getting along good in that.

"Good enough, Fido is on the intruder's track right now," Ken replied, "Let's see which path the dog takes. There isn't much traffic here so the scent should be easy for him to follow, based on how he's been tracking. Let's follow him and bag and tag everything we come to. Ok, go ahead dog."

Fido looked at Jasper and then continued on the scent he had been following.

"Teams, I want you to fan out and look down for suspicious items. Slow the dog down Jasper."

A hundred feet or so and Fido was following a path that had been worn down slightly. As he went down the path, team members would stop and bag items along the way. Soon he came to the fence Shank had mentioned. It was off the path a little and in the middle of a bunch of alder bushes where Fido found a long slit cut in the fence, concealed by the bushes enough for a person to bend back the fence and crawl through.

"Ok," Ken replied. "This is the point of entry the intruder took to get in. Here we check both sides of the fence for anything lost or clothes caught on the fence. Four trips through this opening and there is bound to be something on or around this spot. After this area is checked out, Jasper and myself will go through the fence with Fido and follow the tracks to the road where the intruder probably left a car. We'll gather any other info there might be. We can then all meet in the administration building's meeting room for a wrap-up."

After the area was checked, Jasper, Fido and Ken squeezed through the fence and continued tracking. About fifty feet down the dirt road at a turn, Fido stopped and was hopping up and down at a spot where there was room for a car to pull in. There was what looked like spilled piles of seed on the ground, like the seeds they had been picking up at the corner of the coops.

Ken said, "The damn fool spilled this lethal stuff and never cleaned it up. Jasper, have Fido sweep the area and look for any dead animals or birds within fifty to a hundred feet and go with him. I will pick all of this up so no other animals eat it. We can test it at the lab."

Jasper bagged a dead squirrel, several chipmunks and one bird that Fido had lead him to. They took the animals over to Ken who was taking pictures of tire prints in the sand. "Ken, we found these animals within the distance you mentioned."

"We could probably find more if we made a further sweep, but that will do. I think we can go back now. We have enough evidence bagged to know who this person is. I know we can lift some prints off the beer cans or the cigarette butts. It doesn't look like this guy was any too careful and only used the rubber gloves when he handled the seed. Look, here I found these in the grass, sitting along side this empty Coors beer can." Ken was holding up a pair of rubber gloves that he had bagged along with the beer can.

"Ken," Jasper said. "What does the sheriff's department do with road kill?"

"This isn't road kill. This will go to the lab and I am willing to bet four out of five of these animals were poisoned with arsenic from the seed," replied Ken.

"Yeah, I know these will go to the lab, but regular road kill that the officers find everyday. Where do you put those dead animals?"

"All road kill goes in a dumpster behind the headquarters building in Fort Kent. Every department in the state does it that way. It's a special container with lime in it to prevent smell. Ours is emptied every month or unless we call to have it emptied early. Nothing bigger than a seventy-pound dog are put in it. Moose or large deer are disposed of directly to the health and humane services people. Why do you ask?"

"It just seemed like a large problem for rural communities and I was wondering how they dealt with it," Jasper explained.

"It could be a large problem but the way we do it seems to be the best method. Well, lets get back to the administration building and wrap this up," suggested Ken.

It took him and Ken about a half-hour to get back to the administration building. Jean Barker had gathered everyone's evidence bags and packed them up. She had everyone bag and tag his or her rubber gloves. The last thing she collected were all the reports from the three advisors and put them in her briefcase. She then had everyone go wash their hands and then they could dig into the food Jane had prepared. Ken and Jasper did the same.

Ken took the floor while they were eating. "I'm going to talk while you eat because I know some of you have to be elsewhere and I don't want to hold you up. The first thing is not to discuss this investigation with anyone. That's how rumors get started. I don't want to have to explain this to Sheriff Blaire. I will be sending all this evidence to the lab with special instructions for it to come back to me only. I may use my home address. All of that will take ten days to two weeks. I am sure we will have a person to interview about this when the results come back. I'll stay in touch through Shank if there is anything you all can do."

The meeting broke up and everyone headed off in different directions. Shank had decided to go with Dan to Augusta and they took right off, but not until he talked to Frank LaBreque for a minute. Jasper talked to Frank Cunningham for a few minutes while he waited for LaBreque. Shank had told him to go with Frank LaBreque for the afternoon to get an idea of what he might be doing for the next couple of months. While he had the chance, he talked to Jane and told her about his visiting a friend in Fort Kent and that he would be leaving at about four thirty and not to expect him for dinner.

Chapter 11
A Night Out In Fort Kent

Jasper was on the road to Fort Kent at four-thirty. He had spent the afternoon talking to Frank LaBreque and learning the different operations. His role for the summer was to help Frank in any way he could. According to Shank, Frank knew the overall operation better than Shank himself.

Frank was more than just a foreman, he was head of operations. He had foreman that covered all the other departments. Jasper wanted to trust Frank, but seeing him with the Perry brothers made him a little skeptical. He had the sense that he was on the level and he wanted to trust those senses. There had to be a reasonable explanation for it and Jasper decided to talk to him about it really soon.

It was about a forty minute drive to Fort Kent. Jasper found the sheriff's headquarters with no problem and scouted it out. He saw a couple dumpsters in the back compound behind a security fence.

He continued on to Charlotte's and would visit the sheriff's later. He found the house with no problem and parked in front of it. Charlotte met him at the door and gave him a big hug. Buddy was standing behind her.. He took to Fido right away and looked like he wanted to ride him. They were both invited into the house. Grandma Rosa was introduced and Jasper started talking to her, "Nice to meet you, Grandma Rosa. Charlotte has told me so much about you." He shook her hand. Charlotte excused herself and went into the kitchen to continue with supper

"Yes, well it's nice to meet you young man, just call me Rosa. You did a lot for Charlotte in Bath, and that was nice of you." Rosa said, and she headed for the nearest stuffed chair lead by a cane but moving along pretty well. "Have a seat and tell me a little about yourself."

"Well, I am up here for the summer working on my Grandparent's chicken farm, Steller and Sons. I grew up in Landrush and have come up here a lot of summers and vacations so I know my way around quite well."

Grandma Rosa was about five feet four with blue hair. She had just had her hair done. Probably a once a week appointment that she never missed. She was pleasant and very polite.

"I have a worthless son that works for the Perrys, your competitor. That's Charlotte's father," said Rosa. "Actually if he lost that wife of his and got away from the Perrys, he would have some redeeming qualities."

"It's nice of you to let Buddy and Charlotte stay with you, it seemed to save Charlotte."

"She never had to leave but she wouldn't let Buddy live alone with Karen without her there to watch him. Charlotte doesn't have much use for Karen, Buddy's mother, as none of us do."

"It seems like things are working out here for her. You have a really nice house and it is so picked up and clean. Charlotte seems so happy to be here."

"Oh, thank you. Charlotte and I have never had a problem living together. It's when her father comes around when the problems start. Freddie just has no respect for his own daughter and they fight something awful. It's like she has to fight to get any respect. I've told Freddie that but he's impossible. Buddy starts school this year and then it will be easier for me to help Charlotte manage him better. Charlotte had to drop out of school last year to take care of him at Karen's. She has a better attitude and wants to get back in school and get her diploma. She only has a year left."

"It looks like this is the place for her, and I am glad to see it. You are saving her life."

"Well, I am really glad to do it. But you had an awful lot to do with saving Charlotte with all that money you gave her for the lawyers retainer fee for Buddy's custody case."

"Money for the lawyer's fees? ...Oh, right, I almost forgot. How much money was that fee anyway?" Jasper said, as he remembered the drug money back at Pinetree Campground that Charlotte had promised she'd put back. She's a sly fox, he thought to himself. I'll have to talk to her about that. The truth will set you free. I guess that doesn't apply to her.

"Hey you guys, supper's ready," Charlotte bellowed.

Jasper never got an answer to his question as they got up and went into the kitchen.

After supper, Grandma Rosa went into the living room and settled in to watch the evening news and Buddy and Fido went into the fenced in back yard to play. Jasper stayed in the kitchen and helped Charlotte clean up after supper. "So what is this business you have to do at the Sheriff's office?" Charlotte asked.

He decided to level with Charlotte and tell her what she needed to know in case she wanted to help him. "You know my distrust of Sheriff Blaire." They had talked about him that night back at Pinetree Campgrounds. "Well, he confiscated a couple chickens from my grandfather's farm illegally and sent them into the State Department of Health to try to close him down, but I think he switched them with a couple infected chickens. I want to check his dumpsters and see if there are any dead chickens in them."

"Do you really think he would throw them in such an obvious place?" asked Charlotte.

"You wouldn't think so, but I think he's so arrogant that he thinks he can do anything he wants and people will stay clear of him and leave him alone. I want to find those dead birds and link them to the sheriff. I just can't let it go without looking. I will do all the grub work as far as getting in the dumpster. Do you want to help me?"

"I'll help, but what can I do?"

"I figure we can make up a story to get us in the compound and get a look in the dumpsters." Jasper replied.

"What kind of story do you have in mind? It will have to be something off the wall. They won't just let anyone in there for no reason."

"That's where our acting comes in. I'd like to wait an hour or two when the night shift is on and we are just dealing with a few cops on duty," he said.

Charlotte and Jasper discussed a plan of action to follow when at the sheriff's office.

Charlotte put Buddy to bed about eight-thirty and they were off with Grandma sitting for Buddy. Jasper parked his Grandfather's truck near the entrance to the sheriff's compound so he could grab what he needed in the truck bed. They walked into the sheriff's building with their parts loosely rehearsed. They walked arm in arm with Fido on a leash. "Hello, Officer," Jasper said to the night sheriff behind the desk.

"Hello, son, how may I help you?"

Jasper thought he was ordering hamburgers for a minute, but then brought himself right back to the situation. "Sergeant Burnham," he said, reading his name tag, "My girlfriend has lost two pet chickens and she thinks they may have gotten hit by a fast moving car in front of her house. Has any one reported any road kill chickens in the past twenty-four hours?"

"Chickens are fast and very rarely get hit by cars. When I came on duty I scanned the day report and there were no chickens brought in that I remember." He looked at them closely to see if this was a joke.

"Well, Sergeant we are fairly sure they were hit by a car because my dog tracked them to the road and then we saw a lot of their feathers on the road. When we looked around we couldn't find any dead chickens."

Charlotte cried out, "Oh no! They can't be dead."

"They're probably not honey, we're just ruling that out by checking here," Jasper replied, as he hugged her and patted her on the back.

"They probably got scared by a car and took off," suggested the Sergeant.

"The dog would have been able to pick up their scent and follow them"

The Sergeant looked at Fido questionably and said, "Who has pet chickens anyway?"

"I do. I got them last April for Easter and they were colored, one was red and one was green. The tips of their feathers still had the colors on them, I know it was their feathers in the road," as Charlotte went into a raving fit of hysteria.

Jasper quickly started to comfort Charlotte as did Fido with a low wine and rubbing his head against her thigh. It was a pitiful sight and Jasper said, "Could we at least look in the dumpsters sir, to satisfy her that the chickens aren't dead?"

" I assure you all the road kill is logged in and it would be on this log." The Sergeant said as he pointed to it while looking through it.

"Oh, no question, sir. I believe you. If she just got a look for herself it might help me get her outta here."

Charlotte continued to sob.

"You know that dumpster stinks. It's due to be emptied tomorrow as the Sergeant looked out to where it was. "Is that your truck from Steller's Chicken Farm?"

"Yes, it's my Grandfather's truck," said Jasper.

"Why don't you give her a couple new chickens and she'll be happy?" suggested the Sergeant.

Charlotte then screamed in hysteria, "I want Felix and Tweedy. They're my pets. I don't want any new birds. I would have to train them all over again."

Jasper looked at the Sergeant and shrugged his shoulders and said, "It will only take a second. I brought a hoe in the truck and can fish around to see and then we'll be on our way." He continued to comfort Charlotte.

The thought of them leaving was intriguing to the Sergeant. The noise of this kid over these ridiculous lost chickens was starting to irritate him. Other officers started to look up and take notice. "Very well. I can watch you from here and control the gate. So go ahead and make it fast and then be gone," said the Sergeant. "Who trains chickens anyway?"

"Oh, thank you, sir. You won't be sorry. If I find the chickens, I will come back and sign them out. Charlotte will want to bury them proper if it's all right."

The Sergeant shook his yes. "Just take a quick look and get outta here."

Charlotte turned to Jasper as they walked out and said, "Surely the good Sergeant is right and they won't be in there. I don't want my chickens dead," and she began to sob again. He continued to console her as they walked out.

Once outside, Jasper turned and said, "I thought for a minute I was going to burst out laughing. I can't believe that worked." As they passed the truck, he grabbed his gloves, a hoe, and a plastic bag that he had ready in the truck. He was convinced he would find the chickens. They headed for the back lot, which was in sight of the window. Jasper saw the Sergeant watching and waived to him while pretending to comfort Charlotte.

He got to the dumpsters and Charlotte stood over to the side. He let Fido loose and he was darting around with his noes to thc ground and moving all over like he was tracking, trying to catch a scent of the chickens.

There were two dumpsters. Jasper looked in both dumpsters, one was for regular trash three quarters full and the other was for the road kill, half full with a heavy smell of lime in it. Jay tied his neckerchief to his face and took the hoe and started moving all the dead animals around. There were groundhogs, cats, porcupines, a couple dogs, birds, skunks, but no chickens. The stench got worse as he moved the dead animals around and finally gave up and shut the lid. "Damn it, there are no chickens in that mess," he said to Charlotte. "I guess he put them somewhere else."

At that moment he noticed Fido doing a digging motion around the regular trash dumpster. He was concentrating on the far corner. "Hold on," said Jasper. "I think Fido is onto something. Watch for the Sergeant as I look through the regular trash and see if he comes out." He picked up the hoe and started moving the trash around the corner that Fido had suggested.

"He is lifting up his hands and saying no," she said

"That's all right," he said,as he spotted a black trash bag at the bottom of the dumpster and hooked it with the hoe and pulled it out to look inside. Sure enough there were two dead chickens there. He checked them and they had the leg bands of the Steller Farm. Jasper was excited. "Charlotte, look like you're crying over the dead chickens, will you?" She started to bawl instantly with real tears.

Jasper put the birds in his trash bag and held them out to Sergeant Burnham with a big smile. He was putting on his jacket and looked like he was coming out. He put up his hand and mouthed, I'll come in.

Charlotte said, "Forget that, lets go."

"Now I want to get these chickens in the sheriff's log for evidence that they were found in the dumpsters. You wait in the truck and Fido, great job. You wait out here also. I'll wrap this up and we will head out."

Jasper went into the sheriff's office before the Sergeant could come out. He said to him, "Sir, for some reason they were in the wrong dumpster. My dog sniffed them out so that's why I looked in there."

A couple other officers were milling around and smelled the chickens. "Wow, get them out of here. You'll stink up the building."

"I just wanted to log them in. I can take them, can't I?"

"Yeah, you can have them. Just get them to hell out of here like Charlie said."

"Oh, no. I want to do it legal and everything. Would you put in the road kill log with the band numbers and everything?"

"Ok! Ok! The bands are on there. Read them off," said the Sergeant.

Jasper quickly read the band numbers off to the sergeant.

Charlie, the other officer said, "I saw Captain Blaire put them in the dumpster the other day on the way out to his car. I didn't dear tell him he put them in the wrong dumpster, him being the Captain and all."

"Great," said Jasper. "Can you put that in the log also under where it says finding officer?"

"Well, I don't think I want to get the Captain involved," said Sergeant Burnham.

"Oh, go ahead," said Charlie. "He did it and you can put my name on the line saying that I verified it. Maybe that will get him to be more mindful of what he is doing."

"What is your name officer?" asked Jasper.

"I am Sergeant Charlie Wheeler."

"Ok, are you happy? It's all legal. Now take those stinky things outta here and bury them. Maybe you can get some action afterwards," Sergeant Burnham sneered.

"Yeah, just be careful which bird you bury," echoed Charlie laughing. "I'm going out back. That smell is awful." Charlie then walked to the door behind the desk and the door swung shut behind him.

Jasper grabbed the stinking birds and headed for the door.

"Yeah, Charlie," he heard the Sergeant saying. "I'm coming too, I need to find the deodorizer."

Jasper looked over his shoulder as he opened the door to sheriff's headquarters. The office was empty behind him, both men had gone out back assuming that Jasper was well on his way. He quickly dropped the birds on the steps without going through the door. Jasper turned on his heals and ran over to the desk.

Jasper leaped over it without making a sound and snatched up the ledger containing the log. He could hear the officers digging in a closet or something on the other side of the wall probably looking for the deodorizer. He only had another two minutes at best.

He moved over to the Xerox machine and laid the ledger down on it face up. He hit copy. He could hear Sergeant Burnham moving back toward the door.

Jasper snatched up the copy as it fell in the tray and leaped back over the desk and dropped the log book on the desk. The slam of the book hitting the desk sounded loud to Jasper's ears.

He could hear the door nob turning as he yanked open the exit door and grabbed up the bag of chickens. He marched straight for his grandfather's truck without looking over his shoulder.

He threw the birds in the back of the truck and hopped in behind the wheel. He took that opportunity to look over at the sheriff's office door. Sergeant Burnham seemed unaware as he fired aerosol around the lobby area. Jasper turned the key in the ignition and they soon took off out of the sheriff's driveway and turned towards Route 11. "Charlotte, you won't believe it. I got him to put it on the log. Another sergeant saw Blaire put the birds in the wrong dumpster and he even verified it for me on the log."

"Wow," Charlotte said, "I saw you run back in right at the end. What was that all about?"

"Well, as I was leaving, the two officers went out back. I was afraid that if Blaire found out about our visit, the log might turn up missing. So I saw an opening and I made a copy of the page. It's right here." He held the sheet of paper out to Charlotte.

"Oh, I see," Charlotte said, surprised as she took the copy.

"You don't realize how big this is. It will fry Blaire when we get all the other evidence together. His own staff verifying this, that's huge. I need to take these chickens to Frank Cunningham's house in Soldiers Pond. It should only take about a half an hour. Is that all right with you?" He looked over at her with Fido sitting between them.

"Sure, it's fine with me but who is this Frank guy?" replied Charlotte, as she moved Fido over and sat closer to Jasper and snapped the seatbelt on in the middle of the truck seat with Fido sitting on the passenger side of the truck.

"Frank is a friend of our veterinarian, Dan Cooper. He is another vet that is working on this project and he is holding the evidence and running tests on the chickens and stuff. I talked to him today and I told him what I was doing tonight and he told me if I needed a place to take the chickens, if there were any, to bring them over to his place."

"Ok, well I work at eight thirty but its still pretty early. That is, as long as you don't mind back tracking to bring me home later?"

"Of course I don't mind," Jasper said. "Where are you working tomorrow morning?"

"The animal shelter," Charlotte answered. "It's a pretty decent job most of the time. And if Grandma Rosa isn't up to it, I can usually bring Buddy with me. He plays with the dogs."

"Well, thats good they let you come back."

"Yeah, I only missed one shift with my excursion down south last week."

I need to get myself up at around five am and get an early start at Steller's. They start at the crack of dawn."

"Oh, are you sure you don't mind bringing me home later?"

"No, I invited you. I wanted to talk to you."

"Is there something you wanted in particular?" Charlotte asked flirtatiously.

"No, not really," Jasper said, trying to sound casual. "I just wanted to see how you were making out. I am curious how Buddy's custody stuff is going."

"The custody thing. Oh, that's been started. Grandma Rosa and I have got a lawyer on a retainer and he's working on it. He says that Karen has a long track record with the police and is on probation. We have established a good home for Buddy, so now we just wait."

"Well, you've managed a lot in a short time. Has your father helped with any of this?" Jasper asked as hc turned down route 11 towards Soldiers Pond.

"Actually, Rosa talked to him and he has stayed away from us and just refused to help in any way. I think he wants custody but can't do it because of his situation with Karen and working for the Perrys. Freddie has no backbone and is frightened to death of the Perry brothers. Karen's their sister and he doesn't know which way to turn without getting pushed around."

"It's only been a week since we parted in Millinocket. I'm proud of you Charlotte. You're really getting the ball rolling. Do you think you will get a hearing?"

"The lawyer says it takes time, but maybe there would be a hearing before the school year. He said judges like to get small kids situated before holidays and stuff."

"It must have been expensive to hire a lawyer," inquired Jasper with a sly smile.

"Oh yeah. The money thing. You don't really want to know about it," she said and looked away sadly.

"Look, Charlotte. Do you really think I'm going to turn you in now?"

"You're not mad?" she said turning to look at him.

"I'm not happy about it. I think there is still time left for it to bite us in the ass that you took money from a drug dealer. But I know why you did it, so, no, I'm not mad."

"I really do feel guilty about taking it, but when things are going bad, it just didn't seem like there was any other way out of it. I knew I would need money to get Buddy away from Karen legally and I didn't have the means to do it. So I saw the chance to fix this thing, so I did it. I do understand what you meant about the truth setting me free, but I made this one little detour and I am not going to look back and wish I hadn't done it. I'm glad I did it and it's going to work."

"Well, lets hope you're right. You want to change the subject? Can I ask you something about your dad?" he said as he made the turn onto the road that took them to Soldiers Pond.

"Oh God, I really don't like talking about him. He's such an asshole."

"Just a few things I am curious about," Jasper said, as he was thinking about the investigation that morning at his grandfather's farm. The overheard conversation about Freddie at the Brass Rail in Plastid ran through his mind as well. He knew Freddie was in trouble with the Perrys and probably due for an ass whooping. He kept that information from Sheriff Silvermen because he wanted Silvermen to find out Freddie's involvement for himself. Just so it would be more official.

"Well, ok. What do you want to know about him and what's this all about anyway?" Charlotte said. Her eyebrows narrowed.

Jasper didn't really want to discuss the investigation at the farm with Charlotte. He had to be careful here. "He works for Clinton and Jake Perry, right?"

"Yeah, that's right."

"Do you know what he does for them? Is he a foreman or what?"

"I have never talked to him about his work. When I lived with him and Karen, he would complain to her a lot about them. I don't think he had a very important job though. He was always complaining about doing all the grub work."

"I know you're mad at him now, but was he ever there for you?"

"When my mother was alive, he was ok. He never recovered from her death. I think he blamed himself for it. Then he got the job with the Perrys and met Karen and it was all down hill from there."

"Do you mind talking about it? About your mom, I mean, how she died and stuff?" he asked. They were growing close to Frank Cunningham's house.

"No, I don't mind. It saddens me, but I have grown to live with it and don't mind telling you about it."

"Thanks," Jasper said. "You're a pretty strong person."

"I was born right here in Fort Kent and we lived in Grandma Rosa's house. Crystal, my mother, was a housewife and Daddy lived with us. He was the custodian at the high school. Grandma Rosa had gone to Calais to take care of her sister who was ill for a long time. We rented the house from her and Daddy kept it up nice for her. Life was good for the seven years that we lived there. Crystal and Freddie seemed happy to me. I was just a little kid and didn't have much sense about things. We did family things and stuff. My mother and father owned motorcycles. We used to go all over the place on them and one day Crystal flipped her cycle and died right there on route 11. She was wearing a helmet and all that but the bike went into a skid and into a tree and her neck snapped like a twig. I was on my dad's bike when it happened. I look back and figure my childhood pretty much ended right there. He couldn't deal with anything after that."

"Rosa's sister died that year also and Rosa came home and sort of held the family together. Freddie pretty much gave up on life and lost his job at the high school. He left me with Grandma Rosa and pretty much deserted us. He would come back once in a while, just to dry out. He started to do odd jobs for the Perrys and ended up with Karen and got her pregnant, then married her. I was twelve by then and he needed me to take care of Buddy because Karen couldn't. I thought it might be like it used to be with my mom so I went to Frenchville to live with them and things didn't turn out the way I hoped they would. I had been living there for the past five years and things came to a head in June when I took off and you know the rest."

"Wow, so things were ok for a while with your family in the early years," Jasper said. He was pulling into Frank's driveway now.

"I will take these birds in to Frank and be right out. Are you all right?" Charlotte looked a little misty after telling her story.

"Oh, yeah I'm all right. I just get sad when I think of how things used to be."

"You want me to wait a minute before I get rid of these birds?"

"Oh, no. Go take care of that, I'll be fine."

"Ok. Be right back." Jasper got out of the truck, grabbed the police log and the chickens in the back and took them up to Frank's house.

Frank had seen the truck coming and met him half way up the walk. "Mr. Cunningham, you won't believe it. I got the chickens out of the dumpster at the sheriff's headquarters in Fort Kent and a signed police log to implicate Blaire in throwing Steller chickens into the dumpster." He relayed the rest of the story from the sheriff's office.

"Nice job, Jasper. This will help when we gather the rest of the information from this morning's investigation. I will examine these birds in the morning and write up a report and get it to Deputy Silvermen. We should have a pretty strong case against Sheriff Blaire. Remember to keep this quiet. We want to surprise him and catch him off guard."

"Ok, great. I'll talk to you later. Got to head out to get up early tomorrow." Jasper shook hands with Frank and turned to head toward the truck.

He retraced his path back to Grandma Rosa's house as he and Charlotte talked on about her past and Freddie. "So at one time, your father was a positive person in your life."

"Yes, I have to admit until my mother died, he was there all the time and we were a family. He went all to pieces after that and just never recovered."

"Maybe with some counseling and some positive work he could get his act together."

"That might be possible but he would have to get out of his present situation that he is in."

"Does he smoke and drink?" Jasper asked.

"Oh, yes. GPCs and Coors Light. That has been his trademark."

Jasper made a mental note, it looked like the Perrys sent him out to poison the chickens and he certainly left his trademarks all over the back lot of the Steller's farm. His prints will be all over those cans of beer and cigarettes.

"Would you say he is an alcoholic?"

"Yes," Charlotte said, without flinching.

"Would he admit to it?"

"He might admit it but he would never do anything about it," she said.

"Oh, you never know. Everyone can change. Where does he live in Frenchville?"

"He and Karen live in a doublewide parked in Crosses Trailer Park just outside Frenchville on the county road. They fight all the time and sometimes he stays at the Perrys, in their employee housing, because he can't get along with her for very long."

"What do they do for recreation?" Jasper asked as he turned on to Main Street in Fort Kent, headed for Grandma Rosa's.

"When I lived there, it was Pierce's Pub every Friday and/or Saturday night. Downtown Main Street, Frenchville where all the action is. I am sure they're still on the same schedule."

"Well, I have a feeling things are going to change soon, so don't give up on him," he said as he turned into her driveway.

"What do you mean things are about to change soon?What do you know that I should know?"

"Not much except the fact that I heard the Perrys are unhappy with him and some harm may come to him."

"Oh, that's nothing new. Freddie is always intimidated by them."

"Hey Charlotte, thanks a lot for the help at the sheriff's office and for the good company."

Charlotte unbuckled her seatbelt and moved over close to him and kissed him on the lips and said, "You don't think you can take me out without kissing me goodnight, do you?" She kissed him again and he kissed her back eagerly.

"I guess I can't," he said, and he smiled at her. They made out for a while in Rosa's driveway. When he realized his hands were beginning to creep up her shirt, he pulled back and pushed her away.

"What's the matter, Jasper? Things were just starting to get interesting," she said with a mischievous grin.

"I know they were, but we need to cool it a little,"

"See you later, Jasper. I'll keep in touch."

"I'll call you soon," he hollered as he backed out of the drive. On his trip back to Old Calcutta, he couldn't stop thinking about her. He was glad she was doing a little better and helping her brother. He admired Charlotte's strength in dealing with her drunken father. Then he thought of the GPCs and the Coors Light cans. "How is Freddie getting arrested for poisoning chickens going to effect her custody battle with this Karen person? Probably not in a good way," He said aloud.

Jasper did not realize he had even spoken until he heard Fido make a groan of agreement. He vowed to look more into Freddie Baker's situation.

* * * *

In the morning over breakfast Jasper told Jane and Shank about his adventure at the sheriff's office in Fort Kent.

Shank was dumfounded, "You actually got the night officer to sign and date the log and give you a copy of it?"

"Well, not exactly. He signed and dated the log because I made a stink about signing the birds out officially. I kinda stole the copy."

"You stole it, Jasper? That's not like you," said his grandmother.

"Well, he wasn't exactly going to give it to me if I asked," he said defensively. "The opportunity presented itself when he left the room. I just envisioned Blaire learning about our visit and burning the log to hide the evidence. I couldn't just steal the log book so I made a copy."

"How did you figure the birds would be in the dumpster there?" Shank replied.

"I knew our birds weren't infected. We knew Blaire took them. I was convinced he switched them with infected birds and I asked myself what would I do with two dead birds if I were Blaire. Figuring no one would bother him about them, he threw them in the dumpster at work. He never took the Steller bands off the legs of the birds. He is so arrogant and he thinks he is above the law."

"I asked Deputy Silvermen yesterday morning about where they put all the road kill and he told me in the dumpster behind headquarters in Fort Kent. They douse it with lime and empty it once a month and it was going to be emptied today. So I figured I just had to check it last night because it would be my last chance. I knew Charlotte would help me and I wanted to see her, Grandma Rosa and Buddy anyway."

"I actually wouldn't have found the chickens, but Fido sniffed them out from the regular trash dumpster that they use. It was about thirty feet away from the road kill dumpster. Blaire threw them in the wrong dumpster probably on purpose, figuring they would be hauled off and never seen again."

"Wow, you did good, Jasper. That evidence will support what Dan Cooper and I found out in Augusta yesterday," replied Shank.

"What did Charlie Whipple from the health department have to say?" he asked.

"I was just getting to that. He said the two chickens Blaire gave them were not banded and were infected with the AGL virus. He said they had to recommend to the Attorney General that we be shut down temporarily pending an investigation. With what you have just come up with, I might be able to stop that shut down. I have a friend at the state house. I'm going to call him after my physical therapy and ask for help staving off this shut down. Our farm couldn't sustain a long work stoppage. When it comes to the AGL virus, it would be a long investigation, believe me."

"Man, I don't believe Blaire. Shouldn't we put in a complaint against him or something?" asked Jasper.

"After my call to the state house, I am going to call Ken Silvermen and see what charges we can bring up on Blaire and the Perry farm. Once he finishes his lab work on his investigation at our place and gets the police log report you gave to Frank Cummings, I think we will have the hard evidence he needs."

"I hope so. We have to make Blaire pay."

"Jasper, I have a meeting with Frank LaBreque at noon tomorrow. I want to clear the air about this meeting you saw him at with the Perrys, at the Brass Rail. I also want to see if he found out anything from the old timers on the farm. I was wondering if you wanted to sit in on the meeting and tell him what you found out about their operation after he left."

"Sure," he said, "I'll be there."

"One more thing, who is this Charlotte?"

"Oh she's a girlfriend of mine I met in Bath when I was pedaling up

here a week ago. She's cool, you'd like her."

"I see. You'll have to tell me more about her," his grandfather inquired.

"Well sure, Grandpa. But shouldn't I go meet LaBreque at the administration building?"

"You're right," said Shank. "And I have to get to physical therapy or I'll never make that call to Augusta."

Chapter 12
Shank the Tank

Shank hadn't been in the chicken business for forty years without making some friends in some high places. He had sat on the board of health in animal husbandry in Augusta in an effort to cleanup the poultry industry in terms of protecting the public, workers and birds. In his early years, he had worked hand in hand with some of the state politicians to get bills passed to regulate the poultry industry. He was active in Four H Clubs around the state, always promoting the industry. He worked with OSHA to prevent hazards in the work place and always complied with their strict standards. He had an impeccable record of safety on his farm.

Right now he figured it was payback time for all he had done for the State. All these non-paying committees he belonged to and meetings he had attended and lobbying he had done to pass bills were about to bear fruit. He knew there was a reason he had done all that stuff. Oh, yes it was good for business but it was also good for the State.

Shank had just gotten back from physical therapy and was sitting in his study and picked up the phone to call the state District Attorney's Office. The phone was ringing. "Hello," said the operator.

"Yes, hello," said Shank. "Could I have the District Attorney's Office please?"

"One moment, please." He was on hold before he could blink.

"District Attorney's Office, How may I direct your call?" the receptionist said.

"Yes, Assistant District Attorney, Rockwell Fontaine." Shank had grown up with Rocky Fontaine in Fort Kent when his parents finally settled there. They had gone to high school together and Rockwell had gone on to college when Shank had gone into the Army. They were good friends and had stayed in touch over the years. Rocky had continued on to law school and then worked his way up the political ladder to his present job. Shank had worked with him on several occasions during the early years in the business.

"And whom may I say is calling?"

"Shank Steller from Fort Kent." Click, on hold again.

"He's on another line. Will you hold?"

"Yes, please."

"Thank you." Click, on hold again.

Seven minutes and thirty-three seconds later. "Rockwell Fontaine speaking. Is this Shannon Steller?"

"Watch it, Rocky. You know I don't go by that name, you Fort Kent drop out."

"Hey, Shank. Just teasing. What can I do for you?"

"Rocky, I have a problem I would really like to speak to you about in private and not over the phone. I just don't trust these damn things. I am willing to come to you. It has to be soon"

"Can you tell me the nature of the problem or anything about it Shank?" Rockwell asked as he got a pen and paper ready to write.

"I'd rather not, Rocky. You'll understand why when we talk. Let me just say, I think you will be interested as hell in what I'm going to tell you," Shank implied.

"Well, all right Shank. Let me check my schedule and see if I am up your way
in the next week or so."

"Rock," interrupted Shank, "this can't wait a week. My chicken farm is under fire and it might be shut down by the state for health reason that are unfounded. That's all I can say about it over the phone."

"Ok, Shank, now don't panic. Usually the state moves slowly in these situations and it's Monday morning. Worse case scenario, it wouldn't be till next week before they could get an injunction to shut you down. So we have some time." Rocky had his agenda book out and was checking his schedule.

Shank piped in again, "Not when you're dealing with the AGL virus, Rocky."

Long pause, "I see your point, Shank. They will move a little faster in that case. If you say these allegations are unfounded, I believe you. I have a friend that can put a hold on this for twenty-four hours until we talk. I have to be in Dairy tomorrow. Can you meet me there at about four p.m.? Then you won't have to come all the way down here to Augusta."

"Hey Rock, that sounds great. Look, I really appreciate this."

"Ok then, I should be out of court by three in the afternoon. What do you say we meet at the Pilot's Grill at four o'clock? I know you know where that place is."

"Sounds good to me, and thanks again. You won't regret the meeting."

"Give my regards to Jane and will catch up on everything tomorrow. Bye now." Click.

Wow, that was easy. He sounded in a hurry. I guess District Attorneys are always busy. Shank wrote down the appointment in his address book and picked up the phone to call Ken Silvermen.

* * * *

It was a little after ten a.m. and it was Ken's first day back from a two-week vacation. He had a desk full of paperwork and was wading through it at a pretty good clip. He wanted to be out on patrol from eleven to four, cruising the Canadian border and keeping an eye on things. The phone rang, "Deputy Silvermen speaking."

"Yes, Deputy Silvermen. This is Shank Steller. There has been a development in our recent meeting since yesterday. Could we meet outside the office sometime today to discuss it?"

"I will be patrolling the northern border most of the day. Can it wait until after my shift that ends at five p.m.?"

"Sure, that would be great. You live near Eagle Lake. How about we meet at the turn off to Wallgrass Café, about six o'clock? Is that ok?"

"Great," Shank said. "I'll be there. Thanks."

"No problem," said Slivermen as he hung up the phone.

* * * *

Shank, Frank and Jasper were sitting around one of the round lunch tables in the
large employee lunch and break room at noon. Shank spoke up, "Any of you want
lunch?" Both Jasper and Frank indicated that they hadn't eaten yet, so Shank said,
"Lets get our lunch and meet in the conference room of the café. I think we need
more privacy than this."
The lunchroom was starting to fill up.They all got a lunch from the line and met in the conference room where
Shank came in and shut the door. "I wanted to meet with you both now because I
have a meeting with Ken Silvermen at six this afternoon at the Wall-grass Café. Jasper, have you told Frank about your skit at the sheriff's office in Fort Kent?"

"Yeah, I told him," he answered.

"Good," said Shank. "Is there any news, Frank from the group of old timers
you were checking on?"

"There're a couple of shady characters that I have some of the boys keeping an
eye on. I'm thinking of setting up some hidden cameras in the meat packing section and in some of the other sections that would be easy targets for contamination of the product" Frank said.

"That's a good idea. Let's get security on that right away. I don't think we have to worry about them spreading any more poison around, Jasper already found out who's doing that," Shank said. "Jasper, tell him what you saw and heard at the Brass Rail in Plaisted last week."

"Well," Jasper began, a little nervous. He didn't want to implicate Frank in

anything. "I was pedaling through Plaisted, up Route 11 headed for Old Calcutta and
saw the Steller truck parked outside the Brass Rail there. I pulled over to talk to
whoever was using the truck and then I saw the Perry truck parked in the back.
I saw you there, Frank talking to Clinton. You were just leaving when I got there. After you left, I moved closer so I could hear the Perry's conversation."

Frank interrupted, "Yeah, I was there. I called Clinton Perry and asked for a meeting to see if he was behind this chicken dying thing. I wanted to talk to him face to face, so he told me to meet him at the Brass Rail to talk about it."

Shank jumped in, "I told Jasper that I knew you would have a perfectly legitimate reason for being there. This isn't about you, Frank. Tell us what the Perrys had to say about their role in this."

"They were blowing smoke, telling me stuff I wanted to hear. Like they couldn't believe this was happening and if there was anything they could do to let them know. Of course, denying any knowledge of what was going on. Acting all buddy-buddy and nice. I left there feeling they had everything to do with it," Frank explained.

"That sounds like them. The interesting part of this is when you left, Jasper got up and moved closer to try to hear what they were saying. Jasper, tell Frank what you told me about the conversation of the two brothers."

He went over the whole conversation he had overheard at the Brass Rail. Blaire being on their payroll, the Perrys trying to drive the Stellers out of business so they could monopolize the poultry business in the area and Jasper's suspicions of Freddie doing the poisoning of the chickens. "They even said they were going to zero in on the other end of the business. I took that to mean the packing plant or the shipping dock," he explained.

"I think with that information, I'm glad we are tightening our security up," exclaimed Shank. "If we could catch them red handed trying to pull something off, it would be great."

"Why didn't we tell Silvermen all this sooner?" asked Frank.

"Up until now, it would have been all hearsay. Now with some of the latest evidence, I think we can get Ken to do something substantial about it," said Shank.

"I am driving to Dairy tomorrow to meet with a friend of mine, Assistant District Attorney Fontaine. He is putting a hold on the order to close us down for twenty-four hours until he hears what I have to say. I am going to have him call Ken Silvermen after I meet with him. I think the information Jasper came up with will stop this shut down. It will still take some time to file any kind of charges. With what we have, we can definitely press some charges on Blaire and the Perrys that will stick. I am sure they will hold on to the info until they can make it stick. If we can come up with anything else we can definitely help the situation."

"I will inform some of the old locals to keep an eye on the packing and shipping end of the operation. They're bound to try something there," added Frank.

"I am going to take a trip to Frenchville this weekend to meet Charlotte's father, Freddie. I know where he goes for recreational drinking on Friday and Saturday nights," added Jasper.

"You be careful, Jasper. Don't be doing any detective work that will get your ass in a sling," explained Shank.

"I just want to check him and Karen, his wife out. From what Charlotte tells me he is miserable. He hates his wife, his job, his life, everything. He is intimated by the Perrys. He only stays at home a couple days a week. If I can find out how bad things are and maybe even befriend him and then get Ken Silvermen to put pressure on him to turn,we could have the Perrys in a bind. It's a long shot I want to try out. Like the chickens in the dumpster thing, I just have a hunch."

"Don't forget he works for the Perrys and if he gets word of this thing, he could run to them," Frank said.

"Oh you're absolutely right. At this point, I just want to feel him out and see how desperate he is. I will have Ken Silvermen do all the talking if I think there is a chance of getting him to turn on the Perrys. I saw a picture of him at Grandma Rosa's. I know what he looks like. He doesn't know me from Adam."

"Well, lets all remember this is a police matter and not to take any chances or let anything out. We should meet periodically and compare notes," Shank suggested. They all turned to their cold lunches and ate.

* * * *

It was quarter of six and Shank pulled up to the Wallgrass Café and saw Ken's blazer parked in the front lot. He pulled into the handicapped parking area near the ramp to go into the café and hoped Ken hadn't been there long. He maneuvered his wheelchair up the ramp and into the building. The automatic doors made it easy and he wheeled over to where Ken was sitting and signaled the waitress for a cup of coffee. Ken already had one going. "Hi Ken, I hope you haven't been waiting too long," he said as he held out his hand to shake.

Ken grabbed his hand. "Nice to see you. No, I got out a little early. It gave me a chance to unwind a little. It was my first day back on the job and all. It was a little hectic."

"Well, I didn't expect to be seeing you so soon after everything yesterday but my grandson had this notion about the chickens Blaire took, so he took it upon himself to look into it." The waitress brought Shank's coffee and he stopped talking for a minute.
When the waitress left, Shank continued, "You know I got word from a source in the state house that the two chickens Blaire brought in were infected with the AGL virus, which shocked us all. My grandson Jasper, on a hunch of his last night went with his girlfriend to your headquarters in Fort Kent, looking for the chickens." Shank continued to tell the sheriff the whole story and the evidence in the log that Jasper acquired.

Ken shook his head with a smile. "He was asking me questions about the road kill dumpster yesterday when we were together during the chicken coop investigation. I'll check the log out and see if it will stand up and be strong enough evidence."

Shank thought Ken should know about the conversation the Perry brothers had at the Brass Rail in Plaisted, so Shank told him that

Jasper had overheard the Perrys talking about Blaire being on their payroll, about their intentions to close down the Steller's farm and about Freddie Baker being the person that the Perrys had do the poisoning of the chickens on the Steller's farm.

"Now that would just be ruled as hear say, but with this other stuff like the log from the sergeant's desk and if the beer cans and cigarettes from yesterday's investigation turn out to be Freddie Baker's, that would make it solid evidence and more believable," said Ken.

Shank added, "Jasper wants to go to Frenchville this weekend to where this Freddie lives and meet him." He explained to Ken how unhappy with everything Freddie Baker was and how intimidated he felt by the Perrys. "Jasper wants to go and see how true it is about his state of mind. If it is true then, you might be able to get him to turn states evidence against the Perrys."

"It's not generally a good idea to ask a suspect to turn states evidence. How does he know all this about this Freddie Baker, anyway?" asked Ken.

"The girl, Charlotte, that helped him get the chickens out of the dumpster is Freddie Baker's daughter. She lives with her grandmother in Fort Kent and doesn't have much to do with him mostly because of the stepmother. I'm not sure where Jasper knows her from."

"I don't know if I like him playing detective like this. He could get himself in trouble or alert the Perrys and Blaire before we're ready," said Ken.

"I warned him about the same thing and he told me he just wanted to see what his state of mind was and that he wouldn't let anything slip. Then he'd let you know what he found out."

"We don't want him letting the cat out of the bag and having Freddie warning the Perrys about our investigation either."

"I think we can trust him on this. I've found him to be real smart about this type of thing. If we could get Freddie to turn, it might be all we need."

"You're right, there," agreed Silverman, "but it's important not to move too fast on these things sometimes. It never hurts to let things develop."

"You know the findings from the state health department on the AGL virus I mentioned earlier?" Shank asked Ken.

"Yes, that's a pretty bad virus for a poultry farmer, isn't it?"

"You're damn right it is. It would close us down," Shank said. "That's why I got on the phone to Assistant District Attorney, Rockwell Fontaine in Augusta. I have a meeting with him tomorrow in Dairy at six. He got me a twenty-four hour hold on a presumable shutdown of our farm. That's how serious the AGL virus is."

"Wow, you guys are in trouble. I hope you can get yourself out of this one. How do you know this Fontaine fellow?"

"I went to high school with him and used to work with him a little in the early years when I was lobbying for poultry farmers in Augusta. He knows that if my birds had the AGL virus, I would be the first one closing us down. I'm hoping the evidence that Jasper got with that desk sheriff's log last night will be enough to show him what Blaire is trying to pull off. You know, Ken? Jasper found our band numbers on the birds that Blaire threw in the dumpster."

"Is that right?" Ken said in astonishment

"Yes, that's right and the birds that he turned in to the state had the bands removed. So that's telling me that they weren't our birds Blaire turned in."

"It certainly helps your case. Who was the officer that said he saw Blaire throw the birds in the dumpster and verified it?"

"Jasper made a point of getting his name. It was a Charlie Wheeler."

"That makes a difference, because if it was one of Blaire's boys, he would've flat out denied it, but Charlie Wheeler is an honest man and will tell it the way he saw it. I don't think he can be intimidated."

"I sure hope I can persuade Fontaine to stave off the shut down of our farm with this evidence," Shank said with a worried look on his face.

"I will check the desk log and if it all looks normal, then I will just leave it there and subpoena it when we need it. We don't want to bring attention to it because Blaire will lose it somehow. Chances are it was never brought to his attention and he doesn't even know it's in there. If Fontaine wants to call the Sheriff's office about it, have him call me and I can verify it. I should get to know him anyway because when I have to bring charges up on a superior officer, it would be through the DA's office."

"I will call you after my meeting with Rocky Fontaine tomorrow. It's a late meeting so it will be the next day before I get back to you. Thanks for hearing me out, Ken," said Shank.

"I am glad to be of help. I will be checking things on my end also. Remember, use your security system, double check things, and see if you can put Jasper off on his trip to Fort Kent to see Freddie Baker and have patience. Let things develop." Ken stood up and they shook hands and went outside. They got in their cars and went in opposite directions.

* * * *

The next afternoon, Shank was sitting in the Pilot's Grille restaurant in Dairy at three forty-five for his four o'clock meeting with Rocky Fontaine. He had a scotch and water in a tall glass with plenty of scotch and a little water ready for Rocky and a whiskey and ginger in a tall glass for himself with a couple menus ready for ordering as Rockwell Fontaine walked in and came over to the table. Shank stood up slowly and they shook hands and greeted each other warmly.

"Wow, you remembered," referring to the drink. "Let's order and talk business later. I'm starving after being in court all day with a bagel and a coffee for lunch," exclaimed Rocky. "I see you're recovering pretty well from your heart surgery, Shank."

"Yes, I am, thanks. Ordering, that's exactly what I had in mind," Shank said. They both picked up the menu and started looking them over. The waitress gave them a few minutes and then came over and took their order and left. The two men started talking about old times and pleasant times and current times as the waitress came back and fourth, dishing out their meal, serving them in a timely fashion through every course there was, finishing them off with a pitcher of coffee and a dessert.

"I always liked the service and food in this place," Rockwell mentioned. "And you know? It hasn't changed one bit."

Shank shook his head in agreement. Rocky began to speak, "You know I talked to the director of the Health Department in Augusta, John Carmichael, and he remembers you and all you did for your industry in the beginning when things used to be a lot looser. He appreciates all you did for the industry and was happy to give you forty-eight hours to explain things."

Shank said he remembered Carmichael and set out to explain the whole situation. Not leaving out anything from the unusual death of ten or fifteen chickens dying each day for five day to Jasper's bike ride meeting at the Brass Rail in Plaisted. He showed him a copy of the sergeant's desk log from the Fort Kent sheriff's headquarters that he had gotten from Frank Cunningham the day before, and how Jasper acquired it. He explained details right up to Freddie Baker's role in the case and Deputy Ken Silvermen's involvement. Ken just couldn't start accusing Sheriff Dick Blaire, his superior officer in the sheriff's department, of crimes. In conclusion, Shank said, "The fact that our chicken bands were still on the birds that Jasper got out of the dumpster, where Blaire threw them should be evidence enough that he switched our birds and turned in two unmarked birds to the state. All of our birds are banded and Frank LaBreque has the two serial numbers down as the ones Sheriff Blaire took and threw in the dumpster."

"If all of this information checks out, you should have no problem stopping the shut down of your farm," said Rocky.

"If you have to check anything at the Fort Kent headquarters, call Ken Silvermen. Anything that goes through Blaire will be covered up," Shank added.

"I'll do that all right. The thing is, Carmichael will need to know a couple things. One, who brought the AGL virus into this? Where did it originate? Is someone planning to use the AGL virus again? And where is it now?"

"I can't answer any of those questions," replied Shank, "but I will open my doors to him to come in and investigate."

"He will have to do it legally. What I will recommend is since this AGL virus is so deadly, that John get a statewide search warrant to go into every poultry farm in Northern Maine and investigate for the virus. We can take Blaire and the Perrys by surprise and maybe catch him with a vile of it on premises. I will also be assigning an agent to the case because believe me, this isn't the first complaint we have received against Blaire," said Rocky. "We have cases Blaire's involved in going back years and very suspicious ones with him right in the middle of it. This is all very confidential of course"

"So let me get this straight," Shank said, "there will be a team of investigators from the state health department and an agent from the district attorney's office nosing around within the next couple weeks?"

"Yes, probably more than one state agent from the DA's office. I will be talking to the state District Attorney, Alan Applebee about the case and I think he will want to get on this right away and with some force."

"Great," Shank said.

"My advise to you, Shank is not to tell anyone about this and just let things develop. Some things take a little time but when all the ducks are in order, things will happen fast and this guy will be in the slammer before you know it," advised Rocky.

"Someone else told me that," said Shank.

"What's that?"

"Just let things develop," Shank said, "Ken Silvermen said that to me."

"He's right. Just go about your regular business and let us do our job. I don't even want you to call him. You let me take it from here," Rocky said, as he got up and reached for his brief case. "You go home and take care of that lovely wife, Jane, and tell your grandson to cool his heels and leave things to us."

Shank stood up and shook hands with Rocky and then sat back down in his wheel chair. The two men left the restaurant together, continuing the talk of old times and laughing about old tricks they pulled on each other in the past.

Chapter 13
The Stake Out

Shank met with Jasper and Frank again the next day and passed on the 'let things develop' theme to them. To continue to keep the security up and let the DA do his work. He asked Jasper to hold off on his Freddie Baker weekend if he could.

Things went along as usual at the farm for a while. The health inspectors showed up as expected. There were a couple state agents from the DA's office interviewing the people involved in the Steller chicken deaths. They were keeping a very low profile and not drawing anyone's attention to themselves. They came in the same group as the team from the health department. Word came from Frank Cunningham and Dan Cooper that they had been to talk to them. They'd been very professional and thorough and didn't let out any information. Just gathered facts.

Jasper had been in touch with Claire by phone. The last call, Claire suggested that since he was going to be gone for a whole year that maybe they should 'keep their options open'. Jasper was immediately relieved. Claire was so young and he realized that if things were going to work out with them eventually, then they needed this time away to see other people. If they were going to be together, it would happen. It was like leaving it up to fate, if it was meant to be, it would be.

Jasper had kept up a communication with Charlotte and had even taken her out to the movies and had spent one Saturday afternoon hanging out,talking and listening to music. He went over to the animal shelter where she worked to feed the dogs once as well. Buddy and

Jasper helped clean the cages and put the dogs out in the outside pen for a run. Charlotte was able to finish early so they could make it to a four o'clock matinee, the Return of the Jedi.

Jasper's parents had arrived, bringing Claire along with them to the Steller farm on the weekend of the Fourth of July and were staying for a week. They brought Jasper's trunk of clothes that he had been waiting for. He had a nice week with them and did some tourist type things. The Stellers had a camp on Wallgrass Lake and he and Claire enjoyed boating and water-skiing and other similar type activities. He talked to Claire about her college plans and she had fully decided to go to college instead of doing her senior year. She had a college visit planned for the next week at John Hopkins so she had to get back to Landrush.

Jasper was eager to get back to the situation at hand with the investigation. He had heard some reports about the case and the findings for the Steller farm investigation that they'd all been involved in.

He called Charlotte and had arranged to pick her and Buddy up early Saturday morning. He felt out of it, so he decided the next weekend to go to Frenchville and look up Freddie Baker on Friday night and then spend the rest of the weekend with Charlotte and Buddy at the Cleveland Campground on the North end of Long Lake. It was a family campground in the Frenchville area. It was close enough to the kennel where Charlotte worked so it wouldn't be a problem going over to feed and run the animals on Sunday. She had gotten Saturday off.

When he left the farm, he had asked Jane if he could borrow her Dodge van for the weekend. He wanted a vehicle without the markings of the Steller Chicken Farm on it. He would be in Perry Chicken Farm country and he didn't want any problems with being identified as a Steller.

Jasper took route one from Fort Kent to Frenchville hoping to see Sheriff Silvermen patrolling. He knew it was his patrol and he wanted to talk to Silvermen to see how the investigation was going. Sure enough, there he was with his radar set up on a stretch just east of Fort Kent. Jasper pulled in so he was driver side to driver side and they could talk without getting out of the cars. "Hello, Officer Silvermen. Mind if I talk to you a minute?" he said.

"Hi Jasper. No, not at all. I'm just sitting here waiting for my regular shift to end. I have to work a double tonight and don't get off until one a.m. Then on Sunday, I have to work another double. We get this duty one weekend a month in the summer. This is my weekend. What can I do for you?"

"Well, without appearing nosey, I was wondering how the investigation into the Steller case was going."

He hesitated and then said, "You know that job you did and information you got on the chickens thrown in the dumpster by the chief? It was a really big break. I talked to Charlie Wheeler, the cop who said he saw Blaire throw them in the wrong dumpster. He told me he and this other sergeant saw it together and they will both swear on it. It's all in the log just as you said and hasn't been noticed by anyone other than John Burnham, the night sergeant who wrote it in there while you were there and he's too numb to realize what he did. The State agents have gathered the log for evidence and that caused a stir. Blaire wanted to know why and they just said it was part of an ongoing investigation they were doing and that was it. Blaire couldn't do anything about it and couldn't even look over the log before they took it. Boy, was he pissed. It did alert him to an investigation and he is acting real nervous about it."

"Boy, that sounds good. They've got Blaire looking behind his back now. What about our investigation at the farm? Has all that evidence been confirmed yet?"

"Just as you said. Freddie Baker implicated himself in every possible way. The beer, cigarettes, fingerprints. The State agents are going to pick him up real soon and they want to look his car over to find the poison he used in killing the chickens. They're waiting on some stuff they found in the health department search of their farm for evidence having to do with the AGL-virus. And on top of that they have broken several OSHA mandates and will be fined for some of those charges."

"Wow," exclaimed Jasper. "They are really putting the boots to them."

"You do understand Jasper, that this is all confidential. I am only telling you this because you proved yourself quite trustworthy with your previous help in the investigation. By the way, what are you doing up in this neck of the woods?"

"I'm looking for Freddie Baker."

"Jesus Christ, son. What do you want to do that for? Leave it up to the State agents."

"I want to befriend him. I am kind of going out with his daughter and I want to feel him out and see if I can help patch up the rift between the two of them. The Stellers and the investigation won't be mentioned. I am introducing myself to him as Jay Hawk. He won't even know I am related to the Stellers."

"Well, my better judgement tells me for you to leave well enough alone."

"Ok, how about this? I'll meet you here at midnight and I'll tell you how it went and what he's like."

"I don't know where I'll be at midnight. You could call the station and tell them you're my nephew. Leave a number where I can call you. They'll radio me with the message. But whatever you do, for Christ sake, keep you conversation with Freddie to domestic affairs, meaning his daughter." Ken handed Jasper his business card and said, "Call me and be careful."

"I will, and don't worry." he replied

Ken smiled and said, "Too late for that."

"You sound like my Grandfather. Thanks, and I'll call the office at midnight. Bye." Jasper smiled and waved as they both took off in opposite directions,Ken Silvermen toward Fort Kent and Jasper toward Frenchville.

He arrived at the campground around four p.m. and set up camp. He had picked a site right near the sandy beach of Long Lake. He stowed all his gear in the van, leaving a few things in the tent and fed Fido. Fido ate and did his business in the woods and Jasper took the time to look in his atlas to familiarize himself with Frenchville a little better.

Jasper and Fido then drove to Crosses Trailer Park to find Freddie and see if they could pick up his trail and follow him. He figured it was likely he would end up at Pierce's Pub in downtown Frenchville. According to Charlotte, that's where he spent Friday nights. Charlotte had told him that Freddie drove a '75 Mercury Colony Park wagon, silver in color. Jasper drove through the trailer park looking for the wagon.

He spotted Perry's pick-up truck parked next to a double wide that Charlotte had described. There was no Mercury wagon around. Jasper decided to park outside the trailer park for a while and monitor the traffic in and out of the park. He found a spot near the entrance where he had a clear view and was slightly concealed. To someone just driving by he would go unnoticed. Jasper pulled two sandwiches out of his bag to eat while he sat waiting and watching the traffic. It was five thirty.

Traffic was pretty steady with the five o'clock rush just beginning to slow down when suddenly he spotted the silver wagon turning into the trailer park.

Jasper fired up the van and stayed about fifty feet behind him and slowly drove in. He wanted to see who was behind the wheel. The driver went all the way into where the Perry truck was and parked beside it. The driver was Freddie. He recognized him from the picture that Charlotte had in Grandma Rosa's house.

Freddie was about five feet nine with brown longish hair and an always needed a shave look. He had a six pack of Coors light with two missing in it and one in his hand, and a cigarette in his mouth. He made a beeline for the trailer and didn't notice the van drive slowly by. Jasper was satisfied that he'd found Freddie and would resume his watch outside until he left.

After about an hour, a pizza delivery truck turned into the trailer park and he decided to follow it. Sure enough it stopped at the doublewide. The driver was bringing in another twelve pack of Coors light as well as a large pizza.

Jasper went back to his stakeout position and was thinking what it must be like to be a private detective or a federal agent. They had to do a lot of this type of work. He decided he wouldn't like the inactivity.

He drove the van back to the stakeout spot and was just about to turn off the engine when the 1975 Colony Park wagon tore out of the trailer park, squealing tires and roaring down the road towards Fort Kent like a bat out of hell.

Freddie was at the wheel again, pulling on a Coors Light. Wow, Jasper thought, he is in a hurry. He had to pull a U-turn from his spot to get on Freddie's tail. There were a few cars between Freddie and him by the time he caught up. Freddie had slowed down to regular speed. Jasper was happy with his position on the tail so he maintained a couple car lengths. "I wonder why he is going towards Fort Kent instead of toward Pierce's Pub in Frenchville," Jasper thought aloud. He continued to follow the wagon until they were close to downtown Fort Kent and Freddie took a left onto Grandma Rosa's street. "Oh my God, he's going to Charlotte's house," Jasper said to Fido. "What the hell does he want there? I hope nothing's wrong with Rosa, Buddy or Charlotte."

Freddie had stopped in front of their house and ran up to it, keeping the car running. Jasper parked a couple doors up from the house. He watched as Grandma Rosa answered the door and let Freddie in.

Talking out loud to Fido, he said, "He left the car running. I think he just went inside to get something." They watched.

"Look, he's turned every light on up stairs." They watched another minute. "What, is he searching the place? I think every light is on except Buddy's room. I'm going over to look in a window. I don't trust him," said Jasper.

Fido left out his low, throaty growl that told Jasper the dog didn't agree with his decision.

"What?" Jasper said defensively to Fido. "Let me guess, you think you can spy on someone better than me?"

Fido nodded 'yes'. Of course I can sneak around better then you, thought the dog. It's not even a contest. Fido jumped out of the van after Jasper reached over and opened the door.

"Remember to stay low and keep out of sight," he whispered before shutting the door. He had turned the lights off but kept the car running after parking.

Fido quickly crept up onto the front deck that wrapped part way around the house. He snuck to the side living room window that was slightly open with the blind up. He looked back at Jasper, up the street in the van. He thought he saw Jasper give him a thumbs up. He peered in.

Fido had a good view and could see almost everything, because the living room was the main thoroughfare with the stairs and hall branching off of it. There was a lot of commotion. Freddie was going in and out of rooms. Charlotte was saying for him to stay out of Buddy's room.

"I want what's mine, just looking for something. Don't worry about anything. I just need to get this and I'll be outta here. That's all, it doesn't concern any of you I just want what's mine," Freddie said as he went into another room. Fido thought his words were slurred a little bit.

Grandma Rosa began, "If you'll tell me what you want maybe I can help. This is my house, you know. What are you looking for? Stay out of my room." She walked over to the phone, sputtering, "I'm going to call the police on that damn fool if he doesn't get the hell out of here."

Charlotte went over to Rosa, who had started for the phone, and started to console her, both out of the view of Freddie. Just then Freddie came out of Grandma Rosa's room stuffing a gun in the front of his shirt, and then buttoned his Levi jacket. Neither of the ladies saw his quick move with the gun but Fido did. Oh shit, thought the dog, this just got a hell of a lot more complicated.

Freddie immediately started to make nice with Charlotte and Rosa and was already heading for the door. "Well, I don't think it's here after all. Sorry to interrupt your evening." He was in a hurry to leave. Fido recognized this and decided it was time to get back to Jasper.

The dog turned and jumped over the deck railing to run for the van. Jasper closed the van door behind Fido after he jumped in, right as Freddie came out of the house. Freddie stood there for a minute and talked to Rosa in an attempt to calm her down. Jasper put his binoculars to his eyes to try and get a better look at Freddie. As Freddie turned to walk away his jacket swung open and Jasper saw a flash on silver. It looked like the handle of something. Freddie walked over to his wagon and got back on to route one and headed for Frenchville.

Jasper continued to follow Freddie, two car lengths away. "Well, what happened Fido?"

Fido starred blankly at him for a moment and then shook his head.

"Sorry, I know better than that," said Jasper. He and Fido had a very unique method of communicating. Fido could understand English but that didn't mean he could speak it. Jasper had to ask him 'yes' and 'no' questions and occasionally use a form of Charades to figure out what the dog wanted to say.

"Did he hurt anyone?"

Fido shook his head.

"Did he want something?"

Fido nodded and barked enthusiastically.

"Ok. What did he want? Did he want money?"

The dog shook his head.

"Ummm, booze? Was he looking for booze?"

Fido shook his head and began to growl the growl quickly escalated to an angry fierce growl.

Jasper looked over at him surprised. He could see Fido barring his teeth at him and for a second Jasper was actually nervous that Fido was going to bite him.

Fido must have sensed Jasper's apprehension because he immediately stopped and closed his mouth, but never looked away from Jasper.

Then Jasper remembered the flash of silver he thought he'd seen. He looked over at Fido and the dog, knowingly, nodded yes.

"Freddie was looking for a weapon?" he asked knowing he was right.

Fido nodded and yipped.

"What kind of weapon?" but he already knew, "A gun, is that it?"

The dog nodded again.

"Does he have it jammed in his belt?"

Again, another nod.

"Holy shit, Fido!" Jasper thought about slamming on the breaks right there. But he couldn't just stop following Freddie knowing he had a gun, was drinking and was probably under a lot of pressure from the Perrys. "I need to call Charlotte and get her perspective on what's just happened."

Freddie seemed to be driving a little more sanely now but had to be drunk. He'd been drinking all afternoon as far as Jasper could see. He let another car get between them and saw Freddie's blinker go on. He was turning into a convenience store. "I bet he is buying more Coors Light." Jasper pulled in behind Freddie and waited for him to go in the store. As soon as the coast was clear, Jasper got out and walked over to the pay phone out in front. He dialed Charlotte's number.

"Hello, who's this?" Charlotte answered seemingly a little shook up.

"Hi, Charlotte. It's me, Jasper," he said. "You all right? You don't sound so hot."

"Oh Jasper, it's so good to hear your voice. I'm a little shook up. My father just burst in here looking for something and accusing the Perrys of threatening to beat him up or even worse kill him. When he first came in, he was mad as hell and said that they were after him. He said Karen, his wife and he had gotten into a fight and she started screaming at him to watch his back because her brothers would get him if he didn't watch out."

Jasper said, "Calm down now, Charlotte. From what you've told me she has made those threats before towards your father, hasn't she?"

"As a matter of fact, that's what I said to him and he said this time Karen said Sheriff Blaire was going to get in on it."

"Look Charlotte, whatever you do, don't call the sheriff's office and complain about this. I know a sheriff that isn't associated with Blaire and I will make the call for you. So you sit tight and relax and I will call you back when I have notified the right people."

"Is my father in trouble, Jasper?"

"I'm not sure, but Sheriff Blaire is a crooked cop and you can't trust him. So trust me and I will get someone involved that is honest and will look out for your father, ok?"

"Ok, Jasper. Where are you?"

"I'm on the road, on the way to Cleveland campground."

"What do you mean?"

"I decided to come up to Cleveland campground tonight and set up for tomorrow so everything would be ready and we could get an early start."

"So you're not far away then? Can you come over?"

"I'm just down the road a piece. Well, let me make this call and make sure your father's back is covered and then I'll call you back."

"Ok, wait Grandma Rosa wants to talk to you."

Just then Freddie came out of the convenience store and bumped shoulders with Jasper on his way to the Colony Park. Jasper looked away, hiding his face from Freddie and ignored the "excuse me" Freddie offered. He put the phone back to his ear.

"....on Buddy while I talk to Jasper. I think your father woke him up," Jasper heard Rosa saying.

"Ok, Gram, be right back."

Rosa waited for a few seconds, "Jasper, she's gone. I didn't want her to hear this but Freddie got his pistol out of my room and he has it. I don't want him shot, Jasper. He's no good, but he is my son, he's not all bad. I think he is in trouble, Jasper. Maybe even with the law, but I know the Perrys are after him. He told us that."

"Rosa, I understand," Jasper said whispering into the phone. "I have been following him. I saw him at your house. In fact he is right behind me getting into his station wagon so I should get going if I'm going to follow him. Whatever you do, make sure Charlotte stays home. I will have a sheriff on his tail in a few minutes. It won't be Blaire. Don't trust him no matter what happens. He might come there looking for Freddie. Don't tell him anything. Just say you haven't seen him."

"What do you mean you're following him?"

"It's a long story and I will fill you in, just not now. Trust me, Rosa."

"Ok, Jasper. Take care of my boy. He does love Charlotte, you know."

"I'm sure he does. You know Rosa, Freddie is going to have to cooperate with the law in order to get free of them. You understand?"

"I think I know what you're getting at Jasper, but he can't help if he's dead so you watch over him."

"I understand and I'll call back. Tell Charlotte it may be an hour or so. Bye now."

Jasper hung up the phone and ran back to the van where Fido was waiting. Freddie and the station wagon were gone by now. Jasper pulled back out onto route one and raced off down the road after him. He'd only had a brief head start and within a few minutes Jasper could see his tail lights up ahead.

Jasper tailed him for about ten more minutes. If he remembered the landmarks from his atlas he had examined that afternoon, he believed Freddie was headed toward Pierce's Pub after all.
Jasper watched the wagon pull over on the side of the road. He slowed down as he passed and then watched in his rearview mirror. Freddie appeared to be stopping to pee. Jasper sped back up and then turned into a gas station.

He had left Freddie about a mile behind him and he thought he had a pretty good idea where he was headed. Jasper decided this was probably his last chance to call Ken Silvermen before they arrived at Pierce's Pub.

He dialed the Fort Kent Sheriff's department. He was nervous that he was making a mistake calling, but had no other way of getting in touch with Silvermen. "Hello, Sheriff's Department, how can I help you?"

"Yes, My name is... Rick. I'm Ken Silvermen's nephew. I was trying to reach him."

"Well, I'm sorry he is out on patrol right now but I can radio him a message if it's important."

"It is actually. Could you tell him my car is broken down and I'm worried about my father? He can reach me at this number." Jasper then read off the pay phone's telephone number and implored upon the clerk that it was important for Sheriff Silvermen to get the message right away. When he was finished, he hung up. Jasper looked at Fido and said, "Well, if he gets his messages that should get his attention."

Fido and Jasper waited for what felt like forever. They saw Freddie and the wagon speed by and a few minutes later, the pay phone began to ring.

"Hello, Officer," said Jasper.

"What was all that about?" said Silvermen, sounding worried. "I thought you weren't calling until midnight?"

Jasper went over everything from when he picked up Freddie's trail at the trailer park until now.

"Look, I'm in Van Buren now, about an hour and a half away. I'll put on my music and lights and be there in about an hour or less. You just tail him and if he stops, you stay put. If he has a gun, don't get out and follow him. I'm going to head to the pub. If you end up following him somewhere else, call the station back and have them radio me like you did.... Rick. You understand, Jasper?"

He could hear the sheriff's siren come on and the car squealing out. That relieved him a little, knowing he was on his way. "I understand, but the guy is drunk. He's been drinking since I first picked up his tail and he just stopped and picked up another twelve pack. I figure he's going to Pierce's Pub in Frenchville. What will I do then?"

"Like I said, if he stops, don't go in there with him. Just wait and watch outside. Alcoholics can drink an amazing amount of beer and still seem in control. I'll call for back up and have him stopped and booked on a DWI charge. He still has a thirty minute drive to Frenchville."

"No, Ken. Don't call your office. Blaire will get word of it and pick him up. Then he'll be dead."

"Look Jasper, there are a lot of good cops in the department. I know which ones to call. Besides, one of the cops I'm calling is off duty and he will be in an unmarked car. The longer we talk, the less time I have to get you help, you just follow him and that's it. Bye." He hung up.

"Just like that he hung up, Fido. I don't know what I'll do if Freddie stops. He said not to follow him on foot, but I told Grandma Rosa I would watch out for him and not let them shoot him."

Jasper walked back to the van and got in with Fido. As he was preparing to pull out, a blue Pinto with Charlotte inside pulled in and parked beside him. Charlotte got out and jumped in beside him, sending Fido to the back seat.

"So you thought you were going to do this without me huh, sport?" Charlotte said, as she shut the door and buckled up.

"You shouldn't be here, Charlotte. You need to go home, now."

"No fucking way. I'm in this till the end. Why were you following my old man anyway? Is he in trouble?"

"How are you even here right now?" Jasper asked as he gunned it back out onto route one and sped up to search for Freddie's station wagon.

"I picked up the other line when you were talking to Grandma Rosa," she said casually. "I heard most of what you were saying. So why are you following him?"

"Actually I originally wanted to meet him and get to know him and maybe befriend him to try to get some help for him. I chose this weekend to follow him and maybe meet him at Pierce's Pub to talk to him and invite him to spend the day with us tomorrow and then see what happened. Instead, he threw me this curve ball and headed for Fort Kent and your Grandmother's house. From there, you know what happened. Do you have any idea where he's going? I was thinking Pierce's Pub. Isn't that this way?"

"Yeah, that's down this way. He could also be going to the Rod and Gun club that the Perrys hang out at. It's on Route 162 near Ouellette. They usually get tanked up there and then hit Pierce's Pub. There ain't as many options up here as there are in Landrush."

"Oh great, a Rod and Gun club. That's just what we need. What did Freddie say when he first came into the house?"

"He said he got in a fight with Karen and she told him her brothers were going to put him in the hospital with the help of Sheriff Blaire and he better watch his back."

"You know he got a gun out of your grandmothers room, right?"

"Yes, I heard Rosa tell you that. There he is!" Charlotte said pointing out the windshield at the pair of rear lights that just popped into view. "You see the right tail light is a little dimmer than the left?"

"I can see it. Do you think he would use it? The gun I mean?"

"Well, yes. If he was threatened or shot at he would fire back. Wouldn't you?"

"I suppose so, but it would be stupid of him to go into the Rod and Gun club with the Perrys in there and no one with him. He'd be asking for it. What does he want to do, get it over with?"

"It looks like he is checking the parking lot of Pierce's Pub," continued Charlotte. "He may be looking for the Perrys or his wife. I don't know who he is looking for."

"Lets just wait and watch here and see if he goes in," suggested Jasper. "You keep your head down. Someone might recognize you." Jasper pulled into the parking lot and found a spot half way back and not too far from the road, just incase they needed to leave quickly. "There's a Perry's truck over there. It might be the one his wife is driving. A truck like that was parked in front of their trailer. I just assumed Karen was driving it."

"Look, he's going in," she said. "What should we do?"

"My sheriff friend told me not to get out of the car even if Freddie left did.

"Look, Freddie doesn't know you and neither does Karen. Just go in and scope it out and then you'll have more to tell your sheriff friend. I don't want my father hurt even though he is a dickhead."

"Ok, maybe you're right."

"Do you have a fake ID? They check everyone. They claim it's the law."

"Of course not."

"Just a minute," Charlotte grabbed her purse and fumbled through it and pulled out a fake ID for him. "Take this, they don't check it close they just need one to cover the law."

"What, you carry fake IDs around? What's up with you? What will I find out next?"

"Jasper, cool it. Just get in there and check it out. Don't hang out long, just case it out. I swear if you take to long I'll come in."

"Don't come in. I'll be in and out, I promise. What about getting close and listening to their conversation?"

"It will be to loud to hear anything. They have a band and it's loud."

"What else do you know about this place?"

"There is a five dollar cover charge. Have the five dollars and the ID card ready and just go in, I'll talk to you in a few minutes."

"Give me more time than a few minutes, it will take a few minutes for my eyes to adjust to the darkness." Jasper got out of the van to case the joint and to see what was up.

"I'll be in there in twenty minutes if you're not out," called Charlotte. "It's eleven-ten now. Get out of there by eleven thirty, and oh yeah. The bouncer's name is Bubba. Treat him nice."

Jasper nodded and walked into Pierce's Pub. Bubba stopped him, apparently you did have to show your ID and it did cost five dollars. Jasper got a stamp of a guitar on the back side of his hand. It was dark and the band, "THE WOOS GOWES," were loud.

He said to Bubba, "How you doing, Bubba? Thanks, this is for you. My name is Jay." He put another five in the breast pocket of his shirt. Bubba was a big, mean looking Frenchman with a goatee and muscles so big he had no neck. He reminded Jasper of a huge lumberjack.

Bubba raised his eyebrows and scowled at him for the small contribution and then cracked an ever so small smile and stepped aside for him to pass with no words. It did take Jasper's eyes a few minutes to adjust and he stood just beyond the bouncer until that happened. He took the long way around to get to the bar, observing and scanning the crowded room as he went.

He stopped at the restroom on the way around. He leaned against the wall in the hallway and saw Bubba looking over at him. He nodded. Then he spotted Freddie, Karen and one of the Perry brothers, the middle one, Jake, the dumbest of the lot sitting over across the room. Jake seemed to be sitting up in Freddie face and giving him a lot of shit. Karen kept hitting him in the shoulder every few seconds. Seemingly to drive a point across that Jake was making.

Jasper sensed trouble for Freddie and began making his way through the crowd to get to the table. He had to cross a twenty by twenty parquet wooden dance floor across the front of the band. The table they were at was the closest one to the band, with not a lot of people near it. Jasper had a good view because he was peering straight across the front of the band where no one was dancing.

He jumped on the floor and started in dancing, with his last look at Bubba, who was still watching him. Jasper was glad, he was his back up. The "Woos Gowes" were playing "Joy to The World" and the place was rocking. He didn't look out of place dancing across the floor.

He was ten feet away when he saw a flash of steel come from Jake's hand. It was coming up from under the table. Jake had produced a switchblade and was doing a forward thrust toward Freddie's chest. At the same instant, Jasper leapt and caught the bend of Jake's elbow before it was fully extended. He hit Jake with a solid body block as he pushed into him. Jake in turn pushed into Karen.

They landed in a heap in the corner of the booth, with Jasper on top. In that same instant, Freddie was reaching for the inside of his coat and Jasper knew what was there. He put his foot out and on the bend of Freddie's right arm that was reaching for the gun and stopped him. Attracting very little attention in the close quarters, Jay hollered, "Not here, Freddie. And Jake, I'll take that knife," as he pried it out of his hand.

Jasper could feel Bubba behind him and shouted at them again so Bubba could hear, "You guys can take this outside, there will be know fighting in here. Bubba and I like to keep it peaceful in here. You are to leave now, one at a time unless you'd like us to call the cops," Jasper handed Bubba Jake's knife and gestured who he had taken it from. "You, Jake. Go now and leave. Don't wait for Freddie outside. Just get in your car and go. Bubba, do you want to show this guy out?" Jasper looked at Bubba and raised his eyebrows, hoping for support.

"Yeah, Yeah Jay. Nice job here. You come with me." Bubba reached in and pulled Jake up by the jacket with his feet not touching the floor and walked him over to the band entrance, a few feet away, and threw him out on to the back alley pavement. Bubba walked back to the table and looked down at the three remaining.

No one in the bar acknowledged the incident with the exception of a few dancers. They viewed it as Bubba just doing his job. The music never stopped and the band played on. Jasper had stopped a real serious problem in the bar and Bubba realized it. He said to Bubba, "I'll see these two out and catch you later?"

Bubba looked him over and scowled, "Make sure you do." Bubba turned and walked away towards the front of the pub.

Jasper looked at his watch. Wow! He thought, all of this took just ten minutes. It was twenty past eleven. He had ten minutes before Charlotte came in. "Do you think you two can control yourself or will I need to call Bubba over here again?"

"Fuck off. How do you know us anyway?" Karen said.

"It's our job to know what's going on in the bar. What are you pounding on Freddie for?" Jasper shot back.

"What do you want?" Freddie said. "Who are you?"

Jay smirked "I am just keeping the peace here with Bubba. You, Karen. It's time for you to go. Out this back door and keep on walking. You, sir, can stay there a few more minutes." He indicated to Freddie to stay put. As he walked Karen over to the back door, he looked over at Bubba and signaled to him, and let her out the door.

He went back and sat with Freddie. "Look Freddie, I'll level with you. I'm Charlotte's boyfriend. My name is Jay Hawk. She loves you and was worried about you when you left Rosa's house with the gun you have in your pants. So she called me. It looks like she had good reason. I just stopped you from getting stabbed in the chest. Charlotte's outside in my van. Why don't we go out there and talk things over before you get in a situation where you have to use that gun?"

Freddie looked more than surprised. "You mean you two have been following me?"

"Yes, since you left your mother's. Charlotte called me and we have been on your tail." Jasper saw no reason to get into all the other explanations of why he was following him. "So, what do you say? Lets go talk to Charlotte."

Freddie said, "Fine, lets go."

"We'll wait a minute and make sure Karen is gone."

"I didn't know Charlotte had a boyfriend."

"There's a lot you don't know about Charlotte. Maybe it's time you got to know her a little better. She's a wonderful kid, you know."

"I'd like to go back to the way it used to be but things are different now. I got into a lot of shit I can't get out of and things will never be the same."

"Well, things will never be exactly the same, but they may not all be bad. You stick with Charlotte and me and maybe things will work themselves out. Lets go, Charlotte's waiting."

They got up and Freddie reached for his beer. Jay stopped him. "Seriously, Freddie?"

Freddie gave up on his drink without a fight.

Jasper looked over to Bubba near the front who had been watching Jake and Karen leave.

Bubba nodded that the coast was clear and Freddie and Jasper left through the back door. Bubba watched them leave the pub, still scowling slightly.

Chapter 14
Frenchville

BUBBA met them at the end of the alley and stopped Jasper. "I went along with you but what the hell was that all about?"

Jasper put both hands up and said, "I guess I owe you an explanation. I thought Freddie here might be in trouble and I needed back up and didn't think I had time to explain, so I did what I did."

Just then, Charlotte came up behind them and said, "Hey Bubba, whatcha doing these days?"

Bubba looked over to see Charlotte and a big baby faced grin appeared and they did a high five and continued all the way through to the razzle dazzle handshake and a hug. "What are you doing here girl? Aren't you up late?"

"You gave me tomorrow off, remember? So I am up late. Oh, Jay here is my boyfriend and he and I were looking for my father. Daddy, ah Freddie, Jay, this here is Bubba Stovel. My boss from the kennel I work at."

Greetings were exchanged and Bubba said, "Jay, you handled yourself pretty well in there."

"Well, thanks. I did what I had to do and as fast as I could without a lot of fuss."

"It would be wise to stay out of this place," Bubba added.

"Yeah, you're right. We've gotta get going." They shook hands with Bubba and headed for the van. Freddie was staggering along and it seemed like he might trip and fall, so Charlotte walked him over to the van and they got in the back. Charlotte and her father were talking, but Freddie didn't seem too coherent.

"We should get outta here and find a place to hide your father," Jasper suggested.

"Yeah, I think so too," agreed Charlotte.

Jasper looked in the rearview mirror and saw Freddie slouched over to the side with his mouth open, snoring away. Jasper reached around in his seat and pulled open Freddie's jacket.

"What are you doing?" Charlotte asked.

"I'm just going to take his gun and put it away," he answered as he carefully removed the gun from Freddie's belt. He turned back around and locked the gun in the glove box.

Jasper continued speaking as he pulled the van back out onto route one, "I'm glad he's asleep, Charlotte because I wanted to talk to you and bring you up to date on the trouble Freddie's in. I'd rather he was sober when he hears what I'm about to say. And that won't be till morning."

"He's in trouble with the law, isn't he?" said Charlotte.

"Yes, he is, but how bad it is depends on his cooperation."

"Oh shit, Jasper. Look behind us," Charlotte said with panic in her voice.

Jasper looked in the rearview and saw the blue lights of a Sheriff behind them, trying to pull them over. "Wow, that was fast. We've only gotten a mile away. The Perrys must have gone straight to Chief Blaire. We'll have to stop," he said.

"No, at the house you said not to trust the sheriff," Charlotte protested.

"We can't run and give them cause to come after us," he replied as he pulled over. They both held their breath as they watched the sheriff get out and approach their vehicle.

Jay rolled down the window as the officer approached. He let out a sigh of relief as he saw it was Ken Silvermen. "You scared us to death," he said.

"I saw you pull out of Pierce's Pub, but I wanted to wait till you were a little ways down the road before I stopped you."

"Why? What's going on?" Jasper asked.

"You first, Jasper. Who are these people and what happened back there?"

“This is Freddie Baker in the back and his daughter Charlotte, who is a friend of mine,” he said.

“Jasper, no!” said Charlotte, still sounding nervous.

“Don’t worry, Charlotte. This is one sheriff we can trust, I know him.”

“Tell me what happened back there. Does he still have the gun?”

“No, I took it from him. It’s in the glove box.”

“Here. Why don’t you give it to me so it’s secure,” Silvermen said putting out his hand.

“Sure,” said Jasper as he reached over to rummage through the glove box for the gun. “You don’t need to worry about us using it, I hate guns.”

“I’m sure that’s true Jasper, but it’s a gun,” said Silvermen. “The first thing you do is get the gun and then you know your safe. It was smart of you to put it away like you did.”

He handed the sheriff the gun through the van window.

“Thanks,” Silvermen said with a smile. “Why don’t you get out for a minute and come talk to me at my car. No offense Charlotte, he’ll be right back. I promise.”

Charlotte looked anxious and uncertain as Jasper got out of the car and walked toward the rear of the van. Silvermen took the key out of the van’s ignition as he turned to follow Jasper.

“So listen,” began Ken. “Ten minutes ago, Chief Blaire radioed me. He has put an APB out on Freddie for attempted murder of Jake Perry at Pierce’s Pub. What went on there anyway?”

“Well, about an hour ago, shortly after I talked to you. I ran into Charlotte and we went to the pub together. I went inside to find Freddie. He was with Karen and Jake. They started arguing and Jake tried to stab him. I stopped Jake. Freddie might have pulled out his gun if I hadn’t been there. Then, with the help of bouncer, Bubba Stovel, I quieted things down and Jake and Karen were kicked out. I stayed with Freddie and here we are.”

“I thought I said to stay out of the bar,” Ken said narrowing his eyes. “But I guess I’m glad you didn’t,” he added quickly. “Look, I’m going to be a while. Blaire will arrive at Pierce’s in less than ten minutes. He doesn't realize I was already on my way. I want to steer Blaire in another direction. I want to get Freddie into a safe house before Blaire catches up with him."

"Look, Blaire has nothing on Freddie. Bubba Stovel saw the whole thing."

"Jasper, that doesn't matter with Blaire. He probably wants Freddie dead so he won't turn states evidence. He will shoot him and claim self defense like he did with your friend, Paulsie."

"What?" Jasper said. "You can you prove that?"

"More confidential material, Jasper."

"Look Ken, you can trust me by now."

"I know I can, but I want you to be aware of what I am telling you."

"I understand Ken, I know how to keep my mouth shut."

"Do you? How much does that girl in there know?"

"Only a little, don't worry. I'm not going to blow the whole investigation. Plus, I can trust her. She wants to help her father."

"You tell her what you want about the Steller investigation, but I swear to God, don't tell her a god damn thing about Paul Skater."

Jasper nodded agreement.

Silverman let out a long sigh and said, "The State agents thinks Freddie Baker was at the scene and knows a whole lot about Paul Skater's murder."

"Oh my God, you've got to be kidding."

"They don't kid about those things, Jasper. That's another reason why Blaire wants Freddie... controlled. The state wants to get Freddie into their custody for his protection."

"That would be great, but how do we avoid Blaire?" Jasper asked.

"I hate to put you in harms way, but I'll have to take a little more time and make sure Blaire and his deputies are going in the other direction. I'll catch up with you when I know Blaire has cleared out, and then I want to bring Freddie in to the Eagle Lake State Police barracks."

Ken gestured for Jasper to return to the van and handed him back the keys as he was climbing in.

"Do you know a spot two miles down the road here, east of Frenchville?" asked Silvermen. "Off the road, across from the old abandoned fire barn, there is a stand of trees. You know where I'm talking about?"

"Sort of," said Jasper, not entirely certain.

"I know," Charlotte piped in. "Where that old dirt road runs behind the wooded lot?"

"That's the place," Ken said. "I want you guys to drive there, shut off your lights and stay put. I might meet you there in thirty minutes or it might be a couple hours, but I want you to stay there until I can come for you. It's the only way to keep Freddie safe. You understand, Charlotte? You and your father need to wait there with Jasper if there's any hope that I can help you."

Charlotte and Jasper both nodded understanding.

Ken Silvermen turned and walked back to his truck.

As Jasper put the van in gear and pulled back onto the road, Ken pulled a U-turn and headed back toward Pierce's Pub.

"Look Jasper, I don't want to turn my father in," Charlotte started. "Are you going to tell me what's going on now?"

"We need to talk Freddie into turning himself in. Here, I'll tell you the whole story. Sheriff Silvermen is working with State agents of the District Attorney's office to gather evidence on Blaire to arrest him. Oh yeah, this is all confidential so don't repeat it." Jasper knew Silvermen would shit a brick if he knew he was telling her, but he trusted her.

"Jesus, how much trouble is he in?" Charlotte put her hands to her head in dismay.

"Not as much as you think if he turns states evidence. Now listen and I'll fill you in on all I know."

Jasper proceeded to tell Charlotte everything about the investigation at the Steller farm. He told her about the cigarette butts and the Coors Light cans. How it was all traced back to her father. Jasper told her how Blaire and the Perrys had manipulated Freddie to get back at the Stellers. Fido cringed to himself a few times as he listened to Jasper spill the beans. Fido liked Charlotte despite her occasional dishonesty, but he felt Jasper was too often naive about her.

As Jasper was explaining things, they passed the dirt road turn off from where Silvermen had told them to wait.

"Jasper," Charlotte said. "That was the turn off. Aren't we going to wait for your friend?"

"I would, but I don't want the State agents to take Freddie till we talk some sense into him. No one knows I'm at Cleveland Campground. We'll be safe there. So long as we're not stopped before we get there. I don't think Blaire knows about my vehicle yet."

"Jasper, did you really save my father's life in Pierce's?"

"Well, maybe. But not without Bubba's help. Jake was about to stab him when I jumped in."

Realizing he hadn't explained the events that happened in the bar, told her about Freddie's argument with Karen and Jake. He couldn't help himself and he also told her about Paul Skater's murder investigation six years ago. He now had to ask Charlotte to help him persuade Freddie to turn himself in to the State agents.

"So what's the story? My father will go to jail for poisoning your grandfather's chickens? What's his part in this murder?"

"Well, that depends on whether he cooperates with the police and how involved he was in the murder."

"How would that go?" questioned Charlotte.

"I can't say for sure, " he continued. "Only the sheriff and DA's office can say. I think that if he cooperates fully, he could come out of this with little or no jail time."

"Man, I don't want him going to jail."

"In all honesty, I think this is his best way out."

"He will need to be protected," worried Charlotte. "There are a lot of Perry people out there and he would be in trouble with them and that's not even counting that Sheriff Blaire."

"If Freddie turns states evidence they would put him into a protective custody program," Jasper continued. "He could go into rehab, get some counseling, dry out and be protected while he's doing it. Otherwise he will be arrested and prosecuted with the others."

"He doesn't deserve that. They were using him," exclaimed Charlotte.

"We have to convince him and make sure he knows it's his only chance," he said. "It will be a little ugly but there's no other way. Also, Freddie should to be convinced that you still love him and will stand by him. If he knows you're there for him, he has something to live for. Try not to fight with him."

"That will be a chore. We haven't talked with each other in three years without fighting. You heard us on the phone back at Pinetree Campground in Wiscasset."

"I guess there is no time like the present to start. Here's the campground now," Jasper said.

He turned into the entrance and drove directly to his campsite. It was about a half a mile in the woods on the lake. "Lets get Freddie in the tent and get ready for bed ourselves to get some sleep. I need to get in touch with Sheriff Silvermen. Should you call Rosa before bed?"

"Yes, I should call her. She'll worry all night especially knowing Daddy left with that gun."

"All right, lets get Freddie in the tent and we can leave Fido to guard him. There's a pay phone up near the bathrooms we can use."

They helped Freddie into the tent after a brief stop in the woods for him to pee. He passed out again as soon as his head hit the tent floor. Charlotte and Jasper then left Fido in charge of the site and walked the short distance to the restrooms. It was twelve thirty in the morning by now and the campgrounds was very quiet.

Charlotte called Rosa and told her not to worry. She told Rosa that they had found Freddie and persuaded him to lock the gun away. Charlotte told Rosa that she and Freddie were staying the night at Jasper's grandparents. She promised to call in the morning.

"You lied to her about what happened?" Jasper inquired, raising an eyebrow with a sly smile.

"She'd just worry all the more if she knew Blaire was out to get him. I'll set her straight once Daddy has given himself up to the state agents. She thinks you're Freddie's guardian angel."

"So you think we can convince him, then?"

"Well, that depends on a lot."

Jasper then picked up the phone and called the Sheriff's headquarters as he had done before to reach Silvermen. "Hi, this is Rick Silvermen,

Ken's nephew," he lied. "I talked to you earlier? I'm still waiting to hear from my uncle?"
"Well, sonny," said the operator. "I'm afraid Ken is rather busy on patrol right now. He probably won't have time to call you for while."
"I understand, can I have you give him a new number to reach me at when he has a chance?"
Jasper then gave the operator the number to the pay phone and hung up the receiver.
"Aren't you at all worried that they will trace the call and send Blaire's cronies out to get us?" asked Charlotte.
"Not really," explained Jasper. "First they'd have to realize that Ken was doing his own off the record investigation. Then they'd have to realize he must know where Freddie had disappeared too. I don't think Blaire has any reason to be suspicious of Silvermen. I'm not sure the Fort Kent sheriff's headquarters has the ability to trace a call that easily anyway."
Charlotte simply shrugged her shoulders, not completely convinced and the pair waited for Silvermen to call. They waited for a while, much longer than Jasper had waited at the gas station for the first call. After a half hour, Charlotte was growing restless.
"You see? It was a mistake, he's not going to call back," she said.
"You don't know that," he responded. "He probably has to wait for an opportune time to call us back. If you want to go back to the tent, I'll…."
Just then the phone began to ring. Charlotte was startled and jumped a foot in the air when it did.
Jasper picked it up. "Hello?"
"Hello, Ken Silvermen here, Rick is that you?"
"It's me, uncle. How's work going?"
"Jasper, I talked to the State agents after Blaire left Pierce's Pub. They came by and seized Freddie's car for evidence. They towed it to an undisclosed location. They'd like me to bring Freddie in tonight."
"Can't you serve him the papers later?" He looked at Charlotte and shrugged his shoulders.
"Jasper, the state agents want Freddie, for his own protection. Where did you go? You were supposed to stay put."

"Is it really necessary to pick him up tonight? Charlotte and I can keep him safe." "You bet it's necessary. If Blaire picks him up, he's dead. The agents want to get
him as soon as possible. I explained that he was drunk and passed out and with his family. They agreed to pick him up tomorrow as long as I could assure that he was safe.."
"It seems to me they should pick up some of the Perrys and Blaire and his Deputies."
"That can't happen until they're sure Freddie will turn. So they have to get him first and see what's up. Where are you guys now? I want to make sure Blaire is not in your area. I am responsibility for Freddie's safety now."
"We're going to a friend of Charlotte's that no one knows about. I'll see you tomorrow."
"I should know where he is, Jasper." Silvermen sounded angry.
"I'll call you if anything else develops, Bye." He hung up, feeling a stab of guilt that he was giving Silvermen, who had done nothing but helped him a hard time.
"They want him tomorrow? So he is going to jail?" Charlotte replied.
"No, not jail, protective custody as long as he cooperates. That's our job now, to convince him he's gotta turn himself in."
In the morning, Jasper was up and had a fire going and coffee on. It was eight–thirty. He had started cooking bacon and had fed Fido. It was a really nice morning and looked like it may get hot later.
Charlotte poked her head out of the tent and said, "I smell bacon."
"Well, come on out and have some coffee. The food will be ready in a few minutes."
"I'll do that, but I am going down to take a shower and use the facilities first." She grabbed Jasper's towel of the line and headed for the rest rooms.
When she returned, Charlotte sat at the picnic table with him and ate breakfast.
"You know, we're not going to have much time to talk to Freddie before the agents will want him," Jasper said.
"I know," she replied. "I feel so bad about it that I don't know what to do. He will feel like I sold him out."

"Let's take the approach that the Perrys are after him and Blaire is after him and that the DA's office wants to help him. He can't hide and he should take the safest option."

"Yeah, that sounds easier than it's going to be." Just then, Freddie stuck his head out of the tent.

He saw Charlotte, "Where the hell am I? Charlotte, what the hell's going on? Who the fuck are you?" he said, looking wide eyed at Jasper.

"Hi, Daddy," Charlotte said as cheery as she could. "Good morning, this is Jasper."

"I saw you last night," again refereeing to Jasper. "I don't remember where. Why didn't you take me home, Charlotte? Where are we? I got to go to the bathroom."

Charlotte shot in, "Jasper will take you to the rest area and we can talk when you get back. Then you can have some breakfast."

Jasper grabbed his towel and bath kit and lead Freddie toward the path to the rest area. Freddie went along. "We'll be right back," he said. He nodded to Fido and the dog followed along behind to help keep an eye on Freddie.

They were back shortly and Freddie looked a little better after cleaning up. Freddie walked over to the picnic table,picked up his coffee and sat down in front of bacon, eggs and hash browns. Charlotte gave him two aspirin to start off with.

Jasper walked aside with Fido and knelt down patted him and said, "If Freddie takes off, stop him. Don't hurt him, just scare him and keep him here." He walked over to the table and sat down.

As Freddie was eating, Charlotte told him where he was and explained what had happened last night. "Jake Perry tried to stab you and Jasper stopped him. You were in Pierce's Pub."

"I remember Karen and Jake were giving me a lot of shit and trying to start a fight. He was yapping at me and she kept hitting my chest and then I don't remember what happened. You broke in and next thing I know that big guy Bubba was there and threw Jake out and then Karen left. I don't know exactly how it went," Freddie said as he continued to eat.

"You got it pretty close," said Jasper.

"You still haven't told me why you didn't take me home, Charlotte."
"There are a couple reasons for that and you have to stop and listen closely," said
Charlotte. "Jasper, you tell him. You know more about it than I do."
"Ok, first of all Freddie, I called a friend of mine from the Fort Kent Sheriff's
Department. He told me that Chief Blaire has put out an APB on you to pick you up on charges for the attempted murder of Jake Perry at Pierce's. I know that's bogus because I was there and if anything, Jake tried to stab you. He wants you for something else. Do you know anything about that?"
Freddie got very nervous about that and started looking around like he might run. "I know a little bit about a lot of things and I know I don't want anything to do with Blaire. I'd rather deal with the Perrys."
Jasper put in, "You're safe here, Freddie. That's why we came here last night. My friend said for us to stay put till he could arrange for someone to pick you up and keep you safe."
"Who's your friend?" Freddie asked nervously.
"My friend is a sheriff who works directly with State agents of the District Attorney's office."
"What do you mean the DA's office?" Freddie stood up and walked over to the
tent and looked in it. "What are you doing? Setting me up?"
"If you're looking for that gun, Daddy, it's gone," said Charlotte. "Jasper gave it to his sheriff friend. If you use that gun for anything you will surely go to jail. Listen to Jasper and hear him out."
"You bitch, Charlotte. Turning your own father in," he hollered and started toward her.
Fido was up and between them in an instant, coming out with a deep growl that took Freddie by surprise. Freddie backed away very cautious of the dog.
"Freddie, will you sit down at the table and talk this through?" asked Jasper.. This was a pivotal time to get Freddie to listen.
"I'm leaving," said Freddie as he started to walk away, heading for the path to the rest area and the way out of the campsite.

Charlotte, already standing, started towards him. Jasper held up his hand and signaled her to stop. "Fido will keep him here," he said to Charlotte.

Fido ran over to the path and confronted Freddie with another growl. Freddie turned and started to go through the woods, then picked it up running. Fido shot out after him and fronted him again and really showed his teeth and had Freddie running back towards them.

Jasper told him, "Freddie he won't let you go till you talk this out. And Blaire has an APB out on you. I don't think you would get far. That leaves you no choice but to sit down and listen. You're through running."

Freddie stood there, looking angrily at the dog, then at Jasper and finally at Charlotte.

"Please Freddie, sit down and listen," Charlotte pleaded, "I love you and want you protected from the Perrys and this Blaire cop. It doesn't matter what you've done. Rosa, Buddy and I will be there for you. We can be a family again. This is serious stuff and they will kill you. Jake has already tried and if it wasn't for Jasper, you would be stabbed already.Who knows, you might even be dead."

Freddie hung his head and rolled his shoulders down, looking again in all directions. Dejected, he walked over to the picnic table and sat down quietly.

Jasper started in, explaining the situation to Freddie. "The agents wanted to pick you up last night but we asked them to hold off until we talked to you this morning. They have already confiscated your car out of Pierce's Pub parking lot. They know about you poisoning the chickens at Steller's for the Perrys. The DA has evidence of wrong doings on the part of Chief Blaire and a couple of his deputies. That's why the DA is involved, because he's the head of the department and it can't be handled by any of his subordinates. After they talk to you and if you turn yourself in to them, they will pick up Blaire and the Perrys and they will be arrested and prosecuted. If you don't turn states evidence, then you will be arrested and prosecuted along with them and serve jail time for sure. If you turn, then who knows. You might not have to serve any time at all. That will be up to the state. I know it

will be a lot better if you cooperate with them." Jasper stopped and let Charlotte take over.
"Daddy, please cooperate with them. The state will protect you. They will keep everyone away from you until after the trial. You can make a deal with them to get the very minimum of punishment for whatever you've done. We will visit you if we can and you will be safe for the first time in a while. Life doesn't have to be like it's been. You can be free of Karen and the intimidation by the Perrys. You have already filed for divorce and it will be final by the time the trial is over. You can go into a rehab clinic and dry out and get some counseling and we can be a family again like it used to be before Mom died." Charlotte had hit home with that comment. Freddie was bent over, sobbing and she went over and hugged him, soothing him.
He was a broken man at this point. It had to happen before he could build himself back up. They all sat there and said nothing for a long while. Fido even came up and nudged Freddie's leg. Freddie patted him on the head and then put his head down on the table and cried some more.
Jasper excused himself to use the bathroom and gave them a little time to talk privately. He had told Fido to stay a keep an eye on Freddie. Jasper walked over to the pay phone and called Ken Silvermen at home. Ken picked up the phone after only one ring. "Ken? Freddie's ready send in the agents, but take it easy on him. I think he'll turn."
"How sure are you?" Ken said.
"At least 80 percent as long as you don't spook him."
"Where are you?"
Jasper was still a bit reluctant to give up his location. "Where can we meet you?"
"Jasper, they have an APB out on you as well for helping Freddie at Pierce's Pub. The state agents want you to be picked up also for your protection."
"What? Charlotte's not safe either then."
"The only reason they haven't got you already is because you're driving your grandmother's van. It won't be long before they figure that out."
"What should I do?" he said.

"Where are you now?"

Jasper explained what had happened last night, this morning and where they were. Now that Blaire wanted all of them, no one was safe.

"Why don't they just pick up Blaire and his cronies."

"I've been over that. They need to talk with Freddie, and know that he will cooperate. They have to be sure they have a case. If everything goes right, they'll pick them up on Monday, but they have to get Freddie and know you're safe first. I'll tell you what, stay put and I'll talk to the state agents. Call me back in half an hour. I think we better listen to them. This time don't leave."

"Ok," Jasper said before he hanging up the receiver. He walked over to the campsite and explained things to Charlotte and Freddie.

"What do they have an APB out on you for?"

"Who knows, accessory to this attempted murder charge? He has it out for Freddie. Blaire writes the law around here. Hopefully Freddie will help put him away. Blaire is a real bad cop. Freddie is doing a courageous thing. Believe me."

Freddie added, "Blaire is a murderer, that's what he is."

Meanwhile as they waited, Jasper started to break camp and put things in the van. "We might as well put everything in the van. I guess our weekend is over here." Charlotte started to help and Jasper motioned her to stay and keep Freddie company. When he was finished, he called Ken back.

"Hey, Jasper, we're in a little trouble. Blaire has put an APB out on all Steller vehicles. I'm not working, but I was listening to my police scanner. Plus the state agents have a line in to the DMV. The heard that Blaire called to get all your grandfather's plate numbers, makes and models of all his vehicles. Blaire wants you bad and he knows Freddie is with you. It's in connection with the Pierce's Pub incident. He wants to make an arrest and put you all out of commission."

"What? I don't believe this. That whole list of charges are false."

"We all know that," Ken said, "the state agents have already talked to Bubba Stovel, the bouncer, and are getting his statement now to clear you and Freddie. Tell Charlotte she doesn't have to go to work Sunday. Agent Johnson told Bubba you all would be in protective custody till at least Monday"

"Good, Bubba is the only one who saw what happened," Jasper explained.

"We have two state trooper cruisers on the way and you'll get an escort. Now look, we don't think you should move since you're right in Blaire's back yard. The state agents will meet you at the camp ground and escort you to the state trooper barracks at Eagle Lake. Are you all set with that?"

"I guess we'll have to be. What choice have we got? We'll wait here for the state troopers to arrive."

"Ok, should be about thirty or forty minutes out." Click.

Jasper returned to the site again and brought Charlotte and Freddie up to date on the call. Freddie seemed a little nervous about the wait.

Charlotte said, "Jasper, I'm going to the restroom while we wait, be right back."

"Take Fido with you," he replied.

Fido and Charlotte were gone for a few minutes. Jasper had the van all ready to roll and packed up. They were waiting in it when all of a sudden Fido arrived in a dead run with Charlotte right behind him. Jasper could sense something was not right. He jumped out of the van with Freddie following.

Charlotte gasped for air as she tried to talk and said, "Fido spotted a sheriff cruiser and it's not Silvermen."

"How do you know? You got a look at his face?"

"I know because the license plate said CHIEF on it," Charlotte said still gasping. "If he sees the van, we're toast."

Jasper noticed Freddie's eyes starting to dart around and he looked ready to jump out of his skin. "Ok, let's not panic," Jasper reassured everyone. "We have to conceal the van for a bit to give us a little time." He was thinking out loud so they could follow his thoughts. "Charlotte, you saw the cruiser over that way, toward the entrance, right?" She nodded her head yes. "Let's drive over in the other direction toward the marina." They all got in the van and Jasper headed the way he had mentioned. "Charlotte look at this camp brochure and see what it says about the Goodwill's Marina next door."

Jasper remembered the marina from previous family trips but they had never used it.

The brochure was in the van nook and Charlotte pulled it out and looked through it as Jasper drove down the dirt road slowly. "Ok," she began, "it says here in a back section, you can rent water skis, row boats, kayaks, motor boats, fishing equipment."

"Stop there. What does it say about boats? How big of a boat can you rent?"

"It doesn't say. It just says they're available to rent."

"We can find that out when we get there. We're coming to an end here now. It looks like you can drive right into the marina and park. That's what we can do and it will take them time to find the van, if they do at all. Then we can get away by boat."

"I don't want to be out there in a boat with Blaire after me," Freddie said.

"Well, Freddie, if we stay here he will have us for sure. Look around you guys for a good place to hide the van." The parking lot was half full and right out in the open.

"Look over there, Jasper. There are a lot of boats being stored. We can put the van behind one of those big boats and you can't see it from the parking lot."

"Nice," he said as he drove in about five rows in and put the van behind a big boat that concealed it from the parking lot. "You guys stay here. I will deal with the attendant." Jasper got out to speak with the attendant who was approaching the van.

"Hey, you can't park there," said the attendant.

"I know but I am going in to do the paper work and pick up this boat. I should be out in a few minutes and hooking it up to pull it out of here."

"The paper work takes longer than you think."

"Oh, it shouldn't. I called ahead and talked to the manager and did most of the paper work last week. So it's just a matter of paying and leaving."

"Ok, I guess you should be all set then." The attendant turned and left.

The others got out of the van and Charlotte said, "Boy, you lie convincingly Mr. always do the right thing." Jasper went back to the van and grabbed his backpack.

"Well, sometimes you have to go against your principles when you're dealing with assholes like Blaire. Now Freddie and I will go in because Blaire and his buddies know Freddie. Charlotte, you and Fido sit over there on the porch and look for any cruisers or any sign of anybody hostile."

Freddie and Jasper walked into Goodwill's Marina and he told Freddie to sit down and relax. He wouldn't be long.

Jasper talked to the clerk, who got the manager and Jasper rented a speedboat and bought an extra tank of gas. He pulled a fifty out of his belt and paid for the rental. The manager had one of the attendants go and get the boat ready. The manager told him he had one all set and for them to go down to the dock and they could take off from there. Jasper picked up a map of the lake and the surrounding area.

Just then, Charlotte came in and said softly to him, "I saw a sheriff's cruiser near the road that we just came from. They'll be here soon I think."

"Ok then, I guess we're ready to go," he said, loud enough for everyone to hear. "We'll be back by late afternoon Mr. Franco."

The three of them and Fido went down to the end of the dock where the attendant stood there, proudly displaying the boat they had rented. "This is the best boat we've got for skiing in the marina," he said with pride. "I hope you will enjoy it. Have it back by eight p.m., an hour before dark."

"Oh boy, it looks great. We will probably have it back earlier than eight." They all piled in and Jasper looked back and saw the cruiser checking out the parking lot for the van. Luckily it was still hidden behind the boat in the fifth row of rented boat spaces. Blaire was right on their ass, they just had enough time to get in and get out.

"Thanks a lot," Jasper said and then shook his hand and got in the boat himself. "Freddie, can you drive a boat?"

"Sure," said Freddie as he headed for the captain's seat.

"Go ahead then and go straight to the other end of the lake while I read the map." Freddie took off from the dock quickly and soon had the boat pretty much opened up.

Jasper took his binoculars out of his backpack and looked back to see if he could spot the sheriff. He wanted to get out and away from the marina before Blaire showed up to stop them. Sure enough, Blaire was on the dock with a bullhorn and the blue lights flashing in his cruiser behind him and screaming out at their boat. No one could hear him over the roar of the motor. Charlotte saw him with the blue lights flashing and their eyes met. He put his finger to his lips in a motion not to alarm Freddie. Charlotte nodded in agreement. Jasper handed the binoculars to her and picked up the map he had gotten from Goodwill's.

Charlotte was looking at Blaire through the binoculars as they sped away. "He is radioing someone on his walkie talkie"

Freddie was tearing down the lake. It didn't take long for them to get well out of sight of the marina. Jasper studied the map for a while. Charlotte kept the binoculars pealed on the dock and soon lost sight of it. After about ten minutes, Jasper tapped Freddie on the shoulder and motioned for him to slow down.

Freddie nodded his head ok and brought the speed down so it wasn't near as loud.

"We're in the middle of Long Lake, headed for the Sinclair Locks," he said, pointing at the map. "I noticed on the map that there are a series of five lakes, Long Lake, Sinclair Pond, Cross Lake, Square Lake and Eagle Lake, all connected by locks. You could go to each lake through the locks. In theory we could travel all the way to the Eagle Lake state troopers barracks that way."

"Yeah," said Charlotte sarcastically. "As long as the locks are opened and an insane sheriff isn't trying to kill us."

"Well, I'm not sure what else we can do. The state agents have probably reached the campground by now and discovered we're missing. We have no way of notifying anyone while we're out here. We'll have to try and hope Ken and the agents realize in time what's happened."

"He's right," said Freddie, sounding decisive for the first time. "We were sitting ducks at the marina and not much better out here. We have to try."

Jasper and Charlotte exchanged pleased looks that Freddie was getting involved in his own rescue.

"Two questions," Charlotte said, her voice had lost its sarcasm. "Do we have enough gas? And can we find those locks? Finding them might be a problem."

Jasper added, "We have two tanks of gas, forty gallons, so that should be enough. As far as finding the locks, I have a map and we'll just have to go slow to find our way to them."

"The first two locks are easy to find," Freddie added. "They're both at the end of the lakes as long as you don't miss the dogleg on Long Lake. On Sinclair Pond, just go to the end of the pond and you will run into it. On Cross Lake, Square Lake and Eagle Lake the locks are a little harder to find, they're in the middle of the lakes."

Jasper turned to Freddie surprised by the man's sudden helpfulness. It was as if Freddie was coming out of a once very heavy fog. Jasper said, "All right then, lets get going." He then took back the binoculars from Charlotte and began scanning the waters behind them, looking for pursuit as Freddie sped the boat back up again.

* * * *

DICK BLAIRE was on the dock at Goodwill's Marina with a bullhorn in one hand and his police radio in the other hand. His cruiser lights were flashing and he was watching his APB subjects speeding away down the lake.

"That's right, deputy," Blaire bellowed into the radio. "It's a nineteen-eighty-two black Ford Mustang. It's on official sheriff's department business. Its an emergency situation, I'll explain later. Allow the vehicle to go through. It's will be traveling over the speed limit but it has my permission. Let it pass." There was a short pause while Blaire listened to the voice on the other end. His fat face began to glow red with irritation. "I don't give two shits what you dumb asses thinks is safe. I'm the chief and I'm saying don't stop that vehicle, over."

Blaire jammed his radio back down on his belt and turned to the marina manager who was standing behind him nervously. "So, you sorry son-of-a-bitch you rented a speed boat to three criminals. The least you could do now is show me your office. I need to make a call.

Mr Franco, terrified and wanting nothing more then to appease the overbearing officer gladly showed Blaire to his office and then waited outside.

As soon as Mr. Franco had shut the door, Blaire called Clinton Perry who was at the Ouellette Rod and Gun club, waiting.

Clinton picked up. "Hello, Clint here."

"Clint, this is the Chief. They got away, they're going down Long Lake in a Grady skiing boat, bright red, eighty-five horse power, you can't miss it. Go downstairs and get a standard weapons trunk out of storage." They had trunks all set up with all sorts of weapons for an emergency including a 727-rocket launcher. "Then go to Cross Lake locks and blow that Grady out of the water. Don't miss it, if you do, we'll all end up in prison. I am sure Freddie Baker is turning states evidence. Take out all witnesses after you take him out."

"Ok, Chief. How much time do I have?"

"Probably about thirty minutes. Don't worry about speed, just step on it. I've already called you through on my radio so no other cops will stop your car. If you can hit them out in the lake, it would be easier to cover up. Take the high road off route 161, it's route 162 between Sinclair and Guerette. You can see the whole area from there. It will be like a turkey shoot. They'll either be on Sinclair Pond in the locks or Cross Lake. The trunk has high powered binoculars and scope sites, use them, over and out."

* * * *

Goddamnit, thought Ken Silvermen as he finished listening to the state agent's report over the radio. They had radioed him on the secure frequency of the radio that they had provided him with a week earlier. When the agents had reached the Cleveland Campgrounds they discovered Jasper, Charlotte and Freddie were missing.

At first they had thought that the trio had grown nervous waiting and had foolishly fled. It didn't take them long to realize that they had been forced to leave. The agents had just missed Chief Blaire leaving the Goodwill Marina.

Blaire must have spotted the Steller van in the marina parking lot just like the agents did a few minutes later. According to the manger of the marina, a party of two men, a young woman and a dog matching Jasper, Charlotte, Freddie and Fido's description had rented a boat moments before and tore off across the lake.

The state agents had told Ken that they believe the trio had simply rented the boat to escape and would probably abandon it a mile or so away. Then they would likely be found by Blaire and his cronies before Silvermen or the agents could intervene.

Ken had no doubt that that was Jasper's rationale for renting the boat. It didn't sit well with Ken however, he thought Jasper was a little more resourceful than simply abandoning the boat with no other means of transportation.

An idea occurred to Silvermen and he pulled over to the side of route 161 for a moment to look at his map.

Immediately he saw the pattern. The lakes are connected by locks. The State Trooper's Barracks was right on Eagle Lake. He picked up the secure radio he had been given and called in to the state trooper dispatch. "Notify the ranger station that we need to open all the locks between Long Lake and Eagle Lake. I think Jasper is trying to get Freddie to the barracks by crossing the lakes."

Silvermen soon heard back that the locks were being opened as he suggested. He was also told that the state troopers had a chopper in the air. They wanted to intercept Jasper and the others at the helicopter pad in Guerette, which was a small town right near route 161. The helipad was right near the locks between Long Lake and Sinclair Pond. The agents wanted to pick the group up there because they were not sure what Blaire has planned. The chopper could get there before any other vehicles.

With this new information, Silvermen put on his blue lights and decided to head towards the Guerette chopper pad. He was on the perimeter at Daigle, about twenty miles from Ouellette. He headed his cruiser toward Ouellette on Route 161.

Unbeknownst to Silvermen, the state agents didn't want him involved with the Blaire chase because the DA's plans were to appoint him as acting chief when they brought down Blaire. They were trying to avoid a conflict of interest situation.

Ken was cruising down route 161 at a speed well over the limit but being as safe as he could. There was a call from Sheriff Josh Bugby, one of Blaire's boys, to give a nineteen-eighty-two Ford Mustang the all clear to go over the speed limit on route 161.

Ken had just passed Ouellette and was headed for Guerette. He was making good time and he would be at the helicopter pad before the boat he hoped.

Suddenly the black Mustang came out of nowhere and passed him in his cruiser and waved. Ken sped up and got his plate number. He picked up the State Police radio and had them run the plate. Ken stayed up with the Mustang, keeping it in sight. A few minutes later, the call came back. The plate he had called on belongs to Clinton Perry. Ken heard that and stepped on it. Blaire must have called him, the Perrys had caught wind of their plans and were trying to get there also. Ken kept the Mustang in sight but backed off a little and turned his blue lights off.

Ken told the state troopers to notify agent Johnson and tell him that Ken would be following a Mustang that Clinton Perry was in. He filled them in on the situation and knew that Perry was up to something.

Silvermen was in Guerette and the Mustang turned up Route 162. Ken thought, he's going up to the high road. That's strange? He's probably just going to look and see what he can see. You can see everything from the ridge. He was a couple hundred yards ahead of him, Ken slowed up to make the turn and the Mustang was up the ridge and out of sight. Ken stayed with him and by the time he got to the top of the ridge he saw the Mustang with its hatchback open.

Clinton had wheeled a trunk on a dolly over to a nearby field and out to the ridge. He was looking over the ridge with high-powered binoculars. Ken slowed up and stopped a hundred yards away and got out his binoculars and watched. Clinton was so focused, he wasn't paying any attention to Ken.

Ken looked out across Sinclair Pond and was able to see the bright red Grady sprinting for the end of the pond. He looked back at Clinton and couldn't believe his eyes. He was putting a missile launcher together and Ken didn't have to think twice to know what he was going to do with it. He didn't have much time. An experienced rifleman can put one of those together in seconds.

Silvermen popped his trunk and went around for the scoped deer rifle. It was all set to go Ken grabbed it and the shells and loaded it. He rushed around his cruiser to use the roof to steady his arm for a perch, looked up and saw Clinton aiming the rocket launcher. He was too late to stop the first shot. He grabbed the binoculars and looked out over the Sinclair Pond. The first shot went high and landed fifty feet over them in the water and exploded. He saw the speedboat zig-zag and slow down. The occupants were probably starting to panic.

Ken looked over and saw Clinton reloading. Ken picked up the deer rifle and took careful aim on Clinton, shoot to kill, went through his mind. Clinton had other weapons and if Silvermen only wounded him, he would probably shoot back. Ken did just that as Clinton lifted up the rocket launcher to fire round two which would probably be the fatal round. Ken pulled the trigger and Clinton dropped like a sack of potatoes. He jumped in his Cruiser and drove the hundred yards to the scene. He jumped out and inspected the scene. Clinton was dead. He picked up the high powered binoculars and looked down.

Jasper was nearing the Cross Lake locks. The helicopter was landing. They were so close now. Ken scanned the river and saw another speedboat pushing across Sinclair Pond at break neck speed. It has to be Blaire, Ken thought. He was gaining really fast. Ken looked at the 727-rocket launcher and picked it up. He looked through its scope and could make out Blaire, firing round after round at the red

Grady and he was getting closer and closer by the minute. He had no option but to fire on the speedboat and try to stop Blaire. Ken took aim and let one fly. The rocket missed but it hit the water twenty feet short of the boat and exploded enough to capsize the boat.

Jasper and company were free and clear. Ken watched the red Grady through the high powered binoculars as the occupants looked behind them and saw what happened. They began hugging each other. The boat came almost to a stop as they looked up at where the rocket came from. Ken found Jasper looking through his own set of binoculars. Jasper lifted his arm to wave and Ken did the same.

Silvermen then made gestures with his arms, indicating for them to continue on to the waiting helicopter. Apparently Jasper understood Silvermen's hand signals because shortly after that, they resumed the boat ride to Guerette.

Now Ken could hear agent Johnson on the state police radio. "Have the rangers shown up yet?"

"As a matter of fact, they're just pulling in now," replied Ken after jogging back over to his truck.

Ken heard Agent Johnson calling the Rangers over the radio. He told them to check on the two in the capsized boat and to pull them out of the water. Johnson said that if they're not hurt, to take them into custody put them in the hole, and turn and bail the water out of the capsized boat and toe it in.

Johnson also called the chopper to check in. Everything was going fine with them. They would be arriving shortly at the Eagle Lake Police barracks. He told the officers to put everyone in separate rooms when they got to the barracks and take statements from each one as to exactly what happened in the last two days.

Ken went about the business of wrapping up the situation Clinton Perry had created. He called in a couple of Sheriff's detectives. They would have to check out the scene and write a report. He then called the coroner's office to take care of the body. Then he called the police garage to tow the Perry car to the impound yard along with the trunk of weapons. After all that was done, he decided to go over to the State Police barracks to write his report and check on everything. All of this would take the rest of the afternoon.

Chapter 15
Conclusion

When Jasper, Freddie, Charlotte and Fido arrived at the State Police barracks in Eagle Lake via the helicopter,they were all treated very professionally and asked to go into separate rooms to write out their statements. They wanted the events of the past day and a half, starting with Friday midday. Fido went with Jasper. Freddie was the only one who was read his rights. After Jasper and Charlotte finished with their statements, they were lead to a lounge area with a television and a kitchen nook where they could make up a snack or play cards. Agent John Johnson and Agent Greg Robey came in to introduce themselves and told them they'd like them to stay overnight. If they needed to make any calls, they could make them from a phone he just plugged into the wall. There were a lot of statements that had to be reviewed and they would be having interviews and things. "Police matters such as this always take a while because of all involved. All statements have to be reviewed and cross-checked," explained Agent Johnson. Both Charlotte and Jasper agreed to cooperate and made calls to home.

Later, Agent Robey came in and told them that there would be no further police business today and that acting Sheriff Chief Silver-men would be taking them to dinner and settling them in a nearby mo-tel for the night. They needed to talk to them in the morning. Freddie would be detained and he would explain tomorrow what was going on.

* * * *

In the morning, Sunday, July eleventh, Jasper, Fido and Charlotte had breakfast and headed over to the police barracks. They were put in the same lounge area they'd been in the day before. They were called out separately on several occasions to clarify their statements that were being typed up. They spent most of the rest of the day answering questions for the detectives who were coordinating the case.

It was not until well into the afternoon that Agent Johnson called them in to release them. "You two have cooperated fully and we appreciate it. You will be free to go. Let me explain the situation. As in any ongoing investigation, please do not discuss the case with anyone, especially the press. The wrong thing said to the media could slow up our progress considerably. As far as your individual families are concerned, you can tell them the gist of the situation but ask them to please use discretion and not to discuss this with others, especially the media."

Both Jasper and Charlotte agreed and Charlotte asked. "What will be happening with my father?"

"I will tell you as much as I can," said Agent Johnson. "First, Freddie will be in protective custody until there is a trial. Dick Blaire, Joshua Bugby and Henry Dugan are the three sheriffs that will be brought up on numerous charges, along with Jake Perry, based on Freddie's statements. He has agreed to fully cooperate and seems to know a lot about other happenings in cases dating as far back as the Paul Skater murder and says he can produce physical evidence to prove some really damaging information on the accused."

"Will Freddie have to go to jail?" asked Charlotte.

"Well... yes," said Johnson. "Freddie doesn't get off the hook altogether. He will be detained in a rehab center situation and receive counseling and treatment for his drug and alcoholic addictions. He may be placed in a halfway house after the trial and live there for about six months, then allowed into the community a little at a time for a while. Depending on his progress. Best case situation, he could be out with very little time served. Freddie may be able to prove he was forced to do some of the things he did, at the Steller's based on intimidation by the Perrys and Blaire. As you already know, Ken Silvermen will be acting Chief of the Sheriff's department."

"That's a relief to know that Freddie has a chance. He really is a good man," replied Charlotte.

"Time will tell on that," repeated Agent Johnson. "Jasper, we have taken care of the boat you rented. The department has taken the boat back to the marina. Your grandfather is picking up your van this morning. I also told him he could pick you up. He may even be here now. He said he could take Charlotte home also. As soon as he shows, you both can go. That's all I have unless you have any more questions."

"What about the charges on me and the APB?" asked Jasper.

Johnson chuckled, "All of those charges were dropped and the APB lifted, based primarily on Bubba Stovel's statement."

"What about the rest of the Perrys?" he asked.

"The parents are in a nursing home and Sammy and Susie Mae Perry seem to be completely unaware of any wrong doing. Susie Mae spent much of her time taking care of the parents and the house, meals, laundry, etc. Sammy was in college most of the time. It's possible they had some knowledge of criminal activity, its hard to say for sure but so far they haven't been implicated in any criminal action. That's not to say that they won't be watched. The Perry Poultry Farm business, with proper management, could get back on its feet. They just need to pay the fines that OSHA will be imposing on them and the two youngest could get some sympathy from the courts if they go in with the proper attitude and fight for the business. Clear up the violations OSHA found and display a positive business climate. Time will tell on that also. One last thing, if you think of anything else regarding this case don't hesitate to call Chief Silvermen."

* * * *

Shank Steller had already arrived at the police barracks like Agent Johnson had suggested. Frank LaBreque had given Shank a ride to the Cleveland Campground to pick up the van, then returned to the farm while Shank continued on down to Eagle Lake to pick up Jasper, Fido and Charlotte.

"Well," said Shank, "you guys have had a couple of exciting days. I heard you got shot at by 727-rocket launcher, and Clinton Perry is dead."

"That's true, but he shot at us first and then Ken Silvermen put him down and shot the launcher at Blaire who was gaining fast on us and shooting at us. Ken shot at him with the launcher that capsized his boat...." Jasper continued to tell Shank the whole story, and followed it with, "This is all confidential until after the trial. Especially the media, its hush, hush." They continued small talk until they were at the connivence store where Charlotte had left her car.

They followed Charlotte and went to talk to Grandma Rosa. Shank met her and Buddy. Jasper explained to Rosa how Freddie was in protective custody and all that. He would be getting counseling and be dried out. He explained that he turned Freddie's gun in to Ken Silvermen.

Rosa asked, "Will we be able to see him?"

Charlotte answered, "Not for a while. He is hidden in the protective custody program until after the trial. No one can see him or even write to him for a month. Then his letters will be monitored both outgoing and incoming. He will be all right. We will have him back, Grandma Rosa. His divorce should even be final. It will be a whole new start for us."

Shank and Jasper had to be going and Jasper told Charlotte that he would be in touch and to hang in there. They drove off to the Steller farm.

"Words out you will be heading west soon, Jasper?" Shank asked, as they were driving down route eleven.

"Yes, I mentioned it to Grandma Jane and told her as soon as Robbie came I would be off. Those have been my original plans all along."

"I guess all good things come to an end. It has been great having you spend the summer. You know you saved the farm, Jasper. For that I am extremely grateful."

"I was so glad to do what I could do to help."

"You have great instincts and a real good sense for people. A good head on your shoulders, I know you will always do right by people. Trust those skills and go by them. Are you still doing the bike thing, three thousand miles across the country?"

"Yeah, Gramps I am."

"Would you do me a favor and let me buy you a motorcycle with a sidecar for Fido?"

"Gramps, the bike thing is part of the adventure."

"Yeah, but you can get there faster and start your adventures quicker."

"Ahh, but the biking is the adventure. Your experiences on the road and the knowledge you gain of things not experienced. When will I ever do this again?"

"Never, probably."

"There you go. I will never experience it again so I have to do it now."

"You'll be a stick by the time you get to California."

"I will still eat and I don't go fast. I'll take my time and experience the trip. I'll let nature take its course."

"Do me this favor then. Get a motor bike for your trip back across the states, please."

"Ok Gramps, I'll think about. How's that?"

"Jasper, my boy, my boy. There's no one like you. You take care of yourself." They drove the rest of the way with little said.

* * * *

JONNY SKATER was visiting from Landrush, at the Eagle Lake lodge that was willed to him after his father's death. He said he would be up here the second week of August.

Jasper couldn't believe it was that time already. The summer was flying by. He'd have to start thinking about the continuation of his adventure. He planned to head west in September through Canada. That week, Jonny called him and they made arrangements to visit and Jay stayed at the lodge a couple days.

During the visit, Jasper told Jonny about the situation regarding his father's murder. The District Attorney's office had an eye witness implicating Chief Blaire and two other deputies, along with the Perrys in the Paul Skater murder. There was also some hard evidence that put the sheriffs in the office where the murder happened. The body was moved to the site of the reported shooting and bogus poaching grounds.

From what Jasper could find out, Paulsie had gone to the Ouellette Rod and Gun Club for some ammunition and was going to the bathroom, went through the wrong door and witnessed some drug exchanging.

The amazing thing about the whole situation was that they were watching a home video on a deer hunt that they had been on. When the drug dealers came in the room, Freddie turned off the tape at Blaire's request. Unbeknownst to everyone in the room, including himself, Freddie had turned on the videotape and recorded the drug exchange. He never told anyone and has kept the videotape all this time.

He never trusted Blaire and was afraid of him so he wanted some proof of his wrongdoing. He never expected a murder. He held on to the tape to clear him if he ever needed it, but he made sure know one knew about the tape.

When Paulsie came in, the drugs were laid out on the table and the money was out. He had to know what was going on. Blaire pulled him into the room and bound and gagged him. They wrapped up the deal and the drug dealers left after Blaire assured them that this guy would be taken care of. He said for them "to watch the papers" and laughed.

Blaire checked the building, finding it empty and came back and told Deputy Henry Dugan to shoot him. After the shooting, all hell broke loose and they worked out this cover-up scheme.

Freddie was too afraid to say anything. He had been afraid of this Blaire and Perry clan all this time and intimidated by them in the worst way. Blaire and his deputies were running drugs down from Canada for all these years through the cover of the Rod and Gun Club. That was Blaire's headquarters for his drug operation. There was deer-poaching going on by the Perrys, but Blaire stopped it after the murder so it would like he stopped the deer poaching.

The State Drug Enforcement Agents have looked at the film and recognize some of the players in the videotape as know drug traffickers from Canada.

"Jonny, your father never had a chance. He was in the wrong place at the wrong time. I really feel for you buddy, but now you know that those bastards will pay the price. It doesn't bring him back, but it's got to help clear his name when the real truth comes out. All this has to be a hush job until after the trial."

"Did you ever see the videotape?" Jonny asked.

"No, I haven't and it won't even be discussed until they nail them with it. The accused don't know about the videotape still. That's why it's only been told to the families and it will come out at the time of the trial. Ken Silvermen knew I was going to see you so he told me all of this earlier in the week. He told me to tell you if you wanted to talk to him about the case, to call him, but remember he can't tell you much more about it until after the trial. He said then he would allow you to view the tape if you'd like. He would advise against it, but it would be your choice." Jasper had told Jonny the story earlier during his visit. He and Jonny had discussed parts of it off and on during the stay. Jonny was leaving before noon and Jasper was saying his good byes.

"When will it all come to trial?" asked Jonny, standing there in deep thought.

"Well, all this is being investigated, including the drug stuff so it might be a while. I am headed west so I will have to fly back for the trial to testify some time next winter or spring. I need to keep in touch with the authorities here." Jasper was fiddling with his bike he had peddled down from Old Calcutta.

"I guess I've waited this long to clear my dad's name, I can wait a few more months. Thanks a lot, Jasper. You really did justice here. I will never forget what you did for my father. He never deserved that epitaph next to his name." They shook hands and Jonny gave him a big, teary hug. Jasper left for home, it was eleven a.m. Fido was following right behind.

When he got back from the lodge where he was visiting Jonny, there was a letter waiting for him from Fred Fender, of Wiscasset. Jasper remembered exchanging addresses with him.

Inside there was a newspaper article about a big drug bust in the Bath/Brunswick Times, the paper of the area.

BATH POLICE CRIPPLES LARGE DRUG RING WITH ANONYMOUS TIP

The Bath Police teamed up with the Augusta Police on a tip from an anonymous citizen about a backpack left at the Greyhound bus station in Augusta. The backpack contained a large amount of drugs, paraphernalia, a large amount of cash, and notebook that led police to the location of the source that may extend from Bath all the way into Canada. One of the dealers is Charles Washington Baldwin, he has been arrested and twenty-two other arrests have been made. Baldwin was the head of the trafficking scheme in the Bath area. This led the police to several areas where additional arrests are expected. There will be more on the story as it unfolds in the near future. There is a possible link to drug trafficking out of the Fort Kent area and a drug corridor into Canada.

There was also a note from Freddie Fender, congratulating him and Charlotte for bringing these drug dealers in Bath to justice. He also added, "Your secret is good with me, but there might be a reward in it for you if you think about it." He signed the note Fearless Freddie Fender Bender.

After reading the letter, he called Charlotte and read the clipping to her. "Charlotte, I just can't help thinking that notebook from Charlie Baldwin of Bath might have some names in it and be a connection to the drug dealers with Blaire and his Canadian connection."

"Jasper, what are you saying? You want to report our involvement in that to the police here?" she said.

"Yes, Charlotte. I think we have to. Remember the last thing Agent Johnson said to us? 'If you remember anything that might help the case to contact Chief Silvermen.' It might help stop a whole lot of drugs coming into the state. Look what it's done already in the Bath area, twenty-two arrests. Think about it. Remember my motto, 'always do the right thing'. My question to you is, what is the right thing to do? Look at what Freddie is doing to help stop these drug guys. And, Charlotte, Freddie Fender said there could be a reward in it."

"Oh, Jasper you make things so difficult."

"Does that mean it's ok to call Ken about this?"

"You were going to do it anyway, weren't you?"

"Not really without your ok, but you know Charlotte, you're starting to see the light. Remember 'the truth will set you free'. I think there is hope for you. I'll call you back in a minute. Bye."

Jasper called Ken, he was in and Jasper made an appointment at the Fort Kent Headquarters. He wanted to see Ken before he left and this would be a great thing to leave him with. Possibly more leads to more evidence. Jasper called Charlotte and told her he would meet her at the Sheriff's headquarters building near her house at one o'clock. She knew where that was, they had been there before chasing down dead chickens.

Charlotte was waiting outside headquarters, smoking a cigarette. She saw Jasper coming and put it out. "I thought you quit that habit," he said.

"I quit the real bad habits, not the bad ones I like. I've cut down a lot, so there." She cracked a smile and they walked into the Fort Kent headquarters.

"Look Jasper, I did some bad things back then, I might be in trouble."

"We won't mention that stuff, Charlotte. Boy, there is hope for you. You even have a conscience."

"That's not a conscience, it's being afraid for my own ass."

"Look, Ken Silvermen will work this out in our favor, believe me. You've got to learn to trust people. They don't care that you robbed some drug dealer of his backpack and I was an accessory to your thievery. He'll just want the notebook and he can talk to the Bath authorities. Let me do the talking and see where it gets us. But you know we've got to do this, so lets go."

They walked into Chief Silvermen's office right on time after checking at the desk and being sent in. "Hello, Chief. Congratulations on your appointment," Jasper said and shook hands with him, as did Charlotte. Ken reached down and patted Fido.

"So what brings you two here?" asked Ken.

"A friend of mine sent me this clipping from the Bath/ Brunswick Times." Jasper handed the clipping to Ken and gave him a minute to read it.

"Why did he send this to you? You weren't supposed to discuss this with people. I need to record this. Any objections?" Ken turned on a tape recorder. They both shook their heads, no objection.

"We didn't discuss this with anyone. We had some run-ins with that Baldwin guy. I just thought you could call the Bath police and get that notebook and maybe it will help the Federal Drug Agents with their drug case against Blaire. My friend, Freddie Fender helped us leave there and avoid the Baldwin guy. Agent Johnson told us to see you if we remembered anything that was connected with the case. I had no idea this drug thing went all the way to Bath, Maine. When I got this letter in the mail and read the article I had to turn you on to the notebook."

"I appreciate that but I have some questions. Did either of you buy drugs from these Bath guys?" They both shook their heads no. "That's good, did you both know this Charles W. Baldwin?" They both shook their heads yes. "Are either of you the 'anonymous tip' the paper speak of?" They both nodded their heads yes. "How? You speak, Charlotte."

"Can Jasper tell you the story? He tells it better than I do." Ken nodded his head yes. "Jasper, don't hold back, tell the truth." He looked at her and raised his eyebrows.

"What's gotten into you, Charlotte?" he said.

"You're right. The truth is the only way to go. I'm sorry, I've learned that much, ok?" she said and sat back in here chair and pouted.

“Chief, she’s come a long way. Any truth I tell you about her breaking any law is not serious. It was at the time, but its seriousness has diminished, due to good circumstances beyond our control. I was an unknown accomplice to a point, then she followed my lead so I am the bad guy.”

“Let me see now. Charlotte broke the law and you helped her without knowing it, and when you found out what she was doing, you got her out of it because drug dealers were on to you and Freddie Fender helped you get away.”

“Chief Silvermen, you’re a genius. That’s exactly what happened.”

“Yeah, Jasper but I need the details and not this mambo jumbo crap.”

“He’s right, Jasper. You suck at telling the truth. Let me try, I know I can do better than that,” said Charlotte.

Jasper sat back with a smile on his face because he was a fence sitter and didn’t want to implicate her in the story. He wanted her to tell it.

Charlotte did tell it and she filled Chief Silvermen in about everything that happened, better than Jasper could have told it himself. As soon as she was done, Ken turned off the tape recorder and got on the phone. He was talking to one of the Federal Agents. “Ok, you already have the notebook. That’s good, when I read the article I thought you might be interested in the notebook. But you already have it so never mind then.” A pause in the conservation, “Where did I get the article? We get all the major area papers here. It just takes me a day or two to read them, so I’m a bit behind. Ok then, keep in touch.” He put the phone down.

Both kids looked at him. “You lied to him for us. Why?” Charlotte said.

“Look, Charlotte, what you did was wrong. Like Jasper, I think you learned your lesson. You’ve been truthful with us all through these past couple of weeks. You’re behind your father, you’re taking care of your grandmother and your brother, you’re a good kid. The truth is important. The Feds? They got what they wanted and more. They don't need to know your story. You did tell it a lot better than Jasper did."

"Why did you record our statement?" asked Jasper.

Ken smiled, "Jasper, two things I've learned in the two weeks I have been acting Chief. Number one, always have a tape recorder ready and number two, turn it on whenever anyone wants to confess to anything. It saves a lot of re writing."

"What about that Ken, we did break the law."

"For peat sake, Jasper, will you keep your darn mouth shut?" Charlotte piped in.

"Look Charlotte, I just want to get a cop's point of view, sorry Ken."

"Jasper, yes the law was broken by both of you. Initially more seriously by Charlotte and you Jasper were caught up in it. Like what I told her, you both are good kids, this comes up again, God forbid, you will do the right thing and you won't have to take it this far. Bottom line is we got the big fish and everybody's happy."

"Speaking of catching fish," interrupted Charlotte. "What do you think will happen to my step mother, Karen Baker?"

"As far as this investigation goes?" said Ken, "Nothing. There really isn't enough evidence to name her in anything. It's obvious that she was involved to some degree. She was at Pierce's Pub during the fight and she's been on the periphery of some of these other activities but she's not a key player. It's possible she could get summoned as a witness but thats about it."

"Oh good, I guess," said Charlotte apprehensively.

Jasper and Ken looked at her questioningly until she continued.

"Well, she is my brother's mother," she explained. "I think she's a piece of shit parent but I'd rather her not go to jail. So long as she keeps away from Buddy."

"From what I've heard, you're on the right track Charlotte," said Ken. "Karen has a well documented drug abuse and criminal history. She may not go to jail for any of it but it's enough that if she makes trouble for you or your brother and if it went to court, I think you would secure custody of your brother pretty easily."

"Well," said Jasper. "You got our story. I will be seeing you. I'm headed west in a week or so." He put out his hand and shook with Ken.

Charlotte got up also put out her hand and said, "Thanks for the nice comments about being a good kid. So far I haven't gotten a lot of them except from you and Jasper."

"Well, Charlotte you can take them to heart because they're true," Ken said, as he walked around the desk. "When your father gets back on his feet, I think things will be a lot different for you."

Charlotte suddenly jumped over and gave the Chief a big hug and went out the door before anyone could respond.

"Jasper between you and me I put the recorder on for two reasons. One to put the pressure on both of you especially Charlotte. The recorder kind of puts the right perspective on what you're saying. It kind of makes an honest person tell the truth. The second reason I taped the conversation was in cases like this there are sometimes rewards after the fact. I will be writing up a report about an 'anonymous tip' and sending it in to the state, after all they need to do something with all that drug money, and there was a lot of it. Don't worry I will sugar coat it for the Feds. If anything comes of it I will let you and Charlotte know."

"Ken thanks for everything. You made Charlotte feel so great. I really think she has her act together now. When I first met her in Bath she was down and out."

"Jasper, don't thank me. You're the one who helped her."

"Thanks again and I'll keep in touch and fly back for the trial. I'll stay in touch with Shank so you can always reach me through him. When I get a permanent address, I'll let you know." Jasper waved and left the office.

Charlotte was sitting on one of the benches. She got up and they quietly walked out of the Fort Kent headquarters building.

"You showed some great emotions in there, Charlotte. I'm so proud of you."

"When were you going to tell me you were leaving? I had to hear it in there," she said, wiping the tears from her eyes. "I love you, Jasper." They were in the parking lot between his grandfather's truck and her blue Pinto. She reached up on her tiptoes and kissed him on the lips.

Jasper thought to himself, I tried to be a gentleman and avoid this emotional stuff and here I am again. "I love you too, Charlotte, but I need to go on my way. This is only the first leg of my trip. I can't stay with Shank and Jane. Especially now with my uncle and aunt and there and three kids coming soon, I need to go."

"I know you do, but give me a minute, will you?"

"Lets go over to Jude's and get a sandwich. I have one more tidy bit of information for you." Charlotte jumped at the offer and they took the truck and went the two miles to Jude's Diner and left the pinto in the parking lot of the sheriffs building.

They ordered their sandwiches and ate them without much talk. Finally Jasper told her what Ken said about a reward after the fact.

"Ken really recorded our conversation so he could write a report on the anonymous tip persons. He said that is what they do a lot of times with drug money." They got up and he paid the bill and they walked to the truck. "It will take some time after the trial, but it could come."

"Did you say anything to Ken about me wanting a reward?" she said as they drove back toward the Sheriffs office.

"Ha! No, he mentioned the reward thing to me. He called it an after the fact reward. You know, Charlotte, I will be coming back for the trial so it's not like I am going forever. You will have school, Buddy, and Rosa to take care of. Then there is Freddie to write to. Time will zoom by, you just wait."

"Yeah, I guess I will be quite busy."

"Charlotte, do me one favor. Get all "A's" on your report card. I know you can do it. You have the brains. That's the first thing I will want to see. So make a copy of the first semester report card." Jasper parked beside her Pinto and they sat and talked.

"Jasper, you're impossible. Always demanding."

"Charlotte, the trial will probably be in the winter. If it's later than that in the spring, I want you to apply to University of Maine, Fort Kent or University of Maine, Presque Isle.

"What are you talking about? College? That's not for me."

"Of course it is. That's why you want all 'A's.' That will prove you can do the work. When you write up your college letter, explain what you went through to get those grades."

"What do you mean?"

"Tell them how you held down a part time job at the kennel, and that you took care of Buddy, and Rosa your eighty-two year old grandmother. How you got meals and did laundry and still maintained an "A" average, even though you were on welfare. Welfare is made for people like you. You can show them that you're working hard to get off the welfare of the state. All of that will have to make them believe in you. God knows I believe in you. You will even be able to go to college almost for free."

Charlotte jumped over and kissed him and said. "By God, I'll do it. I'll work my sexy little butt off and do it."

Jasper thought to himself, it sure is. Sometimes I wish I wasn't so good. "That's the spirit girl, I know you can do it, and now you know you can. Your only choice is which college. I vote for UMPI. There is nothing like getting away for school. You start to develop a sense of independence. You need that Charlotte, you really do."

"Oh Jasper, I am going to start tomorrow. I'm going to the school to see what my classes are and start right in." She opened the truck door and so did Jasper. They hugged, kissed and she got in her Pinto.

"Go to guidance right off and give them that attitude and they will help you for sure," he said through the car window.

"I'll do that," she said, as she peeled out of the sheriff's parking lot, lighting up a cigarette. She was gone. If she had stayed another second, she would have cried her eyes out.

* * * *

Jasper had just come in from saying his good byes to Charlotte after a sad drive home from her house. He wouldn't be seeing her again for a while. He walked in the door after noticing a strange SUV sitting outside. To his surprise, Uncle Robbie was there with his wife Bea and their three kids.

"Uncle Robbie, Aunt Bea, how you all doing? I didn't expect you guys till September. What's up?" Jasper went over and hugged them all, including the kids, Billy 13, Sally 9 and Shannon 6.

Robbie explained, "I got this early release from the Air Force. Since my discharge date was coming up and my career field was full and I am in the middle of my twenty-first year, the Air Force let me go with no penalty. We've been out for a month. We spent some time with Bea's family, did a little vacationing and came here to start our new life and relieve dad and mom from the burden of every day work."

"That will be great, but it might be hard pulling both of them out from under the business totally," said Jasper. Jane came and bustled the kids outside with a plate of sandwiches.

"That will never happen, we can always use their help and guidance. It's going to be a slow takeover and probably never a total one. I want to thank you personally for your help in saving the business from the Perrys. From what I understand, they were doing their best to shut us down. We can probably turn the tide on them and do them in."

"Clinton was trying to shut us down, but their business doesn't have to go under. Sammy and Susie Mae Perry may still be interested in it. They could bring it around with some solid management. They are young but from what I've heard they weren't involved with their brother's plans. Clinton Perry was the total brain behind this with Blaire. I think the younger Perrys deserve a shot at bringing the business back. It definitely wont hurt us. Competition is good and they still have family to think about. We might even be able to help them get on their feet."

Shank had come in and had heard what Jasper had said. "So what are you saying, Jasper? After what they pulled, we should help them out?"

"Yes, Grandpa, I would give them a shot. Set up a meeting with the two remaining Perrys, Susie and Sammy and feel them out. See what their attitude is and if they want to take on running the business. It would be nice to just open up some communication with them. Even help and advise them. They don't have to be our enemies the rest of our lives. I think Clinton was the evil one and dragged Jake in with him. Jake will be serving some time so he will be out of the picture for a long while and those two can maybe turn things around."

"Boy, Jasper. You would just go and help them out rather than work on shutting them down?" said Shank.

Robbie stepped in. "Jasper might have a point, Dad. A meeting with the younger kids wouldn't hurt. We could find out their plans, what direction they're going in. Best case scenario, they can bring the business back and worst case scenario it will fold on its own accord."

"There's always the scenario that they may be hostile to our family," put in Jasper. "At one time when we were younger and I was up visiting, Dan Cooper, myself and a couple other town kids used to hang out with Susie. We used to go to the Fort Kent municipal swimming pool and swim together. Older brother Sammy was always close by and we all got along, with the hostility of the rest of the family not an issue. I would be happy to go over there and talk to them together and see if there is any animosity there. However, it might not be the right time being so close to the death of Clinton."

"I think you're right there, Jasper. It's too early. We can wait till the time is right and maybe make some type of overture," said Robbie. "It's going to take some time for them to get back on track. I think there is bound to be some feelings. Wrong or not, we were the victims of Clinton's wrath and he did pay dearly for it. They won't be looking at the situation like we are. He paid the ultimate price for his stupidity. That won't sit well with them."

Everyone sort of nodded and that seemed to be the end of that conservation. Rob was the take charge type of guy and that would be good for Shank and Jane. They could retire as much as they wanted to, without worrying about anything. Rob's career with the military was over and he could devote all of his time to a business he grew up with. Things would be really nice around here.

Shank already seemed more relaxed than he did a month ago when he had those series of meetings with LaBreque, Silvermen and Rockwell, and that damn AGL virus was looming over his head. Yes, things did look better. Jasper would have no problem leaving on his next adventure.

His next plan was to cross the Trans Canadian Highway and peddle to the West Coast before winter. He wanted to settle in Southern California or even Mexico. Warmth was what he was looking for during half of November, December, January, February and half of March. He figured he could get a job for four or five months and then his plans were to bike the midsection of the country to the East Coast and then head south to Florida, New Orleans, across Texas and possibly down into Mexico.

He was also thinking hard of a motorcycle with a sidecar that Shank had suggested. Maybe in the spring. He would see. There was no timetable and wherever he was in June, he promised Claire he would comeback to Landrush and that's what he planed to do.

Made in the USA
San Bernardino, CA
23 February 2015